M
STREETS

'A walk on the wild side of 1920s London. Dark, atmospheric and utterly compelling.'
Jake Arnott, bestselling author of
The Long Firm* and *The Fatal Tree

'Phil Lecomber's jaw-dropping debut is exactly what I want from a historical hardboiled novel: passionate nihilism and a tough-as-nails loner making his way through a depraved underworld whose darkness goes all the way down.'
Duane Swierczynski, *New York Times*
bestselling author of *Lion & Lamb,*
California Bear* and *Secret Dead Men

'I really enjoyed this book. Lecomber creates a strong sense of time and place, and has a unique voice… Very highly recommended!'
Denzil Meyrick, bestselling author
of *Murder at Holly House*

'I loved this fast-paced, atmospheric adventure through the smoke and neon of 1920s Soho, vividly written and rich with historical detail. The twists and turns will leave you reeling.'
Alex Pavesi, bestselling author of *Eight Detectives*

'If Patrick Hamilton and Dashiell Hammett had got hammered in some boozer in old Soho, *Midnight Streets* is the novel they'd have come up with… All of London (low) life is here. A cracking debut.'
Martyn Waites, author of the Joe Donovan crime series

'A polished story set in a vibrant and colourful London between the wars. Full of twists, it gradually unveils a horrific set of crimes. The dogged George Harley will appeal to anyone who loves a private detective story.'
Mick Finlay, author of the Arrowood Mysteries series

'A gripping mystery, steeped in the deliciously seedy side of Golden Age crime.'
Lucy Barker, author of *The Other Side of Mrs Wood*

'A clever mix of *Silence of the Lambs* and Dennis Wheatley, all set in the dark and dangerous world of Jazz Age Soho.'
Stuart Douglas, author of *Death at the Dress Rehearsal*

'Absolutely terrific – incredibly gripping… brought the seamy streets and seamier denizens of 1920s London to brutal life.'
Ajay Chowdhury, author of *The Waiter* and *The Cook*

'Set in London in 1929 – prime Golden Age territory – *Midnight Streets* is as dark as any noir classic. In this book, evil has its gloves, and its monocle, off, and we see the darkness we knew was there.'
S. J. Rozan, co-author of the Judge Dee and Lao She mysteries

'An atmospheric thriller set in 1920s London, which reveals Lecomber's keen ear for the off-beat rhythms of the city… Immersive and mysterious, this debut will delight historical crime fans.'
Jo Furniss, author of *Dead Mile*

MIDNIGHT STREETS

PHIL LECOMBER

TITAN BOOKS

Midnight Streets
Print edition ISBN: 9781835411995
E-book edition ISBN: 9781835412008

Published by Titan Books
A division of Titan Publishing Group Ltd
144 Southwark Street, London SE1 0UP

First edition: March 2025
10 9 8 7 6 5 4 3 2 1

This is a work of fiction. All of the characters, organizations, and events portrayed in this novel are either products of the author's imagination or are used fictitiously. Any resemblance to actual persons, living or dead (except for satirical purposes), is entirely coincidental.

© Phil Lecomber 2025.

Phil Lecomber asserts the moral right to be
identified as the author of this work.

No part of this publication may be reproduced, stored in a retrieval system, or transmitted, in any form or by any means without the prior written permission of the publisher, nor be otherwise circulated in any form of binding or cover other than that in which it is published and without a similar condition being imposed on the subsequent purchaser.

A CIP catalogue record for this title is available
from the British Library.

Printed and bound by CPI Group (UK) Ltd, Croydon, CR0 4YY.

For Susie, Jack and Ned.

But most thro' midnight streets I hear
How the youthful Harlot's curse
Blasts the new-born Infant's tear
And blights with plagues the Marriage hearse

—William Blake, 'London'

1

London, 1929

GEORGE HARLEY LOCKED eyes with the fox which stood motionless in the frowzy Soho courtyard, the silver lustre of moonlight giving it the appearance of a bronze sculpture left out for the binmen.

'How's your luck, mate?' he said softly, then tossed it the remaining nub of saveloy from the hasty supper he'd grabbed from the all-night café in Lisle Street. He'd always felt a certain affinity with these urban scavengers, who eked out their living among the city's shadows.

The fox gobbled up the offering then slunk past him to peruse the dustbins with the cool insouciance of the streetwise.

Smiling, Harley sucked the grease from his fingers and got back to the job in hand. He took out the photograph of the runaway. She looked the epitome of a well-brought-up suburban girl. God only knew what the kid had had to endure in the last few weeks on the streets of the capital. Still, if his information was correct, he might have her safely back home by the following evening.

He transferred his trusty brass knuckleduster to his side pocket, sparked up a smoke from a pack of Gold Flake and made his way towards the iron staircase in the corner of the yard. The stairs led to the Pied Piper nightclub – though calling such a drab little joint a nightclub was stretching it a bit. This particular dive was not much more than a 'bottle party' open to anyone desperate enough to hunt it out in the dingy back streets of Soho.

Once inside the club, Harley took stock of his surroundings. It was a meagre affair: a simple, rectangular room; wooden tables and chairs scattered around a small dancefloor; the musty tang of sweat, alcohol and tobacco smoke. The standard of punter was equally uninspiring: wide-boys and petty criminals; a few down-on-their luck musicians and theatrical types; a group of provincial travelling salesmen (looking the worse for wear in their cheap, ill-fitting suits) and two university students, whose cut-glass accents and drunken braying would no doubt single them out for special attention at the end of the night. And then there were the 'hostesses'. In some of the more fashionable West End establishments these would have been professionals of a different type – genuine graduates of social and theatrical dancing schools, employed by the club to offer their skills to the good-time Charlies and jazz-mad scions of the upper classes. But in the Piper their provenance was of a far more dubious nature, and they wore their credentials on their louche, powdered faces.

It didn't take Harley long to spot the pimp Vern Slater. There he was, leaning against the makeshift bar in the typical wide-boy uniform: the garish checked suit with its oversized lapels, the gaudy American silk tie – the ubiquitous toerag ponce, keeping an eye on his new acquisition, no doubt. But where was she? It was likely he'd have attempted to change her appearance somehow, but a quick scan of the club failed to reveal anyone who looked remotely like young Alice Pritchard from Woking.

Harley looked back at Slater and noticed he'd been joined by a forlorn-looking character in a decaying lounge suit. The newcomer was pointing in Harley's direction while whispering in the ponce's ear. Slater hitched his waistband and began to saunter over.

He'd been clocked.

'Well, well. What have we here, then?'

'Evening, Vernon,' said Harley, offering a casual smile while surreptitiously teasing his fingers into the heavy brass knuckles in his pocket.

'Oh, *Vernon*, is it? Well, I don't know you, pal. But my mate over there reckons you're the sherlock who's been sticking his fat nose in where it don't belong.'

Keeping his smile, Harley looked over to the door, to make brief eye contact with the club's strong-arm – a young West Indian named Jensen, known to have a calm head on his well-developed shoulders.

'The smart thing to do here, Slater, would be to play nice with me. See, I'm here to help you resolve your little problem. But I guess you demonstrated your reluctance to do the smart thing when you bought that suit.'

The ponce sneered at him.

'What little problem?'

'The one you're about to have with the bogeys, when I tell them your latest acquisition is only fifteen. You probably didn't even know – they look so grown-up in their glad rags, don't they? But now you do know, I'm sure you won't mind me taking Alice off your hands, so I can get her back to her old mum. What d'you say? After all, a bit of poncing's one thing, but corruption of a minor? You don't want to be getting your collar felt for that kind of thing.'

Slater's response was to conjure a cut-throat razor from his inside pocket – the lower portion of its blade covered in sticking plaster, to make it easier to wield. This was hardly a surprise to Harley – with this kind of lowlife a razor was almost a given.

But before the private detective could respond to the threat, the impressive figure of the club's bouncer appeared, looming large over Slater's shoulder.

'Everything alright here, gents?'

'Nothing I can't handle thanks, Jensen.'

'Glad to hear that, George. But this can't be happening in here.'

'You'd better explain that to Sweeney Todd,' said Harley, keeping his eye on the blade in Slater's scrawny fist.

Jensen turned to the ponce, retaining his beatific smile. 'Vernon, I'm afraid you're going to have to leave now.'

Slater tried his best to give the bouncer a dismissive once-over – made all the more laughable by the contrast in their stature.

'Oh yeah? And who's going to make me?'

Jensen answered this with a quick flash of the machete tucked into his waistband.

The pimp curled his lip and spat on the floor, then pushed his way through the small crowd which had gathered to watch the altercation.

'Did that cockroach come in with a girl tonight?' asked Harley.

'Yeah,' said Jensen. 'A clean-cut little number. Looked a bit green for one of Vernon's pals.'

'That sounds like her.' Harley offered a cigarette. 'Where is she now?'

'Left with a punter. 'Bout twenty minutes before you came in.'

'Anyone we know?'

The bouncer lit his smoke on the proffered match, then shook his head. 'No. But the boss mentioned something about the fella. I got the feeling she didn't like him too much.'

Harley made his way over to the small dancefloor, where the proprietor of the club – an ageing platinum blonde by the name of Shelly Carboys – was attempting a foxtrot with one of the theatrical types.

'Mind if I cut in?'

'George! What a nice surprise. We've not seen you in ages.' Carboys' make-up looked a little more Hackney than Hollywood at close quarters. 'Business or pleasure?'

'Business, I'm afraid, Shelly.'

'No peace for the wicked, eh? What can I do you for?'

'Vern Slater.'

She pouted with disdain. 'Oh, that little toerag. No doubt it's about that new little mott of his.'

'You got it in one. Jensen tells me she went off with a punter a little while back. Someone you know?'

'Tell me, George – how old is she?'

'Fifteen.'

Carboys let out a weary sigh then led Harley to a secluded table in a darkened corner, where she slumped into a chair and splashed a generous slug of gin into her glass. 'Fifteen? I swear I'm getting too long in the tooth for this game.' She took a restorative gulp of her drink then placed her hand on Harley's. 'Listen. The bloke that poor kid's gone off with? He's a wrong 'un.'

'In what way?'

'In quite a few ways, I'd say. His name's Turpin, Alfred Turpin. He used to be a regular at the Fitzroy Tavern, that is until Pop Kleinfeld barred him. He got obsessed with Pop's daughter, Annie. Started bombarding her with gifts and letters. Oh, it began all innocent enough – romantic poems and such. Turpin fancies himself as a bit of a tortured artist, you see. Anyway, Annie didn't want anything to do with him and told him as much, in no uncertain terms. Well, that's when things started to get ugly.'

'How so?'

'Well, instead of love letters, Annie started to receive these creepy packages. Queer stories that Turpin had penned, and obscene drawings, all featuring poor Annie as the victim of some demented killer. And there was other stuff in the parcels too. Clumps of his hair, toenails and...' Carboys gave a little disgusted shake of her shoulders and paused to cleanse her palate with another swig of gin. 'Anyway, a few of the regulars at the pub decided to take the law into their own hands; went round to Turpin's one night to warn him off. Things turned a bit nasty and Turpin pulled a gun; shot one of the lads in the hand.'

'Did he do time for it?'

'No. Not for that – the family had some fancy brief who got him off on a claim of self-defence. But when the bogeys searched his place, they found all sorts. Dirty books and pictures – and not just those saucy smudges they knock out in Old Compton Street; real perverted stuff, you know? And more of the drawings he'd made, and the stories, not just about Annie but about other girls as well. There was enough evidence to have Turpin put away for a while in the funny farm. But he's been back in Soho a couple of months now. And by all accounts he's as loony as ever: preaching in the street from some paperback novel as though it were the Bible. Looks like he hasn't slept in weeks. I don't know what Jensen was thinking, letting him in here, really I don't.'

'And this is the punter who's just gone off with my client's fifteen-year-old daughter?' Harley grabbed his hat from the table and stood up. 'Where does this character live?'

'Not far from here. Above the newsagents in Bridle Lane. He's got the set of attic rooms. But be careful, George. I'm telling you, Alfred Turpin's not right in the head.'

* * *

The lock on the communal street door next to the newsagents was a simple latch affair and offered little resistance to Harley's deft application of a small strip of celluloid, which he kept in his jacket for just such occasions. After a quick check of the list of named bell pushes it was just a matter of a quiet climb to the top floor.

On reaching Turpin's apartment, he took a moment to catch his breath.

There came a sharp squeal from inside the room.

He placed his ear to the door: a man's voice, cursing... a plaintive sobbing... and, underneath it all, a kind of low hiss.

What *was* that? Like the sound of a gas bracket before it's lit. Was this madman trying to gas himself, and take little Alice with him?

Harley made a quick assessment of the door: two locks on this one, both of a superior quality to the latch on the street entrance. But the doorframe had seen better days – patched and filled from a previous forcing by the look of it.

The first hefty kick did significant damage: there was the satisfying sound of splintering timber and the door yielded a quarter of an inch or so. But the locks weren't fully breached yet and now he'd shown his hand.

'Turpin!' he shouted, hearing panicked scrambling from inside. 'Give the girl up and I promise it'll end there!'

Another boot saw the bottom third of the frame break free. He took a step back, hurled himself against the door... and he was in, stumbling across the room, grabbing at the foot of the bed to steady himself.

There, amongst the tangle of soiled sheets, chained to the bedstead by her ankle, lay a girl. Pale and thin. Naked, apart from a cotton shift, rucked up to reveal a white thigh as slender as a hare's. It took a moment for Harley to work out what was wrong with her face. Then he realised where the hissing was coming from.

He ripped the rubber mask from her mouth and shut the valve on the cylinder. The sweet, sickly odour hung in the air. Ether. Enough to knock out a horse. He placed a finger to the carotid artery – to his relief, he found a pulse, surprisingly strong in the circumstances. But this wasn't Alice Pritchard.

He took stock of the room. The wall above the bed was plastered with pages torn from a book, notes scribbled in the margins, and phrases ringed and underlined. Other walls were adorned with sketches and paintings, and poetry scrawled in erratic capitals. Most of the artwork was figurative – nudes, executed in a naive style with a bold hand; but their poses and distorted genitalia hinted at a fevered brain. Harley thought he recognised the unconscious girl on the bed in a couple of the more shocking images. He glanced over at her forlorn figure, hoping they hadn't been drawn from life.

A cold draught blew in from the corner of the room, where a rickety flight of steps led up to an open door. It was almost certainly the way Turpin had escaped, but Harley decided to make a quick check of the kitchenette first – he didn't want to be crowned with a frying pan on the way up.

Less than a minute later, he was tentatively stepping out onto a flat roof, slick with a light rain that had just begun to fall on the Soho night. The building was high enough to catch a glimpse of the illuminated billboards of Piccadilly Circus, the neon light fizzing and squirming in the distance.

'Get out, copper! This is private property!'

Harley span around to find Turpin balanced on the parapet wall. His jacket had been slung over a grubby vest, his eyes were wired with bloodshot veins. Around his neck there was a noose; expertly tied by the look of it. A prop for his sick fantasies? Or part of the plan for some dramatic final scene? The other end of the hemp rope was hitched to an iron ring bolted to the chimney stack.

And there, clasped tightly to Turpin's side, was little Alice Pritchard. Her eyes were fixed, unfocused, her face set with a sickly pallor; this may have been due to shock, or a dose of Turpin's ether. Whatever the reason, the girl seemed dangerously unaware of the fatal drop behind her.

Harley made a lightning assessment of the situation, his brain fizzing like the neon in the distance. Force was out of the question.

'Listen, Alfred. I'm not the police. My name's George, George Harley. I'm here for *her*, for Alice.'

'You can't take her. It's her destiny, together with the other one. My work...'

Harley noticed Turpin's focus drift. His head jerked to the side, as though he were listening to something.

'Your work? Yes, of course. Are those your pictures in there? They're good, you know, you've got a talent. And the poetry, is that yours?'

Turpin gave a derisive laugh and hitched Alice up to get a better hold of her, both of them stumbling a little closer to the parapet's edge. He took a deep breath, turning his face up to the rain and mumbled something to the night sky.

'What was that?' With Turpin's gaze diverted, Harley risked taking a step closer.

'I said, it's not *my* poetry, it's from the universe. But it's hidden, don't you see? Hidden by our banal rationale.'

'The poetry of the universe, eh?' Harley took another surreptitious step forward. 'Sounds interesting. Explain that to me.'

Turpin chuckled. 'The pale girls lay chained in dreamy languor in the starlit loft.' He fixed Harley with a delirious grin and repeated the line, bellowing it out to the night: 'The pale girls lay chained in dreamy languor in the starlit loft! Don't you see? The starlit loft... the girls...'

Harley tensed as Turpin's hand disappeared into his jacket pocket.

'Cassina has it all in here!' he yelled, pulling out a tattered paperback. 'He's given us instructions. You just have to know where to find them.' He pushed the book against his forehead and closed his eyes again. 'At first, I didn't know how, couldn't work it out. But then it came to me. It's so simple, really. So simple. You just have to *stop looking*, d'you see? Embrace the randomness!'

Turpin's yell seemed to rouse Alice and, although still groggy, she began to squirm a little in his tight embrace. The artist stuffed the book back into his pocket and grabbed at the girl's wrist. The rain was falling harder now and he continued to shout, so he could be heard against its clattering.

'I allowed the universe to reveal its messages to me!'

'I'd like to know how you did that.' Harley moved another step closer, watching Turpin's feet, which were beginning to slip on the lichen-covered coping stone.

'I'm no amateur, you know, Harley. I've been to Paris. Met with Breton and the Dadaist Ernst. Supped at their table, drank it all in: the automatic drawing, the dream reading, expressions of the subconscious. But my work was still dross. Hackneyed, clichéd…' He paused to rearrange his grip on Alice, who had begun to moan and toss her head about. 'But the moment I read Cassina's book, I knew it held a message for me. A key to unlock it all. I went back to my notebooks from Paris, you see. And there it was, *Le Cadavre Exquis* – the *Exquisite Corpse*, creating random poetry. So, following Cassina's lead, I allowed it to guide me. My *life* became the work of art—' He stopped abruptly, snapping his head around as though expecting to find someone behind him.

'Alfred?'

Harley watched anxiously as Turpin released his grip on the girl in order to pull the noose tight around his own neck.

'The *Exquisite Corpse*…'

'Alfred, no!'

Turpin nodded, thrust Alice away from him, grasped at the wet rope and stepped back into the night.

With a desperate lunge, Harley just managed to grab a handful of damp trouser tweed. He clung doggedly to Turpin's right leg as he scrambled back to his feet beside the parapet. Turpin was thrust out horizontally before him, his body suspended by the noose attached to the chimney stack, one hand clutching desperately at the rope just above the knot. For a moment the man lay still, a look of perplexed surprise on his face. Then he began to kick out against his saviour.

'Cheese it, you bastard!' growled Harley, fending off the blows from the artist's free foot.

The delivery of a swift punch to the stomach soon put a stop to his struggling. Winded, Turpin lay still again, his face turning a shade of puce.

As the slate sky cracked to unleash its full torrent of freezing rain, Harley hooked his hand around the artist's belt and began to haul him in. It was then he cast a glance over at Alice.

The girl was on all fours on the parapet wall, heaving up the contents of her stomach in a watery stream.

'Alice! Get off the wall!' he shouted. But she seemed oblivious to her surroundings, rising clumsily to her feet.

'Get down, girl!'

As if in a dream, Alice closed her eyes and thrust her hands out to her side, her fingers splayed out in the torrential rain. Then, to Harley's horror, she began to stagger along the slippery parapet.

It was at this moment that Turpin began to lash out again with his feet. Harley parried the blows for a while but, by now, with the girl in such jeopardy, it had become a case of priorities.

He released his grip and vaulted across the roof to drag the fifteen-year-old to safety. On looking back, he found Turpin gone, the wet rope taut over its new load.

Once he'd secured Alice in the safety of the apartment, Harley returned to the roof's edge. There was Turpin below him – a gruesome pendulum swinging in the dismal night; his pallid face scuffed from its collisions with the brickwork.

'What a sodding mess!' he muttered, then got out of the rain to spark up a cigarette, before going off in search of a telephone.

2

'JESUS! AM I glad it was you that turned up, John,' said Harley, watching the detective inspector as he searched with meticulous care through the drawers in Turpin's dresser.

DI John Franklin was a rare breed: a straight bogey. Here was a CID officer who – to the best of Harley's knowledge – had never taken a bribe, mislaid corroborating evidence or forged a witness statement. And though Harley's complicated relationship with Soho's underworld meant they would never exactly be on the same side of the fence, he knew Franklin was a copper who could be relied upon to play it straight down the line.

'I mean, I thought I might be getting my collar felt for this mess; or, at the very least, have to spend a night down the factory, answering a lot of awkward questions.'

'Well, George,' said Franklin, taking a contemplative pull on his Bulldog briar pipe, 'I will need you to pop into the station to make a formal statement in the next couple of days. But, as you know, Turpin had form for this kind of thing. I see no reason to doubt your version of events. As a matter of fact, you've done us all a favour.'

'How so?'

'Well, I didn't want to say too much in front of the doctor, but that poor girl who was chained to the bed? She's Mia Janssen, the niece of the Dutch ambassador. She's been missing for just over a month now. We'd just about given up the ghost on her, to be honest with you. The whole thing has turned into a bit of a diplomatic nightmare. Over here studying Art, you see. One Saturday afternoon she tells her flatmates she's off to visit the National Gallery and then she simply disappears. Now we know why.'

'Art student, eh? Well, it looks like she became Turpin's muse, in a twisted kind of way.' Harley nodded to one of the grotesque sketches pinned to the wall above Franklin's head.

'Indeed,' said the policeman, with a disdainful sniff. 'God knows what she's been put through, the poor thing. I take it you've seen the box of photographic plates over there? Pornographic. No doubt destined for the smut pedlars of Soho. I would imagine the same fate awaited your Pritchard girl.'

'Yeah. She'd been slipped some kind of opiate, apparently,' said Harley. 'How she didn't fall off that roof I'll never know. But the doc thinks she'll recover quickly enough. Physically, anyway.'

Franklin sighed then turned his attention to some strips of paper laid out in front of him. 'Tell me about this theory of yours.'

Harley joined Franklin at the dresser and picked up one of the paperbacks stacked in a small pile there.

'Well, this book, *A Reflection in the Ice*. We've found, how many of these so far?'

'Ten at the last count.'

'Exactly. Now, this Turpin was as crazy as a clown in a nut factory, but who needs ten copies of the same story? I think for him this was more than just a novel. I think it had become a kind of bible, an instruction manual for his crazed life.'

Franklin picked up one of the books, turning it over to look at the photograph printed on the back cover. 'I've heard about this fellow, Alasdair Cassina. Bit of an agitator, by all accounts. Wants to stir things up.'

'I've not read the book myself,' said Harley. 'But, according to the newspapers, it's a bit controversial.'

'All good for sales.'

'No doubt. The story's about a priest who loses his faith and starts to question whether things can be morally right or wrong. He begins making decisions based on random events.'

'What do you mean?'

'Well, he starts to use the Bible to dictate his actions – flicking through the pages and stopping at random, interpreting the text he finds there as instructions. Think about it. That Old Testament has got more sex and violence in it than Villiers Street on a Friday night. You can imagine what this character gets up to.'

'So, are you saying Turpin was using the same method?'

'Kind of. But in a sort of more artistic way.'

'Artistic?'

Harley nodded. 'Open that novel, flick through the pages.'

'This looks like it's where these strips of sentences were cut from.'

'Exactly. Cut out and mixed up, to construct poems. Now look on the mirror there.'

Franklin took a pair of spectacles from his jacket pocket and peered at the lines of text pasted to the mirror. '*The pale girls, lay chained in dreamy languor, in the starlit loft...* I see: our two victims, this attic apartment.'

'Turpin recited that one to me just before he jumped. Now go and read the one above the sink in the kitchen.'

With a slight groan in acknowledgement of his lumbago, the policeman got up and crossed the room.

'*The blue artist, swings against the velvet shroud of night,*' he read. 'So, what? You think Turpin had planned his suicide, as some kind of work of art?'

'I can't say for sure. But who keeps a professionally tied noose in their bedroom? Apart from maybe one of those dodgy knocking shops in Mayfair.'

'Well, I don't profess to know much about art,' said Franklin, applying a match to the bowl of his Bulldog. 'To be frank, some of this modern stuff just leaves me with a ruddy headache. But I'll have the station photographer make records of all the walls before they're cleared, just in case there's some relevance to them. And as for the pornographic photographs, I suppose there's a small chance they were just for his personal use, but I think we have to assume they're already in wider circulation. One for C Division. God only knows what we're going to say to the ambassador.'

The policeman gave a sigh, producing a small cloud of aromatic pipe smoke.

'But I think one thing we can say, with some conviction, is that this Turpin character was a dangerous lunatic. Society's better off without him, in my opinion. And it's thanks to a damned good bit of detection work on your part that those two young girls will sleep safely in their beds tonight. Let's hope there are no other maniacs out there wanting to take instruction from this infernal book of Cassina's.'

3

JESSICA DAWSON'S FACE glimmered in the reflected neon from the billboards. She knew the diversion through Piccadilly Circus would add another quarter of an hour to the taxi journey home, but she'd felt a sudden desire to take in the spectacle, hoping the thrill of modernity might prolong her holiday spirit for a while longer. It had been less than an hour since they had disembarked at Paddington, but already she could feel the small nip of anxiety, worrying away at her insides. She knew it would only become more insistent the nearer they got to that dull, suffocating house.

The two weeks at her parents' had proved such a tonic. Oh, there had been the usual awkward questions about Rupert's business trips, her father labouring the point about the importance of strong role models for the children and the like; but, for the most part, she had relished the respite.

'Don't worry, Sophie, we've got a way to go yet,' she whispered, noticing the children's nanny had woken and was gazing out of the window in confusion. 'Go back to sleep, dear.'

As usual, Sophie had been a godsend while they'd been away. Jessica felt a little pang of guilt at the way her children seemed so physically at ease in the young woman's sleeping embrace: little Alice sucking her thumb and mechanically stroking the bridge of her snub nose, and Billy... well, Billy looking like a contented, normal child for once.

Whatever was to be done with Billy? There could be no denying that in these past few weeks the strangeness of his behaviour had begun to intensify. The habitual stretching of the truth was one thing, but of late his little 'pranks' (as Rupert chose to call them) had exceeded mere whimsy and, in her opinion, were now bordering on the downright abnormal. And to think he'd be going away to school next year. Something must be done soon about the child, or else... or else, what? Well, she wasn't sure, but she could sense its presence, looming, just out of sight. She sighed quietly and felt another little anxious flutter in her gut.

The cabbie slid open the glass partition. 'There's a dray that's lost its load up ahead, missus. We're gonna 'ave to take another slight detour.'

'Very well. If it can't be helped. Only I really should be getting the children to bed soon.'

'Don't you worry, lady. We'll 'ave the little tykes all snuggled up and sawing logs in no time at all.'

'Much appreciated,' she said, forcing a smile. But secretly she was in no hurry to return home, no hurry at all.

South of the river, the streets grew shabbier. As the cab pulled up at a traffic light, Jessica's eyes were caught in the hollow stare of a mangy terrier, gnawing at a bone in the entrance to a butcher's shop – a look repeated in the rheumy eyes of the vagrant attached to it by a filthy piece of string. The medieval-looking headgear slumped over the old man's head reminded her of the Breughel print above the fireplace in the drawing room. She sat there transfixed as the tramp took a shuffling step towards the vehicle, holding out a grimy hand in a half-hearted manner. It was as if the unknown presence she'd felt looming in the shadows had revealed itself for a brief moment. The cab started off again and when she looked back through the rear window, the man remained standing there, his hand held out to the night.

* * *

Sophie pushed the front door closed behind her with her foot and dropped the last of the luggage on the hallway runner. 'Gosh! You were right, madam,' she said, rubbing her hands together. 'Just feel how cold it is.'

'I gave Justine the fortnight off,' replied Jessica. 'The house has been empty since we've been away. You get the children off to bed and I'll lay a fire in the drawing room. They can have the paraffin heater on in the nursery, just until it warms up a little.'

Suddenly wide awake, Billy tossed his cap in the general direction of the hatstand. 'Bagsy I light it!' he chirped, dashing up the stairs.

'Absolutely not. Billy!' Jessica yelled after her son. 'No matches, do you hear me?' She turned to Sophie with an exasperated look.

The nanny scooped up Alice and made for the stairs. 'Don't worry, madam. Billy, you wait up now!'

Before long, Jessica had the gas mantles hissing and popping in the drawing room, and with the fire built and beginning to take, she turned to the tantalus of decanters on the sideboard. She was just in the act of pouring herself a generous sherry when her attention was drawn to one of the heavy damask curtains, which had given a flutter, as though caught in a draught. The pair of curtains weren't quite drawn to, and she could see the French windows, leading to the back garden, had been left slightly ajar. *Damn that girl!* she thought, assuming that the maid, Justine, had been so desperate to get off to Brighton with her latest beau that she'd neglected to make the final checks of the property. No wonder it had felt so cold when they'd first arrived.

With a little dramatic huff of exasperation, Jessica placed the stopper back in the decanter and began to make her way over to the windows. But as she did so, her eye caught the Breughel print, and she was overtaken by an immediate sense of foreboding.

She stopped and took a step back.

What if they'd been burgled? Who was to say that at that very moment some brute wasn't behind the curtain, lurking there with murderous intent?

Keeping her eye on the French windows, Jessica backed towards the fireplace and grabbed the poker from the companion set.

'Sophie? Would you come down here for a moment?' she called towards the open doorway.

The nanny came into the room, drying her hands on her apron. 'I'm afraid Alice is still suffering from the effects of all that chocolate yesterday and— Oh! Whatever is it, madam?'

Jessica lowered the poker, not wanting to cause any unnecessary alarm. 'Hopefully nothing.' She nodded towards the curtains. 'It would appear that Justine was in somewhat of a hurry when she locked up last week.'

'Or…'

'Yes?'

'Or we might have been broken into. After all, Justine may have her faults, but I really don't think she'd—'

'No, perhaps you're right,' said Jessica, raising the poker again.

'Should I run and get a constable?'

'Not just yet. We need to make sure it's not just a silly oversight; after all, nothing else appears disturbed, does it?'

The nanny, now looking decidedly pale, shook her head. Then she steeled herself. 'We could look together, madam? I'll pull back the curtain, if you could...' Sophie nodded towards the two feet of wrought iron in her mistress's hand.

'Well done. Brave girl. Come on, we'll link arms.'

Having made a cautious approach, Jessica felt Sophie's taut frame relax a little.

'Oh, thank goodness! Look.' She pointed towards the pair of children's patent leather shoes which protruded from the hem of the curtain, then unhooked her arm and stepped forward. 'Billy! You're a wicked little devil, giving us such a fright. What are we to do with you?'

Her mistress, however, wasn't quite as reassured by the sight. 'Wait a moment,' she said, as the nanny grabbed at the damask. 'Those aren't Billy's shoes—'

But it was too late. Sophie had already whipped aside the curtain to reveal the grisly tableau, destined to replay in both women's nightmares for years to come: the child's corpse dressed in a pristine sailor's suit, propped sitting up against the wall, its once-innocent face now blue-black with putrescence, the vulgar wound encircling its neck puckered with crude stitches.

As Jessica Dawson stood in her suburban drawing room, deafened by the piercing screams of her children's nanny, she found herself pondering one uncanny detail in the abomination laid out before her. 'It's too small,' she murmured. 'The head – it's too small.' It was a puzzle she was still mouthing when the constable arrived, ten minutes later.

4

Harley stopped at the entrance to Meard Street and tapped out a smoke from the packet of Gold Flake. He nodded towards the lamplight, where a few frayed wreathes of smog had begun to gather.

'I told you we were in for another London Particular, didn't I? I can always sense it coming. You get that taste like iron filings at the back of your throat.'

Cynthia pulled her coat collar up against the night chill and gave him a frown. 'Alright, my little Geronimo, there's no need to look so delighted about it.' She rubbed her upper arms, trying to produce a little warmth.

Harley took a long drag on his cigarette and regarded his girlfriend, who at that moment – standing beneath the gas lamp in her suede-down overcoat and velvet toque hat – was looking rather glamorous. Not for the first time he posed a silent question to himself: *What on earth was she doing with him?*

Now, George Harley was no diffident youth. During his formative years on the tough streets of Shoreditch, and the subsequent action he'd seen in the war, he'd cultivated a respectable amount of self-confidence. He was quite aware he had a sharp brain, and a set of skills which allowed him to successfully navigate the sometimes-perilous day-to-day existence of a private detective working in the underbelly of the city. And though under no illusions of possessing matinée idol features, he *had* managed to survive his time in the trenches without receiving any disfiguring injuries – something that couldn't be said for a lot of the poor buggers you saw on the streets – and he'd been told, on more than one occasion, he had a certain 'rugged charm'. So, what was the problem? The problem was one of class: Cynthia Masters' formative years hadn't been spent on the tough streets of Shoreditch, but in leafy Hampstead. She was the cultured offspring of a wealthy, middle-class family (albeit a slightly bohemian, liberal one), one of the first female members of the Queen's Hall Orchestra. And therefore, although all the evidence suggested they had a strong and genuine relationship (among other things, they shared a love of books and a sardonic sense of humour), Harley could never fully quash the niggling doubt that he might be just some kind of entertaining social experiment.

He was brought round from his reverie by a poke in the ribs.

'Hey! Corporal Harley. Do you really mean to make a girl wait out in the cold and fog whilst you finish your cigarette?'

'Sorry. I was just thinking.'

'What is it, Einstein? Got cold feet all of a sudden?'

'What d'you mean?'

'Well, here we are at your current favourite watering hole, the famous Shabaroon. Full, no doubt, of your colourful villainous cronies and very probably the odd former sexual conquest.'

'Now, hold on a minute—'

'And I was just wondering whether you mightn't be a little embarrassed at the thought of revealing me to the throng.'

'Why the bloody hell would I be embarrassed?'

'Oh, I don't know,' she said with a theatrical sigh. 'Perhaps I'm a little too humdrum? Too respectable?'

'If you must know, I was just thinking that maybe we should have chosen somewhere a bit more upmarket. I mean, meeting your sister for the first time – I want to make a good impression, right? And the punters in the Shab are... well, let's just say that one or two of them are little more than just "colourful".'

'I wouldn't worry about Lilian. She's led rather a different kind of life to me. I told you she was adopted? Well, in her case, nature has had a bigger influence than nurture. She left home at nineteen, under somewhat of a cloud. Fell in with a few colourful types of her own, as a matter of fact. No, I don't think the Shabaroon will hold any surprises for Lilian.'

Harley killed his cigarette under his shoe. 'Now I *am* intrigued. Come on then, let's get you in out of the cold.'

'What *is* a shabaroon anyway?' asked Cynthia, linking arms with him as they approached the pub, which gleamed with welcoming promise in the gloom of the Soho street.

'It's a milestone-monger. Someone who looks like they're on the George Robey,' said Harley, grinning because he knew what was coming next.

'Very good. Now once again in English please?'

'A tramp. Well, actually, anyone who looks a bit filthy.'

'Shabby?'

'Exactly,' said Harley, stopping to open the swing doors of the pub.

* * *

The sight which greeted Cynthia on entering the saloon bar of the Shabaroon was that of a fine, handsome London pub. The L-shaped room was flanked on either side by long leather bench seats and rows of circular tables. The ochre-tinged pattern on the oil-cloth flooring – originally designed to mimic the neoclassical mosaics of a stately Georgian mansion

– was now so distorted by a collection of faded patches, scuff marks and dubious stains as to leave it looking more like an extended version of the Turin Shroud. The crimson-papered walls were lined with a selection of Gillray's most grotesque and bawdy caricatures, interspersed with mirrors which extolled the virtues of various spirits and ales. As yet, only a low rumble could be heard emanating from the public bar next door, but there was still plenty of drinking time left for its small cast of taxi drivers, costermongers and navvies to develop a more bellicose soundtrack for their neighbours in the saloon bar. But the main focus was the bar itself; there, at the centre of things, in all its grandeur of polished brass, lacquered mahogany and shimmering glass, it was a vision as exciting to a thirsty punter as a schoolboy's first glimpse of a fairground carousel. And then there were the Shab's customers, at least half of whom sat drinking alone, dotted around the bar in meditative attitudes, as if posing for a life-drawing class for students of a Cockney Toulouse-Lautrec. Individuals who might pass for perfectly ordinary in the crush of the underground carriage or tram, but who here, singled out for scrutiny, all appeared to be advertising the promise of an entertaining backstory.

'We could go through to the lounge bar, where it's quieter,' said Harley.

Cynthia shook her head, momentarily transfixed by an elderly woman with a towering bird's nest of hair, who had just produced a small pug dog from her voluminous handbag and was now feeding it like a newborn from a bottle of stout.

'What, and miss the main event? No fear.'

'Alright then, let's get you a drink.'

'Here he is – Georgie Boy!' exclaimed the barmaid, her accent as brash as her bottle-blonde hairdo. 'And *you* must be Cynthia. He's told us all about you, dear.'

'Has he, now?'

'Cynthia, this is Juney,' said Harley, trying to ignore his girlfriend's withering look. 'It might have Hal's name over the door,' he pointed to the portly man in a checked waistcoat and unconvincing ginger toupée who was serving at the other end of the bar, 'but it's Juney here who really runs the place.'

'Please to meet you, Juney,' said Cynthia.

'Oh, but she's lovely, George. And don't she talk nice? I'd say you're punching a little over your weight with this one.'

'Alright, steady on.'

'Oh, go on with you, I'm only pulling your leg.'

'Hold up. Is that Teddy Gables that Hal's chucking out?' said Harley, watching the landlord, as he escorted a skinny youth with a Hessian sack to the door. 'What's he been up to this time?'

'Spectacle cats.'

'Whatever are spectacle cats?' asked Cynthia.

Juney laughed, shaking her head. 'It's his latest hare-brained scheme. He's got two white kittens in that sack that he's trying to flog, with little spectacle markings around their eyes. Teddy swears it's a freak of nature. But you can still see the hair dye on his fingers, the pillock. He certainly ain't got his old man's nous.'

'His dad, Sonny Gables, is a big name in knocked-off gear,' Harley explained to Cynthia. 'He could sell balloons at a funeral, that one. But Teddy? Well, I reckon the midwife must have given him a big whack with the stupid stick when he came out.'

'Ain't that the truth?' said Juney. 'Now, what'll it be, love?'

'Whisky and a splash for me, and a gin and French for Cynthia.'

Having received their drinks, they retired to one of the small tables by the windows. Cynthia unbuttoned her coat, giving Harley a nudge with her elbow.

'Penny for your thoughts.'

'Sorry, I was just thinking about the Turpin case.'

'Those poor girls. Have you heard how they're faring?'

'Alice is doing alright, by all accounts. I had a long conversation with her father on the phone yesterday. Mia Janssen is convalescing in hospital. She'll be returning home when she's strong enough. By the way, I got a nice surprise from the ambassador.'

'Really? What was it?'

'A healthy little cheque, plump enough to bring a smile to the face of my morbidly depressed bank manager. That, along with the fee from the Pritchard case, means… well, I should be on velvet for a good couple of months at least.' Harley took a sip of his Scotch. 'So, silver linings and all that.'

'Mercenary,' said Cynthia, poking the end of his nose.

'By the way, I meant to ask you: this author, Alasdair Cassina – just how well do you know him?'

'Well, he was part of the crowd I used to hang around with, some four or five years ago.'

'Would that be during your Bright Young Things phase?' asked Harley with a smirk.

'Really, at times you're so—' Cynthia suddenly lowered her voice to a whisper at the sight of the woman approaching the table. 'Hello, who's this coming over?'

The newcomer appeared to be somewhere in her mid-forties; she was a little overdressed for a pub, and her faltering step suggested that the drink she clutched in her hand might not be the first of the day. She slumped herself down on the bench seat beside them, letting out an exhausted sigh.

'George, darling. How simply *wonderful* to see you.' Her voice was smoky, a little mannish and had a monotone suggestive of habitual ennui. 'Life looking after you, I trust?'

'Oh, mustn't grumble, Dora. You're looking well.'

'Really, d'you think so?' She offered a feline smile and touched a hand to her hair, which was dyed a cardinal red and worn a little longer than the current trend. 'One does one's best with the materials provided.'

'This is Cynthia, Dora.'

'Please to meet—' began Cynthia, but stopped as the older woman bobbed out of sight, finally appearing again with a pair of Mary Jane shoes, which she dropped onto the table.

'That's better. They've been pinching like buggery for the past hour or so.'

'Been on your feet all day?' asked Cynthia.

'On my back mostly, if you must know,' said Dora, producing a packet of Black Cat cigarettes from her clutch bag. 'At Claridge's; one of the penthouse suites. My darling little Arab is over at the moment, you see. Quite a voracious appetite, for a small man...' She gave Cynthia a slow wink. 'But he is so incredibly *thankful*. And he's got the wherewithal to prove it. I shan't have to work for at least another fortnight. Hence the celebrations.' She raised her glass in a perfunctory toast and downed its contents in one. 'I'm sorry, dear – not shocking you, am I?'

'No, not at all,' said Cynthia, hoping she'd managed to modify her expression in time.

Dora lit her cigarette and placed a half-crown down on the table. 'George, do be a darling and get another round in. The usual for me.'

'Whisky and peppermint? Right you are. Cyn, you want another?'

'Not just yet, thanks. I don't want to get squiffy.'

'Good grief!' said Dora. 'Whyever not?'

As Harley went off for the drinks, Dora leant on the table, a ribbon of cigarette smoke escaping through her crimson lips. She regarded Cynthia with her painted almond eyes, languid and world-weary. 'You know, you really shouldn't pity me, dear.'

'Oh, but I—'

'Really, there's no need to explain,' said Dora, placing a hand on her forearm. 'I caught the look – see it all the time. But it's not such a bad life. I'm not actually "on the pavement", as they say, like all those Piccadilly daisies.'

'Oh,' said Cynthia, caught a little off guard by Dora's nonchalance. 'Are there many girls like that, would you say?'

'In the West End? Simply droves of them, my dear. The area's notorious for it. Oh, but don't be too concerned, we're not all fallen women in need of salvation.'

'Why then, would you say…' Cynthia struggled to find the best way to phrase her question. 'How does—'

'How does a girl end up whoring?' Dora smiled at the colour she'd raised in Cynthia's cheeks. 'Oh, there are countless reasons for that. For most, though, I'd say it's a conscious decision to improve their lot. Granted, there are those poor wretches who turn to it out of desperation, but they're by no means the majority. You see, many girls come here to London from different parts of the country in search of work. Well, they soon discover that our game is far more lucrative than going into service or working their fingers to the bone in some godforsaken factory. They come from all types of backgrounds. Some girls are weak in intellect, others are the most cunning little cats you'll ever meet. But there *is* a hierarchy.' She took a leisurely draw on her cigarette.

'Hierarchy?'

'Of course. At the very bottom of the ladder are those desperate enough to have to use the streets to both attract and perform their business.' Dora showed her disdain for this conduct with a little wrinkle of her nose. 'Then there are those girls who solicit on the streets but take the punter back to a rented room, or the "lumber" as they call it – by far the most common practice, I'd say. These girls are usually enslaved to some awful pimp type, of course. Then we have the fillies in the stables of the more serious villains.'

Dora made a quick check around her and leant in close. 'Like those dreadful Manduca brothers, for example.'

She sat back, dabbed an elegant finger to her tongue and smoothed one of her pencilled eyebrows.

'And at the top of the profession are those such as yours truly. We rely on personal introductions, you understand. It's mostly the top-end hotels, or their place, if wifey's away. As well as the professional fee, I'll be wined and dined; sometimes there's an expensive gift. You get used to anything if you do it long enough. And, God knows, I've been doing it long enough. We all sell ourselves eventually, in one way or another, body or soul. You know, once upon a time, I was one of those dutiful little housewives. Difficult to picture, I know, but there you are. The perfect little homemaker – dinner on the table, attending to the needs of hubby. Well, if you ask me, I'd say there's not much difference between that game and the one I'm in now. Except, of course, now I get to choose what I spend the ill-gotten gains on.'

Dora lounged back in her seat, exhaled a plume of smoke and treated Cynthia to one of her arch smiles.

Up at the bar, Harley was being attended to by the landlord, Hal Dixon.

'By the way, George, Franklin was in at lunchtime.'

'Was he?' As usual, when conversing with Dixon, Harley was trying his best not to be caught glancing at the notorious hairpiece, which was a completely different hue to the publican's remaining hair and was nestled atop his scalp like a hibernating woodland animal.

'Good plainclothes man, that one,' said the landlord. 'As rare as hen's teeth, these days, more's the pity.' He placed Harley's Scotch on the bar and took the money. 'He was asking after you. Said he wanted to see you about something.'

Harley made a quick check of the bar for eavesdroppers. After all, he could ill-afford to acquire the reputation of a copper's nark. 'Thanks for the tip. I'll get on the blower tomorrow and see what he wants. Oh, and keep schtum, eh?'

'Goes without saying,' said Dixon, tapping his finger to the side of his nose. 'But it's not exactly a secret you've been working together, is it?'

'What do you mean?'

'Well, it's in the paper.'

'What's in the paper?'

'Here,' said Dixon, producing a copy of the *Daily Oracle* newspaper from under the bar, already folded open at the article. 'I was just showing Juney. It's that Turpin affair, the kidnapping of the ambassador's daughter. You get a mention.'

'Jesus, no! Show me.'

'Don't worry,' said the landlord as Harley scanned the report. 'You come out of it well, I'd say.'

'That's not the point, though, is it? This game relies on discretion. Anonymity. I can hardly work undercover if my ugly mug is staring up at the world and his wife from their bleedin' chip paper, can I? I can't believe Franklin would have sanctioned this. There must be a leak at the station.'

'There's no photograph. You know, you could look at it another way, it might be good for business. After all, it was a decent result.'

'Good for business? Oh yes, and what about certain local characters, the ones who aren't exactly fans of His Majesty's Metropolitan Police Force?' Harley checked no one else was in earshot and lowered his voice. 'The seasoned villains I rub shoulders with on a regular basis won't think it's good for business, will they? Turpin was my case, worked in the usual way; just solo sherlocking. The bogeys only got involved after the fact, to help clean up the mess. To read this article you'd think I was working for them as some kind of special constable.'

'I understand what you're saying, George, but you're overthinking it. Nobody will remember the details of that article, not with that kiddie murderer all over the front page.'

'Kiddie murderer? Sorry, I was working a late one last night, missed the morning edition. Hang on, is this the Clapham thing? I heard someone talking about it on the tram. What happened exactly?'

Dixon folded the newspaper to the front page and pointed at the headline.

NURSERY BUTCHER! MONSTER AT LARGE IN CLAPHAM!

'That's what's happened. And it ain't pretty reading, I can tell you.'

'Blimey! That's awful,' said Harley, tipping his hat back after skimming the first few paragraphs of the story.

'Ain't it just?' said Dixon. 'Just imagine finding that in your parlour. Two young women on their own, an' all. Doesn't bear thinking about, does it?'

'And the dead kid?'

'The police haven't identified the body yet. Least, they're not saying if they have. Go on, take the paper with you, I've finished with it. Although you might want to spare your young lady the more gruesome details. It reads like one of them old penny dreadfuls. The little mite's heart had been torn out, apparently.' He handed Harley his change. 'Puts me in mind of when Old Jack was raising Cain around Whitechapel. You'll be too young, of course.'

'The Ripper?'

'Yeah. I must have been around nine or ten, at the time.' The landlord gave a sigh as he hooked his thumbs into the pockets of his tight-fitting waistcoat. 'You know, to me the most terrifying aspect was thinking of them poor buggers who discovered the bodies. To be on your own, in the dark, stumbling across all that horror laid out before you. Used to give me the willies, I don't mind telling you. I still think on it from time to time, especially when we get a thick old pea souper. When that fog comes in... well, I dunno, it's like something evil is descending on the city.'

'It's coming in out there right now.'

'Well, let's hope we haven't got another one of them homicidal maniacs on our hands, eh?'

'Too right. Though, I must say, on first impressions this reads like—'

Harley was interrupted by a huge hand clamping down on his shoulder.

'Christ, Solly!' he exclaimed, turning to discover Solly Rosen standing behind him. 'What have I told you about creeping up on a bloke like that?'

Rosen was one of Harley's oldest friends. A former middleweight champion of Great Britain, he now worked for Mori 'The Hat' Adler – the Jewish mobster who controlled a large part of the West End underworld.

'He's right, you know, Hal,' said the ex-boxer, poking a thumb at Harley and addressing the landlord with a wonky grin. 'You've got to tread careful with this one. He learnt all that fancy hand-to-hand combat malarkey in the war. He'd break your neck as soon as look at you, would Georgie Boy.'

'You're a funny man,' said Harley, swatting his friend's hand from his shoulder. 'You ought to be working the variety houses, you know? You'd make a killing.'

'Oh yeah?' Rosen made a brief feint with his right hand, then slapped his friend playfully on the cheek. 'Anyway, you're the only celebrity round here, as far as I can see.' He pulled a rolled-up newspaper from the inside pocket of his coat. 'George Harley, *the Soho Sleuth*.'

'You've seen it, then?'

'Yup. I'm guessing it weren't your idea.'

'Anyone mentioned it yet?' asked Harley.

'Mori's asked a couple of questions. But don't worry, I fought your corner for you. He knows you've always been staunch.'

Rosen sniffed and took a quick look around him. 'The Maltese might be a different story, though.'

'The Manducas? I've never had any dealings with them. Why should they worry?'

'Because that Turpin used to make a bit on the side by taking smutty pictures for them, that's why. A bit stronger than the usual schtick, apparently: weird set-ups, bizarre costumes.'

'Featuring the kidnapped daughters of foreign ambassadors, by any chance?'

'Yeah, well, Victor Manduca ain't going to worry about that, is he?' said Rosen. 'The more perverted the better, as far as the Spider's concerned; the man's an animal. But what he *is* worried about is the box of photographic plates found by your bogey mates at Turpin's flat the other night, after you'd marked his dance card up on the roof. Apparently, through some paperwork in the box, they've managed to trace the smut back to the Manducas' printing business.'

'Shit!'

'Exactly. They were raided by C Division yesterday. Destroyed a load of stock and slapped a hefty fine on them. What makes it worse is that Manduca's already bunging C Division a decent whack to leave him alone, but because the find came from DI Franklin's department, they had to show willing.'

'Please don't tell me Manduca's blaming me for all this?'

'I don't know yet. But if he sees that article in the paper…' Rosen finished the sentence by breathing in through his teeth. 'But listen,' he continued, noticing the concern on his friend's face. 'Why don't I have a word with Mori? They do a bit of business from time to time. See if he can't smooth things over for you.'

'Would you?'

'What are pals for? But in the meantime, I'd keep your head down, Georgie. Those Maltese don't play nice.'

'Understood. What are you drinking?'

Having furnished Rosen with a foaming pint of Burton's, they returned to the table, where the ex-boxer – who'd always possessed a breezy, ingenuous charm – proceeded to chat away freely with Cynthia as though they'd known each other all their lives. Having expounded further on the Shab's clientele, recounted a number of embarrassing stories from Harley's youth, and regaled her with some highly embellished accounts of his career in the ring, he'd just got around to producing photographs of his children, when he looked up towards a group who had just entered the pub.

'Ah! Now, here we go, Cynthia. Here's a proper local character for you. You might even have read about this one in the papers.' He nodded towards a woman of Junoesque stature surrounded by a small entourage of elegantly dressed young Chinese men.

'Limehouse Lil,' said Harley, taking over the commentary. 'She runs a roaring trade from above her restaurant in Chinatown, supplying all the little snow-birds in high society with their happy dust.'

'Do you mean cocaine?' asked Cynthia. 'Are you sure?'

'Positive. And she's doing well on it, by all accounts.'

'She's certainly doing well on something,' said Rosen. He sat up in his seat, straining to get a better view. 'What was it they called her in the paper, George?'

'*The High Priestess of Unholy Rites.*'

Rosen gave a quiet whistle.

Having scanned the room, the subject of their interest now made a beeline for their table, the swish of her Chinese satin brocade clearly audible above the hubbub of drinkers.

'She's coming over,' said Rosen, as he whipped a comb from his pocket and gave his slicked-back hair a quick tidy.

Much to Harley's surprise, Cynthia stood up to greet the new arrival.

'Lilian.'

'Cynthia, darling.'

'George,' said Cynthia. 'Meet Lilian Lee, née Masters – my big sister.'

'Oh, there's no need for introductions. George and I go way back, don't we George?' said Lil, giving Harley a peck on his astonished face.

5

IN 1918 BLAKE Harley had been legally declared dead, seven years after he'd gone missing while on expedition in Peru. The subsequent reading of his will revealed he had bequeathed his townhouse in Fitzrovia to his favourite nephew, George, who, after returning home from the war in France, took charge of his inheritance. Along with the Bell Street property came an extensive and eclectic reference library – which would go on to serve Harley as an invaluable aid to his investigations – and a vast collection of curiosities and treasures, amassed during Uncle Blake's adventuring around the globe.

Cynthia now stood in the sitting room of Harley's townhouse, studying a hand-tinted photograph on the mantelpiece, which depicted Uncle Blake dressed in traditional Turkish costume.

'I should like to have met your uncle. He seems to have been a remarkable character.'

'He was.'

'And to have left you this house and all these wonderful things. It must have been reassuring.'

'Reassuring?'

'Well, after all that horror you saw in the war. Wasn't it a consolation, of sorts, to have a solid base here to start again from?'

'Now you put it like that, I guess it was.'

'And of course, you had Moloch here to keep you company. Come here, you grumpy old thing.' Cynthia gathered up the tatty black tomcat and sat him on her lap. 'What?' she asked, seeing Harley's look of mild astonishment as Moloch squeezed his one green eye closed and began to purr loudly.

'I still can't get over the way he lets you manhandle him. He'd knock lumps out of me if I tried that.'

'You obviously haven't got the magic touch,' she said, chucking Moloch under his chin. 'Boys are so very easy to control, you know. You've just got to find what makes them tick.'

'You think so, do you?'

'Didn't I prove the point last night?' She tucked a lock of raven-black hair behind her ear. 'Why, Corporal Harley, are you blushing?'

'Give over!'

'You *are* blushing. Well, I never. Who'd have thought it, Moloch?' she whispered into the cat's ragged ear. 'The hardened trench-raider, blushing like a choirboy.'

Harley gave a little self-conscious chuckle and lit a Gold Flake. 'It's just that… well, I still haven't got used to your, you know – *frankness*.'

'I thought you were fully signed up to this new enlightened age?'

'Yeah, yeah, alright. Maybe it's a class thing.'

'Oh, we're there again, are we?'

'I don't know. Growing up around all those Hampstead bohemians; maybe you're just more relaxed talking about this stuff?'

Cynthia snatched Harley's cigarette off him and took a drag. 'Your friends at the Shabaroon the other night didn't seem too worried about discussing things of a carnal nature. Dora insisted on giving me tips on technique at one stage, and those two girls at Piccadilly Circus that we bumped into afterwards, well…'

'Vera and Gracie? I'd hardly call them girls. They're jaded nymphs of the pave. I'm just saying, your typical, decent, working-class girl wouldn't be as uninhibited as—'

'Hold on a moment!' she exclaimed, putting Moloch on the floor and standing up. 'Are you insinuating I'm not "decent"? Just because I'm able to discuss perfectly normal, adult topics, without pandering to outdated Victorian prudery?' She took a furious puff of the cigarette. 'Or is it because I allowed you to bed me so easily?'

'Whoa, whoa!' said Harley, his hands held up. 'Where did this come from? I wasn't saying you weren't decent. I mean, look at you.' He grabbed her around the waist. 'Who could be more decent? Miss Cynthia Masters, lead cello with the Queen's Hall Orchestra.'

She blew a small gust of smoke into his face. 'The phrase is "Principal Cello", philistine. And, anyway, I'm only Sub-Principal, that little weasel Humbert Fotheringhay is Principal. Lord knows why.'

'*Humbert Fotheringhay?* What kind of sodding name is that? I bet he got picked on at school.'

'I suspect Humbert went to a very different kind of school to you – that's assuming you actually went to school?'

Harley gave her an old-fashioned look. 'Of course, appearances aren't everything. I mean, you give it all that head girl schtick, but secretly you're the sister of the notorious Limehouse Lil. Who'd have thought it?'

'I've told you – don't call her that.'

Cynthia returned to the sofa.

After a period of quiet reflection, she said: 'I had no idea, you know – about the drug peddling. Although I must admit I had a sense she might be involved in something illicit. You see, Lilian's always been so evasive about... well, about most things, to be honest.'

'Well, Lil's got a profitable business down there in Limehouse; she's running a tight firm, which garners a lot of respect. Make no mistake, your big sister's a force to be reckoned with – with some powerful connections in society, by all accounts.'

'I don't see how that makes it any better.'

'Did you really have no idea about the stories in the papers?'

'It might surprise you, but I don't read the *Daily Oracle*.'

'Well, you're not missing much there.'

'Yes, I rather gathered that. Have they run many articles about her?'

'Just a couple. Last year. And, of course, they didn't publish her maiden name; she was Limehouse Lil or Lily Lee.'

'Do you know, I've never actually met her husband, Sammy.'

'Really?' said Harley.

She shook her head. 'It's only in the last year, since Mother died, that we've been back in contact – they had a terrible falling out, you see, when Lilian was in her early twenties. Mother forbade me to get in touch with her after that. Oh, we'd meet up secretly now and again, but then we had our own little spat. Nothing serious, just the usual sisterly squabbling. It was obvious by then that Mother was dying, and, well, I suppose I was feeling disloyal by going against her wishes. Since Mother's death we've met up a few times, usually in a tea room somewhere. She brought the girls along with her on a couple of occasions. That did raise a few eyebrows.'

'Because they're half Chinese?'

'Yes,' said Cynthia, looking a little abashed. 'Oh, but, they're super kids. And then, of course, there's the other business. I mean, I shouldn't imagine I'll be meeting Sammy any time soon.'

'You know he's in prison, then?'

She stubbed out her cigarette. 'Yes, but that's all I know. Lilian refused to give me any more detail – apart from insisting on his innocence, of course. To tell you the truth, I think I was a little too shocked at the time to pursue it any further. I almost daren't ask, but – do you know the full story?'

Harley nodded. 'Sammy's a lovely bloke. Salt of the earth.'

'Then why is he in prison?'

'Mainly for being in the wrong place at the wrong time. You see, Sammy and Lil bought themselves a restaurant, and worked it up into the best little dumpling house in Limehouse. But it got shut down, after a bunch of drunken sailors tore the place apart in a brawl. One of them, an officer, testified that Sammy was running janes from a flat above – all a load of madam of course, because Sammy's no ponce. But he lost his licence and the restaurant. Sammy got a job as a chef in another Chinese restaurant and Lil got a part-time job and, after a while, they'd managed to buy back the restaurant and bribe someone in the know to get the licence renewed. They then spent all their spare time and cash doing the place up, while Sammy continued to work in the other restaurant by night. But the guvnor of this other place ran a spieler in the basement – you know, an illegal gambling club. Anyway, the place got turned over by the bogeys one night and Sammy gets lumbered along with everyone else. When they found out he was married to a white girl – well, it didn't go down too well with some of the coppers, nor with the judge. And because he had some previous, they landed him a three stretch – three years – in Wormwood Scrubs. That rag the *Oracle* got hold of the story and painted him as some kind of oriental criminal mastermind, you know, the whole Yellow Peril, Fu Manchu schtick. God knows what kind of time he's having inside.'

'I can't imagine,' said Cynthia.

'Now Lily really was on the ribs,' continued Harley. 'Her old man in stir and two small girls to fend for. So, she decided to use her entrepreneurial skills. Having moved in some colourful circles before she settled down with Sammy, she knew there was a demand for dancing powder on the party circuit in the West End. With those old society contacts and her new links to the Limehouse docks, she figured it would be easy for her to buy the stuff at trade and make a good profit. The rest – according to the *Oracle*, anyway – is history.'

'I must say, the whole thing's like something from the movies. A million miles away from how we grew up.'

'Well, so am I, aren't I?' said Harley with a smile. 'It obviously runs in the family.'

'To be honest with you, George, I'd say you appear a little humdrum in comparison to my sister's antics.'

'Is that so? Humdrum, eh?' Harley consulted his watch. 'Well, I can't stand around here all day taking insults, I've got an appointment.'

'Yes, Detective Inspector Franklin. And what do you suppose he wants with you?'

'It'll be about some job. Don't worry about me, Miss Masters. After all, I'm not the one with criminal relatives.'

He dodged the swipe of her hand and kissed her on top of the head, savouring for a moment the scent she always wore, Gizemli (which she'd explained was Turkish for mysterious), a luxurious melody of bergamot, ambergris and night-blooming flowers.

'Right, I'll catch you later.'

'It'll have to be tomorrow, I'm afraid,' Cynthia called after him as he left the room. 'I've got a rehearsal.'

'Righto – Abyssinia!'

* * *

As with most Theatreland cafés, the teashop in Greek Street had its usual smattering of out-of-work performers, eking out a three ha'pence cup of tea, while carping on about the hours spent huddled outside agents' offices, hoping for an engagement. The table opposite Harley's displayed a fair example of the species: two bottle-blonde chorines, a dwarf with an oversized mouth organ stuffed into his top pocket and a juggler balancing the meagrest of pencil moustaches on his upper lip. The latter was annoying his fellow starving artistes by playing with three matchboxes, repeatedly tossing and catching one between the other two.

'Can'tcha give it a rest, Gus?' said one of the dancers. 'You're getting right on my wick.' She went back to gnawing at a raw stub of thumbnail. Her anaemic pallor suggested it might be the closest she'd come to a meal recently.

'Got to keep my hand in, ain't I?' said the young man. He appealed to the diminutive musician for some support. 'I had my cigar boxes pinched last week from the digs, see.'

'What you telling me for? Do I look like a copper?'

The juggler gave a sigh and pocketed the matchboxes. 'I was sure old Kramer would have an engagement for me this morning,' he said, resorting to doodling in some spilt sugar.

'That one?' said the second chorus girl, the schoolgirl pitch of her voice sounding at odds with her world-weary face. 'He wouldn't give you the drippings off his nose.'

'Afternoon, George,' said DI Franklin, slipping into the seat opposite Harley. 'Taking in the cabaret?'

'Hello, John.' Harley offered his hand. 'I was just thinking – they all look like they could use a bit of gainful employment.'

'Hmm.' Franklin took a puff on his Bulldog pipe and regarded the little motley troupe. 'I wouldn't be surprised if in the next few weeks I encountered one of them in a professional capacity. The girls especially look as though they're teetering on the edge of a slippery slope. Unless they have that rare lifeline of a loving family to return to, it won't be long before some wide-boy ponce is hovering around, with his soft-soap spiel and his hollow promises.'

'No doubt it would make your job a little easier if there weren't so many empty bellies about.'

'Indeed. I'm with Monsieur Voltaire on that one: *Work saves us from three great evils: boredom, vice and need.*'

'Wise words. You want a cuppa?'

Having dealt with the refreshments, Harley suggested they move tables to the back of the teashop. 'The conversation might be a little more private here,' he said, breaking open a new pack of Gold Flake. 'Which leads me on to that soddin' article in the *Oracle*. I hope that wasn't your idea?'

'It certainly wasn't. I can only apologise, George. I realise publicity isn't ideal for someone in your profession.'

'I can't afford to get a reputation as a copper's nark. Especially with this turf war between Mori's mob and the Elephant and Castle boys. Seems like every other night there's some idiot cutting chunks out of someone with a razor. I don't want anyone coming to the wrong conclusions. You know yourself that the McDonalds have a couple of bent bogeys in their pockets.'

'And we both know that your friend Moriel Adler has the same. It's like the force has succumbed to some damnable infectious disease, with all this corruption. I tell you, I shan't be sorry to see the back of the whole affair.'

'What do you mean? You're not going anywhere, are you?'

'Retirement. I've got six months before I collect that gold watch and they put me out to pasture.'

'Get out of it,' scoffed Harley. 'What'll you do with yourself?'

'Whitstable.'

'Come again?'

'The good lady wife and I are going to open a B&B in Whitstable. Had it all planned for a couple of years now.'

'You won't last a season. You'll be dead of boredom within the first month.'

'That's a risk I'm willing to take,' said the policeman, clamping the bit of his pipe between a smile.

'Aright. Maybe I'll come and see you down there, eh? We can go paddling together.' Harley took a gulp of tea. 'So, what is it you wanted to see me about?'

'It's about your pal, Solomon Rosen. I hear that he's working for Adler nowadays, supplying a bit of muscle?'

'Come on, John. Solly's a good mate of mine. And even if he wasn't, if you think I'm stupid enough to put the squeak in on one of Mori the Hat's crew then you're—'

'Listen,' interrupted Franklin. 'I'm not asking you to inform on anyone. In fact, it's the other way around. I've got some information that might be beneficial to Mr Rosen. I saw him fight a couple of times at Premierland, you know. What was it they used to call him? The Yiddish Thunderbolt?'

'That's it,' said Harley with a laugh. 'That or "Solly the Smoke".'

'The lad had talent.'

'Yeah, he started off there as a kid. Built himself up, getting paid ten bob for six rounds. Ended up as British Middleweight Champion,' said Harley, with some pride.

'It's a pity he gave it up, especially as he's ended up working for that mobster Adler.'

'Well, to tell you the truth, to a certain extent he was working for Mori even when he was still in the ring, if you know what I mean. That was the problem with our Solly. He was always susceptible to other incentives. Used to drive his poor trainer mad.'

'Taking a dive, you mean?' asked Franklin.

'You know the fight game. Use your imagination. Thing is, that malarkey's all well and good for some old punchbag of a prize fighter, but there was no need for Solly to get his hands dirty like that. As you say, he had real talent. I tried telling him at the time, but he wouldn't listen to reason. He's like a big kid when he gets something stuck in that thick skull of his. Impetuous, always has been.'

'Well, let's hope he listens to reason this time. You see, I have it on good authority that Solly Rosen will be getting his collar felt in the near future.'

'Oh yeah?' Harley took a quick look around and leant in closer. 'On what charge?'

'Serious wounding. Don't look so worried, George, your boy didn't do it. It's trumped-up, that's why we're having this conversation.'

Harley sat back in his chair and hid his relief with a pull on his Gold Flake. In his experience, Solly Rosen was capable of just about anything in the heat of the moment. Thump now, think later – that was Solly's motto. And those middleweight's paws had done plenty of serious wounding in their time, that was for sure.

'What's the story?'

'Well, as you were saying earlier – there's a feud between Adler and the McDonald brothers. The McDonalds' Elephant and Castle mob have been flexing their muscles a little recently, making tentative moves further into the West End.'

'And treading on Mori's well-shod toes in the process,' added Harley.

'Right. One of their recent targets was a drinking club by the name of the Hot Penguin.'

'In Little Denmark Street, I know it.'

'Well, the Elephant Boys bowled up there one night, mob-handed, intimating to the owner that it would be within his interests to let them provide "protection" for the club.'

Harley whistled. 'They've got some neck. In Mori's manor?'

'Yes,' said Franklin. 'And that's just what the proprietor of the Hot Penguin pointed out to them.'

'Jimmy Pascoe. He's got balls of brass, that one. Jimmy would have told them how things stood, that's for sure.'

'Unfortunately, he did – and ended up in hospital for his troubles. Concussion, ruptured kidney, a handful of broken ribs. His own mother wouldn't have recognised him the next morning.'

'Dirty cowsons,' said Harley.

'When the local beat bobby dropped in on him in hospital, Pascoe fingered the McDonalds for it, and said he was willing to sign a statement to that effect.'

'Just as I said – balls of brass.'

'Well, let's not get ahead of ourselves. You see, a certain CID Detective Inspector stood down the two junior PCs assigned to take Pascoe's statement, insisting that he'd handle it himself. When he returned – surprise, surprise – the name of the assailant had miraculously transformed into Solomon Rosen.'

Harley shook his head and stubbed out his Gold Flake. 'Pascoe must have come under some real pressure to finger Solly, they're good pals. Not to mention any comeback from Mori. Who is this DI? Sounds like he's firmly in the pocket of the McDonalds.'

'I'm telling you this in confidence, because I know I can trust you. And also because I can't abide this type of bent coppering. But if it ever got out that I—'

'Hey,' interrupted Harley. 'This is strictly *me and you*. To be frank, I'm slightly offended you felt you had to point that out.'

'Alright then, just so we understand each other. The officer in question, is Detective Inspector Aloysius Quigg. He's relatively new to the station, turned up out of the blue a few months ago. But he's not wasted any time making a name for himself.'

'Quigg? Yes, I've heard rumours about him,' said Harley. 'I was in Alberto's café the other night. Some of the regulars were saying he's been making a nuisance of himself around the Circus. Pressurising the ponces into letting him have his pick of the girls for nix. So, this Quigg's in the pay of the McDonalds?'

'It would appear so,' said Franklin. 'But it's not quite as simple as that. You see, he's also managed to get in tight with the superintendent. I would imagine because they're both "on the square".'

'Freemasons?' Harley pulled a face. 'I hate all that secret society bollocks.'

'As do I. But I'm afraid it's something we have to put up with in the job. Its influence runs deep through the Yard; you never quite know who's in and who isn't. Apropos Quigg, it means I'll need to tread extremely carefully.'

'I see. So, let's get back to Solly and this trumped-up charge. What can he do about it?'

'As I see it, he simply has to get himself a decent alibi for the twenty-first of September; that and a good brief. I'm sure his employer, Mr Adler, can help with that. I'll sow a few seeds of doubt about the charge at the station. I can't promise anything, but if we take those precautions – and Solly has nothing to hide in the way of knocked-off gear at the homestead – well, I don't think a magistrate will look twice at it. I'm sure that Quigg will be satisfied with the McDonalds being off the hook; as long as he isn't implicated in any way himself, of course.'

'Sounds like a plan. Thanks, I'll get on it right away.' Harley started to get up.

'Hold on, George,' said Franklin. 'There's something else I need to talk to you about.'

'And there was me thinking all this was out of the goodness of your heart.' He dropped his hat on the table and sat back down. 'I'm guessing there's a favour due in return, right?'

Franklin smiled as he relit his pipe. 'There's not much gets past George Harley, eh? Well, you're quite right, I do need a favour. I think I may need your assistance with an investigation.'

'What's the case?'

Just then the waitress came to clear their table. Franklin waited until she'd returned to the counter then leant forward, his voice barely above a whisper. 'The Nursery Butcher murders.'

'What, that dead kiddie found in Clapham? Hold on – what do you mean, *murders*. Have there been others?'

'It looks like it,' said the policeman, checking that the waitress wasn't listening in. 'You see, the head of the corpse found at Clapham didn't match the body. It had been sewn on, and rather crudely at that. And so, we have *two* dead children. Both still unidentified.'

'Bloody hell! So where do I come into all this?'

'Well, they've put me in charge of the case; made me up to acting DCI. Stationed me at the Yard.'

'I know I should be congratulating you, but your face is telling me otherwise. You're none too pleased with the promotion, then?'

'No, I'm not,' said Franklin. 'Here I am, six months from retirement. We get lumbered with a case involving dead children and defenceless women terrorised in their own home. A case that, unless it's solved within a couple of weeks, with all the ends nicely tied up in a neat bow, will have the popular press and the great British public baying for the blood of an incompetent Metropolitan Police Force. And, lo and behold, suddenly they choose this exact moment to recognise all the hard graft that Detective Inspector John Franklin has put in over the years and promote him to lead detective on the case. I'm being offered up as a sacrificial lamb, I'm in no doubt about that. Someone who can be quickly swept away under the carpet of early retirement when it all goes wrong.'

'Hmm,' said Harley. 'I see your point.'

'But it's worse than that,' said Franklin. 'You see, my appointed second-in-command is none other than Aloysius Quigg. I wouldn't be at all surprised, what with his influence over the superintendent, if it was Quigg who suggested me as a scapegoat in the first place – he knows I've got his number, you see. And I have my strong suspicions that, as well as being on the payroll of the McDonald brothers, DI Quigg has a rather questionable relationship with the press; to be more precise, with the *Daily Oracle*'s lead reporter, Enoch Craster.'

'Craster?' said Harley, with a dismissive sniff. 'That cowson is always stirring up trouble in that sodding column of his, blaming the woes of the world on the Jews, or the socialists, unmarried mothers – or whoever else might be the target for his bile that particular week. Some of his articles have almost caused riots in the East End. Hold on, are you saying Quigg leaked that story to Craster about me being on the Turpin case?'

'Highly likely. And it was Craster who first ran the story on this Nursery Butcher murder,' said Franklin. 'A whole day before the rest of the papers got wind of it. And his article was full of little details that could only have come from someone close to the case. Such as the missing heart. And I know for sure that Mrs Dawson and the nanny have refused to speak to the press. Although he doesn't seem to know about the decapitation yet; or maybe his editor feels that might be a little too much gory detail, even for the *Oracle*'s readership. And there are other significant details he hasn't reported yet, so I'm hoping he isn't privy to everything.'

'Such as?'

'Well, along with the heart, the toes of the left foot had been removed from the body.'

'Trophies, d'you think?'

'Possibly.' Franklin checked the other occupants of the café, making sure he couldn't be overheard. 'And rather oddly, a key had been placed in the mouth.'

'What kind of key?'

'An old iron door key. An antique-looking thing.'

Harley took a contemplative sip of his tea. 'All part of his message, no doubt.'

'Message?'

'Well, the whole thing sounds so staged: dressing the kid up like that, sewing the head on. And this key thing. It's like one of those old grisly fairy tales. This bastard is playing a sick game. My gut tells me it's going to be a bugger to solve.'

'Why do you think we're having this conversation?' said Franklin, with a guarded smile.

'So, you want me to do a bit of sherlocking for you, right? I come straight to you with anything I uncover, bypassing our friend Quigg, and therefore the press. That about the size of it?'

'Spot on. I know you're about the best private detective we have in the city. And then there's your specialist training, of course.'

Harley shrugged and kept a straight face. 'What specialist training?'

Franklin looked over at the waitress, who was busy filling up the urn. He opened his notebook and scribbled on the page: *MI5*.

'Oh, that's just a load of old gammon. I don't know who started the rumour, and sorry to disappoint you, but it simply ain't true.'

Franklin smiled and shook his head.

'I've seen the official papers; don't ask me how, but I have. I know that after the war Corporal George Harley, DCM, entered the ranks of Military Intelligence. Now, I don't know what you did there, or why you left, but I do know you were in MI5.'

Harley leant back in his chair, crossed his arms and shrugged again. 'All I can say is, there must be another George Harley out there.'

'Alright, I get it. Mum's the word. Let's just agree you're a very useful man to have around in a fix. And I'm in a fix. So, I'd like to engage you – unofficially, you understand – to work this nasty little murder case with me. But I need you to play to your strengths. Utilise those special contacts you have; the ones that even the most wily of coppers couldn't ever hope to develop. Well? What do you say? Do you accept?'

Harley took a moment to think this over. He had long understood that to be an effective private detective in the metropolis he couldn't avoid dealing with its nefarious underworld. A good number of the contacts and informants that he'd built up over time would no doubt feature heavily in Franklin's case notes back at the station. He also knew that any hint of a close association with Scotland Yard could easily be misread by such types as a betrayal, thereby squandering years of reputation and trust building – not to mention the risk to his personal safety. Thanks to the article in the *Oracle*, there was a good chance he already had one unscrupulous villain – Victor Manduca – believing he was in cahoots with the police. God only knew what a mobster like Mori Adler would do to him if he got labelled as a copper's nark. He knew the most prudent thing to say at this moment would be: *Thanks for thinking of me, but I'm afraid I'm going to have to decline the offer.* But George Harley was a man of pride. It had been the making of him – and could so easily become his downfall. He had just been told by an experienced detective chief inspector that one of the oldest police forces in the world needed his personal skills to help protect the innocent and bring the most abhorrent of child murderers to justice. Him. A little old wide-boy from Shoreditch. So, what he actually said was:

'Normal rates, plus expenses?'

'I suppose I'll be in charge of the case budget, so, yes, normal rates plus expenses.'

'Alright, DCI Franklin,' said Harley, offering his hand across the table. 'You've just hired yourself a sherlock.'

6

As on most mornings, Billy Loveday had been yanked from a blissful sleep by the shrill scolding of his alarm clock. After a quick sluice with ice-cold water, he'd left his little room in the run-down Fitzrovia boarding house and trudged the fifteen-minute walk to the butcher's shop in Brewer Street in a sleepy daze.

Seven o'clock Soho. He didn't think he'd ever get used to the look of the place in the morning. It was like walking into a café and catching one of the showgirls from the revue bars without her make-up: scrubbed and pale and robbed of all the magic. Shopkeepers sweeping rubbish from the gutters; the pavements wet from hosing-downs by puffy-eyed Italian waiters; punters from the spielers slumped on the pavement with their head in their hands, trying to summon the courage to skulk back home to their wives with an empty pay packet.

And there! There she was again. That belladonna-eyed jane, slinking back to her digs.

Loveday stood for a while, vacantly scratching his head

as he watched the young streetwalker sashay her way into Wardour Street.

But she was soon out of sight, and once again he was unlocking the door and hooking the awning down with the boat hook. Another Soho morning with a dozen jobs to do before the boss and his son turned up in their pristine white aprons for another day's trading in the bloodied carcasses of beasts.

As the butcher's boy strewed the floor with fresh sawdust, he tried to visualise the diagram of the cow displayed behind the counter, attempting to reel off the names of the cuts of meat he was supposed to have memorised:

'Topside, silverside, rump and sirloin,' he chanted, dipping his hand into the sack of shavings again. 'Forerib… forerib…'

But the bovine illustration had given way to an image of those belladonna eyes, and the sway of those hips, with their hint of swagger that was still so alluring, even after a night of… of what? He could hardly imagine. That was the trouble.

He looked up at the clock. Seven twenty! And he hadn't even started on the sausages yet.

He quickly finished off the sawdust and went to unlock the cold store to get the pork for the mincer. Mr Roberts had had electricity installed the previous year – at vast expense, he never tired of pointing out. But in Loveday's opinion the huge blocks of ice they used to have delivered from Chatham had always kept the store colder. And now one of those damned new lamps had blown again.

He swung open the heavy steel door to try to let in a bit more light and pushed his way past the carcasses, which hung by vicious-looking hooks from the ceiling.

He winced as the smell hit his nostrils.

'Cor! Blimey!'

There was always a gamey whiff about the place, but this was something else – the distinct tang of rotten meat. Something had obviously gone wrong with the new-fangled refrigeration system. Old Roberts was going to be livid. If only he could get a bit more light in the place, he might be able to work out if it was just the one bad carcass – maybe get it out before it contaminated the rest of the stock.

He flinched and batted at his head as a fat bluebottle droned in his ear.

As he ducked and weaved to avoid the assault from the insect, Loveday bumped into one of the large quarters of meat. The air immediately erupted with the electric buzz of flies and the full-blown foetid reek of corruption. Gagging at the stench, he fumbled in his pocket for a box of matches.

He struck the match and held it up in front of him.

Having expected a gangrenous side of beef, it took Billy Loveday a second or so to make sense of what he now found dangling before him in the gloom. Then it was all too obvious.

The corpse of a child.

Dressed in a sailor suit.

Strung upside-down by the ankles.

Its once-cherubic face now swollen and blackened by putrescence.

And frozen in each of its soulless pupils, his own Munch-like scream of terror.

Loveday dropped the match and staggered out to empty his stomach on the freshly laid sawdust.

7

FLANKED BY THE soot-blackened tenements of Limehouse, Cruickshank's Yard stood forlorn and neglected in the failing light. The faded sign on the gates read: JEREMIAH CRUICKSHANK – SHIPS' CHANDLER, but Jeremiah was long-dead, and the vacant warehouse within bore its own signs of terminal decline. The character now shambling towards the gates of the yard seemed well-suited to such surroundings. Swathed in a voluminous overcoat, with an ancient-looking beaver hat crumpled upon his head, he might have been mistaken for some Victorian revenant – perhaps the ghost of old Jeremiah himself? But the tremorous hands which clutched at the rusty latch were corporeal enough, and the perennial stoop, the fingerless mittens and unkempt facial hair had more of the casual ward about them than the graveyard.

'Mr Perrine?' said Horace Treamer, emerging from the shadows, as the old man opened the gate.

Although still in his early thirties, the estate agent had already acquired the jaded demeanour of a middle-aged undertaker. He stood in his long black overcoat, his hands clasped behind his back, like an oleaginous crow.

'It *is* Mr Perrine?'

'Yes,' said the old man, sounding a little unsure of the fact, as he pushed his blue-tinted spectacles back to the bridge of his nose.

'My name is Treamer, from the agency.' Treamer produced a large keychain from behind his back and jangled it in the air by way of credentials. 'I'm here to hand over the keys.'

'Ah!' said Perrine, shuffling towards the estate agent.

Treamer detected a hint of stale spirits as he dropped the chain into the mittened hand.

The warehouse at Cruickshank's Yard had lain vacant for as long as he could remember. Although relatively close to the thriving West India Docks, the setting out of a new road system at the beginning of the century had left it malingering at the dead end of a tangle of narrow back roads, rendering it unappealing as a commercial dockside premises. And yet the organisation that Perrine worked for had signed the lease and paid a full year's rent in advance, before even seeing the property. For Treamer this, combined with the disreputable appearance of the old man, imbued the whole affair with the whiff of something illicit. Not that this should necessarily pose a problem – as estate agents and rent-collectors working in one of the most prosperous ports in the world, Treamer and his father were finely attuned to the slightest opportunity of a little hush money for turning a blind eye.

'May I ask your intended use for the property?'

'Our gentleman requires it for storage. It is, after all, a warehouse, is it not?'

'Quite so, quite so,' said Treamer, squeezing a thin smile from his lips. 'But what *exactly* is it that you'll be storing here? The agency has a certain reputation to uphold, you understand, a moral obligation to the fine officers of His Majesty's Customs and Excise.'

Treamer fell silent, distracted for a moment by the wad of notes which Perrine had produced from his overcoat pocket.

'On the other hand, for certain discerning clients, we offer a most discreet service, ensuring that your privacy will be respected at all times.'

'I can assure you our gentleman is *most* discerning,' said Perrine. He licked a grubby thumb and peeled off one of the large white notes. 'How much privacy would five pounds buy us, would you say?'

'Five pounds?' The agent's smile suddenly became more convincing as he plucked at the note with bony fingers. 'Why, for five pounds you'll be positively ignored. Left to your own devices. I'd say, for five pounds, Mr Perrine, you'd become invisible.'

'We're very pleased to hear it,' said the old man, fishing out a battered hip flask from the inside of his coat.

Treamer folded the note and placed it carefully into his wallet, surreptitiously wiping his fingers clean afterwards on a pristine white handkerchief.

'Tell me – might we have met before? You seem somehow familiar.'

Having partaken of his nip of brandy, Perrine wiped his mouth on the back of his sleeve and took a moment to contemplate the question.

'Not that I'm aware of, sir, no.'

'Never worked in the vicinity of the Pool of London before?'

'Never.'

'Native to London?'

'You ask a lot of questions, my friend.' Perrine tapped the cap back on his flask with the flat of his hand and stowed it back in his pocket. 'Some while back I was a Punch and Judy man. We'd sometimes work the capital in the spring. Maybe you remember me from one of my shows? As a child, perhaps? Now, I believe we agreed on the fee. You have the money. If you don't mind, I'd like to sample a little of that privacy you promised.'

'Of course. Forgive me, I shall just—'

'Good evening, Mr Treamer.'

And with that, Perrine ambled off to the main warehouse door and began to fumble with the rusty lock.

8

BRENDAN COLLINS – LITERARY agent and good friend of the *enfant terrible* author, Alasdair Cassina – entered the green room at the BBC's Savoy Hill radio studios and approached the distinguished-looking, tweed-clad individual who sat engrossed in a book in the far corner of the room.

'Professor Morkens?'

Morkens pushed his half-moon spectacles to the top of his bald head and took a moment to focus on the younger man.

'Collins?'

'Do forgive me for interrupting you. I wasn't sure if you'd remember me.'

'Dear boy! How could I forget such a diligent and attentive student? Not to mention a former member of the Blind Bard Society, of course.'

Osbert Agamemnon Morkens was Professor of Ancient History at Brasenose College, Oxford, where Collins had studied Classics. Cassina himself had also initially been a Classics undergraduate, but had changed course after the first year to

English language and English literature. Both students had attended the professor's storytelling club, the Blind Bard Society, which assembled in Morkens' rooms on the last Friday of every month, so the members might recite a few self-penned stories while enjoying a choice selection from the professor's private wine cellar. Always a popular tutor with his students, Morkens was somewhat of a polymath. Along with Ancient Greek and Latin, he was fluent in several modern languages; he was an accomplished actor; a talented musician; and, as a younger man, had competed at county level in athletics. A natural and enthusiastic communicator, of late he had become something of a regular for the nascent BBC's radio programming, recounting accessible versions of the Greek myths and representing academia in debates on questions of societal change and modern culture. It was in this latter capacity that he was currently attending the Savoy Hill studios, where the popular programme *The Social Looking Glass* was soon to debate the cultural significance of the recent horrific child murders.

'So, Collins, are you working for the Corporation now?'

'No, no. I'm here with Alasdair. You remember – Cassina? I'm his literary agent.'

'Ah yes! Young Cassina. Our fellow panellist this evening.' The professor gave a contemplative tug at his white, caprine beard. 'Literary agent, you say? You know, I've a couple of new books in the pipeline myself. Populist ancient history, that kind of thing. Not sure if it's right for my current publisher. I wonder if you might take a look? See what you'd recommend?'

'I'd love to. In fact, here's my card,' said Collins, pulling up a chair. He took a quick look around the room and leant in close, lowering his voice. 'But, just now, I wonder if we mightn't have a quick word about Alasdair?'

Morkens looked a little puzzled. 'About Alasdair?'

'Yes. I've always trusted your opinion, Professor. I'm frightfully worried about him, you see. Especially about his performance tonight. What he might say. And as you'll be in there with him… well, I thought you might intervene.'

'Intervene?'

'If you felt he was about to say anything inappropriate.'

'I see. And what exactly might he say, do you think?'

'Lord knows. He's been acting increasingly erratically lately. Positively maniacal at times.' Collins sighed and sat back in his chair. 'Oh, Alasdair's always been something of an egotist, but lately, with all the public interest in the novel… well, I think he truly believes that his books can change society somehow. I wouldn't be surprised if he's on the brink of some kind of narcissistic breakdown.'

'I see.'

Morkens removed his glasses from his head and placed them in the top pocket of his jacket.

'You know, have you considered the possibility that Alasdair might be right? After all, ideas found in books *can* change societies, can't they? Foment revolutions? Topple kingdoms?'

'But that would make it all the more worrying. You see, some of Alasdair's ideas are, frankly, terrifying. Brilliant, yes. Inspired. But nonetheless terrifying. Have you read *A Reflection in the Ice*?'

'Yes. I thought I better had, before tonight's programme. I can see why the man in the street might be a little exercised by its premise.'

'Well, I can tell you, the moral dilemmas in that are nothing compared to some of his new ideas.'

'Really? He was always such a bright lad. Do you fear his mental faculties might be compromised?'

'No, not compromised, exactly. But definitely altered. At times he's unrecognisable. Like some kind of lunatic-genius. The constant drinking doesn't help, of course. And lately… well, I'm afraid he's fallen in with rather a bad crowd.'

'Bad? In what way, exactly?'

Just then a member of the studio staff rushed in with a clipboard and hurried over to their corner.

'We have ten minutes to broadcast, Professor. If you'd follow me, please.'

'I'm sorry, Collins. I'm afraid I have to…'

'Yes, of course. But if you feel he is about to go off on some messianic rant, try to calm him down, would you? Prevent him from hanging himself on national radio. I'm sure he'd listen to you. God help us if he doesn't.'

Morkens patted Collins on the shoulder as he got up to go. 'Now, don't you worry, dear boy. I'm sure everything will turn out just fine.'

* * *

A blue-grey haze of cigarette smoke hung above the four men sitting in the curtain-lined room. Above the door, the red electric lamp began to flash, prompting the presenter to sit up and clear his throat. Decked out in evening dress, with the presence of a seasoned repertory performer, he now leant towards the lozenge-shaped microphone to address the nation in an assured, thespian tone:

'Good evening, ladies and gentlemen. This is Peter Gibson, and I welcome you to another edition of *The Social Looking Glass*. With a decline in church attendance, an increase in civil unrest and the decadent influence of American jazz, some social commentators have warned recently of a crisis in western civilisation. Some have even gone so far as to predict the coming of a new Dark Age. Could we perhaps see the recent horrific child murders in London as a symptom of such a collapse of society? With me in the studio this evening to discuss this question, we have a panel of eminent commentators: the Reverend Charles Ruxton, fellow of St John's College, Oxford; Alasdair Cassina, author of *A Reflection in the Ice*; and Professor Osbert Morkens, Camden

Professor of Ancient History at Brasenose College, Oxford. Alasdair Cassina, perhaps we might start with you? You were recently quoted in a national newspaper as suggesting that the staging of these horrific murders held some kind of artistic merit. Isn't that a rather glib comment to make, given the nature of these crimes?'

The author took a sip of his whisky and soda, and swept away a flop of fringe from a face that, although handsome, still retained traces of the precocious child.

'Glib? How so?' he said, affecting a bemused look.

'Well, what if the parents of these unfortunate children were to see your comments?'

'As I understand it, the victims have yet to be identified. We can't even be sure that they have parents, can we? Anyway, I was talking in an objective, theoretical way. About the staging of the murders. After all, one doesn't go to watch *Titus Andronicus* and worry about the appetites of the mothers in the audience.'

'But that's drama, entertainment. This is reality, it's—'

'I disagree,' interrupted Cassina. 'It's only reality to those immediately involved. To the vast majority of people, to Edna and Ernie sitting at the breakfast table, reading about it while eating their boiled eggs, why, it's pure entertainment. And as such, you must admit the grotesque nature of the staging has a certain unique allure.'

Gibson raised a quizzical eyebrow at the novelist and turned to the clergyman. 'Reverend Ruxton, do you view such transgressive crimes as an example of the waning of the Church's influence on the morals of the nation?'

'Good evening, Peter,' said Ruxton. 'And good evening to your listeners. I thank you for asking me this question, which, of course, rests upon the supposition that we need religion – and therefore, God – to provide us with a moral code.'

'Moral code?' scoffed Cassina. 'Your church's moral code is nothing more than the fear of God's punishment, or the longing for His approval. And, as such, it is totally inapplicable to those of us who deny his existence.'

'Alasdair, come now' said Professor Morkens, with a calming tone. 'You will admit that, even for the atheist, there is a need for morality? Any kind of human society, from the smallest tribe to the largest city, needs a set of rules to maintain cohesive stability. We even see it in the animal kingdom, do we not? What colony of ants could function without a set of rules?'

'Yes, but that's my point. They're not ordained from above. One may want to *act* morally – or to be *seen* to act morally – to attract a mate, say, or to fit in with one's peers... or simply to avoid imprisonment.'

'That's a rather cheerless view of your fellow man, is it not?' said Ruxton.

'I'd say it's equally as honourable as adhering to a moral code simply because one's terrified of divine retribution, wouldn't you?' replied Cassina.

'You know, Reverend,' said Morkens, hoping to diffuse the atmosphere a little. 'Your question of whether man needs a divine authority to set his moral code has a precedent in ancient history, of course. Polybius, in *The Histories*, says that a scrupulous fear of the gods was the very thing which kept the Roman commonwealth together.'

Ruxton nodded in gratitude. 'There you are, then.'

'Although he does go on to say that if it were possible to form a state wholly made up of philosophers, such a custom would perhaps be unnecessary.'

Cassina barked a laugh at this and took another swig of whisky.

'But what about *objective* morality? Hmm?' retorted Ruxton. 'The fact that certain things are good or evil, regardless of whether an individual believes it or not. For this deeper kind of morality, God is indeed necessary. In the absence of God, good and evil would become mere illusions, just man's creations.'

'That's exactly what they are,' said Cassina.

'I believe you touch on this idea in your latest – some would say, controversial – novel,' said Gibson, referring to his notes. 'Isn't the main protagonist a defrocked priest who styles himself a *moral nihilist*?'

'Indeed. Father Cassidy has a kind of epiphany, after stumbling across the writings of Nietzsche in his college library. This eventually leads him to regard the concept of choosing good actions over evil ones as absurd as saying one prefers a shoehorn to a tin of corned beef.'

'A point of view which leads him to commit a string of heinous crimes, and indulge in an orgy of violence and perversity, does it not?' said Ruxton, who was becoming rather red in the face.

'It is only a story. Fiction. A mere experiment in thought.'

'Yes, but one that may well do an awful lot of harm to young, impressionable minds. Take the recent case of this artist chap in Soho. Turpin, wasn't it? By all accounts he'd styled himself on your protagonist. It would appear your book acted like a kind of—'

'That's slanderous nonsense!' snapped the author, leaning forward in his seat and poking a finger at the clergyman. 'I can't possibly be held responsible for the actions of every lunatic that reads one of my books. And might I just point out the great number of atrocities carried out in the name of religion?'

'Perhaps we might return to the point in hand, gentlemen?' intervened Gibson, only too aware that his producer in the gallery had begun to gesticulate madly at him. 'Professor Morkens, given your area of expertise – and I'm sure our listeners would appreciate you not going into too much detail, here – but, would you say there is any *ritualistic* significance in the manner in which these terrible atrocities were committed?'

'Ritualistic?' Morkens sat back in his chair and tugged at his beard. 'Well, there are numerous examples of the child as a sacrifice in antiquity: in Phoenicia, Carthage, and of course, there's the great Ammonite god, Moloch, to whom thousands of infants were sacrificed as burnt offerings.'

'Are you, erm…' Gibson gave another nervous glance at his producer. 'Are you suggesting that these murders may be some kind of pagan sacrifice, Professor?'

'Well, if we take the removal of the victims' hearts – as reported in the newspapers – that's perhaps analogous with the Aztec sacrifices. They would pluck out the hearts of the victims whilst still alive, you understand. Since antiquity, many cultures have regarded the heart as the seat of vitality, you see. They believed that if you consumed one, you would take on the victim's energy, his attributes; and, in the case of an infant, his innocence. For this reason, the human heart—'

'Please, Professor, the listeners?' said the now-panicking host, pulling at his shirt collar.

'Forgive me. Well, I was just going to say that the heart has often featured as a key ingredient in certain magical preparations. There's some evidence to suggest it formed part of the Mithraic sacrament, and there are apocryphal texts relating to Simon Magus consuming the heart of a dead infant before performing his flying spell. Of course, this is all just speculation, you understand.'

'Well,' said Ruxton. 'I do hope you're wrong. To think of those poor defenceless creatures being slaughtered for such unholy reasons.'

'What reasons *would* be acceptable?' asked Cassina, getting increasingly animated. 'And for that matter, why is it more horrific that the victims are children? In realistic terms, wouldn't it be more of a loss if the victims were mothers, who had large families relying on them? Or perhaps businessmen who employed scores of workers? These children weren't old enough to have contributed anything to society yet, so why is it so tragic that they've been removed from it?'

Gibson turned to Ruxton. 'Reverend, maybe you could answer that question?'

'Well...' the churchman thought for a moment. 'Children have yet to be corrupted by the world. They have all the potential of life before them; the possibility to grow into beautiful, loving, generous adults. They have yet to fail at this – as *we* all have failed, to a certain extent. Maybe it is this that we mourn in their passing?'

'Good God, man!' said Cassina, shaking his head in pity. 'You sound like some mawkish epitaph on a Victorian tomb. Yes, children might delight us because they are archetypes of innocence and defencelessness. But, taking a page from the professor's book, if we look back through history, we see so many examples of man's bestiality towards them: marauding troops ripping babies from their mother's womb, impaling them before their mother's eyes, roasting them in fires.'

'Mr Cassina, please!' said Gibson, concerned at the delirious glint which had appeared in the author's dancing eyes. 'And would you sit down, sir? The microphones are—'

But Cassina was shouting now, seemingly ignorant of his host's protestations or, indeed, of anyone else in the room.

'I believe it's their very *helplessness* that leads to such brutality – the innocent lamb tantalising the voracious wolf, provoking him to tear, to rip and gorge! I think it may well be the stirring of this primeval, bestial bloodlust inside ourselves that we sense when we contemplate such victims. Perhaps the true horror is not the actual crime, but the thought that we may be capable of committing it ourselves!'

And at that moment listeners around the country were puzzled to hear *The Social Looking Glass* suddenly replaced by the dulcet tones of Jack Payne and His BBC Dance Orchestra.

9

NIGHT SETTLED ON Piccadilly Circus. The neon hoardings shimmered into life, beacons to the thrill-seekers and the dispossessed. Harley emerged from the Underground station, weaving his way through the last straggles of office clerks and shop assistants heading home after the working day. He made his way into Shaftesbury Avenue, through clusters of suburbanites 'up town' to marvel at the delights of the West End: the excited chatter of foreign tongues from open doorways; the glimpse of theatrical types, still in costume, emerging from stage doors; the medley of alluring, unfamiliar smells wafting from the restaurant kitchens. But Harley was heading deeper in, into the dark interior of Soho; only a few hundred yards from the bright cheer of the department store and the Lyons Corner House, but a million miles from all that was safe and mundane.

Following Franklin's instruction, he had begun to utilise his close contacts within the capital's demimonde and, knowing that the DCI and his colleagues were busy rounding up all the known pederasts for questioning, Harley had consulted his own mine of information for all things sexually nonconformist – Dora. Earlier that afternoon, ensconced in the snug bar of the Shabaroon – fuelled by a plentiful supply of whisky and peppermint, and Black Cat cigarettes – Dora had waxed lyrical about her experience of sexual deviation in the capital of the Empire. After a string of salacious stories in which she'd recounted a catalogue of perversions and fetishes (some of which had even shocked the cynical and streetwise private detective) Dora had recommended that Harley visit a friend of hers – Madame Leanda. Dora explained that Leanda had worked for a time at the Berlin Institute of Sexology, under the tutelage of the 'Einstein of Sex' Dr Magnus Hirschfeld. Having been educated in the sexual pathology of the modern city dweller, she had returned to London to set up an exclusive service, administering to the sexual deviations of her many well-heeled clients. Dora explained that Leanda had devised her own unusual method of treatment. She would hire prostitutes and encourage her clients to re-enact their wildest sexual fantasies, so that she might deconstruct their obsessions to discover the original triggers. Sometimes she even engaged in the roleplay herself. Perhaps unsurprisingly – after all, the social mores of Weimar Berlin bore little resemblance to those of stuffy old Blighty – this had led to a run-in with the authorities, the closure of her business and a hefty fine.

Her clients were distraught. Cheated of their regular sessions with Madame Leanda, where now could they vent their pent-up sexual tension without the risk of violence, arrest or both? They began to bombard her with messages, imploring her to see them privately at double, triple the original fee. And so, Leanda had decided to adapt her original business model and relocate to the illicit shadowland of Soho. Reducing the therapeutic element of the sessions, she now offered a clandestine bespoke service. For those lucky enough to be able to afford this service – and pass the rigorous vetting process – Madame Leanda would analyse the essence of their sexual obsession and then curate a collection of 'treatments': meticulously staged engagements with the capital's most highly skilled sex workers, out-of-work actors, animal trainers, struck-off doctors, professional sadists or anyone else who might be able to help recreate the client's sexual fantasies.

'I'm telling you, George,' Dora had said, in her husky voice. 'If anyone can explain to you the inner workings of the deviant mind, Madame Leanda can.'

And then she'd added something that had really struck a chord with Harley.

'You know, she did mention something to me the other day. Something that might be relevant. You see, she was explaining about this craze she'd encountered when she'd lived in Berlin – this strange, mystery sect thing. Sex magic, she called it. I said: "If you mean one of those orgy clubs, dear, I've been to a few similar things here – ghastly, awkward affairs; about as erotic as a naked whist drive. But, no, she said, this was different. It was hosted by a charismatic leader, a mesmeric character, by all accounts. The members had to undergo some kind of rigorous training. They had their own scripture, one of these new-fangled religion things, I suppose. But there had been talk, you see. Rumours going around Berlin that, at these gatherings, the sect performed abhorrent acts on *children*. Never any proof; so, it might all be nonsense. But, you see, Leanda has seen him recently – this mesmeric leader of the sect.'

'Over here?'

'Yes. In Soho. It was only a glimpse, across a crowded street. But he's very distinctive, this German. Quite handsome, apparently. Swarthy, continental-looking. Anyway, she was convinced it was him.'

And so, Harley now found himself at Duck Lane, a dingy back street formed by the rear elevations of two drunken rows of Georgian townhouses, which ended in a litter-strewn dead-end. Not the most inviting of locations, but no doubt Madame Leanda's clients appreciated the anonymity. A gas bracket with a blue-glass shade cast its paltry light on a single, unmarked door. This, he had been told by Dora, was the sign for the fetish curator's clinic.

As Harley stopped to spark up a Gold Flake, someone in a light mackintosh exited the door and made his furtive way up the alley. He glanced up as he passed the private detective, offering a clear view of his appearance: Homburg hat, doughy complexion and pebble-lensed spectacles so thick that they magnified his watery eyes to nightmarish proportion. Not the kind of character you necessarily wanted to bump into in a dark alley such as this. Harley tried hard to stop himself contemplating exactly what kind of special 'treatment' the fellow had just enjoyed at Madame Leanda's.

Let's hope she's washed her hands, he thought as he tugged on the bell pull.

* * *

'So, you have some questions for me? How intriguing.'

Madame Leanda had led him up a narrow staircase to a first-floor suite of rooms. Because of Dora's reference to her time spent in Berlin, Harley had imagined Leanda to be German. But her cut-glass accent was pure Home Counties.

'I must say, you're not what I was expecting at all, Mr Harley. The phrase "private detective" summons up an image of someone skulking about in hotel rooms, trying to catch out adulterous husbands. Someone a little ferret-like, in a cheap suit.' She flashed a beguiling smile at him.

'I'm sorry to disappoint.'

'Oh, believe me, it's no disappointment.'

Madame Leanda was a bit of a surprise herself. For some reason Harley had imagined her as a slightly frumpish, professorial type. In fact, she was stunning. A strawberry blonde with deep blue eyes, exquisite skin and the kind of bone structure that was hard-wired in the psyche as a model for beauty. He found himself smiling like an idiot as he drank it all in.

'So, Mr Harley? Your questions?'

'Ah yes, of course.'

He stubbed his cigarette out in the ashtray and pulled out a notepad.

'Well, I'm on a case, you see. A case that may involve a suspect with deviant sexual feelings.'

Madame Leanda raised an exquisitely shaped eyebrow. 'That's rather a broad church. Could you be more specific?'

'A sexual attraction to small children. In your opinion, why is it that children, young boys in this case, might become objects of sexual desire?'

'Oh, the reasons are multiple and complex. Sometimes the sexual exploitation of the child is opportunistic, or due to a lack of normal inhibition – the inebriated father sharing a bed with his young daughter, for example. Sometimes it is because the perpetrator finds it difficult to form a relationship with an adult sexual partner – because they are feeble-minded or possess some disagreeable social characteristics. And then, of course, there are those who have a persistent and focused sexual attraction to pre-pubescent children. But of this last group it is by no means guaranteed they will act upon these urges. You see, Mr Harley, most sexual obsessions are fixed in the mind at a very early age. Some event in their early childhood eroticises a morbid attraction to a person, situation… even an inanimate object.'

'Inanimate object?'

'Indeed. You know, I had one former client – a highly successful industrialist as it happens – who was a closeted infantilist. He spent a small fortune on the construction of a private nursery, equipped with sexual apparatus, all fashioned in the form of old toys from his childhood. Most of the work I do here is focused on channelling such deviant obsessions and allowing them to be played out in a safe environment.'

'What if those fantasies included the murder and mutilation of small boys?'

Madame Leanda narrowed her eyes. 'Exactly what is this case you're working on? It isn't to do with the recent discovery of those poor children's bodies, is it?'

'I'm afraid I can't say. But tell me something. Do you think any of your clients, past or present, could commit such atrocities?'

The telephone began to ring.

'Do excuse me.'

Harley wondered whether the sashay across the room was for his benefit, or her normal form of locomotion – whatever the answer, he found that he couldn't take his eyes off the play of the satin dress across Madame Leanda's thighs. As she turned to pick up the receiver, she caught him watching her and once again narrowed her eyes at him.

'Yes?' she said. 'Yes, that's correct. Oh, if you must... Yes, I've left the door on the latch.'

'Another appointment?' asked Harley, as she replaced the receiver in its cradle.

Madame Leanda sighed deeply. 'I'm afraid not.'

She took a cigarette from a box on the desk, her carmine lipstick leaving the ghost of a kiss on the white paper.

'I can only apologise, you know. Please don't take it personally.'

'Apologise for what? Have you got other commitments?'

She slid up onto the desk, where she sat, gazing across the room, as though she were addressing someone else. 'You see, pretty soon after relocating here, I learnt that when you move to the jungle, you had better make friends with the tigers and the crocodiles. Lest they gobble you up.'

Harley sat up as he heard the front door slam.

'Who's that coming up the stairs?'

'As I say, I do apologise. But there really wasn't anything I could do about it. They seemed to know you were coming.'

The door burst open to reveal two burly individuals. Wide check suits, gaudy silk ties. One in a billycock hat, wielding a small hatchet in his wiry-haired fist, the other in a green fedora, playfully slapping the end of a two-foot lead pipe into his open hand.

Trouble. The painful kind.

'George Harley?' said Billycock, pointing with the hatchet. 'We've got a little message for you, from Mr Manduca. Up you get. And let's keep those hands where we can see 'em.'

10

HARLEY STOOD FLANKED by the two heavies, his brain whirring through possible escape strategies. Although full of the usual bluster, the pair seemed slightly agitated, as if they were unsure of exactly how to conduct the whole affair. His guess was that these boys weren't actually on Manduca's payroll, but just a couple of hired hands brought in on the fly. Well, that was to his advantage – there'd be no staunch loyalty to contend with.

'Listen boys,' he said, keeping his tone calm and measured. 'There's obviously been some mistake here. I thought it had already been explained to Mr Manduca, but obviously not. But I realise you're not to blame. What say we come to some arrangement, eh? Think about it. Mr Manduca will soon be told what really happened at Turpin's, you can make a few extra quid, and everyone ends up happy. What are you getting paid for this? I'll add a suitable bonus.'

He watched as Fedora's pencil moustache twitched nervously. The lad was obviously contemplating the offer, tipping his hat up a little to get a better view of Harley's face.

'Cut that old gammon!' barked Billycock, prodding at Harley's shoulder with the hatchet. 'We've been sent to give you a message and that's what we're going to do.'

'Yeah,' added Fedora with a show of bravado, covering his embarrassment at nearly falling for the ploy. 'You cost Victor a flock of dough. You got to pay up, or else.'

'How much?'

'A couple of hundred should do it,' said Billycock, with a smirk.

'Oh, is that all?' said Harley, tapping at his jacket inner pocket as if it were normal to carry around more than the average annual wage in small change. 'Hold on, I'm a bit light. Maybe I could wire him the money?'

'Don't worry, we'll just get it out of you another way,' said Fedora, pushing Harley back against the fireplace with the lead pipe.

'Wait!' snapped Madame Leanda, who had been pouring herself a sherry. 'I was promised that nothing would happen here. I'm not clearing up after you boys. Take him elsewhere.'

She walked over to the open door and directed them out.

'Well, go on! Don't just stand there gawping.'

During Harley's trench-raiding forays in the war, rather than firearms, the order of the day had been spiked clubs, knives and knuckledusters; all silent and deadly in confined combat. The trench-raiders had also been taught that, in a fix, any suitably hard or sharp object could be utilised as an improvised weapon. As he was now frogmarched to the open door, it was this hard-won experience that drew Harley's eye to the bottle of sherry held in Madame Leanda's left hand.

Why hadn't she put it down before walking over? Was she possibly helping him in a way that wouldn't lay any blame at her door? Whatever the reason, here was a lifeline.

A glance at the mirror on the opposite wall told him that Billycock was immediately behind him, with Fedora making up the rear. That was good – Fedora was more likely to panic if left on his own.

'Come on, get a move on!' grumbled Billycock, as the detective stopped at the doorway and turned to Madame Leanda.

'Where are your manners, pal? Madame Leanda,' he said, holding out his hand, 'I just wanted to say – no hard feelings, eh?'

'That's very noble of you, Mr Harley.'

Was it his imagination or had she just given the bottle a little waggle?

Another glance in the mirror.

She took his hand.

Harley yanked her arm.

She screamed.

He snatched the bottle with his left hand, spun around and swung it like a club, covering his eyes with his forearm. The base of the heavy glass bottle exploded against the side of Billycock's head. One deep guttural groan and the big lump was over, gurgling on the rug in a mess of blood, broken glass and sherry. As Harley had hoped, Fedora just stood gazing in astonishment at the casualty at his feet, the lead pipe hanging useless at his side.

Harley was off, springing for the open door and taking the stairs two at a time in a perilous descent. As he reached the bottom there came a savage roar from behind. He had just managed to get through the front door when the lead pipe came hurtling down the stairs, embedding itself in the timber frame. And then he was away, out into the night.

* * *

Harley guessed the Maltese would be too busy regrouping to come after him immediately. But, just to be certain, he'd spent an hour or so in the relative safety of a dimly lit cellar bar in Fitzrovia. However, although he'd escaped immediate danger, this problem was certainly not going away on its own. Victor Manduca – aka 'the Spider' – was a serious villain who had his fat, well-manicured fingers in all the seedier pies baking in the cauldron of the city's underbelly. One thing was for sure, the private detective had to find a way of persuading Manduca that he hadn't been responsible for the raid on his business. And he had to do it quickly. So, having made a thorough recce of the surrounding area after emerging cautiously from the cellar bar, Harley found himself a phone box and proceeded to make a series of calls to discover the current whereabouts of Mori Adler.

* * *

The small private room of the Frith Street restaurant had just the one table in it, set for two. One of these seats was occupied by Adler. Standing by the door, keeping a close eye on the new arrival, was the mobster's right-hand man. Scrawny build; pasty, pock-marked complexion; expensive suit. Benjamin Dalston, aka Benny Whelks – named for his penchant for pickled seafood – an artful 'chiv-man', expert with a taped-up cut-throat razor and, despite his sickly appearance, probably one of the deadliest characters in the city.

Adler looked up from the large bowl of pasta. He pushed his fingers through his thick hair and beamed a smile that offered a glint of gold.

'There he is – George Harley!' He kicked the empty chair out from the table and pointed at it with his chin. 'Sit, sit!'

Harley made a quick check around him, his street sense on high alert. He felt Whelks' hand on the small of his back.

'Sit down, G-G-G-George,' said the chiv-man, battling as usual with his chronic stammer.

Harley took the seat, surreptitiously patting his jacket pocket to check for his brass knuckles; remembering with dismay that they'd been confiscated by Manduca's heavies.

'You eaten?' asked Adler. 'You want I should get Franco to knock up a little nosh for you?'

'I'm good thanks, Mori.'

Adler splashed some wine into a glass and pushed it over to Harley. 'I'm glad you popped in to see me. I wanted to thank you.'

'Thank me?'

'Sure. For tipping us the wink about that little business with Solly. Thought we'd show our gratitude.'

Whelks appeared at Harley's side and placed a small roll of notes on the table.

'No, you're alright,' said Harley, sliding the money away from him. 'Solly's a mate.'

The beaming smile fell from Adler's face. He nodded, then plucked the gold toothpick from the chain around his neck and worked away at a molar for a while.

Harley knew too well the probable consequences of taking money from a villain like Adler – that was a slippery slope he'd always been keen to avoid. 'So, Solly's got his alibi sorted, has he?'

'For sure,' said Adler. 'Cast-iron. An old married couple are swearing blind that Solomon met them on the night in question, to arrange a boxing demonstration for charity. Nice touch that – my idea.' Adler refilled his own glass. 'Kosher, too – civilians, of unquestionable character. You see, an old Jew can always be relied on over a yok to tell a decent ghost story to the bogeys. Know why? They all remember the brutality of the Russian authorities. When they sign that witness statement, it's not a CID man they see across the table, it's a Cossack.'

Adler tossed back his wine, then produced a double corona from his inside pocket. 'So, George,' he said, nipping off the end of the cigar. 'How's the sherlocking working out for you? Must be doing well for yourself if you can afford to knock me back like that.'

'Come on, Mori,' said Harley, using the excuse of pulling out his packet of Gold Flake to make a quick check of where Whelks was lurking. 'I'm not knocking you back. It's no show of disrespect, if that's what you're thinking. In fact, it's the opposite.'

'So, enlighten me.'

'Well, me and Solly go way back, don't we? We've been hanging out since we were snotty-nosed kids. You ask Benny, here. What's an old mate like that going to think of me if he finds out the only reason I've given him the tip-off is to earn a few shekels?'

Adler sat thinking about this as he warmed the end of his cigar. After a while, seemingly satisfied with Harley's explanation, he gave a slow nod and pocketed the roll of money.

Sensing the mobster might be in a favourable mood, Harley decided to seize the moment.

'But, you know,' he said, taking a sip of the wine. 'There is a little something you could do for me.'

'Oh yes? Go on then, try me.'

'Victor Manduca.'

'The Spider? What about him?'

'You on good terms?'

'We do a little business from time to time. Why do you ask?'

Harley was convinced that Adler knew only too well why he was asking, but he played along.

'Oh, it's just that, erm, I think there's been a little misunderstanding. You see, I get the impression that our Mr Manduca thinks I might have been somehow responsible for him getting raided by C Division the other day.'

'You don't say. Well, that can't be right, can it? I mean, you're staunch. Everyone knows that.'

'Exactly. So, what say you have a word with him for me? Explain the error of his ways?'

Adler tipped his head back a little and scrutinised the private detective's face.

'Before I answer that, I have a question of my own. Who was it that slipped you the information about Solomon's imminent arrest?'

Harley took a long drag on his Gold Flake and studied the ceiling for a while. 'Do I have to answer that one?'

'Oh, I'd say it's within your best interests to. Wouldn't you agree, Benny?'

Whelks gave a silent nod, a small tic worrying the muscle beneath his eye.

'And remember, Georgie Boy,' said Adler, 'Uncle Moriel has eyes and ears everywhere. On this you should reflect before answering.'

'DI Franklin. Though he's actually a DCI now.'

Adler leant forward, his Havana clamped between his teeth. 'Good boy!' he said, gently slapping Harley's cheek. 'See? Honesty's the best policy, every time. Yes, that's what I heard: DI Franklin. Now, as far as I know, John Franklin is as straight as they come, and unless I'm very much mistaken, you're no copper's nark. But you could see how people could jump to the wrong conclusion. So, tell me, why does Franklin pick George Harley to spill the beans to, eh?'

'Cos he knows Solly's a mate of mine. And he can't be seen talking directly to you boys, can he? As you say, he's as straight as a die – he's got a reputation to keep.'

'That's all well and good, Georgie Boy. But why should a bogey be worried about some ikey wide-boy getting his collar felt in the first place, eh? Is it skin off his nose, such a thing should happen?'

Harley thought fast.

'He used to follow Solly when he was in the ring. I dunno, maybe he's still got a soft spot for him from then. Plus, Franklin doesn't like bent coppers, especially this cowson, Quigg. I s'pose he wants to queer his pitch with this trumped-up charge scheme. You know about this new DI, right?'

'Quigg?' Adler sent a smoke ring barrelling up to the ceiling. 'Of course. A shicer of the first water. Word is the Elephant Boys have got him all buttoned up.'

'He's also got his feet under the table with the superintendent at Vine Street. Lodge brothers.'

'Interesting. Might be a bit of leverage there. But you see, I think there's another reason that Franklin is sharing such information with you.'

Harley made a quick check to see if both of Whelks' hands were still empty.

'Oh, yes? And what's that?'

'Maybe it's because you're helping him to sniff out the perverted son of a bitch who's going round offing these little kiddies.'

Harley jumped as he caught a sudden movement from Whelks in the corner of his eye. But he was relieved to find that the chiv-man was just in the midst of a particularly animated nervous tic.

'Alright, Benjamin. Just breathe,' said Adler, holding his hand up. 'So, George, what do you say to that? And I'll remind you of what I said about my eyes and ears being everywhere.'

So here it was. Stuck in a room with two of the most dangerous villains in the city. About to confess he was working for Scotland Yard. And he didn't even have his brass knuckles for company.

'It's true. I'm working the case for Franklin. Unofficially. As a sherlock.'

Adler looked at Harley.

He took a draw on his cigar.

He looked over at Whelks.

Then back at Harley.

Then nodded.

'Good.'

'Sorry?'

'I think that's right and proper.'

'You do?'

'For sure. You're one of the best in the game. And some of those momzers at the Yard don't know their arse from their elbow. As I'm sure you know, I'm a family man myself. When that first poor kiddie was found in Clapham it was bad enough. But at least it was south of the river, right? Like it was happening in a foreign country.'

Adler paused to look over at Whelks, who had just made a little groaning noise.

'But this latest one?' he continued. 'On our own doorstep?'

There was another groan from Whelks, the tic under his eye was twitching convulsively now.

'Those beautiful little boys, molested by that sick bastard? Messing about with their little dead bodies like it was some fucking game. And now they're saying in the paper that he's been swapping their heads. I mean, what kind of dirty paskudnik does that to a kid, eh?'

Now both Harley and Adler jumped in their seats as Whelks, seemingly in a fit of uncontrollable rage, punched the panelled door, moaned once again and then rushed out into the restaurant.

'Is he alright?'

'Benny lost his sister a few weeks ago. They were close. Took it bad. And then the whole business with this kiddie murderer?' Adler held out his hands and sighed. 'Well, it's opened up some old wounds, I think.'

The mobster pushed back in his chair.

'But getting back to business. Let's say, for now, you've got my blessing to work with the bogeys on this. But you'd better get a result, son, and quick. 'Cause I'm not having this on my manor, you understand me?'

'Perfectly... and Manduca?'

'Well, as you know, I'm a reasonable man.' Adler paused to wet the end of his cigar. 'But if I do this thing for you with the Maltese, there's something you've got to do for me in return.'

Here it comes, thought Harley. He turned to see Benny Whelks slip back into the room, his tic now calmed to a series of slow winks.

'A little bird tells me,' continued Adler, 'that you're tight with Limehouse Lil.'

'Don't take this the wrong way, Mori, but you heard wrong. I know Lil well enough to have a drink with, but that's as far as it goes.'

'We both know to what I'm referring, so if you don't mind, I'll ask you to save that old madam for some other mug.' Adler flashed his gold tooth again. 'Now, I've got a lot of time for Lilian. She's respectful. She don't tread on toes. Up until now, I've chosen to keep my nose out of the dope game. Dealing with all those socialite snow-birds and hop-heads? Oy!' The mobster spread his beringed fingers. 'Who needs it? But our friends the McDonalds don't have such qualms, and the cackle on the street is that they're thinking about diversifying. And we both know those Elephant Boys won't be so respectful in their dealings, right? So, as I see it, it's of mutual interest that Lil and I have a little pow-wow, to see if we can't come to some arrangement. See where I'm coming from?'

'I think I've got it. And if I happen to bump into Lil, I promise I'll mention what you've got in mind.'

'Well, seeing as you're cased up with her little sister, I reckon it's stone ginger that you're going to bump into her, don't you?'

'I told you: *it ain't like that—*'

'Listen to this one – it ain't like that. That's exactly what it's like.'

Harley put his hands up in submission. 'Alright. I'll do my best to get the message to her.'

'This I want very much you should do.' Adler tapped the glowing plug of ash from his cigar. 'So endeth the lesson. Again, thanks for the steer with Solly – it was a mitzvah. Someone will be in touch about the Maltese thing. Benny, see our old friend out, will you? And after that, send Fayvel in with the books – Esther wants a new outfit, so help me. They say you can't buy love. Well, that may be so. But, believe me, you can sure as hell pay for it – and how.'

11

THE DAY WANED. The city slowed. Night spread its pall over the streets.

In Shadwell, Benny Whelks stood at the window of his top-floor room, looking out across the blackened rooftops and listening to the melancholy sounds of the boarding house as it settled for the night.

The sparsely decorated room was as neat as a pin. In the stained-oak wardrobe, three identical suits hung alongside a row of freshly laundered shirts; shoes lined up, just so, along the skirting; a starched collar for each day of the week ready in the chest of drawers.

Whelks moved to the small washbasin and contemplated his reflection in the mirror which hung above it. Deep-sunk, eldritch eyes stared back at him from above hollow, pock-marked cheeks. It was a face hard to love.

But someone had loved it.

He placed his fingertips on the photograph tucked into the mirror's frame – two small Edwardian children in their

Sunday best; a brother with his hand placed protectively on the shoulder of a younger sister. Sweet Margaret. Innocent. Unsullied.

Whelks felt the swell of grief in his chest; and behind it, the simmering rage, triggering the tic in his cheek and a craving to caress that mother-of-pearl handle.

His fingers found the cut-throat razor on the washstand. He pulled the whetstone from the shelf and, as he began to hone the blade, he cursed in whispers, recalling the fear of those nights, so long ago, with little Margaret clinging to him for protection in their tiny bed. And through the rage, with each sharpening pass, he could hear the blade calling to him, demanding its tribute.

* * *

Five miles away, in his Mayfair penthouse, Alasdair Cassina emptied the last of the cognac into his glass, adding to it three drops of opium tincture and a teaspoonful of sugar. He swirled the contents to dissolve the sugar a little and then saw it off in one draught.

The author fell back in his chair and closed his eyes, anticipating that ecstatic moment when the drug would swell again inside. Overwhelm. Transport him.

The seconds passed.

He fidgeted.

Pinched at his cheek.

Pressed his nails into the flesh of his arm.

Damn it! Where was it?

He was just reaching for more of the tincture when the first waves of pleasure began to lap at his brain...

Then – how much later? – he found himself at the large ormolu mirror above the mantelpiece, his face bathed in the golden glow of the candles.

He pushed a greasy lock of hair from his eye.

If you were to empty all the galleries in Mayfair, he thought, *and decorate this room with their works, you couldn't make it as beautiful as it looks now – nor improve upon the masterpiece I see before me.*

He took up the ceremonial kukri, hanging from a chain on the wall, and removed his damp shirt, the sweat on his pale skin glistening in the candlelight.

'Man is but a step below the angels,' he mumbled (or thought he mumbled). 'One simple leap of faith and all glory is ours.'

He rolled back the large Persian rug before the fireplace, revealing the circle painted on the floorboards there – the Goetic circle, with its alchemical symbols and demonic names. Placing his bare feet within two smaller circles encompassed by an inner triangle, he removed the dagger from its sheath and began to chant aloud:

'Io Pan! Io Pan! Pan! Pan! Pan!'

And there, in the heart of the West End, with the dying embers glowing like infernal jewels in the ornate grate, Alasdair Cassina was once again convinced he felt the veil of the universe withdraw.

He opened his eyes wide and prepared himself for terrible wonders.

'I renounce and deny God, the blessed Virgin, the Saints, Heaven, earth and all that is in the world!' he roared, with maniacal exaltation.

'Goat of thy flock, I am gold, I am God!
I rave and I rip, and I rend.
Everlasting, world without end.
In the might of Pan!
Io Pan! Io Pan!
Pan! Pan! Io Pan!'

* * *

In the gloomy office at Cruickshank's Yard, Martin Perrine was reading an article in the *Daily Oracle*, which recounted, in salacious detail, the heinous crimes recently committed at Clapham and in the Soho butcher's shop, and proposed that such frightful atrocities might portend the death of British values and Christian morality.

When he'd finished the piece, the old man gave a croaking chuckle, then balled the newspaper in his mittened hands and threw it across the room. He pulled himself up from the dilapidated chair – the light from the paraffin lamp affording him a decrepit, Hogarthian demeanour – and, taking the lamp with him, made his way down the stairs.

At the bottom step he stopped to look around the warehouse, the light casting a feeble halo on the littered floor. Most of the storage bays were empty, bar the odd broken crate, but the one opposite contained a large bulky item, covered by an old tarpaulin.

Perrine cursed and kicked out as something small and black scurried around the penumbra of his light. Then he shuffled his way over to the covered item.

After struggling for a while, he managed to remove the tarpaulin, revealing a robustly constructed metal cage, similar to those used for transporting wild animals.

Perrine dragged across a bale of straw and cut the twine on it with a penknife, before scattering a few handfuls across the floor of the cage. He then produced a new padlock from the voluminous pocket of his overcoat and threaded it through the hasp and staple on the door, snapping it shut with a metallic clunk which resounded in the dark empty space.

'Yes,' he said, rattling the bars of the cage door. 'That should do nicely.'

12

Rose Muller touched her husband's arm as he passed her in the tiny kitchen.

'Sidney, can I have a word before you go, please?'

'It'd better be quick,' he said, grabbing the wax-paper package from the dresser. 'If I ain't at the front outside the dock gates, there'll be no chance of me getting picked.'

Rose went to the door of the parlour, where her two children were playing on the rug in front of the small grate.

'Ooh, Mum, I've taught Eddie that song Uncle Bert was singing. D'you want to hear it?'

Rose gave her daughter a brief smile. 'Maybe later, Milly. Mummy's busy just now.'

'Well, what is it?' asked her husband, once she'd closed the parlour door.

She stood drying her hands on her apron, her eyebrows knitted in concern. 'D'you think you'll pick anything up today? You've only had two full days of work in the past fortnight. We're down to our last scuttle of coal.'

'Don't you think I know what state we're in?'

'Sid, keep your voice down. The kids…'

'Well, it don't help you coming on my ear'ole all the time. I'm doing my best, ain't I? There just ain't enough work to go around.'

'Can't you go to the union? Isn't that why you pay the dues?'

'We already had that handout last month, remember? The relief fund's shrinking all the time. Too many lads on their uppers.'

'Well, we've got to do something.'

'I bleedin' know we've got to do something,' he growled. 'And the longer you keep me here nagging at me, girl, the less chance I've got of doing that something.'

Rose picked up the dirty breakfast plates from the table and took them to the sink.

'I could always write to Father.'

'I am not going to that bastard, cap in hand. D'you hear me?'

Milly poked her head around the kitchen door. 'Mum, Eddie wants you.'

'Go back inside, there's a good girl,' said Rose, ushering her daughter back into the parlour.

'Don't fret, love,' said Sidney, seeing the promise of tears in his wife's eyes. He offered her his handkerchief. 'Something'll turn up, you'll see.'

'But the rent's due soon. And I can't get any more credit at the corner shop.'

'Right,' he said, purposefully buttoning his coat. 'I'll sort it.'

'How?'

'I'll go and see Treamer. See if I can get him to postpone the rent for a bit.'

'Will he do that?'

'Old Man Treamer wouldn't. But Horace is a different kettle of fish. He's open to persuasion. Some of the lads have buttered him up in the past with a bit of knocked-off gear.'

'Oh, but what if you get caught?'

'It'll be fine. Everyone does it now and again. The trick is not to get too greedy. I'll promise him something from the next shift I'm on. It's got to be worth a go, ain't it?'

Rose grabbed the thick lapels of his docker's peacoat. '*Please* be careful. We can't afford for you to get in trouble with the law.'

'Don't you worry about me. I'll be alright. And don't you go writing to your old man – promise?'

'Promise.'

He held up the wrapped sandwich. 'What we got?'

'Dripping again, I'm afraid. That's all there was.'

'Well, beggars can't be choosers, eh?'

He gave her a kiss on the top of her head before heading out the door.

* * *

Three hours later, Rose was at the kitchen table, still contemplating the family's precarious domestic situation, when she was roused by a knock at the door.

'Oh, Mr Treamer,' she said, trying to disguise the note of alarm in her voice at the sight of the rent-collector. 'We weren't expecting you today.'

'Fear not, Mrs Muller. This is merely a social visit.' Treamer forced his thin lips into a smile.

'Oh, then perhaps you'd better come in.'

'Most kind,' said Treamer, removing his bowler to reveal an unnaturally pale parting through the centre of his Brilliantined hair.

'Please go through to the kitchen. I have some tea in the pot.'

'Delightful.'

Treamer placed his hat in the centre of the kitchen table and removed his leather gloves.

'I had the pleasure of spending a little time with your husband this morning, you know. He was explaining your current situation: the fact that you find yourselves a little… financially embarrassed.'

'Yes, we've been finding things a little hard recently,' said Rose, colouring a little as she poured tea into one of the two 'best' cups and saucers from the dresser. 'There seems to be so little work about, you see.'

'Indeed. Your husband is a stevedore, I believe?'

'Yes. Fully registered, with lots of experience. But that seems to matter little nowadays.'

'Hmm.' Treamer added sugar to his tea and began to stir it with a slow, precise action. 'My father has some contacts with the Port Authority. Maybe I could look into it.'

'Oh, would you? Would you, really? We'd be most grateful.'

'Yes, I'm sure you would. I couldn't promise anything, of course, but…' Treamer flashed another thin, obsequious smile and then took a dainty sip at his tea.

'Well, anything at all would help at the moment.' Rose took a surreptitious glance in the bread bin. 'Would you like a slice of bread and margarine with your tea, Mr Treamer?'

'No, that's quite alright, thank you. Wouldn't want to spoil my luncheon.' He placed the cup on its saucer and pushed it away as though making a move in a game of chess. 'Of course, if the authorities were to hear about your husband's injudicious offer to pass on goods he was planning to steal from them, I fear it might have grave consequences for his future career, if not his liberty.'

The blush now drained from Rose's face.

'Oh, I'm sure he didn't mean it. It's all just hot air. He's desperate, you see. So desperate to provide for his family. Sidney's a good man, Mr Treamer, really, he is.'

'No doubt he is, Rose – may I call you Rose?'

'Yes, of course.'

'Well, Rose, that's all very well. But you see, if it gets out that I've been accepting bribes from our tenants... well, it could prove very sticky for everyone. Very sticky indeed. Do you understand?'

'Of course, Mr Treamer.'

'Call me Horace.'

Rose smiled nervously, concerned at the rent-collector's change of tone.

Treamer stood up and took his cup and saucer over to the sink.

'It was foolish of Sidney to be so indiscreet,' he said, tutting and shaking his head. 'But I have so enjoyed our little tête-à-tête. And, so, I'm willing to overlook it this once. And I shall also endeavour to secure Sidney some guaranteed shifts at the docks. However—'

Treamer's speech was cut short by the appearance of Milly, who now rushed into the kitchen, holding a shabby rag doll.

'Mum, Eddie's scribbling on the walls again. And Dad said next time he found him doing it, he'd give him what for.' She stopped in her tracks on seeing the stranger at the sink.

'Hello. And who do we have here?'

'Answer the gentleman, Milly,' said Rose, as her daughter began to cling to her skirt.

'Millicent. Millicent Muller.'

'Pleased to meet you, Millicent,' said Treamer. 'And Eddie – that would be your brother, yes?'

'My *little* brother. I'm the eldest. I'm eight and three quarters.'

'Oh, yes. I understand. Eight and three quarters. And tell me, Millicent – do you happen to like currant buns?'

Milly looked up at her mum, who gave a little hesitant nod of approval.

'Yes. Though I've not had one in ages.'

'And Eddie – does Eddie like currant buns?'

''Spect so. Couldn't say for sure.'

'Well then, here's thruppence to help you find out. You know Jennings' on Pennyfields?'

The little girl nodded enthusiastically, her eyes clamped on the coin that had appeared between the rent-collector's fingers.

'I happen to know they have a fresh tray of currant buns in the window. They're probably still warm from the oven. Why don't you take little Eddie along there and get a couple to try, eh? And bring one back for your mother, too.'

'Ooh, can we, Mum?' Milly squeezed her mother's hand in excitement.

'I don't know,' said Rose, trying to fathom the look in the stranger's watery blue eyes. 'There's a fog blowing in from the river. Maybe you should wait a little.'

'Oh, *please*, Mummy. I've been to Pennyfields on errands *loads* of times.'

'Come on, Rose. It's only just around the corner,' said Treamer. 'A smart girl like Millicent, here. I'm sure they'll be just fine.'

'Alright,' said Rose, reluctantly. 'But *do* be careful. And straight back, mind.'

Milly grabbed the thruppenny bit and dashed out of the kitchen.

'Put your coats on!' Rose called out. 'And don't dally!'

'Well, we don't want them to be too quick now, do we?' said Treamer, unbuttoning his black overcoat. 'After all, we have some important things to discuss, you and I.'

'What do you mean? What things?'

'I'm about to offer you a chance to redeem your young family from homelessness and destitution, for a mere trifle of your time. I expect you'll jump at the chance. But, then again, I understand such decisions can't be rushed.'

Rose took a step away from him, backing up against the dresser. 'I'm not quite sure I fully understand you, Mr Treamer.'

'Oh, don't be coy. We both know exactly what I'm talking about. I mean, why would I be tempted by the odd carton of knocked-off cigarettes, when your husband has such a treasure to negotiate with at home? And remember, it's *Horace*. There's no need to stand on ceremony, is there? Not when we're destined to become such good friends.'

* * *

Milly snagged the last few loose currants from the bottom of the paper bag, then, with a sigh, scrunched it around the remaining bun and stuffed it into her coat pocket. She turned to her brother, who was dawdling a few paces behind.

'You going to eat all that?'

Eddie wrinkled his brow and thought for a moment, then enthusiastically nodded his head.

'Well, don't dally then.'

Walking on a few paces, she noticed a young Chinese girl, scrutinising her from the doorstep of the Yeung Sung General Store. The girl was roughly Milly's age, dressed in a simple white shift, with scuffed black boots, a couple of sizes too big for her.

Sidney Muller had warned his daughter on numerous occasions to stay away from the 'chinks'. Influenced by the fictions of Sax Rohmer and the *Daily Oracle*'s Yellow Peril scaremongering, he was of the opinion that within their ranks there lurked a mysterious criminal syndicate, intent on luring white girls off the streets into a nightmare world of addiction and abuse.

Despite her father's Sinophobic prescriptions, Milly – being a bright and curious child – found herself fascinated by Limehouse's Chinese community. Here, on Pennyfields, among the grubby pubs and drab terraces, there had blossomed a cluster of shops and cafés, each offering bizarre wares with names that couldn't be found in her mother's

Pears' Cyclopedia. It was as though they'd grown from some exotic spores brought in on the foreign cargo ships. Even the short bob of the inquisitive child watching her from the shop doorway was so unlike her own hair as to appear fashioned from some curious fabric – so glossy and blue-black, even in the fog-thickened air.

'What you looking at?' said Milly, giving the girl her best pout.

'Dunno, the label's fell off, ain't it?'

The Cockney cheek of the reply – sounding as though it had come straight from the mouth of one of her own little friends in Dolphin Lane – caught Milly by surprise; she couldn't help but laugh out loud.

'I'm Milly,' she said, taking a step closer. 'And this here's little Eddie. What's your name?'

'Jing.'

'That's a funny name, ain't it?'

'So's Milly.'

Milly thought about this for a moment. 'It's short for Millicent. What's yours short for?'

'Jing,' said the girl, with a calm detachment. She pointed at Eddie, who stood chomping his cake. 'He's enjoying that, ain't he? Currant bun, is it?'

'That's right,' said Milly. 'Want a bit?'

Eddie shook his head vehemently, hiding the remnants of the bun behind his back and eyeing Jing suspiciously.

'S'alright.' Jing directed a thumb at the shop behind her. 'This is our place. I can help myself to sweet cakes whenever I like. As long as Ma ain't in a mood.'

'Cor! Really?' Milly rushed to push her nose against the shop window. 'What's them things, there?'

The girl joined her at the window.

'Chrysanthemums.'

'Can't be.'

'Are so.'

'But they're all shrivelled up. Who'd want *them* in a vase?'

Jing tutted. 'Not for vases, for *tea*.'

'Whoever heard of making tea out of flowers? That's stupid, that is.'

'T'ain't stupid at all. Tea's just leaves from a tree, ain't it? Why not petals then? Besides, we invented it, so I says we can do it how we like.'

'Who did?'

'The Chinese.'

'Get off it! Tea's British as anything.'

'It's not. Emperor Shen Nung, that's who done it. He was sitting under a tree and the leaves blew in his pot of boiling water. Thousands of years ago, that was.'

'Don't believe it.'

'Suit yourself,' said Jing with a shrug, and went back to her step.

Keen to make a new friend of this curious creature, Milly walked over to her little brother and wiped the crumbs from his cheek.

'I taught Eddie a song. D'you want to hear it?'

Jing gave another shrug.

Not to be daunted, Milly bent and whispered in Eddie's ear.

'Don't wanna,' said Eddie, picking the goo from his teeth.

'*Eddie.*'

The younger Muller child had learnt that it was best to offer just the mildest of objections to his sister's demands – especially when she had this particular look on her face. So, he gave a sniff, hoisted up his trousers and began his little performance.

'Don't walk about without your cady on – Ginger, you're barmy! Get your hair cut! They all begin to cry. With nothing on your napper, oh, you are a pie.

Pies must have a little bit of crust, why don't you wear a cady?
If you want to be a don, you want a little something on, to take orrrff to a lady!'

Jing jumped up from the step and clapped enthusiastically. Her broad smile and twinkling eyes were such a contrast to her previously stony complexion that Milly couldn't help but giggle with delight.

'Good, ain't it? Harry Champion, that is. Our Uncle Bert knows him, you know.'

'We've got a parrot,' said Jing, ready now to make friends. 'You want to see it? He talks sometimes, if he's in the right mood.'

'Where?'

'In the parlour. Come on.'

Milly grabbed her brother's hand and went to follow Jing through the shop door. But Eddie vehemently refused to enter such strange foreign territory. For a few seconds, Milly hesitated – after all, she had been well-schooled by her mother in her responsibilities as an elder sibling. But the lure of all the curious-looking jars that could be glimpsed through the open door proved far too tantalising and, with a hurried instruction to her brother not to move from the spot, Milly went dashing after her new friend. Little Eddie was left standing on the pavement, with the fog painting a wash over the derricks and warehouses of the Limehouse skyline behind him, like the backdrop from some cheap melodrama.

* * *

While Milly had been in Jing's shop, the streets of Limehouse had become swathed in a thick blanket of yellow-brown smog, which had billowed in from the river. She now stood on the doorstep, looking in wonder at the transformation, the turbid air muffled to an eerie silence.

Then, with a sudden stab of panic in her chest, she realised her brother was nowhere to be seen.

'Eddie?' she called out; quietly at first, the potential consequences of having lost him in such a clear act of selfishness taking her breath away.

'Eddie!' She was shouting now, running to the middle of the street and spinning around, trying to catch a glimpse of him in the swirling mist.

'Eddie! Stop mucking around, do you hear?'

And then something cold was squeezed into her clenched fist.

She looked down.

It was her brother's damp little hand.

'What you playing at? I told you not to move, didn't I?'

'I thought I saw Dad.'

She could see he had been crying, had been frightened by something. He would have to be mollified on the way home, or else tales would be told.

'Dad's at work, silly. He won't be home till supper.'

'But it looked like him.'

'It's the fog. Probably just another docker, they all dress the same, don't they? Come on, let's get home. It's taters out 'ere.'

They ran the last fifty yards or so to the house, adding their own little billowing clouds of breath to the murky air.

The letterbox was slick with condensation as Milly pushed it open to fish for the string that held the latchkey. But as she bent to peer through the opening, she saw something that made her snatch her hand away and take a step back onto the pavement.

'What's the matter?' asked Eddie, holding his hands under his armpits to warm them. 'Ain't the key there?'

But Milly was too busy trying to unravel what she'd just seen.

'Why don'tcha just knock? Mum's in, ain't she? I'm going to knock.'

'No, Eddie!' Milly's shriek made her little brother jump. 'Don't do that! We... we can't go in just now. Mum's busy.'

'But I wanna—'

'She's busy, I tell you! Come on,' Milly grabbed Eddie's hand, and began to pull him up the street. 'We'll go back to Jing's.'

Eddie slipped from her grasp. 'I don't wanna go back there. It's scary.'

'What's scary? Here, maybe she'll give us one of them sweet cakes she was on about? You'd like that, wouldn't you?'

Eddie stamped his foot. 'No!'

'You can't stay here. Come with me to Jing's.'

'No!'

'Alright. Suit yourself,' said Milly, turning her back on him and striding off into the fog.

She needed to get away from the house. Needed time to reason what exactly her mother had been doing with that strange man. It wasn't until she had reached the corner of the high street that she realised Eddie still hadn't joined her.

'Oh, the little idiot.' She turned on her heels and began to run back, calling his name, worried he'd be knocking on the door, peering through the letterbox.

'Eddie? Where are you?'

But little Eddie Muller had disappeared, swallowed up by the thick, acrid fog.

13

IN CONTRAST TO Harley's sitting room – eccentric and exuberant with Uncle Blake's curiosities – Cynthia's apartment was the last word in tasteful contemporary design: a monochrome colour scheme highlighted with geometric prints and oriental touches. It was a reflection of her own innate elegance; something which had always intrigued Harley. Sometimes, watching her perform the most mundane task – drinking tea, say, or writing a letter – it was almost hard to believe they were of the same species. There was nothing haphazard or inefficient in her movements. To experience her playing the cello in full flow, lost in some piece by Dvořák or Elgar, was fascinating; she almost seemed to meld with the instrument itself.

'What's this one?' asked Cynthia, after Harley had placed another platter on the gramophone.

'Jelly Roll Morton – "New Orleans Bump". What d'you think?'

'Well, it certainly has *energy*.'

'Is that all you can say about it?'

'It's just difficult for me to escape my training; to hear it with fresh ears. I've been playing Busoni all day.'

'They'll be studying this stuff in universities one day. You mark my words.'

'Perhaps they will,' she said with a smile. 'But, for this evening, can we please make this the last one?'

Harley gave a little huff and pulled the needle from the record.

Cynthia sighed, then tapped the newspaper she was reading. 'It says here that the little boy that went missing in Limehouse could be another victim of the Nursery Butcher. What do you think?'

'We're not treating it as such. Not until we have a body.'

'Those poor parents. I can't imagine what they're going through, can you?'

Harley had slipped the disc back into its sleeve, but now stood gazing absent-mindedly at the label.

'George?'

'Sorry. It's just this case. We're still no further forward than when we started. And God only knows what that bastard's going to present us with next. We've got the *Oracle*, publishing all the gory details for the nation's entertainment. And then there's DI Quigg, rotten to the core. You can bet your life he was where Craster got the lowdown about the children's heads from. Franklin's furious.'

She grabbed his hand and pulled him towards her.

'I do wonder why you chose such a profession in the first place.'

He shrugged. 'Well, it kind of chose me, in a way.'

'But you pursued it, excelled at it. You must have done, for Scotland Yard to want to employ you as a consultant. Why this? You could probably turn your hand to most things.'

'That's easy for you to say. I mean, unless you went to the right school, or come from the right family, there ain't too many options open, are there? You see it all the time, all those useless demobbed officers who immediately fell into cushy little numbers after the war. The Old Boys' Club.'

She pulled her hand away. 'I'm not getting into another debate about the British class system. Come on, there must be something that made you stick to it. Really there must.'

'Maybe…'

He thought for a moment.

'Soho and Piccadilly, the places I mostly work in, they're… what's the word? Like a border between worlds.'

'Liminal?'

'Liminal, yeah. Well, I feel like that – always have, in a way – in between worlds. I suppose it's a prerequisite for being a decent sherlock. But there's more to it than that.'

'Such as?'

'I dunno, I've not really said this to anyone before.'

'Then I shall be flattered, Corporal Harley. Go on.'

'Well, since coming back from the war,' Harley paused, rubbing at the back of his neck. 'Having survived, relatively unscathed. I've had this deep sense of, I dunno, *guilt*, I s'pose you'd call it.' He gave a little embarrassed laugh. 'Oh, I know you'll say it's illogical; but that don't make it any easier to deal with. Actually, it's more than just guilt. It's more like this sense of impending doom. Like something's looming out there, waiting in the shadows. I can't put a name to it. I mean, it ain't a sniper's bullet anymore, is it?'

He took a glance at his reflection in the mirror.

'Anyway, soon after becoming a sherlock, I came to realise it was important to me to work those cases where the victims were the most vulnerable. The unchampioned. The snatched kid, the murdered young woman…'

Cynthia nodded, keeping silent, waiting for him to continue.

'Because, after what I'd seen in the trenches, I somehow wanted to prove to myself that that type of criminal was an aberration, a monster. I don't know, it sounds like the ravings of a madman when you say it out loud.'

'Not at all.'

'But the thing is, it always turns out that these shicers are just like the rest of us. Just weak and stupid – just human. But with *this* case – with the beheadings, the desecration of those little bodies? I worry I might finally be getting what I wished for.'

'You think this one really is a monster?'

'Maybe, in a way. And if he is, well, I'm still the poor bastard who's got to help bring him in.'

She smiled and squeezed his hand affectionately.

'Anyway, that's as far as I'm prepared to go today, Dr Freud.' He smiled and went over to peruse an array of photographs in ornate silver frames displayed on the piano: groups of androgynous Bright Young Things, picnicking on some country estate, drinking champagne at a well-heeled ball, punting on a river.

'Is Cassina in any of these?'

'No, I don't think so.'

'You know, after his performance the other night, I'm not so sure the BBC will be inviting him back on the airwaves any time soon. Do you think it was all an act? I mean, some of the stuff he was saying sounded quite intelligent to me.'

'Oh, Alasdair's always had a quick brain. The trouble is, he knows it.'

Harley moved to the drinks cabinet.

'Handsome, is he, your rebellious author?' he asked, passing her a glass of amontillado.

'Why, you're not jealous, are you?'

'Get out of it.'

'Handsome? Well, he's acceptable, I suppose – in a boyish kind of way. But he doesn't have your rugged good looks, Corporal Harley.' She made him lean down, so she could deliver a kiss on his cheek. 'Besides, between you and me, I'm not wholly convinced he's all that interested in girls. Oh, he had plenty of girlfriends but… well, it might just be rumours, but I remember there was some talk amongst the gang about him and his friend, Brendan.'

'Really?'

'I don't know if there was really anything in it. This chap is his literary agent now. They were at school together. It seems a lot of the boys had their little dalliances at school.'

'Not at Deal Street, we didn't.'

'Hmm… anyway, you never really know with Alasdair. Most of the things he does are simply for effect.'

She offered him a cigarette from a Bakelite box adorned with an Assyrian relief.

'No, you're alright,' he said, flashing his packet of Gold Flake. 'I'll stick with these. Were there any other rumours about Cassina?'

'What do you mean?'

'Well, you said he had girlfriends. Were there any stories about how he treated them, for example? Or any strange interests he might have had, things that might be considered, I don't know – somehow deviant?'

'Deviant?'

Harley noticed Cynthia's cheeks had coloured a little.

'Just how close were you two, anyway?'

She suddenly snapped at him, a flash of anger in her eyes. 'What is this exactly? Because it's beginning to feel a bit like an interrogation.'

'Whoa! Slow down there,' he said, holding his hands up.

'I was joking when I asked you whether you were jealous, but really, it's a most unattractive trait, you know.'

'Actually, I've got a good reason for asking.'

Harley went over to his coat and retrieved a letter, which he handed to Cynthia.

'Delivered to the station. Anonymous. And Franklin says it's not the only one they've had.'

'*The author Alasdair Cassina is a depraved individual,*' she read out loud, in a mocking tone. '*Wicked. Ungodly. He is known to be actively involved in a clandestine, orgiastic sex cult.*' She glanced up at him, her face now confused, incredulous. 'This is just muck-raking, George. Why are you even showing me such drivel?'

'Read on. The bit about the doctor.'

Under duress, Cynthia continued with the anonymous letter, which went on to accuse the author of various nefarious practices. But it was when she reached the account of how, when at university, Cassina had allegedly been in league with a certain doctor, who had performed abortions for him on the unfortunate young victims whom the author had molested after incapacitating with a cocktail of drink and drugs that she stopped reading and looked up at Harley with a flash of anger in her eyes.

'Wait a moment.' She waved the letter at him. 'You're not suggesting this might have happened to me, are you?'

'Don't be daft. I just thought it might jog your memory or something. The link to the doctor might be significant. And I've had another, independent lead on this sex cult thing, I—'

'Rubbish! It's that stupid male ego of yours. You've been acting jealously since the moment I mentioned I knew Alasdair.'

Harley took a consolatory pull on his Gold Flake, a little taken aback by Cynthia's reaction.

'I happen to be investigating a serious child murder case, here.'

'Yes. And don't we all know it.'

'What's that supposed to mean?'

'Let me tell you, it's not much fun playing second fiddle to the great crusade.'

'Don't be like that, Cyn. Can't we just—'

'No!' she said, batting his hand away. 'I think you ought to just go home. I've got a long rehearsal in the morning and I'd like to get some rest.'

Harley nodded to himself, stabbing his cigarette out in the ashtray. 'Like that, is it? Alright, I'll see you tomorrow then, when you've calmed down a bit.'

She held out the letter. 'Here, don't forget your precious evidence.'

* * *

When Harley arrived back at Bell Street – still licking his wounds from his spat with Cynthia – he noticed a figure lurking by the steps to his front door. He quietly slipped into a nearby darkened doorway, his hand automatically feeling for his brass knuckles (which he'd replaced that morning from his collection of war paraphernalia, kept in a large suitcase under his bed).

Finding nobody at home, the mysterious visitor now began to walk back down the road towards him. Harley made a quick check up and down the road for any hidden accomplices or suspicious parked vehicles, and then stepped out onto the pavement.

Standing there under the gaslight, with her Marcel-waved, strawberry-blonde hair framed by an elegant black cloche hat, and her voluptuous figure hugged by Parisian haute couture, Madame Leanda looked every bit as alluring as at their previous encounter.

'Well, Mr Harley. Aren't you going to invite me in?'

* * *

'Quite a remarkable place you have here,' said Leanda, now comfortably ensconced in Harley's parlour with a whisky and soda. She was looking with puzzled interest at the display of Uncle Blake's curiosities. 'But then again, you're full of surprises, aren't you, Mr Harley?'

'Call me George,' he said, offering her a cigarette.

'Thank you, George.'

She caught him for a moment in the lustrous azure of her eyes, making him falter a little with the lighted match he held to her cigarette.

'What do you mean, full of surprises?'

'Well, the way you handled yourself with those brutes back at Duck Lane. I'd say that's the type of performance that comes with experience and training.'

'Well, it didn't hurt having you waggle that bottle under my nose to use as a weapon. What happened? Did you have a change of heart?'

'Come now. I explained to you that it was nothing personal. Believe me, I was put under intense pressure by that Manduca creature. You look like a man who would understand the principles of self-preservation.'

She took a drag on her cigarette and regarded him silently for a while, allowing the smoke to escape from her painted lips in a meandering ribbon.

'Actually, when I realised that you might be involved in the investigation of these horrific child murders... well, let's just say I've been feeling tremendously guilty about the whole affair ever since.'

She took a sip of her whisky and then set the glass down on the table.

'So, I thought a little more about your question – about whether any of my clients might be capable of such appalling violence against a minor.'

'And?'

Harley sat forward, watching with anticipation as Leanda removed a Manila envelope from her bag.

'And I came to the conclusion that the answer was probably no. But I do have a series of photographs of a client at one of my sessions.'

'Taken in secret?'

Leanda gave a shrug.

'Working the black, eh?'

'Blackmail?' She wagged a finger at him. 'Shame on you, for thinking so little of me. No, it's more a question of insurance. You see, I only photograph those clients who I feel might pose a risk, to either myself or the professionals I engage.'

'And you felt this one posed such a risk?'

She placed the envelope on her lap and tapped it for a while with an immaculately painted crimson nail.

'You must understand I could never repeat this in a court of law. Nor in the presence of the police. Such a breach of confidence goes against one of the fundamental tenets of the service I provide my clients. My reputation would be in ruins. Not to mention the threat to my personal safety.'

'Of course. I understand,' Harley was trying to sound nonchalant, but he sensed he might be finally close to a breakthrough. 'You only need to tell *me*, Leanda. I'll do the rest.'

She gave a resigned sigh. 'Very well. But my name *must* remain out of it. You'll recall I spoke of a client who was an infantilist?'

Harley nodded. 'The one with the private nursery.'

'Exactly. Well, our friend here is another. Though he has decidedly more sinister tastes: a morbid obsession with young children, especially boys. And a penchant for violence.'

'Do you have a name for me?'

She gave a chuckle.

'Nobody gives their real name. He books in as "Mr Brooks", but I wouldn't get distracted with that.'

'Can I see the photographs?'

She took another pull on her cigarette and narrowed her eyes.

'Not until I've left. I shan't be divulging any more information than is absolutely necessary.'

'Understood. But can you tell me *why* you suspect him?'

'I don't. Not really. But there is one thing I feel compelled to tell you about. At one session – some two months ago now – our Mr Brooks related a recurring fantasy he's been having off and on since puberty. A dark fantasy. Sexual and violent. Now, that in itself isn't anything remarkable. These kinds of forbidden thoughts are universal. Indeed, I firmly believe that if we try to repress such thoughts, or are filled with self-disgust for having them, then we run the risk of doing damage to our mental health. It's an integral part of my work. But most of us would never act upon our forbidden impulses; and I'm not suggesting I know for sure that Mr Brooks has. But, you see, his fantasy was about decapitation. The decapitation of children.'

'Christ! And this was two months ago? Well before the first victim was discovered. Can you tell me anything else about him, Leanda?'

'I'm afraid not.'

'But there must be—'

'No, George!' she said. 'There's simply nothing else I can tell you that would help you with your investigation.'

She looked at her watch then stood up, smoothing down her skirt before offering him the Manila envelope.

'There you are. Don't open it until I've gone. I'm sorry I can't be any more help.'

'I understand. Thank you anyway. This could be significant. But there is one more thing I need to ask you.'

'Oh, yes?'

'Dora mentioned a German you'd spotted. Someone you recognised from Berlin. The leader of some secret sex cult?'

Harley thought he'd glimpsed a flicker of concern on Leanda's face, just before it eased into a broad seductive smile. 'Dear Dora, gossiping as usual. That was just a little idle tittle-tattle. It's really no concern of yours.'

'It might be. Especially if this German fella has started up his cult over here. Do you have a name for this character?'

'I've said far too much already.'

'What about the author, Alasdair Cassina? Do you know if he might be involved with this German's cult?'

She walked towards him with a determined look in her eye and placed her fingertip on his lips.

'I'm not saying any more today. Why don't you come and see me in Duck Lane? Perhaps we could discuss *your* little fantasies.'

'I'm not sure I have any.'

Madame Leanda raised herself up on tiptoes.

The kiss was long and sensual, perfumed with her expensive scent, the subtle flavour of her lipstick, and the faint tobacco and whisky on her breath. He felt those crimson nails lightly rake his hair, and the slight pressure of her breasts pushing into him.

Then she pulled away from him and blinked languidly.

'How about now?'

But before he could answer she was walking towards the door, waggling her fingers in the air in farewell.

'Goodnight, George. I'll see myself out.'

Once he'd heard the front door shut, Harley walked over to the mirror and wiped Leanda's vermilion lipstick from his mouth (although he failed to erase the smug smirk that had stuck there). He then sat down in the armchair by the fire and tore open the envelope she had left him.

Inside were five photographic prints, all slightly out of focus and underexposed. But the images were clear enough to make out a male in his early thirties, in various stages of undress. One showed him bent over a child's rocking horse, his pale buttocks exposed to the camera. In another he was seated at a small desk, eating a boiled egg. But it was the last photograph in the collection that caught Harley's attention. In it the mysterious 'Mr Brooks' was looking directly into the camera – which Harley guessed had been concealed behind a two-way mirror. There was a look of abject self-loathing in his otherwise unexceptional face. But it was the outfit he wore that was the most significant thing for Harley: a sailor suit, complete with a V-fronted collar and a cap with ribbons – almost an exact replica of how the Nursery Butcher's victims were dressed.

14

CONTRARY TO WHAT she had told Harley, Cynthia hadn't retired to bed for an early night after he had left her apartment. Instead, she had slipped out to hail a cab. Having read the anonymous letter to the police, there was something important she needed to do.

Now that cab was pulling into a narrow East End side street, lined either side with a row of dilapidated houses. It was a far cry from her exclusive mansion block in leafy Hampstead.

'You sure you got the right address, miss?' asked the cabbie.

'Yes, I believe so,' she said, checking a scrap of paper in her handbag.

'You got someone meeting you here? Someone you can trust?'

'I'm sure I'll be just fine,' she said, putting a brave face on it as she paid the fare. But as she made her way through the dank alleyway, dodging the unsanitary puddles and little rotting heaps of refuse, Cynthia wasn't at all sure that such confidence was well-founded.

Feeling a little self-conscious in her brand-new Bond Street overcoat, she entered the tenement block's darkened stairwell and made her way up to the first-floor landing. The sounds of communal living played out around her: the thin strains of a gramophone – Vesta Victoria singing 'Daddy Wouldn't Buy Me a Bow-Wow'; the screaming of a distraught child; a relentless bout of bronchial coughing; someone repeatedly shouting the name Betsy from a floor above.

She found the door to number seven and rapped sharply on the knocker.

There was no reply.

Glancing around nervously, she tried again.

This time she thought she heard a murmur from inside.

After the third attempt, the door was cracked open to reveal a face which had once been considered beautiful, but now looked older than its years, wan and sickly with dark halos around the eyes. A face Cynthia had known in its prime, before it had been ravaged by addiction. Who would have thought it? The Honourable Pamela Chisholm, darling of the society columns, ending up in such a dismal state?

'Oh, it's you,' said the woman, mechanically. 'What do you want?'

'May I come in, Pamela?'

'No.'

'But we need to talk. About those letters – the ones you've been sending to the police.'

Cynthia could see this registered a slight reaction, but still the door remained only partially opened.

'How do you know about the letters?'

'One was shown to me, in relation to something rather serious.'

'Really? How intriguing.'

Pamela's inherent sarcasm was obviously undiminished; but her eyes had become blank, lifeless mirrors. And Cynthia found the unnatural ageing of the once-exquisite features disconcerting – as though she were conversing with some older Chisholm sibling.

'How can you be so certain they were from me?'

'I recognised the handwriting. And there was all that stuff about Dr Jeakes; it was obvious, really.'

Cynthia looked behind her as she heard footsteps on the stairwell.

'Look, can't we talk about this inside?'

'What is it, dear? Feeling a little guilty?' A flash of anger briefly illuminated Pamela's eyes. 'And so you bloody well should! If it hadn't been for you and Constance wearing me down, convincing me it was the only sensible course of action, I wouldn't have gone through with the wretched affair.'

The truth was Cynthia did feel a little ashamed about Pamela. She had tried to help at first, to keep in touch, offer assistance where she could. But then the rumours had started to circulate: the embarrassing scenes in public, the arrests, the stealing from friends. It had simply become more convenient to slowly drift apart. After all, Pamela had never been the easiest person to like. She had always had her spiteful side, far too eager to mock when others encountered some kind of failure; it was difficult not to experience a little *schadenfreude* at her own dramatic fall from grace. But for all that, they *had* been friends.

'You would have been stuck with a baby, out of wedlock,' said Cynthia, trying her best to keep a reasonable tone. 'Whose father you couldn't stand the sight of.'

'Do you think that could have been any worse than this? It was that bastard Jeakes, you know. With his oily bedside manner; Douglas Fairbanks in a lab coat. "Just a little something for the pain," he said. And there it was. He had me. Next thing I knew, I'm back there every week for my little prescription. Spending everything I have. Family washing their hands of me, friends deserting me.' She fired another vicious look at Cynthia.

'Grubbing around for shillings. Of course, it was about more than just the money for Jeakes. He's an addict himself, you know. But I'm sure you didn't come here to listen to this.'

'I really am dreadfully sorry, Pam. If there's anything at all I can—'

'Oh, I don't want your sympathy. If it will make you feel better about yourself, you can lend me some money.'

'Why, yes, of course. I'll—'

'Five pounds. Just until I've sorted myself out.'

'Erm, righto. Would a postal order do?'

Pamela nodded fervently.

'But about these letters, dear. Why *did* you send them? You do realise you might have put Alasdair in an extremely difficult position with the police. And what if they start to investigate them? Mightn't it lead to problems for you? Given your condition?'

'I'm beyond caring. I heard him on that damn radio programme, the self-aggrandising pig. And all the fuss about this new book of his. He doesn't deserve it all.'

'You're perfectly entitled to feel bitter, after the way he treated you. But all that nonsense about a secret sex cult? With Alasdair's recent comments about the child murders, it could really land him in some deep water, you know.'

'If only it *were* nonsense. I've seen it all with my own eyes. And more besides.'

'You were involved yourself, in this cult thing?'

Pamela nodded. 'The Ancient Order of the Unicursal. The AOU. You wouldn't believe the things I've had to do.' Pamela placed a hand to her ashen face. 'The depths I've stooped to. Seeing you standing there, as innocent as ever, the perfect English rose.' She paused, as if something had just occurred to her. 'Do you have money for a taxi?'

'Why, yes, but—'

'I'll take you there. Then you'll see what Alasdair is capable of. And Jeakes. He's mixed up with it all too, you know.'

'Now?'

'Yes! You'll be quite safe with me. Or aren't you interested in discovering the truth?' Pamela gave a little sigh, as though the conversation had exhausted her. 'You do owe me, remember?'

'Well, I suppose. If it's not too far.'

Cynthia looked around at the drab tenement, wondering how she'd slipped into such a precarious situation.

'Don't worry, dear, it isn't around here. It's in Belgravia. All highly *civilised*. I'll just get changed, though.'

'Pamela!' Cynthia called, as the door was closed on her. 'Must I really wait out here?'

She was left standing awkwardly on the doorstep for a good ten minutes, where she began to wonder what Pamela might be up to inside. She had read in lurid novels about people 'overdosing', but she hadn't a clue of what one might have to do in such a situation. If the police were involved, would she be classed as an accessory?

Having made herself anxious she rapped on the door. 'Pamela? Are you alright in there?'

Good grief! Why on earth had she put herself in such a compromising position? Why hadn't she just explained to George about Pamela and Cassina, and let him sort out the facts? After all, he was the professional. Here she was, a silly meddling amateur in a disreputable part of town with – for all she knew – the corpse of an old friend on the other side of this cheap, chipboard door.

'Pamela, dear! Do answer me, *please*!'

She was just about to try to force her way in when she heard the latch turn. The next moment Cynthia was presented with a fair imitation of the Honourable Pamela Chisholm from before her fall – if a little manic-eyed and overly made-up for the daughter of a viscount.

'Right!' said Pamela, with exaggerated bonhomie, her speech a little slurred and her pupils the size of saucers. 'We're off! The Ancient Order of the Unicursal awaits its newest acolyte!'

15

'You sure I can't interest you in a Hanky Panky?' asked Cassina, flourishing a pair of coupe glasses.

'No, I need to keep a clear head,' said Collins. 'I've a meeting with the publishers in the morning. We'll be discussing the advance on your next book.'

'How perfectly dedicated you are.' Cassina dashed some Fernet-Branca into a shaker. 'Are we feeling optimistic?'

'Well, the sales are going well on *Reflection*, helped – for the time being, at least – by your constant exposure in the press.'

'One tries one's best,' said Cassina, toasting his agent with his freshly made cocktail.

'Yes, I've noticed.'

Collins was keen to discuss Cassina's recent outburst on national radio, but he'd learnt from bitter experience that such confrontations had to be handled with kid gloves.

'By the way, Rosemary Dukas is throwing a safari party this weekend, at her place down in Wiltshire. We all dress up as wild animals, big game hunters, that kind of lark. Sounds a bit of a hoot, actually. I think most of the gang will be there.'

'No doubt.' Cassina stifled a yawn. 'The same old pedestrian daredevilry, all that forced shrieking and self-conscious dissipation. Sounds unbearable.'

'Well, we all know your tastes are a little more *avant-garde* nowadays.'

'You know, Brendan,' said the author, sipping his drink at the patio windows, gazing out across the rooftops of Mayfair. 'You really ought to come out with me again some night. There was a time you used to enjoy our little escapades.'

'Indeed. But...'

'But?'

'Well, don't you think you ought to rein it all in a little? A bit of gossip about a freak party or two in the society columns is one thing; in fact, in the early days it did wonders for your career. But if the press were to get wind of some of these other things you've been dabbling in...'

'Nobody's dabbling here.'

'Precisely. And if it got out... well, you could kiss goodbye that publishing deal of yours. There might even be a prison sentence in it.'

'Oh, your father would always put in a good word for me. Government minister and all that. He's always had a soft spot for little Alasdair, hasn't he? He wouldn't stand by and see me hang.'

'I'm deadly serious. Just think of what some of those characters you've been associating with would say, if offered money for their stories. After all, everyone has their price.'

'I fear you may have succumbed to a rather serious strain of growing up, Brendan,' said Cassina. 'If this is what engagement has done for you, then I shall telephone Barbara immediately and have her call the whole thing off. After all, it will only be exacerbated by actual wedlock.'

'If you did call her, she'd be telling you exactly the same thing. She cares for you as much as I do – although God knows why we bother.'

'Well, I know why you bother – it's that damned fifteen per cent.'

'Seriously, I've been mopping up the mess from that little outburst on *The Social Looking Glass* all week. You really do need to moderate your opinions when in the public forum. God knows what Professor Morkens thought of it.'

'Why should I care what that old duffer thinks?'

'Oh, come on! He's partly responsible for you having a career as a novelist in the first place. He was most encouraging when you began writing at university. You must recall how he helped with all those stories for the Blind Bard Society.'

'Yes, and we all know why, don't we? Closest thing the poor old dinosaur got to an erotic encounter – huddling up in the dark with a bunch of excitable undergraduates telling ghost stories. You remember how he used to try to get us all squiffy.'

'That's unfair, and you know it.'

Collins lit a cigarette and sat in silence for a while.

'Listen, old thing,' he said, having calmed his frustration a little. 'We really do need to discuss the content of the new book. They're bound to ask me about it tomorrow.'

Cassina emptied his glass then walked over to the cocktail cabinet to replenish it from the silver shaker.

'Fire away.'

'Well, are you still insisting on this occult setting? All the Black Mass rituals, and the like?'

'I should say so. I've put in the best part of a month's research on it already.'

'And you're sure the Great British public are ready for such material?'

'Fuck the Great British public, this is art! And don't act all shocked and outraged. I'd like to know what the Great British public – let alone your fiancée – would think of your dirty little secrets if they ever came out.'

'What on earth do you mean by that?'

'I know you better than anyone, Brendan Collins – don't ever forget that.'

Collins was about to respond to this, but thought better of it when he saw the menacing glint in Cassina's eye.

'Hang the damned publishers,' continued Cassina. 'If they don't have enough backbone to support my choice of material, then they don't deserve the privilege. Good God! This nation of maiden aunts, hobbled by their ridiculous sense of propriety. Cowering in their closets, terrified they might catch a glimpse of a naked crotch. What do I care if they think my ideas outrageous? You've seen the letters, the fan mail. We're turning lights on in brains out there. Changing the way people think. This new book? It's my best yet, I tell you. We'll attract hordes. They'll gather around me. We'll be hundreds of thousands strong!'

Now genuinely concerned for his friend's state of mind, Collins smiled and nodded encouragingly.

'Alright, then. Why not show me something now? Just a few pages, so that I might get an idea of the tone.'

'No!' barked Cassina, pushing his fingers through his hair. 'It's not ready. There are still things I need to work out.'

'But I've got to have *something* to show the publishers.'

'They'll just have to wait. They can keep themselves occupied counting their profits from *Reflection*.'

Knowing it would be futile to try to push Cassina any further, Collins got up and poured himself a large measure of gin.

'I thought you said you needed to keep a clear head?'

'You would drive a nun to drink.'

Cassina laughed at this and delivered a boisterous slap to his agent's back.

'Come on, old man! Let's not fall out over this. I'll have something for you soon, I promise. I know, let's have champagne! I'll pop down to Filippo's and get us a bottle. We'll have a toast to the new book. Yes?'

'Why not?' said Collins, submissively.

But once he'd heard the front door close and the lift motor whirr into life, Collins slipped quietly into Cassina's study. The author's desk was in its usual state of chaotic creativity. Teetering piles of books, scattered sheets of paper, empty brandy bottles and overflowing ashtrays, all crammed in around a monstrous Underwood typewriter. Collins picked up a notepad that Cassina seemed to be currently using, and by doing so revealed a small book which had been hidden beneath it.

The book was old. To his classicist's eye, possibly seventeenth or even sixteenth century. It was bound in leather of a mottled terracotta hue, and had hand-sewn end bands. Tooled upon the front was a single design, a complex geometric device picked out in black pigment.

As Collins picked up the book, he noted a strange tactile effect – the binding felt greasy and inexplicably warm, and the whole thing was unusually pliable. It was the most curious sensation, a little like holding a small hairless creature.

Strips of paper had been inserted as bookmarks at various pages and, at the top of each strip, Cassina had pencilled a reference number. One of these numbers corresponded to an underlined heading on the notepad. Collins opened the book at this marker.

Although a little rusty, Collins still had a good grasp of Latin and a tolerable understanding of Ancient Greek, having read Classics at Oxford; but he struggled to even identify the alphabet that had been used for the faded handwritten text. Some form of Hebrew, perhaps? Aramaic? Whatever it was, Cassina clearly had enough knowledge of it to perform a translation. Beneath the reference number on the notepad, after a few crossed-out earlier versions, were the following lines:

For he who has bathed in ordure and filth, the innocence of the child supplieth that which is wanting, and the Holy Archons are much pleased with its purity.

Part of Cassina's research for the new novel, no doubt; and on the face of it – although not exactly Hodgson Burnett material – not too devastatingly awful.

But when Collins began to flick through the rest of the book, the shock of what he saw there made him throw it down, as though it had delivered a bolt of electricity.

After a few moments, with his heart now racing, he reached out a tentative hand and began once more to turn the thick vellum pages. There, interspersed with the paragraphs of indecipherable text and tables of alchemical signs, were the most abhorrent illustrations. The majority of these depicted, in graphic detail, forms of torture performed upon young children; children whose angelic faces, framed by Botticelli curls, gazed down with lustful glee at the horrific violence being enacted on their innocent bodies. And it was these leering expressions on the children's faces – so inherently evil and beyond their years – that affected Collins the most, filling his soul with a creeping dread.

Conscious he hadn't much time before Cassina returned, he took a clean sheet of paper. With a soft 2B pencil, he began to take a rubbing of the archaic magical symbol embossed upon the cover of this despicable work.

16

Having arrived in Belgravia, Cynthia now waited anxiously on the pavement outside a large Corinthian-columned townhouse. At the door of this imposing edifice, Pamela was negotiating with a rather austere-looking footman. She'd seen a telephone box on the corner of the elegant square and was sorely tempted to slip away to make a quick call to Harley. But as there was no appliance installed at Bell Street, this would mean telephoning the Shabaroon pub and leaving a message for him there; she was no expert, but she imagined this wasn't how such things were done in the world of undercover investigation. Before long the decision had been taken out of her hands – Pamela was beckoning her up the steps of the grand portico.

After their coats were taken, they were ushered up a cantilevered stone staircase to a large first-floor salon, guarded by a doorman of gargantuan stature. The room had a lofty ceiling and heavy purple drapery, and together with the shoulder-height candelabra, a lingering aroma of incense and the mosaic of the

Qabalistic Tree of Life on the marble floor, the overall impression was that of the inner sanctum of some ancient temple, rather than the drawing room of a Georgian townhouse. Adding to this effect was the strange company assembled there.

Forgetting for a moment her precarious situation, Cynthia found herself gazing at these guests with fascination. A proportion of those present would have seemed perfectly at home at any high-society function: men and women in conventional evening dress – possibly the cultured representatives of old aristocratic families or the suave scions of the nouveau riche. But interspersed with these were a number of eccentric-looking individuals dressed in pseudo-Egyptian garb: white cotton gowns, tied at the waist with a golden rope, and a diagonal sash embroidered with hieroglyphs. Their feet were bare and on their heads they wore a simplified version of a pharaonic headdress in blue and gold silk. She quickly concluded that these must be current members of the order and noticed some of them seemed to be instructing what she took to be prospective neophytes with the aid of a small pamphlet.

'I don't see Alasdair,' she said to Pamela.

'Alasdair? Oh no, *he* won't be here. He's far too important to mess around with the new recruits.'

'But hang on a moment! I thought you said that—'

Cynthia was cut short by the approach of an extraordinary individual in a tuxedo – dark-haired and beetle-browed. She might have considered him handsome, but for the disconcerting, penetrating eyes.

'How *wonderful* to see you, Pamela,' said the man, his thick German accent tinged with a hint of sarcasm. 'I thought you were taking a little holiday from us, no?'

'Oh, Fedor. Don't be silly! How on earth could one stay away from you for very long?'

Pamela held her hand out defiantly. After a short hesitation, their host took it to his fleshy lips.

'And, anyway, I simply had to introduce you to my good friend Sibylla. She's exceptionally curious about our little gatherings, you see. Sibylla, this is Fedor, Fedor von Görlitz.'

'Please to meet you, Mr von Görlitz,' said Cynthia, wishing Pamela had chosen an easier pseudonym for her.

'Enchanté, my dear,' he purred, regarding her with a look a wolf might reserve for a new-born lamb. 'Sibylla – such a beautiful name; like the Greek prophetess, no? Is this your real name?'

'I might ask the same of you, Mr von Görlitz,' said Cynthia, surprising herself with her boldness.

The German laughed heartily. 'Oh! But she's delightful, Pamela! First rate, as you English say.'

He paused to draw his hand under Pamela's chin; an act which quietened her and left her with the look of a contented feline.

'You have done well, my dear,' he whispered into her ear. 'Go and find Jeakes and tell him I said that you deserve a reward.'

With a smile of desperate delight, Pamela gave a squeeze to Cynthia's hand before disappearing into the crowd.

'I say! Pamela?' Cynthia called after her.

'Now, don't concern yourself,' said von Görlitz. 'You're quite safe here.'

Cynthia turned to find a colossus of a figure looming over them.

'And just where have you been hiding this delightful creature, Fedor?' he asked, a plump tongue wetting his rouged lips.

'Oh, I assure you, she's quite the latest arrival. This is Sibylla. My dear, let me introduce you to a very old friend of mine, Victor Manduca.'

'Manduca?' repeated Cynthia, blanching. She remembered Harley's description of Manduca the Spider – the infamous Soho pornographer. *Like an elephantine Nero*, he'd said. She'd chuckled at the time. But looking up at that hideous countenance, with its fleshy, powdered jowls, she wasn't laughing now. 'Such an unusual name,' she managed.

'Maltese, originally,' he purred in a cut-glass accent.

'Victor is a very important local businessman. A pillar of the community. Does so very much for charity, you know. And, of course, he has achieved the fourth-degree grade in our order.'

'Delighted,' said the Spider, grasping Cynthia's elegant musician's hand in his huge paw. An ostentatious ruby glinted from a cluster of rings squeezed onto his sausage-like fingers. 'My my, you're quite the vision. Angelic bone structure. Classical figure. Have you ever considered sitting as an artist's model, my dear?'

'Uh-uh!' said von Görlitz, playfully slapping at Manduca's wrist. 'Hands off, Victor. There's a good boy.'

He quickly led her away from the giant Maltese, across the room to a large table, displaying an impressive array of alcoholic drinks. 'Might I get you something? Perhaps something you won't have tried before?'

'How do you know I won't have tried it?'

The German laughed, as though it were amusing to think there might be anything he didn't know about her. He picked up a large ornate silver wine jug.

'Here we are: Hippocras. An ancient cordial of wine, sugar and bruised spices. Is this the correct word, *bruised*?'

'Possibly.'

'Well, good enough, perhaps. Named after the Hippocratic sleeve, through which alchemists would drain their magical concoctions.'

Von Görlitz poured two glasses of the deep purple wine. Cynthia waited until her host had taken a drink himself and then risked a sip. It was delicious – a little like mulled wine, but more complex, perfumed almost. She took another, more adventurous gulp in order to steady her nerves.

'So, my dear. What is it you are so curious about, hmm? Let me guess. It is because you have heard we are a *sex* cult. And you desire,' he placed a firm hand on her bare arm at this word, 'to know what this means. Am I right?'

'Perhaps.'

Cynthia hoped he hadn't seen the colour she could feel rising to her cheeks. She took another quick sip of the drink.

'Well. The sexual content is only part of our teachings. But an important part, nonetheless. You see, any religion that chooses to suppress the passions of sexual desire – and so many do – risks breaking a covenant with the gods. Masturbation, copulation, ecstatic release… Ah, no!'

Von Görlitz took a step closer and touched her arm again.

'You must overcome your childish embarrassment, my dear. Keep eye contact. Listen carefully. Masturbation… copulation… ecstatic release…' he enunciated carefully, 'these are all transcendental acts, fundamental to the human spirit. And with the correct training and technique such acts can unlock the hidden secrets of ancient esoteric wisdom.'

'I say, I do wonder where Pamela has got to,' said Cynthia, a little shocked at the sudden turn of conversation.

'I'm sure you will be reunited again soon. Ah! There! Listen… do you hear it, my dear?'

Cynthia looked around her, trying to find the source of the music that had begun to play. It was Oriental-sounding: the soft rhythmic pulse of a drum and tambourine, and a haunting ancient melody played on some kind of reeded instrument.

'I didn't see any musicians,' she said, hoping to change the subject. 'Where are they?'

'There's another room. Adjacent to this one. We'll go in there soon. Perhaps we will find Pamela there? How is your Hippocras?'

He smiled at her, the candlelight flickering in the bottomless pools of his eyes.

Remarkable eyes. Not in the least bit frightening, as she'd first thought.

The smile seemed to go on for much longer than was normal. Then von Görlitz began to sing softly to the music, a simple, repetitive phrase of strange, foreign-sounding words:

'*Sicofet, Cenalif, Oramaro. Sicofet, Cenalif, Oramaro…*'

It was like listening to an old familiar nursery rhyme, comforting and nostalgic. She nodded in time and sipped at her wine, marvelling at the strangeness of it all, her nervousness fading.

Yes, she decided, he *was* handsome. Extraordinarily so.

'You mentioned ancient esoteric wisdom, Mr von Görlitz – what did you mean, exactly?'

'Perhaps if you were German, my dear, you wouldn't find this such a remarkable idea. The Christian church has always found it harder in my country to totally eradicate the heritage of our pagan past. Show an Englander an image of Cernunnos and he sees Satan, whereas the Bavarian peasant would recognise the symbol of a sacred sexual deity, a god of nature and wild abandon.'

'Cernunnos?'

'Cernunnos, or Pan, or Baphomet. Here, let me show you.'

Von Görlitz stopped one of the passing cult members and asked for her instructional manual. She was a large woman in her late fifties, with a pronounced paunch and a mane of frizzled grey hair poking out from under her headdress. She handed over the booklet then seized the German's face in her manly hands and delivered him a passionate kiss.

'Thank you,' he said, nonchalantly, as though she'd merely offered him a light for a cigarette.

He turned back to Cynthia and opened the pamphlet to an illustration of an alarming-looking mythical creature – a winged, goat-headed hermaphrodite.

'This is the Sabbatic Goat, my dear. A cipher, to be unravelled by the subconscious. Look…'

Von Görlitz now held the book up so that his piercing eyes were in line with the image.

'The beast's head expresses the horror of the sinner. It is the great god Pan – he of the voracious, divine lust, whose death, some say, left a vacuum to be filled by the Christ child.'

The German's silken voice seemed to have grown louder somehow, dominating her attention. The general hubbub of the room had faded into the background. But curiously the rhythmic pulse of the drum was still there, punctuating his words.

'Or perhaps it is the Egyptian Banebdjedet?'

Boom-Bah-Bah-Boom went the drum.

'Or Ba'al?'

Boom-Bah-Bah-Boom.

'Or Cernunnos?'

Boom-Bah-Bah-Boom.

Her peripheral vision was fading now, blurring at the edges, tunnelling into those piercing, mesmeric eyes.

'You see, we all share a collective memory of such horned deities.'

Boom-Bah-Bah-Boom.

'Don't you feel it, stirring within you?'

Boom-Bah-Bah-Boom.

'Yes,' she murmured, and her voice was someone else's.

'Christians seek to suppress these powerful effects, by transferring these attributes to their own great horned adversary, Satan. But this is mere propaganda. Do you understand, my child?'

'Yes, Fedor.'

His warm hand was once again on her arm. She closed her eyes.

Boom-Bah-Bah-Boom.

'And what could be more natural? More sacred...'

Boom-Bah-Bah-Boom.

'... than the miraculous rite of sexual congress?'

Cynthia felt the fingers crawl up her neck, the downy hairs there aroused in anticipation.

And then the hand was gone.

'Ah! I must apologise. One moment.'

She opened her eyes, expectant, confused by the abrupt interruption, to find the German's attention had been caught by a dishevelled character in a voluminous overcoat and crumpled hat, who had just slipped into the room and was now talking conspiratorially with the doorman.

'I need to speak to someone, my dear. It shouldn't take long. Stay here and finish your wine. Oh, and Sibylla?'

'Yes, Fedor?'

'Don't go into the other room, will you? Not until I get back. Is that clear?'

She nodded her head slowly. 'Yes, Fedor.'

Von Görlitz tapped her lightly on the arm with his index finger and then made his way over to join the dishevelled-looking Martin Perrine, who looked so incongruous among the other attendees of the occult gathering.

* * *

Fedor von Görlitz was not, in fact, German, but Hungarian. He had started life as Agoston Popović. Born into a long line of circus performers, the young Agoston worked his way up through the carnival and music-hall circuits to become a successful stage clairvoyant. Changing his name to something more Germanic, the showman relocated to Vienna, where he began to train in hypnotism, and to inveigle himself into the city's social scene. Before long – now as Fedor von Görlitz – he became the acclaimed sensation of the cocktail-party set, helped in no small part by his extraordinary animal magnetism. Playing to his natural talents, von Görlitz worked up an act based on erotic suggestibility, hypnotising well-heeled female volunteers and commanding them to perform lewd acts before their astonished – and often highly titillated – fellow guests. News of his unique skills spread, and he was subsequently lured to Berlin (then at the height of its Weimar Republic decadence) where he became entangled in the city's murky world of mystery sects. With his innate sexual charisma and expert mentalist stagecraft, von Görlitz soon rose to prominence, eventually launching his own occult sect: the Ancient Order of the Unicursal. This began to attract members from some of the highest echelons of European society, lured by its leader's erotic take on Thelemic mysticism. And now, here he was, a few years later, exporting the same clandestine mysticism to stuffy old England. But in the interim years the order had adopted a somewhat more serious agenda, mainly due to its association with the wily character who had just arrived, whose bumbling, tramp-like appearance belied a menacing, dangerous nature.

'So, what news from Berlin?' asked Perrine, sitting down behind the desk in the small office off the main salon.

'Things are going well,' said von Görlitz. 'Many of Grosche's followers are leaving the Fraternitas Saturni and coming over to us now.'

'Good, good. It is, of course, thanks to the war that we have such fertile land in Germany, in which to sow our seed.' Perrine took a sip of water. 'Any sign of our little watercolourist?'

The Hungarian shook his head. 'Not in person. Herr Hitler has too high a profile nowadays. But he writes from time to time, asking my opinion on things.'

'Try to keep him close. Such individuals can be easily dismissed, but I wouldn't underestimate him. The fact that you have his ear could prove most helpful. Most helpful indeed. But you should also consider the possibility that, in the future, he may regard you as a threat.'

'A threat?'

'Of course. After all, you have knowledge of some of Herr Hitler's most intimate secrets. Do you still have those photographs of him, taken at the ceremonies? You may need them some day, for insurance purposes.'

'Yes. The roll of film is safely stored. It's here in London, actually. I've asked Victor Manduca to produce some high-quality prints from it.'

Perrine nodded. 'Very good. By the way, that Berlin dog of yours, the one you brought over to deal with our little sexologist? I've been told he's a kind of sadist for hire.'

'Yes. The Bulgarian, "Mr Whispers". One of the best.'

'Mr Whispers? He's professional, I trust?'

'Naturally. And extremely discreet. Why do you ask?'

'I may need someone else to help with the next delivery. And other things. Do you think you might lend him to me?'

'Of course. But the two AOU brethren I supplied you – there has been no problem with them, I hope?'

'Oh, they've been quite adequate, Fedor. But I fear we may have exhausted their resources by now. Burnt them out, so to speak. The work is quite gruelling, psychically speaking.'

'Of course. I'll have the Bulgarian report to you immediately.'

'Excellent.'

'And what of our *gentleman*?' asked von Görlitz, arching one of his thick eyebrows dramatically. 'Will he be making an appearance soon?'

The old man smiled.

'Patience, Fedor. He is making great strides in his experimentation. But this is lofty work, such things can't be rushed.'

'But are we close, do you think? The inner circle grows eager to perform the ritual.'

'Yes, we are close.' Perrine pushed his blue-tinted spectacles back up his nose. 'We have now chosen our little goat.'

'Really?' Von Görlitz rubbed his hands together. 'Excellent! And I believe you have something for me, yes?'

Perrine nodded and produced a small, circular golden pot from his pocket.

'*Lamiarum unguenta* – the infamous witches' ointment, with which the good women of the night were said to have anointed their broomsticks and naked bodies.'

Von Görlitz's bushy eyebrows arched in surprise.

'*Die Hexen*? Flying ointments? Surely, our gentleman doesn't believe in such *Hokuspokus*?'

'We're not talking about some pantomime spell here, Fedor. This is the ancient craft of *veneficia* – the mixing of herbal and other arcane ingredients to produce physics which have the most powerful effects on the mind and body. Effects both beneficial and detrimental. After much research, we have arrived at the conclusion that the night flights on brooms, the animal metamorphoses, the demonic congregation and other extraordinary acts attributed to the witches of the sixteenth century were all just fantastic visions brought about by the *lamiarum unguenta*'s hallucinogenic properties.' The old man tapped the lid of the pot. 'But as well as being used to bring on these mind-altering states in the witches themselves, it is our belief that these powerful ointments were used to control others.'

'Control others?' said von Görlitz, suddenly becoming more interested. 'How so?'

'By inducing a dreamlike trance in the subject, in which they might be open to any suggestion. And by warping their sense of reality, so they might attribute greater powers to the witch.'

'Or wizard,' mused von Görlitz, picking up the small golden pot. He unscrewed the lid, revealing a bright green unguent.

Perrine held up a hand. 'Careful.'

'Is it so dangerous? What is in it?'

'Ah, that would be telling,' said Perrine, with a smile.

'It smells strongly.' Von Görlitz flared his nostrils. 'Like churches.' He took another sniff, adopting his stage persona.

'Incense... the dusty robes of priests... fungus... herbs... dark forest floors... the damp pelts of animals.'

'Most poetic, Fedor. Don't touch it, though, there's a good chap.'

Von Görlitz put the pot down carefully. 'Just to touch is enough?'

'Of course. One of the desired effects. So it can be administered transdermally.'

'Through the skin?'

'Exactly.'

'Then how would you give it to the, erm...'

'Victim? You must first apply some petroleum jelly mixed with a little antidote to your own hand, to act as a barrier. Here is the antidote.'

He placed a small, blue-glass bottle on the table.

Von Görlitz's dark eyes glinted with malicious delight.

'So, with your witches' ointment, we could summon for them the demonic goat of nocturnal orgies,' he said. 'Or have them consort with those pale *incubi*, who project their cold seed into the black of the skies!'

Perrine chuckled. 'You've got the idea. And, of course, they'll be an absolute *slave* to your bidding. Now, why don't you try it out on a few of your acolytes, and report back on the results, hmm?'

Von Görlitz gave a formal bow.

'Tell our gentleman I shall be delighted. In fact, waiting for me out there right now, I have a delightful creature who would make the perfect subject for such an experiment.'

17

CYNTHIA AWOKE.

Her brain began a panicked scramble to get a fix on the here and now.

She was standing in the middle of a strangely ornate room. She looked down at her hands. In one was a glass of wine, in the other, a pamphlet whose cover was decorated with a strange design: a hexagram of unusual proportions, like two arrowheads intersecting each other, one pointing up, one down.

Things snapped into focus.

Von Görlitz. That velvet voice. The penetrating, mesmeric eyes.

The Hippocras! It was almost certainly drugged. She could feel its effects – a muddying of her reasoning, a slight dizziness when she turned her head. But away from the German's hypnotic influence its effects were weakening.

She remembered it all now – the trip to Pamela's flat; her insistence that a visit to the AOU gathering would expose the truth about Cassina. But Alasdair wasn't here. And where was

Pamela? It was looking suspiciously like the only reason she'd been lured to the cult was so Pamela could ingratiate herself once more with Fedor von Görlitz.

Handling it as though it were a glass of hemlock, Cynthia placed the Hippocras on a table and began to frantically search the room.

She noticed the hideous Manduca, fixing her with a predatory gaze from across the room. He lifted his glass, his loose jowls wobbling beneath pursed lips.

Ignoring him, she purposefully approached a young woman not far off her own age; demure-looking – apart from the fact that she was exposing a little too much cleavage in her Egyptian robe.

'Excuse me, but have you seen Pamela?'

'Pamela? I'm sorry, but I don't think I know her. Is she your assigned mentor?'

'Erm, yes. I suppose she is,' said Cynthia, trying her best not to stare at the woman's prominent nipples. How strange she couldn't seem to keep her eyes off that shapely body. 'I lost track of her a little while ago, you see. I became somewhat distracted.'

'I saw you talking to Fedor,' said the girl, giving her a knowing look. 'I'm afraid he can have that effect, especially if it's your first time.'

Just then the Oriental music started up again in the adjacent room. Cynthia turned to the double doors with ornate cut-glass handles.

'Actually, I think Pamela might have gone in there. Is it alright if I just check?'

'Oh no, you can't do that, not until the induction.'

'You could come with me. It wouldn't take long. I need to find Pamela. There's something important I need to tell her.'

'Well, I *suppose* we could.' The young woman looked a little unsure. 'Have you signed the papers of confidentiality?'

'What? Oh yes. Fedor has already taken me through all of that,' said Cynthia, relieved to feel her wits returning.

'In that case, I should think it would be alright. Just for a short while, though – I'm meant to be helping in here, you see.'

The woman cracked one of the doors open just enough for them both to slip through.

It was much darker in this room, the only illumination supplied by two large candelabras and a number of smoking braziers, packed with fiery red coals. It took a while for Cynthia's eyes to adjust after the bright lights of the salon. The air was overheated, oppressive and thick with the heady perfume of incense.

'Stick close now,' said the young woman, slipping her hand into Cynthia's. It felt cool and strangely pleasing.

Cynthia looked around, sensing someone close by, staring at her. It was a man standing at a table to their right; tall and vaguely handsome, in formal evening dress. As they passed him, she saw he was removing things from a large Gladstone bag and laying them out on the table: syringes, vials and glass bottles with pharmaceutical labels, as though preparing for a medical operation. She wondered whether this might be the infamous Dr Jeakes.

'Careful you don't trip on anything,' said the young woman, pulling her gently forward into the darkened room.

Cynthia now saw the shadowy objects dotted around were in fact luxurious divans, and Persian rugs scattered with large, embroidered cushions. Some of these were already occupied by cult members, naked, apart from a transparent chiffon gown and a black domino mask. As her eyes began to adapt to the low light Cynthia realised this partial nudity did not necessarily result from a need to advertise to the world a perfection of form: although there was the odd Adonis and Aphrodite amongst their throng, Cynthia found herself gawping at a profusion of pot bellies, shrivelled genitalia and pendulous breasts, albeit softened a little by the diaphanous material.

'Do you see her anywhere?'

'Sorry?'

'Your mentor, Pamela.'

'Oh, no,' said Cynthia. 'Not yet. But do tell me something – the author, Alasdair Cassina, is he a member, do you know?'

The young woman smiled and shook her head. 'I'm afraid we can't talk about our fellow members, not with neophytes.'

The girl pulled her further into the room; the hypnotic music grew louder.

As they turned the corner Cynthia let out an audible gasp.

There in front of them, standing on a raised dais, illuminated by the infernal glow of the brazier's coals, was an imposing alabaster statue, depicting the same winged, goat-headed hermaphrodite that von Görlitz had pointed out in the pamphlet.

The young woman by her side giggled and made a playful curtsy to the horned god.

'Love is the law, love under will,' she chanted.

It wasn't just the commanding idol that had caught Cynthia's breath, but also the group of sprawling bodies around its base. Four men and three women, naked, lost in lustful abandonment – the sweat on their skin glistening in the flickering light as they rutted like animals in the zoo.

She felt giddy at the sight, her head muggy with the oppressive heat and the overpowering incense.

The young woman moved in close behind her.

'I don't think your mentor is here, is she?' she whispered, her breath hot in Cynthia's ear. 'No matter. There'll be many other willing volunteers for your induction; you're such a beautiful thing.'

The cool hands were on her hips; then moving down her thighs.

'Why don't we get you ready? Out of these stuffy clothes and into your chiffon.'

Cynthia was suddenly struck by a moment of clarity. She looked around her, now desperate for a means of escape.

'I, erm, I'm afraid I need the powder room, first.'

'Of course, dear. The door's just over there, behind that curtain. But don't be too long, now, will you?' she giggled.

As soon as she was inside the bathroom, Cynthia slipped the lock and slid to the floor with her back against the door. Her heart was racing – the nature of the ordeal that awaited her at the hands of the wanton cult members now all too obvious.

The young woman was probably compliant enough to allow her back out into the salon. But what then? The doorman was a giant. And what if von Görlitz reappeared? Could she really trust herself to resist the German's mesmeric influence?

She stood up and brushed herself down. There was nothing else for it – she'd have to take her chances, bluff it out, speak loud and confident, raise a fuss with the doorman.

After all, this is London, she thought. *Not the back streets of Cairo.*

She walked to the handbasin and doused her face with cold water, slapping her cheeks to rouse herself, knowing she'd need her full wits about her. Then, rehearsing a few lines of reasonable argument in her head, she took a deep breath and went to unlock the door.

'Sibylla? Are you in there?'

Her hand jerked from the door handle as though she'd received an electric shock.

It was von Görlitz.

She stood stock-still, holding her breath.

'Sibylla? You're needed out here, my child.'

And now the pulsing drumbeat was back in her head.

Boom-Bah-Bah-Boom.

And she could almost see those black, penetrating eyes, boring through the timber panel of the door.

Boom-Bah-Bah-Boom.

He began to sing.

'*Sicofet, Cenalif, Oramaro…*'

And it was as though he were in the room with her.

'*Sicofet, Cenalif, Oramaro...*'

The lilting, silken voice seeped into her mind. Her vision began to tunnel, the bathroom fading around her. She knew she had but a few seconds more.

'*Sicofet, Cenalif, Oramaro...*'

Turning in desperation to the sink, Cynthia looked up and saw her chance.

'I shan't be long!' she shouted, steeling herself.

She rushed to the large sash window and heaved it open, feeling immediately invigorated by the dank night air that rushed in. The window looked out onto the garden at the rear of the property. A few feet below her, she could just make out the flat roof of the adjoining building.

Denying herself time to think too clearly about what she was about to attempt, Cynthia kicked off her shoes and grabbed the hem of her silk skirt, yanking with all her might. Having torn a rent large enough to allow her legs free movement, she clambered up onto the side of the bath and crawled out onto the window ledge.

The cold drainpipe was greasy and slick with condensation. Startled by the loud thumping on the bathroom door, she almost lost her grip; somehow her stockinged feet found a purchase on the wet brickwork and, after a few terrifying seconds of uncontrolled sliding, she found herself close enough to the edge of the flat roof to thrust out an exploratory leg. On the second attempt she managed to summon enough courage to make the leap and, although barking her shin badly in the process, she made it safely. She took a moment to catch her breath, then wiped her grubby hands on her skirt and lowered herself over the edge, her bare feet feeling for the cold galvanised steel of the dustbin lids below.

And then Cynthia was away, fleeing for her life through the damp night, her heart pounding in her chest, cursing her own naivety and thanking the gods – horned or otherwise – for her timely escape.

18

'THAT'S ONE UGLY brute you've got there, George,' said John Franklin, looking at Harley's tomcat, Moloch, who was scrutinising him from on top of the bookshelf. 'The way he's looking at me, with that one yellow eye of his, you'd think he owned the place.'

'Well, in a way he does. He just showed up one day and laid claim to the place. I didn't dare argue with him.'

'He puts me in mind of a wrestler I once arrested. A big Russian old-timer – the *Baltic Behemoth*. Bit a landlord's ear off in a pub brawl. Swallowed it whole. When I was taking his statement, he stared at me across the table just like that.'

'Oh, you'll be alright,' said Harley, handing the policeman a cup of tea. 'You like coppers, don't you, Moloch?'

'Yeah, I bet,' said Franklin. 'With a little vinegar, and a slice of bread and butter, no doubt.'

Harley laughed and slumped down in the battered old wing chair. They were in the attic room at Bell Street. In front of them was an easel holding a blackboard, on which Harley had chalked up some of the details of the Nursery Butcher murders. Also displayed were various black-and-white photographs, pinned to the board with clothes pegs.

After applying himself to his cup of tea, DCI Franklin got up to give the blackboard a once-over. 'This something you learnt in MI5, then? Oh, sorry, you can't talk about that, can you?'

Harley allowed the policeman a brief smile.

'Decapitation, eh?' said Franklin, looking at the photographic copies of illustrations from reference books.

'Yeah. Some of the famous cases. I take the photographs myself. It's a bit of a hobby of mine. I've got a little darkroom in the under-stair cupboard.'

Harley got up to point out some of the examples. 'This is Judith beheading Holofernes... Salome with the head of John the Baptist... David and Goliath...'

'Didn't know you were so religious.'

'I'm not. But our killer might be. Anyway, this is just an ideas board, a tool to get me thinking a certain way. I pin all the references up, stare at it for a bit, listen to a bit of jazz. It helps to stimulate the old subconscious, you know?'

'Well, it's not a technique covered in the detective's handbook, but I suppose I can see what you're getting at. After all, there's more than one way to skin a cat – no offence, Moloch.'

'So, come on then,' said Harley, sparking up a Gold Flake. 'Don't keep me in suspense here. What's the verdict on that head from the butcher's shop victim?'

Franklin nodded. 'The pathologist has confirmed it matches the Clapham victim's body. And vice versa.'

'So, we have our two victims. Any closer to identifying them?'

'Not as yet, I'm afraid.'

Harley shook his head.

'And what's more,' said Franklin, 'the key planted on our new victim is identical to the one found at the Clapham scene.

Antique, possibly mid-eighteenth century. Any new thoughts on those keys? I assume they're some kind of message.'

'Well, it's almost too corny to believe, isn't it? As though he's nicked the plot from some Victorian Gothic melodrama. "The victims hold the key to the mystery." I'd say our man is one arrogant shicer.'

'Or a criminal lunatic.'

'Maybe both. Do you think you could get me an exact copy made? One that would turn the lock if we ever found it?'

'Shouldn't be a problem.'

'Good,' said Harley, getting up to chalk the details about the keys on the blackboard.

'So, any news on the Muller kid?'

'Nothing yet. Do you think it was our man?'

'I'd say it's unlikely, wouldn't you?' said Harley. 'The other victims have been so anonymous. And we still don't have a body.'

'I agree. But let's keep an open mind.'

'I wish Craster would keep an open mind.' Harley held up the front page of the *Daily Oracle* newspaper. 'The bastard's already got little Eddie Muller decapitated and dressed in his sailor suit.'

'I know. I can't begin to think what effect it's having on the parents.'

'So, you've had the post-mortem back then?'

'Yes. I've brought along a copy for you.' Franklin pulled a folder from his briefcase. 'It makes for grim reading, I'm afraid.'

Harley took a moment to scan through the report.

'Same MO, then,' he said, when he'd finished reading. 'The heart and the toes of the left foot missing. And we're still no closer to knowing who these poor sods are.'

'We've had a few more parents with missing children come forward, but they've all failed to identify the bodies. It's not as if there was anything left on them to help; no labels sewn into the clothes, nothing.'

'That's because they were just costumes. All part of the staging of the thing.' Harley sat back and took another look at the post-mortem report.

'You know, I'm not sure this is in-depth enough for what we need. What are the chances of getting Sir Bernard Spilsbury to take a look at the bodies?'

'What, the chap from the Crippen case?'

Harley nodded. 'He's supposed to be the best pathologist in the country.'

'Well, he's a bit of a celebrity nowadays, but I might be able to swing it. But to what end?'

'To help us identify our victims. If we know where they're from, it might lead us to our man.'

'Alright, if you think it'll help, I'll see what I can do.'

'How's it going with potential suspects?'

Franklin shook his head. 'We've had a dozen men in for questioning – all of them known pederasts, or with some previous for sexual deviancy. We'll be keeping a couple of them under observation, but so far there's nothing to link any of them to the crimes.'

'I realise you've got to do the legwork, but I don't think you'll find our man on any list of usual suspects. This one's something different.'

'Someone who can turn murder into an art form, you mean?'

'Are you thinking of our old friend Alasdair Cassina?'

'Yes, I am. What with the newspaper articles, that damned radio programme, and those anonymous letters… well, the superintendent wants him looked into.'

'What for? Incitement?'

'There could be an argument for that – as well as the Turpin affair, we've had recent reports of a teenager arrested for animal cruelty who cited that damned book of his as inspiration. But, no, the super wants Cassina looked at as a potential suspect for the murders.'

'Seriously? But I've told you about those letters. They were sent maliciously. The Honourable Pamela Chisholm is hardly a reliable witness.'

'How is Cynthia, by the way?'

'Still a little shaken,' said Harley, scowling at the thought of his girlfriend's recent escapade. 'But to tell you the truth, I think the most serious wound is her bruised ego.'

'I'd say she was extremely lucky. It could have been a damn sight worse. A slip of a girl like that, playing at detectives.'

'Hold on, John,' said Harley, flicking his cigarette butt into the fireplace. 'Personally, I'd say she showed a lot of bottle, wouldn't you? And some nous for getting out like she did. Although, granted, she could have thought about taking a little more backup.'

'Well, perhaps. But I certainly wouldn't want either of my daughters associating with such people. You're sure you don't want this black magic outfit raided? I'm not sure we could secure any arrests, but we could at least ruffle a few feathers.'

'Believe me, I'd love to go over there and knock a few heads together. But I think we should keep our cards close to our chest for the time being. From what Cynthia's told me, this Fedor von Görlitz character is high up in the cult. That means it's probable he's the same German that Dora was talking about. He could well be linked to the murders. If you go wading in there half-cocked with a troop of flatties, he'll just disappear back to Berlin. But this AOU outfit definitely needs looking into. Have a look at this.'

Harley unclipped a pamphlet from the blackboard.

'Cynthia got that at the AOU gathering. It's a kind of beginners' manual for the new members. It's got some gibberish about rituals, and then at the back…'

'Good Lord!' exclaimed Franklin, having turned to a set of explicit illustrations, showing sexual positions. 'I would imagine we could get a conviction under the Obscene Publications Act for this.'

'I know, but just hold your horses. Look at those illustrations.'

'To be honest with you, it's hard not to.'

'What I mean is, look at the *style* of the illustration. Doesn't it remind you of something?'

'I don't quite follow. Wait! My word, yes! They look like that lunatic Turpin's work. Do you think they were done by him?'

'I'd say there's a good chance. And there's more. Guess who else was at that AOU orgy? None other than Victor Manduca. I'm sure you've heard of *him*.'

'Indeed, I have,' said Franklin. 'The Spider. Maltese national. Arrived on our fair shores, along with his brother Spiru, a few years ago, after they'd both been expelled by the Egyptian authorities for running a chain of highly successful bordellos in Alexandria.'

'That's him.'

'And, of course, he's now set himself up in a similarly profitable business in Soho, and has expanded into pornography and extortion. I believe there was even a rumour that he might be involved in some kind of white slavery – ensnaring young girls in the West End and shipping them off to his pals in the back streets of Alexandria. Most of this is just conjecture of course. As well as having the morals of a sewer rat, the fellow's also damned clever at covering his tracks. Hides his illicit dealings behind a number of legitimate businesses. We've had him in at Vine Street a couple of times, but we've yet to make anything stick. So, this damned AOU cult has links with the likes of Turpin and Manduca. You know, if Cassina is a member, then maybe we *should* be looking at him as a potential suspect.'

'The thing is,' said Harley, pouring out some more tea, 'we still have no hard evidence he *is* involved with the AOU. And it was only a bit of second-hand gossip from Dora that linked them to a rumour of using kids in their rituals in the first place. All we've got so far is a lot of hearsay.'

'Well then, I think we should pay Victor Manduca a visit. Put some pressure on him to reveal what he knows about this German von Görlitz and his nasty little cult.'

Harley couldn't help wincing at this, knowing what a mess he was already in with the Maltese mobster. He realised he was going to have to act shrewdly – strike a fine balance between an effective investigation and streetwise self-preservation.

'Maybe. But you said it yourself – the Spider's meticulous in concealing all the bent stuff. You're hardly going to stumble across any hard evidence by just dragging him and his brother down the nick. Let me have a go first, work it from the street level. I've got a few contacts.'

'Hmm… well, alright. But if you don't get anywhere, I'm going to have to take a more formal approach.'

'And what's that going to look like, just after I've been quizzing him about the same thing? Believe me, we don't want to go upsetting the apple cart in the West End underworld at the moment. Not with everyone so jumpy over this turf war between Mori's gang and the Elephant Boys. If I'm going to be of any use to you at all in this investigation, we need to keep all my usual lines of communication open. If the villains start to think that associating with George Harley is going to lead to a night of interrogation in Vine Street, then I won't get anywhere at all – apart from to the bottom of the Thames in a hessian sack.'

'Well, let's hope you get a result, then. Listen, I'll do my best, but I've got to be honest with you, for some of this my hands will be tied. The super's keeping me under intense scrutiny on this one – thanks to the influence of that weasel Quigg.'

'Yeah, and look who your super fancies for it – Alasdair Cassina. Listen to your copper's gut. You don't really believe such a public figure could be involved, do you?'

'I suppose not,' Franklin said with a sigh, beginning to fill his pipe. 'But you have to admit, he does keep cropping up like a bad penny.'

'Listen, the more I learn about our privileged little author, the more I dislike him,' said Harley. 'But if we discount those letters, I don't see what evidence there is to associate him with any kind of crime at all.'

'That may well be the case but, nevertheless, the super wants him looked at. And what the super wants, he gets.'

Franklin held a match to his Bulldog briar and was lost for a moment in a small cloud of smoke.

'Actually, I've already approached his literary agent – Brendan Collins – requesting an interview. This Collins is a reasonable enough chap, but he's highly protective of his client. Not heard anything back yet. Cynthia knows Cassina, doesn't she? Do you think she might persuade him to talk to us?'

'I'll give it a go,' said Harley. 'But I'm not promising anything. As you can imagine, it's all a bit of a touchy subject with her at the moment.'

'Well, God knows we need some kind of break on this case.'

'Funny you should say that.' Harley rubbed his hands together. 'I might just have something along those lines for you right now.'

He leant over and pulled the envelope which contained Madame Leanda's photographs from under his chair.

'I have it, on reliable authority,' he said, handing it to Franklin, 'that the man in those photographs is a known sexual deviant. One who has regular violent fantasies about the decapitation of children.'

'Good God!' exclaimed the policeman, having arrived at the print of the mysterious Mr Brooks dressed in his V-necked sailor suit.

'Exactly. Now, I'm told he goes by the moniker of "Mr Brooks". But that's moody, for sure. If we can discover his true identity, I'd say we might just have our first decent suspect.'

'But I already know who your Mr Brooks is, George,' said Franklin, looking a little nonplussed.

'You do?'

'Yes.'

The policeman took another astonished look at the photograph.

'For Christ's sake, John! Are you going to leave me hanging here?'

'Sorry. It's just that this is a photograph of Brendan Collins, Cassina's literary agent.'

'What? Are you sure?'

'Positive. I was speaking to him, face to face, only yesterday.'

'Then, what are we waiting for?' said Harley, jumping up and grabbing his jacket from the back of the door. 'Let's go get ourselves a warrant and pay Mr Collins a visit!'

But Franklin had remained firmly seated.

'I'm afraid we can't do that.'

'What? Why?'

'Because, as well as being Cassina's agent, Mr Brendan Collins is the son of the Right Honourable Sir Hugh Collins, Parliamentary Under-Secretary of State for the Home Department.'

Harley snorted and hung his jacket back up. 'Oh, I see,' he said, looking far from impressed. 'And that makes him untouchable, does it?'

Franklin puffed defensively on his pipe. 'All I'm saying, is we'll need to handle this with kid gloves. After all, we're talking about telling my guvnor's guvnor's guvnor that his beloved son is a crazed sexual deviant who has been murdering innocent children and mutilating their bodies. And there's me looking forward to a quiet retirement.'

'Yes, but if he *is* a crazed sexual deviant who's been murdering innocent children, surely we need to pull the shicer off the streets as soon as possible?'

'Now, let's just slow down a bit, shall we? Sit down a moment and let me think. The first obvious question is where did you get these photographs from?'

Harley rubbed his chin and flopped back down into his seat.

'I'm afraid I can't divulge my sources. It was one of the provisos for handing them over in the first place.'

'Well, there's a problem straight away,' said Franklin. 'I mean, it may be my copper's cynical nature, but these look to all intents and purposes like they've been procured with the intent to blackmail.'

'Yeah, I know,' said Harley, dejectedly sparking up another Gold Flake. 'That was my first thought.'

'And it will, no doubt, be the first thought of the eye-wateringly expensive barrister that the Right Honourable Sir Hugh instructs upon hearing the news that the fruit of his loins has been arrested for child murder. Unless we have a statement from a credible witness to back up your allegations it'll never get to court.'

'She's credible, alright. She's just not willing to give a statement.'

Harley took a long pull on his cigarette.

'Listen – the super wants you to investigate Cassina, right? So why can't we use that as an excuse to do a bit of digging on his agent? Use that as our in.'

Franklin thought for a moment, tapping the tip of his pipe stem against his teeth.

'Alright then, here's the plan: I'll do some preliminary checks on Collins under the premise of investigating Cassina. I'll also try to get Sir Bernard Spilsbury to take another look at the bodies. You concentrate on von Görlitz and the AOU cult. Go and see Manduca, pump him for what he knows about it;

find out whether there's anything more than just salacious rumour to this child sacrifice mumbo jumbo, and whether there's any link to Alasdair Cassina. Oh, and work on the source who provided you with these photographs; see if you can't persuade her to make a statement about Collins.'

'And can I take a look at Collins as well?'

'Not just yet. As I said, we need to handle him with kid gloves.'

'Alright,' said Harley, taking back the photographs of the literary agent and pinning them to the blackboard. 'But don't go soft on me now, John. I know you've got your retirement to think about but, if Collins is our man, we've got a duty to bring the bastard in; even if he is the son of the Right Honourable Sir Hugh.'

Next to the newly pinned-up photographs Harley chalked the words: *Brendan Collins, No.1 Suspect.*

19

OVER THE YEARS, Alberto's all-night café bar in Lisle Street had proved an invaluable source of information for Harley's investigations. It attracted the sort of dissolute night creatures who were more than willing to share the latest gossip from the street for the price of a cup of weak coffee, or a dubious saveloy with bread and margarine (the ubiquitous 'sav and a slice'). The clientele at this time of day, though, were of a completely different breed: the streetwalkers, ponces and petty criminals – now sleeping it off in the flop houses and bedsits of the capital – having been replaced by shoppers and staff from local businesses.

However, as he peered through the fogged-up window, Harley did recognise one customer from Soho's shady demimonde; the broad-shouldered outline was unmistakable.

'How're you doing, son? That kosher, is it?'

Solly Rosen looked up from the bacon sandwich he was devouring. 'Very funny! You want a cup of rosie?'

Rosen held his mug up to the waitress who was wiping down a nearby table. 'Another two, Maria,' he said, pushing the last of the sandwich into his mouth. 'So, how are you getting on with the case? Any leads yet?'

'And which case is this?'

The ex-boxer leant over and whispered melodramatically. 'The Nursery Butcher, of course. Word is you're giving the bogeys a hand.'

Harley gave a long sigh. 'Brilliant. I suppose you heard that from Mori?'

'Yeah. And I'd say it's a good job you're on board. In my experience, those CID boys ain't worth a fart in a colander.'

'Right. Well, keep schtum about it, won't you? I know how leaky you are – I don't want the world and his wife knowing.'

'Me, leaky? Never. Anyway, all the boys already know about it.'

Rosen laughed at the expression on his friend's face.

'It's in your own interests.'

'How's that, then?'

'Bit of health insurance, ain't it? Mori tipped us the wink so no one would think you'd turned nark if they see you knocking about with Franklin or his cronies. A good idea, seeing as you queered the pitch with the Maltese on that Turpin case. By the way, I hear you went to see Mori about calming the waters with Manduca.'

Harley sighed. 'Yup.'

'What are you looking like that for? If Mori said he'd have a word, he'll have a word – it'll be sorted.'

'The thing is, Sol, I need a bit more than just calming the waters. I now need to interview Manduca, to do with the case.'

'You don't think the Spider's involved with those kiddie murders, do you?'

'Not directly, no. But he might have some information that could help. Only I can't go back to Mori just yet.'

'Why's that? Oh, hold on, here she is!'

Rosen placed his hand on the behind of the waitress, who had just arrived with the teas.

'The beautiful Maria.'

Maria slapped his hand away. 'Don't touch what don't belong to you, Mr Yiddisher Thunderbolt.'

Laughing, Rosen slipped off his chair onto one knee.

'Ah, come on, Maria. When are you finally going to give in to your secret desire and run away with me, eh? I mean, what's that big lump Pietro got that I haven't?'

The portly Maria retrieved a soup spoon from her apron pocket to give Rosen a sharp rap on the top of his head.

'Ow!' he yelled, returning to his seat.

She waved a finger at him as she walked back to the counter. 'That's right. You just think about that lovely wife and those two beautiful bambinos you got at home.'

'You quite finished, have you?'

'Oh yeah. Sorry. So why can't you ask Mori to sort out the thing with Manduca?'

'Because your boss has asked me to do him a favour.'

Rosen sucked his teeth. 'There ain't usually much *asking* where Mori's concerned.'

'Don't I know it? Trouble is, I'm not sure I can deliver this particular favour.'

'Sounds like it might get painful. What's the favour?'

'He wants me to organise a pow-wow between him and Limehouse Lil. See if they can't work out a little collaboration.'

'Well, that should be easy enough,' said Rosen with a grin. 'Seeing as you're now part of the family.'

'That's just it. Cyn would crucify me if she found out I'd been encouraging her big sis to expand her dope-dealing empire.'

Rosen gave a little whistle and kicked back in his chair. 'Blimey, what's happened to the great George Harley, DCM?'

'What's that supposed to mean?'

'Well, you spent most of your time over in France creeping into enemy trenches at the dead of night, armed with nothing more than a paperknife and a knuckleduster. Now you're bottling it over what some judy might say about a perfectly reasonable bit of business.'

'Cyn ain't just some judy.'

'Alright. Maybe she ain't. But think of it this way – you do the boss this favour and you're the golden boy again. You can ask him to sort out the sit-down with the Spider, and maybe give you a bit of backup if it all turns sour. And, who knows? This info might help you find that bastard child murderer and deliver him into the hands of old Jack Ketch, right?'

'Well, we don't know—'

'On the *other* hand,' said Rosen, interrupting. 'You can be the gallant gent and avoid upsetting the lovely Cynthia – by pissing off one of the most dangerous men in London and risking the death and mutilation of countless other innocent kiddies. I can see it must be a difficult decision.'

Rosen reached into his trouser pocket and slapped down two pennies on the table. 'There you go. There's a phone box round the corner. Do yourself a favour – go and give Lilian a call.'

Harley sighed. 'Alright, Rockefeller. Put your money away. I'll do it, straight after we're through here.'

Rosen grinned, flipped one of the coins in the air and then thrust them back into his pocket.

'Tell me something,' said Harley, after sipping at his tea. 'Have you noticed anything strange about Benny Whelks recently?'

'Anything strange? He's Benny Fucking Whelks! Everything's strange about him.'

'I know. But when I went to see Mori the other night, he was *really* uptight, you know? Even more than usual. Fizzing and sparking, like a soddin' Roman candle. At one stage he had to walk out of the room just to calm himself down.'

'It's his sister, Margaret, ain't it? She passed a few weeks ago. Finally drank herself to death.'

'That's what Mori said. They were close, right?' Harley offered Rosen a cigarette.

'Ta. Yeah, real close.'

'There was some problem with the stepfather, wasn't there? I can't really remember the details.'

'That's because it was all hushed up when we were kids,' said Rosen, lighting both cigarettes. 'But a few years ago, I got the full story from Mori. And I tell you, it'd be enough to turn anyone doolally.'

'Go on.'

Rosen took a quick look around him and lowered his voice. 'This is strictly *me and you*, mind. I don't fancy getting on the wrong side of Benny Whelks – especially when he's having one of his funny turns.'

'Listen to him. As if I'm the leaky one.'

'I told you, I ain't leaky!'

'Just tell me the story, Sol.'

'Well. As I said, Benny's always been real close to his sister. In a way, I reckon the love he had for that girl is the only normal thing about him. But it don't come from a normal place.'

Rosen took a gulp of tea and drew heavily on his smoke.

'You see, when they were little – Benny must have been six or seven, Margaret a couple of years younger – their old man just upped and left. Probably on account of his wife, Betty. Do you remember Benny's mum, Betty?'

'Vaguely,' said Harley. 'Liked a drink, didn't she?'

'Not 'alf! Probably where Margaret got it from. Betty Dalston was a bit of a looker when she was younger, by all accounts – Benny obviously took after the old man – but she was always in the pub on a Saturday night, getting a little too friendly with anyone who had the wherewithal for her next gin. Anyway, as I say, one day the old man had enough of it all and took a run-out powder. Needing someone to put food on the table, Betty took up with a bloke called Tyler. He was in the Merchant Navy. Right nasty piece of work. Little too quick with his fists with Betty and the kids, especially when he'd been out on the hops. But they made it work somehow – probably because Tyler was away at sea most of the time. Well, Betty falls pregnant and, before you know it, Benny and Margaret have got a little stepbrother and there's another mouth to feed in the house. Only this kid's not quite right in the head, see – probably due to it being pickled in the womb with all that gin. Doesn't sleep properly, bit feeble-minded, and he's terrified of his father. But little Margaret dotes on him – which is probably just as well, because his mother is still spending far too much time in the boozer. By the time the lad's five they've moved into a bigger place with a separate bedroom for the kids, which makes things a little easier at night, right?'

Rosen leant in close on his muscled forearms.

'But then, one day,' he said, adding a dramatic note to his voice, 'this shicer Tyler returns from a two-month voyage at sea. He goes straight from the ship to the pub and spends all night on a monumental bender. By the time he gets home in the early hours, he's got the madness on him. Crashes into the bedroom in a drunken frenzy and falls on Betty like a wild animal. Of course, with all the commotion the kids wake up next door, and the little one starts to whine, terrified of what this big brute might be doing to his mother. Margaret tries desperately to hush him up, knowing that for all their sakes it's better just to hide under the bedclothes until it's all over. But she can't get through to him. He's hysterical, just keeps howling, louder and louder until the door crashes open. And there's Tyler. Drink-crazed. Yelling his head off. Clutching a bread knife in his fist. But the kid just keeps wailing and wailing and kicking and screaming, and so this dirty bastard, he rips his own son away from little Margaret's arms, holds him out like a chicken for slaughter and slits his throat.'

'Jesus Christ!'

'Yeah, I know. Imagine seeing that as a kid, right? Apparently, Margaret was never the same afterwards. Like all the joy had been wrung out of her. And you know what Benny turned out like.'

Rosen took a gulp of tea.

'There's more, though.'

'More?'

'Yeah. See, the official story was that, after a few minutes of dazed confusion, Tyler comes to from his drunken rage and, seeing what he's done to his own son, does away with himself in a fit of remorse, using the knife on his own throat.'

'But?'

'Well, the truth is that was just a story Betty told to the coppers to protect her own. What really happened was that Benny waited until the bastard had fallen into a drunken stupor and then did the job for him.'

'How old was he?'

'Eleven.'

Harley sighed. 'So starting an illustrious career as a blade-wielding maniac.'

'Exactly.'

'Hold on!' said Harley, his brow furrowed in thought as he stubbed out his cigarette in the ashtray. 'Did you say that Tyler had gone straight out from the ship that night?'

'Yeah, why?'

'Well then, there's a good chance he'd have still been in his matelot's uniform.'

'What's that got to do with the price of eggs?'

'Think about it. Benny's sister died a few weeks ago, right? A sister he'd formed an especially close bond with due to a shared traumatic event.'

Rosen shook his head. 'Still not with you.'

'That's because you haven't let me finish yet. Mori told me these child murders had touched a nerve with Whelks, "opened up some old wounds", he said. The first body was found in Clapham a fortnight ago, right? *After* Margaret's death.' Harley tapped the table. 'Dressed in a *sailor suit*.'

'What? Benny Whelks is the Nursery Butcher?'

'Shush!' hissed Harley.

He looked around the tables to see if anyone had heard the outburst.

'No. I'm not saying that. I'm just saying there's a bunch of coincidences here. And I don't like coincidences. They give me indigestion. Now, you need to keep schtum about this, while I look into it. Don't mention it to anyone. Got it?'

'Got it.'

'I'm serious, Solly. No one.'

'I've got it, I tell yer!'

'Good. And you let me know if you notice anything out of character with our friend Whelks in the coming days.'

Harley stood up and put his hat on.

'Alright. I'm off to give Lily Lee a call about that pow-pow with Mori. I'll be in touch. Abyssinia!'

'Yeah, Abyssinia, George,' answered Rosen, looking a little shaken as he stared into his teacup.

20

TERRY RAWLINS FINISHED his mug of tea and took the last drag on his breakfast cigarette. The staff canteen at the St Giles Circus terminus was empty apart from Dougie, the ancient night-watchman, who was dozing on the opposite side of the room, his grizzled black mongrel curled faithfully at his feet. Rawlins checked his watch. Within an hour or so, the depot would be a hive of activity. He'd play his own part in this – pitching in with the gentle ribbing of colleagues, sharing snippets of gossip. But it wouldn't come easy. It would take a level of concentration and effort that this peaceful start to the day helped him maintain.

He stood up to examine his reflection in the mirror. He set his conductor's cap to the correct angle, dusted his shoulders off and adjusted the straps of his ticket machine. It had taken him a while to get used to wearing a uniform again, but now he was proud of how it made him look – like someone with a sense of duty. In the first few weeks at the clinic, after his return from the front, just to hear the word *duty* had been enough to bring on an episode of violent facial spasms. This tic – which, according to one doctor, was due to Rawlins' horror at having bayoneted an elderly German infantryman through the cheek – was just one of the symptoms of his 'male hysteria'. He remembered shuddering on first seeing that diagnosis in his medical records. If he did have to speak about it nowadays, he preferred to use the term 'war neurosis' – in his opinion, far more accurate than that awful *Boys' Own* cliché 'shell shock'. But why would anyone want to speak about it? The seizures, the hemiplegia, the years of deadening shame; not to mention the additional indignities of the treatments themselves (he still winced at the buzz of the tram's pantograph, because it put him in mind of his electroconvulsive sessions). Still, that had been over ten years ago. And though he'd wasted eight of those years hiding away from the world, here he now was, holding down a decent job; a job with responsibilities, something he could be proud of. A job for life, some might say.

Rawlins made his way out into the main depot. It was still dark outside, and the pendant lamps cast a lattice of shadow across the silent ranks of parked trams. He stood for a moment, relishing the tranquillity of the hangar-like space, before seeking out the Number 81, his footsteps echoing around him. This was his favourite part of the day. He'd make a thorough inspection of the vehicle, then sit on the top deck, smoking quietly, observing the depot coming alive around him as his workmates drifted in for the day's shift. The first job was to reset the destination blinds; a process he always found strangely satisfying. This done, Rawlins carried out his external inspection and then climbed on board to check the lower deck. Finding everything clear there, the conductor climbed the narrow spiral staircase to the upper deck.

He noticed the hat box immediately. It had obviously once been an item of quality: fabricated from ox-blood leather, with wide riveted straps – the type a gentleman might pack his opera hat in when travelling. But it had seen better days – the leather was scuffed in places and one of the strap clasps was missing.

Oh dear, thought Rawlins. *Someone's going to be kicking themselves this morning when they wake up and find they're missing a piece of luggage.*

Perhaps it *was* a little remiss of the nightshift not to have spotted such a large item, but who was he to judge? The Lost Property Office wasn't open yet, of course, but he could write a brief note of explanation and leave it on the counter; he still had plenty of time before his driver was due to arrive. After all, this was one of the reasons for giving the tram a thorough inspection before they took her out for the day.

As Rawlins took hold of the hat box it was immediately obvious that its contents were far too heavy for just a hat.

His initial reaction was one of mild excitement. He recalled a story told to him during his training about a conductor discovering a shoe box on a tram which had been stuffed full of money, and it was with some eagerness that he now unfastened the one good clasp that secured the lid.

Rawlins was discovered twenty minutes later by his driver, wedged between two bench seats on the upper deck of the Number 81, in the grip of what the doctors later diagnosed as a 'violent, psychogenic non-epileptic seizure' – a resumption of his former medical condition, brought on by a significant psychological shock. On the floor beside him, having been dislodged from the satin-lined hat box, was the item responsible for the former infantryman's traumatic relapse: the decapitated head of a cherubic young boy. If he had ventured past the rear of the upper deck, Rawlins would have made another shocking discovery – a child's corpse, propped up in the front seat, dressed in a pristine knickerbocker suit. The first passenger of the day, with an antique key in his hand, but neither a valid ticket to travel… nor a head.

21

HARLEY PADDED DOWN the hallway in his stockinged feet and opened the front door.

'Morning, Mr Aitch. Got a message, from Limehouse Lil.'

The twelve-year-old Alfie Budge (who'd acquired the nickname Squib due to his firecracker nervous energy) plucked off his oversized pancake cap to reveal a folded piece of paper lodged within his shock of red hair.

'Summit smells good.'

'Does it, now?' said Harley, taking the note from his diminutive visitor's grubby hand.

On the paper were a few cryptic lines from Lily Lee, confirming that she was prepared to enter into discussions with Mori Adler about the possibility of collaborating on some mutually beneficial business.

As Harley read the message, Budge stood on the doorstep, performing an involuntary nervous jig. His fidgeting was alleviated a little by the production of a coin from the private detective's pocket.

'Much obliged,' he said, giving the sixpence a lucky rub before secreting it in his shabby knickerbockers.

Harley rubbed his chin and studied his young visitor for a moment. The lad's appearance had given him an idea.

'Listen, Squib. You had your breakfast?'

'Me?' Budge's freckled face adopted an air of hopeful expectation. 'I had a puff on a Woodbine earlier.'

'Alright, come on then. I've got a couple of bangers I was saving for the cat, but you look like you've got more need of them.'

'Hold on. *It* ain't in there, is it?'

'What?'

'That bleeding devil moggy of yours, that's what. Almost had my head off last time.'

'I'm sure he was only playing with you. Don't be so milky. In you go. Wipe your feet.'

Installed at the kitchen table (having first made a cautious check behind the door to see if Moloch lay in ambush), the young messenger was soon ravenously attacking a thick sausage sandwich.

'So, my little Hermes, what's the cackle on the street?' asked Harley. 'Any news I need to hear about?'

'Hmm, let me see now…' Budge paused to tussle with a lump of gristle which had got stuck between two wonky incisors. 'Fingers Flynn is walking about with a couple of smashing lamps at the moment, as a result of being roughed up by that new bogey, wossisname – Quinn, is it?'

'Quigg. You be sure to steer clear of that one. He's a wrong 'un.'

'Oh, that's stone ginger. We've all got the measure of him, don't you worry.' Budge took a noisy slurp from his mug of tea. 'Then there's Teddy Gables – you know Teddy, Sonny's youngest – well, he's giving it the big "I am" at the moment. Flush with gelt from knocking out dirty pictures. Actually, Mr

Aitch, there's a connection with your good self there.'

'How so?'

'Well, Teddy boy got hold of the negative plates for these smudges from some bent copper in C Division.'

'No doubt a connection established by his old man,' said Harley. 'As a fence, Sonny Gables has his mucky fingers in all sorts of pies. It's a wonder he don't carry a Royal Warrant. But what's that got to do with me?'

'Well, apparently, the plates in question were part of the haul the bogeys took from that nutcase Turpin's flat – you know, where you sprung those judies from.'

'Really? Well, if I were Teddy, I wouldn't go shouting that from the rooftops. That merchandise belongs to Victor Manduca. If the Spider gets wind that Teddy's making a flock at his expense, he'll be after his pound of flesh.'

'Teddy won't see it like that. He ain't quite right in the head, if you ask me. Don't tell Sonny I said so, though.'

'I make you right there. So come on – what else you got?'

'And there's me thinking you were filling my kite out of the kindness of your heart. What exactly do you want to know?'

'What about these child murders? Heard any rumours?'

'The Nursery Butcher?' Budge gave a little theatrical shudder. 'Blimey, gives me the collywobbles just thinking about it. They say it's the Ripper, come out of retirement. D'you think that's true?'

'No, I don't. That's just a ghost story to sell more newspapers, and don't you go spreading it around for them either.' Harley lit up a Gold Flake.

'Ooh, any chance of an oily? I'm down to my last dimp.'

'No, there ain't. You're too young to smoke.'

'That's funny – I was managing it alright earlier.'

'Finish up your grub. And less of the backchat.'

Budge gave a little dismissive sniff and went back to munching on his sandwich. 'What about that latest one? That head in the 'at box. Coo! But they reckon in the papers it ain't the Muller kid, is that right?'

'It's not Eddie Muller. It's been confirmed by the parents.'

'Well, that's one thing at least. Kind of makes it worse when you know their name, don't it? Though I don't expect Ma and Pa Muller thanked the bogeys for making 'em look on such an 'orror.'

Harley smiled and revisited a previous conjecture that young Alfie Budge was wise beyond his years.

'The worst thing about it, is it's little kids he's after. I mean, as if we ain't got enough to worry about.'

'What d'you mean?'

'Well, I dunno whether you've noticed, but it ain't exactly the land of milk 'n' honey out there. It's hard enough trying to earn a decent crust, without having to worry about some ghoul snatching you off the streets so he can pluck your heart out and slice your head off, like you was no more than pie filling. I dunno about you, but when I finally go off to meet me maker – touch wood' – Budge gave a quick rap of his knuckles on the kitchen table – 'I want me giblets still intact, not under a blanket of pastry in some cannon ball's pie dish.'

'Hold on a minute. No one's said anything about cannibalism, did they?'

'Well, what else is he doing with them kiddies' hearts? Playing cricket?'

Harley gave a sigh and took a long drag on his cigarette. 'See, this is exactly what this shicer wants. To become a bogeyman, the stuff of nightmares.'

'Yeah? Well, he's going about it the right way, if you ask me.'

'Anyway, a bright lad like you should be in school, not out on the streets all day. You're not supposed to leave until you're fourteen nowadays, are you? If you finish your schooling now, there'll be more chance of you getting a decent job in the future. You've got to think of the long game, son.'

'With respect, Mr Aitch, if I ain't out there every day, grafting, there ain't going to be no long game. I'm at me sister Maud's at the moment. She's got two nippers and another on the way. Plus a fella who can't stand the sight of me. So, we ain't exactly playing happy families, if you know what I mean. If I go home empty-handed, I go to bed empty-bellied. Some can't afford the luxury of sitting in a schoolhouse listening to teacher rattle on about King This and Queen That, and how many apples Johnny's got in his sodding basket.' Budge gave an involuntary jerk of the elbows and then conjured a weary dog-end from the inside of his cap, the pitiful sight of which prompted Harley to relent and offer the youngster a Gold Flake.

Budge sparked up and took a long, satisfied draw on the cigarette. 'You're a gent.'

'But coming back to the Nursery Butcher…' said Harley.

'Do we have to? It ain't good for the digestion, you know.' As if to validate the point, the lad let out a resounding belch.

'Listen, Squib—' Harley was interrupted by the sound of the front door slamming.

'It's only me, George!'

'That's Cynthia,' said Harley, lowering his voice. 'Hide that fag! And keep schtum about that message from Lil. Got it?'

'Righto, guv!' Budge hastily pinched out the Gold Flake and secreted it under his cap.

'Alfie!' said Cynthia, bustling in with an armful of parcels neatly wrapped in brown paper and string, which she dropped with relief onto the kitchen table. 'What a pleasant surprise. And how are we this morning?'

'Oh, mustn't grumble, miss,' said Budge, sitting up straight in his chair and wiping the grease from his chin.

'And to what do we owe the pleasure?'

'Well, I was just, erm… I was just passing, like, and I, er…'

'I asked Squib over to pick his brains about the Nursery Butcher's victims,' said Harley, clearing the lad's empty plate from the table, and taking the opportunity to shoot him a quick, meaningful glance.

'Do you really think it's a suitable subject to discuss with Alfie?'

'I do, as it goes. Squib's got his ear to the ground. He hears all sorts. Don't you?'

'That I do,' said Budge, puffing out his little cock-sparrow chest.

'So, tell me, son, what do you make of the fact that no parents have claimed the victims yet?'

'Well, that's a queer thing, ain't it? Seeing as they were little toffs.'

'How d'you figure that?'

'On account of them sailor suits. There ain't many from *my* manor togged up like that.'

'And if they were from poorer backgrounds?' asked Cynthia, sitting down at the table and pulling off her calfskin gloves. 'Would it still be strange then – for them to go missing without anyone reporting it?'

'Well, I must say, miss, I'm very honoured you value my opinion. Let me see, now…'

The youngster pouted his lips in concentration.

'I'm gonna say *no*,' he said, after giving the question due deliberation. 'I don't think that would be strange. There's plenty like me – orphans, right? Plenty sleeping rough, or in the workhouse. I've had a taste of that myself, you know.'

'There you are, Cyn. I told you.'

'The workhouse? Good grief!' exclaimed Cynthia. 'I thought we'd seen the end of such places a long time ago.'

'Oh, they serve a purpose, miss.' Budge leant back in his chair, relishing his new role as adviser. 'I was in there when mother was still alive, you see. Only for a few months – whenever she was taken too bad to put food on the table. They used to feed us alright, and we had a bed an' all. But there were some cruel so-and-so's in there, I can tell you. Proper nogoodniks. And I reckon the stench will stay with me forever. Horrible, it was – all carbolic and stale bread.'

'Oh, you poor thing!' Cynthia reached out and touched her fingers to the back of the lad's grubby hand, which made him start a little.

'Nah! I'm alright, miss,' he said, blushing. 'I'm a survivor, ain't I? But them other poor buggers? The Butcher's victims?' Budge shook his head and gave a soft little whistle.

'Alright,' said Harley. 'What about the idea that he might be getting his victims from the workhouse or children's homes?' asked Harley.

'You know what? I bet kids are disappearing from them places all the time. I mean, what would they care? It's one less to look after, ain't it? And, course, no one would notice a *street* kid go missing, neither; apart from their mates. And *they're* not likely to go crying to the bogeys now, are they? Yeah, there's plenty of wrong 'uns about, alright. And a lot of them with enough money to help people turn a blind eye.'

'Goodness! What a world,' said Cynthia.

She thought for a moment, then added: 'You know, George, I have an old school friend, whose sister is on the board of a children's charity. *You'd* probably find her a little too churchy, but she has a good heart. The charity is concerned with the prevention of cruelty to children; and I believe this includes visiting children's homes to monitor the welfare of the inmates. Perhaps I should talk to her, ask her opinion on whether children could just disappear from these institutions? She might even be able to organise a visit to one.'

'I think that's a sterling idea. As long as you're sure you want to get involved. After – you know…'

'After my last little adventure, you mean?' said Cynthia, smiling. She nodded her head, reassuringly.

'Great! You know what, Miss Masters? Against all the odds,

you're turning out to be more than just a pretty face.'

This comment earned Harley a smart slap from one of Cynthia's gloves.

Chuckling, Harley got up to put the kettle on the hob. 'You want a cup of tea?'

'Oh gosh!' said Cynthia, looking at her watch. 'No, thanks. I didn't realise the time. I've got to be at the rehearsal rooms in an hour, and I've left my score at the flat. I only stopped by to drop these packages off. I'll pick them up this evening, if that's alright?'

'No need. I'll bring them over to yours later.'

'Will you?' she said. 'Thank you!' Then, with a quick kiss on his cheek and a wave to Budge she was out the door.

'So,' said Harley, taking the tea caddy down from the shelf, 'apart from this messenger lark, what else are you doing for work?'

'Oh, this and that,' said Budge, relighting his cigarette which he'd already retrieved from his cap. 'As it happens, I've just started doing a bit of running for Sonny Gables.'

'You watch yourself with that one. He'd sell his own mother if the price was right.'

'That's what you call business acumen, Mr Aitch.'

Harley laughed and shook his head. 'Alright, Mr Tycoon, as it goes I've got a business proposition for you.'

'Go on,' said Budge, sitting up in his seat, looking like a dog who has just smelt a steak.

'Do you know who Benny Whelks is?'

Budge clucked. 'Course I do. He's Mori the Hat's right-hand man. The most fearsome chiv-man in the whole of London.'

'Very good. And you've seen him about, have you? Know what he looks like?'

'Oh yeah,' said Budge, with a grimace. 'He looks something 'orrible, don't he? All pockmarked and haunted, like. Don't repeat that to anyone, though.'

Harley smiled and nodded. 'That's it. And what about where he hangs out? His usual watering holes and such?'

'Let's see now.' Budge scratched away at his mop of red hair. 'The Twelve Ten club, Gregorio's on Frith Street… the Crown and Apple Tree… the Blue Posts… the Pie and Mash shop in Bridle Lane… Oh yeah! And he's a frequent visitor to the little seafood stall that pops up on the corner of Berwick Street and Oxford Street. Hence his nickname.'

'I'm impressed. You're obviously the right man for the job.'

'Thank you very much. Hold on!' said Budge, looking a little perturbed. 'What job?'

'I want you to tail him for a few days. See if he goes anywhere out of the ordinary.'

'Who?'

'Benny Whelks.'

'Get out of it!' said Budge, with a reactive jerk of his elbow. 'Not in a million years. D'you think I'm soft in the 'ead?'

'What's he going to do to a kid? You're no threat to him,' reasoned Harley. 'Besides, I reckon you could tail anyone through the streets of this fine city without them noticing.'

'That's very nice of you, but it's muggins 'ere who'll get carved up if your confidence in me is ill-founded.' He gave an adamant shake of his mop of red hair. 'I ain't doing it.'

'Half a crown a day, plus a bonus if you turn up anything interesting.'

'When do I start?' said the youngster, sitting to attention.

'Straight away.' Harley fished some coins out of his pocket. 'There you go, there's an advance. But listen – rope in some of your mates, work in shifts. That way you'll alleviate the risk of Whelks clocking you. They don't have to know what you're getting a day, so you can still make a bit out of it when they're working.'

Budge nodded, adopting a look of grave concentration. 'Understood.'

'Only, keep the numbers small and just use those you can trust. This is important work, Squib. And I want results. Leave a message behind the bar at the Shab if you discover anything. I telephone in there a couple of times a day to check if there's anything for me. Alright then, Private Budge. Clear about your orders?'

'Sir!'

'Right you are. Dismissed!'

And with a little salute Budge hopped off his stool to disappear out of the kitchen in a flurry of elbows.

As he watched him go, Harley suffered a brief qualm at the thought that he'd just sent a child out to shadow a ruthless killer. But then he quickly reasoned that Alfie Budge and his team of urchin chums probably had more street sense than all of the hard-nosed bogeys in the Yard put together.

22

Even in this final year of the Jazz Age, there were still many back streets of Soho seemingly impervious to the glitzy draw of the nightclub and the revue bar. Here successive waves of immigrants had failed to make an impression on the shabby Georgian buildings. Instead of nightlife venues and foreign restaurants, these dingy streets were populated with the more utilitarian businesses – watch-menders, wigmakers, haberdashery shops and solicitors' offices. In such a Soho backstreet, under a sky which hung low above the city with sulphurous intent, Harley stood before a sign advertising the most unglamourous of businesses: *Pollock & Greene – Surgical Instruments & Appliances*. He was there for a meeting with the Spider, Victor Manduca – organised by Mori Adler, in recognition of Harley persuading Limehouse Lil to consider a collaboration between their two firms.

The shop window displayed a frightening array of wares, some of which might have been mistaken for apprentice pieces made for the Spanish Inquisition: bunion springs, surgical boots, umbilical trusses and gastrostomy plugs, all arranged with theatrical panache around an alarming collection of surgical instruments: fracture braces, bone saws, bowel scissors and scalpels. It was enough to send the more faint-hearted browser scurrying back to the dazzling temples of commerce in Regent Street and Piccadilly.

The sprung bell having announced his arrival, Harley waited no more than a few seconds at the counter before a bald, diminutive figure in a brown warehouse coat appeared.

'Good afternoon, sir.'

'I have an appointment...' said Harley, looking around him and wondering if he'd been made the butt of an elaborate practical joke. '... with Mr Manduca?'

'Ah,' said the shopkeeper, with a grave nod of his gnome-like head. 'Very good, sir. This way, if you will.'

Harley followed the man through a small workshop, cluttered with packing cases and half-completed medical appliances, towards a set of poorly lit backstairs. It was the type of vertiginous staircase originally intended for domestic staff, and the Georgian architect's ambivalence towards the working classes was admirably demonstrated by its extreme pitch and constricted access.

'It might be wise not to rely too much on the banisters, sir,' said the shopkeeper over his shoulder, as he puffed and groaned his way up. 'And I always find it advantageous to avoid the temptation of a rest. Take her in one go, as it were.'

'Does Mr Manduca use these stairs?' asked Harley, remembering the Spider's famously large stature.

'Oh, bless you, no, sir. There's another entrance, you see, with a lift.'

They've obviously brought me in this way to deny me the knowledge of a quick getaway, thought Harley.

'There you are, sir,' said the little man, puffing energetically after leading Harley to the second floor. 'Carry on up the passageway, and then through the door at the end. There's a small waiting room there. Someone should be along to collect you in a short while.'

The waiting room was more in keeping with what Harley had expected: a plush red sofa and chairs, parquet flooring and a small ormolu coffee table. After all, Manduca's little empire of pornography and exploitation was bound to be lucrative. In fact, it wasn't a waiting room as such, but the lobby for another flight of stairs – far grander than the one Harley had used. He guessed Manduca's office was behind the polished oak door to his left, displaying the brass nameplate: *Rivista Publishing Ltd*. To his right was another door, with a large vision panel of Muranese glass, on which was painted *Administration*.

There seemed to be some activity in the administration office. Harley could see figures moving around through the obscured glass. After a little while, it was obvious that what had started as a low rumble of conversation was turning into a heated discussion.

Harley moved quietly to the door.

Raised voices... now the sound of a scuffle... furniture being overturned... gasps, grunts...

Then a desperate scream, quickly stifled.

He could no longer see any obvious movement, but he could hear something. The unmistakable sound of someone being choked.

Here he was, in the headquarters of a violent criminal, one with a reputation for cruelty and double-crossing. Harley knew the sensible thing would be to quietly disappear, back down the rickety staircase and out into the safety of the Soho back streets.

But instead, he tried the door handle – and found it unlocked.

Harley recognised the pale, androgynous-looking youth straight away. Stimps Stephen was a dilly boy – one of the troupe of male prostitutes who worked the streets around Piccadilly. Harley had used him as an informant on the odd occasion. Stimps was in trouble. The Spider's younger brother, Spiru Manduca, had him backed up against the wall, his large hands clasped around the boy's slender throat, throttling the life from him.

'Put him down!' Harley shouted.

Without releasing his grip, the Maltese snapped his head around, his face a leering mask of fury.

'Stay out of it! Or you're next,' he growled, then doubled his efforts.

The lad's frantic slapping of the wall abruptly ceased, his face now a lurid purple.

Harley slipped on his brass knuckles and delivered an excruciating blow to Spiru's kidney.

With his attacker now groaning on all fours on the carpet, Stimps slumped down on his backside, his eyes unfocused, staring at the floor.

'Come on, son. Stay with me, now,' said Harley, gently slapping the boy's cheek.

'Get the fuck away from that nancy boy!'

Harley let go of Stimps and held up his hands as the cold muzzle of the mobster's gun bit into the back of his neck.

'Easy now, mate. Let's not do anything hasty.'

Spiru pulled in close to whisper in Harley's ear, his breath sickly sweet with stale alcohol. 'First you're going to tell me who the fuck you are. Then I'm going to take you out the back and croak you.'

A voice resonated from across the room, deep and peppery.

'That'll do, Spiru. Put that thing away and help Mr Harley to his feet.'

Anyone who had actually met the Spider would have realised that his nickname did not derive from his physique – there was nothing even faintly arachnid about Victor

Manduca. Six foot two and twenty-four stone, he stood dominating the space, his obese frame clothed in an expensive Savile Row suit, and a pristine cashmere coat slung cape-like across his shoulders.

Revived enough to realise he was out of immediate danger, Stimps now scrambled over to hug Manduca's tree trunk of a leg.

'I told you about him, Victor,' he gasped. 'I swear he'd have killed me this time.'

Manduca ruffled the lad's hair.

'There, there, Stephen,' he said. 'I'm sure there's just been some misunderstanding. But we'll discuss this later. I have some business to attend to with Mr Harley.'

'Hold on, Vic,' said Spiru, taking a step towards his brother. 'This baghal has the nerve to jump me in my own office, and you just—'

'Mr Harley is here by arrangement with Moriel Adler. And therefore, he will be offered the respect such an endorsement deserves. Now please, I'll ask you again to put away the firearm.' The Spider's flabby jowls hung around a charming smile, but his eyes flashed a look of blackest anger.

Pocketing the pistol, Spiru stormed out of the office.

Manduca turned to the burly young man waiting in attendance in the lobby.

'Andre, would you take Stephen up to the apartment and get him cleaned up? And then sit with him for a while. He's had quite a shock, we wouldn't want him doing anything foolish. Understand?'

'Got it, boss.' Andre gave a short whistle, as though summoning a dog. 'Come on, you, out!'

Stimps got up sulkily and went to leave, but stopped in the doorway and turned to Harley. 'Thank you, George,' he said, tears welling in his spirited blue eyes. Then he disappeared up the staircase, closely followed by Manduca's heavy.

* * *

'I must apologise for my brother,' said Manduca, now installed in his office, behind a highly polished mahogany desk. 'Spiru has always been a little hot-headed. But we must forgive our loved ones for their little foibles, don't you think?'

The villain's voice had an extraordinary quality to it: unctuous and urbane, the accent so polished as to remove any hint of the foreign that it was somehow beyond posh; the kind of accent that would be deemed the epitome of Englishness by anyone except the English themselves.

'Well, it's none of my business, but the kid was right – a few more seconds and he'd have been a goner. Not exactly a fair fight.'

'I'm afraid Spiru shares the same prejudices as most of society when it comes to the likes of Stephen.' Manduca let his gaze drift off to the distance for a moment. 'Of course, in Ancient Greece the catamite was a socially accepted role. Honourable in a way. Ah, well.'

As he'd remarked to Cynthia, Victor Manduca's fleshy pout and his habit of using the merest hint of rouge on his flabby cheeks always put Harley in mind of a painting he'd once seen of the emperor Nero. He noticed that on the mobster's desk was a photographic portrait of a young woman, attractive in an obvious, debutante, kind of way; and another similar framed photograph hung on the wall opposite. Considering Manduca's comments about the androgynous youth, Harley wondered what relationship this woman might be to him.

'First of all, Mr Manduca. I just want to apologise for that mix up with Turpin. I hope you understand that any disruption to your business was purely unintentional. I was just trying to track that young girl down for her parents.'

'Moriel has explained it all to me. He tells me that you're very good at what you do, Harley. I do sincerely hope you're not investigating *me*?'

'Of course not.' Harley returned the charming smile but couldn't help wondering what debt he'd placed himself in for kidney-punching the villain's younger brother. 'I just need a little information from you, that's all.'

Manduca nodded. 'Well, now. You may, of course, ask me what you wish, but I'm afraid I can't promise you that I'll necessarily give an answer.' He took a toffee from a jar on the desk and began to slowly unwrap it. 'I'm a slave to my sweet tooth. Would you like one?'

'No thanks,' said Harley, taking out his packet of Gold Flake.

Manduca nodded. 'So, what is it you wish to know?'

Harley sparked up and drew deeply on his smoke. He knew he'd need to tread carefully, especially after the altercation with Spiru.

'Well, first of all, are you aware of the work Madame Leanda does at her clinic in Duck Lane?'

Manduca popped the sweet into his mouth and smiled.

'A little disingenuous for your first question, don't you think? Seeing as it was at Madame Leanda's clinic that you assaulted one of my employees the other night. Yes, of course, I am aware of her work. She falls under my jurisdiction, so to speak.'

'I see. And would you say she's running a racket there? Working the black on her clients?'

'Blackmail? Madame Leanda? No, no.' Manduca shook his head. 'I would say that's highly unlikely. In my experience she is the epitome of professionalism.'

'That's good to hear.'

Harley placed the pamphlet that Cynthia had taken from the AOU on the desk in front of Manduca.

'Do you know anything about this outfit?'

The Maltese looked at the pamphlet without touching it at first, the wobble of his heavy jowls keeping a steady rhythm as he slowly chewed his toffee. Then, with a sniff, he picked it up and gave it a cursory look.

'I didn't have you down as an erotic art fan, Harley.'

'What about Herr Fedor von Görlitz? Ring any bells?'

'I'd say you're wasting your time here. You appear to already know the answers to your questions.'

'Not quite all of them.'

It was obvious that the villain wasn't going to simply volunteer any useful information. There was nothing else for it, he was just going to have to jump right in.

'No one's getting into any hot water here, Victor. A little information, that's all. I just want to understand what this Ancient Order of the Unicursal is all about. So why don't you educate me?'

Manduca shrugged, turning over an enormous, fleshy hand.

'Oh, it's all quite harmless, really. Fedor is from Berlin, you understand. The Berliner is not frightened to confront the transgressive side of human sexuality. You'll find many such clubs there, places where sex is regarded as a religion, rather than just a bodily function.'

'And are you a member of von Görlitz's club?'

Manduca's smile was now serene and malevolent in equal parts.

'I'm afraid I shan't be answering any *personal* questions.'

'What about the author, Alasdair Cassina? Is he a member?'

'I couldn't tell you.'

'Because you don't know?'

'Because such things are a matter of confidentiality.'

Harley took a pull on his Gold Flake and studied Manduca. He knew that the only answer his next question would receive would be a reaction on the villain's face, and he was keen not to miss it.

'Apparently, there are rumours in Berlin about the AOU. Rumours that their rituals may involve the abuse of young children. Do you think that your friend von Görlitz could be capable of such a thing?'

Manduca's eyes were devoid of emotion. Over-moist and bovine. Impossible to read.

'What possible incentive could one have for answering such a question?'

Harley's brow furrowed. 'What? Apart from saving the pain and suffering of some little kids, you mean?'

Manduca gave a sinister chuckle. 'Come now. That's no concern of mine.'

'Maybe I can think of a possible incentive for you.'

'Really?'

'What if Scotland Yard got their hands on your mate's little booklet here?' He waved the cult's pamphlet in the air. 'I mean, those illustrations could definitely be construed as contravening the Obscene Publications Act, don't you think? Then C Division would have to raid their premises in Belgravia. I'm sure they keep a list of members.'

The Spider raised an eyebrow. 'My my, was that a threat?'

'Not at all. I'm just saying that if you tell me all you know about von Görlitz's cult – about those rumours of child abuse, or sacrifice, or whatever it is – then I'm sure we could avoid a troop of bogeys traipsing their dirty size nines through all your affairs. Doesn't that sound like an incentive?'

Harley sat back and watched Manduca carefully. He took a long drag on his Gold Flake and tried to look as nonchalant as possible. There was just no way to judge how this had landed.

'I think our little interview is over, Mr Harley.'

The villain pushed a button on the side of the desk, then took a small implement from his jacket pocket and began to attend to his cuticles. Having inspected his work under the angle-poise lamp, he helped himself to another toffee from the jar, sat back in his chair, and resumed his serene and malevolent smile.

Harley had known there was a strong chance that the interview would yield no results and that he'd probably be sent away with a flea in his ear. He also knew that – for the time being, anyway – he had Mori Adler's support, and so had been relatively relaxed about the threat of any physical reprisals from the Maltese gang. But when the door now burst open to reveal Manduca's brother Spiru and the burly sidekick Andre, he began to have his doubts.

Doubts that were confirmed when he once again felt the chill kiss of Spiru's Beretta on the back of his neck.

Manduca now stood up, dominating the room like some pin-striped colossus.

'This meeting was never about answering *your* questions, Harley.'

'No?' Harley kept eye contact, while surreptitiously reaching into his pocket for his brass knuckles.

'Hands on the desk!' barked Spiru.

Harley killed the stub of his cigarette in the ashtray and placed his hands flat out in front of him.

'You see,' continued Manduca. 'I have a question of my own. Namely...' He leant over the desk, close into Harley's face, bringing with him the strong scent of rose oil and a hint of caramel from his moist, full-lipped mouth. 'What have you done with those negatives?'

'Negatives? Hold on – do you mean the photographic plates from Turpin's place? CID took those. Why would I want to nick them? I mean, I'm not planning on going into the dirty book business, am I?'

Harley winced as Spiru dug the barrel of the pistol into his neck.

'You know full well I'm not talking about the photographic plates,' said the Spider. 'A Leica film canister, thirty-five-millimetre format. Sealed in a brown envelope with German writing on the front. I at first assumed that the police had seized it along with the rest of my property. But I have been reliably informed that it was never entered into the property register at the station. And as we have had no subsequent visits from the Special Branch... well, the only obvious solution is that you pocketed it yourself, before the police arrived. I must commend you. You look remarkably cool for someone in such a dire situation.'

'That's because I haven't a clue what you're going on about.'

'A sudden bout of amnesia? Well, let us see what we can do to cure you of that little ailment. Spiru, take our friend here down to the—'

Manduca was interrupted by the shrill and distinctive clanging of the bell from a Metropolitan Police Q car. He went to the window, splitting the net curtains to see a phalanx of plainclothes officers, decamping from two black Wolseleys.

'Now I see why you might not be too concerned,' he said, flashing the private detective a black look. 'It appears your friends from Scotland Yard have arrived. You'll pay dearly for this, you despicable rat.'

23

DETECTIVE INSPECTOR ALOYSIUS Quigg stood before Harley, the Manduca brothers, Andre the heavy, the gnome-like shopkeeper and two frightened office workers, all of whom had been corralled in the surgical appliance workshop. All around them CID officers were searching diligently for any evidence of the Manducas' illegal enterprise. Quigg was busy flicking through a Pollock & Greene – Surgical Instruments & Appliances catalogue, pulling a face like a duchess emptying a bed pan; but, to his great frustration, the policeman could find no actionable pornographic material in the publication. He threw it testily to one side.

'Come now, Manduca. This would all be so much easier for you if you just tell us where you've hidden the smut.'

'Smut, Inspector?' said the Spider, his face the very essence of perplexed innocence. 'I've absolutely no idea to what you're alluding.'

Quigg approached him.

'What about your whores, then? I've heard you fancy yourself as some kind of business wizard. No doubt you keep detailed records. I'm sure all will become apparent once we've had a close look at the books.' The policeman peered up at the huge slab of face. 'Are you wearing cosmetics, man?'

'A mere trifle,' said Manduca, not batting an eyelid. 'To cover the effects of a hormonal condition, you understand.'

'Damned odd,' said Quigg, with disgust.

He now moved along the line to Harley. 'And you're this private detective chummy, are you? DCI Franklin's special informant, or whatever it is you are to him.'

'Informant?' said Harley, noticing the looks this comment had garnered from the Manducas. 'You know that's not what I am. Does Franklin know you're here today, playing your little games?'

Quigg took a step closer, his face colouring with anger.

'You, my friend, should be very careful. For the moment, at least, my hands are tied, but let me tell you if it were up to me, you'd have no part in this investigation whatsoever. Now, you'd best be on your way. After all, you've served your purpose, leading us to the lair of our Maltese friend here.'

Harley glanced at Manduca – all remnants of the Spider's suave façade had disappeared, replaced now by black, murderous intent. There was no doubt he was staring at a whole bucketful of woe with the Maltese for the foreseeable future. All because of this poisonous cowson, Quigg. He'd only been a few months in the manor and already this shicer had made it to the top of Harley's hate list.

'Inspector?' said Manduca, studying his fingernails. 'I wonder – might I have a brief word? In private?'

'Well, I suppose so,' said Quigg, checking the three burly CID men were still behind him, just in case things turned ugly.

His curiosity piqued, Harley kept a close watch on Manduca as he led the policeman to the back of the room. The huge villain bent down to whisper conspiratorially in Quigg's ear. And there it was! Over in a few seconds, but undeniably there. The huge hand had slipped in to deliver a clandestine handshake. Perhaps it was no surprise that Victor Manduca, pimp, publisher and pornographer was also 'on the square'.

'Well now, Sergeant,' said Quigg, after returning from his conflab with a flustered look on his face. 'Manduca here has just furnished me with some very interesting information.'

'Pertinent to the case, sir?' asked the CID officer.

'Oh yes. Quite pertinent. So, I think we can wrap things up here for today.'

'Stop the search of the premises, sir?'

'Yes, Watkins. Stop the search of the premises, get the men back in the car. Chop chop!'

'Very good, sir,' said the puzzled sergeant.

'And you!' said Quigg, pointing at Harley, his wobbling dewlap giving him the air of an irritable turkey. 'What in God's name are you still doing here, man?'

As Harley exited the building, he was approached by an odd-looking individual, whose wiry frame, receding chin and prominent front teeth gave him an unattractive, rodent-like appearance.

'George Harley?' said the man, with an obsequious smile. 'Enoch Craster, lead reporter for the—'

'I know who you are, pal,' said Harley.

'Really? Well, well. Jolly good. Might I have a word?'

Harley's only answer was to clamp a Gold Flake between his lips.

'I have it on good authority, Mr Harley, that you're acting as some kind of special adviser to Detective Chief Inspector Franklin.'

'I'm sure your chum Quigg has filled you in. Probably gave you the lowdown at your last Lodge meeting.' With ill-concealed contempt, Harley spat out a small strand of tobacco that had stuck to his tongue.

'It's a little unconventional, wouldn't you say?'

'What is?'

'Well, the Metropolitan Police engaging the services of an amateur such as yourself. I mean…' Craster closed his notepad. 'I'm sure you're competent in finding lost pets and conjuring witness statements for sordid little adultery cases, but child murder? A little out of your league, wouldn't you say?'

Giving Harley a sly leer, Craster turned and thrust two fingers beneath his buck teeth, whistling to his photographer, who was currently slumped against a wall, eating a wilted cheese sandwich. The pale youth pocketed his lunch and rushed across the street, wielding his boxy Rolleiflex press camera. 'What's up, skip?' he asked, still sucking the bread from his back teeth.

'I'm thinking of doing a feature on Mr Harley here. Take a couple of snaps, would you?'

'Certainly,' said the photographer, rubbing his hands clean on his trouser leg. 'Alright then, Mr Harley. Why don't we have you in that doorway? D'you want to lose the fag, or keep it in?'

'What's your name, son?' asked Harley, pleasantly.

'Johnny. Johnny Gaskill.'

'Come here a second, Johnny.'

Grinning eagerly, Gaskill dutifully slung his camera back on his shoulder and walked over to Harley, who leant in close to whisper in the photographer's ear.

'If you take one smudge of me, I'll grab that camera and ram it so far up your jacksie you'll need surgery to remove it. Got it?'

Gaskill gulped. 'Got it.'

'Sure?'

'Clear as day, chief.'

'Good,' said Harley, hitching up his trousers. 'Right, gents. I think we're done here. Why don't you toddle off and annoy someone else?'

***

A few hours later, Harley was sitting at the bar of the Shabaroon, enjoying a ham sandwich and a consolatory pint of beer.

'Bad day?'

'You could say that, Juney,' he replied to the barmaid, trying his best to summon a smile.

'Well, it might not be over yet.'

'What do you mean?'

'There's a lad asking for you in the public bar – a little lavender, looks like he's been in the wars.'

'Alright. Send him over. I think I know what it's about.'

A few minutes later Harley was ensconced in one of the snug bar booths opposite Stimps Stephen, whose slender neck bore the evidence of his violent encounter with Spiru Manduca.

'Cheers!' he said, holding up the glass of whisky the lad had just bought him.

'Oh, it was the least I could do. I swear, you saved my life earlier. It's as simple as that. You're a dorcas, really you are.' He took a delicate sip of his gin and put a tentative hand to the bruises on his neck. 'Does it look awful? Tell me the truth now.'

'It'll be gone in a few days, I'm sure.'

'I suppose I could resort to a silk scarf, go all Gloria Swanson…' the lad gave a half-hearted laugh then slumped back in his seat. 'I shan't be going back, though.'

'I don't blame you. Were you working there?'

'Victor has these little obsessions with pretty boys.' Stimps gave a coy smile. 'It seems I'm his favourite at the moment.'

'Well, you can't be much of a favourite. He didn't seem too upset that his brother was trying to kill you.'

'Oh, I don't kid myself. I know we're just playthings. I shan't go into too much detail, but the work isn't all that strenuous. More looking than touching, which is probably just as well, given the logistics of the whole thing. I mean, you've seen the size of him, right?' He gave another little chuckle, more genuine this time, then took some more drink. 'Actually, he can be quite sweet at times. Better than some of the rough trade I've had in the past. And the dinarly's good, of course. Oh, but that brute of a brother.'

'What started him off? He looked off his nut.'

'Spiru? Oh, he's like that most of the time. Proper screw loose. And, of course, he can't come to terms with the fact that his brother – the great Victor Manduca – is an omi-polone.'

'Did you hear what happened later, with the bogeys?'

'To tell you the truth, that's why I'm here.'

'What do you mean?'

'Well, luckily, I'd managed to give that numbskull Andre the slip, otherwise I might have been pinched with the rest of them. But I went back later and got the whole story from Victor's secretary. How this sherlock called Harley had put the squeak in to the bogeys about the whole operation. Only, I know you're no copper's nark. And I also know that DI Quigg is the nastiest piece of work to come out of Vine Street in donkey's years. It's obvious you've been dropped in it, George.'

'It might be obvious to you, but it's Manduca I've got to convince.' Harley gave a sigh and downed his Scotch.

Stimps sat thinking for a moment, swirling the last mouthful of gin around in the bottom of the glass. 'I might be able to help you there.'

'Go on.'

'The thing is, you've got to swear you'll use this information to help both of us.'

'I promise to do my best. What is it?'

'Well, when you asked what triggered Spiru's murderous little outburst today, I wasn't completely honest with you. You see, it was something I said to him. He'd been rattling my cage, saying the most disgusting things. I couldn't help myself.'

'What did you say?'

'I let slip that I knew what he's been up to.'

Stimps checked around him and leant forward.

'Victor Manduca has a niece, you see,' he continued, in a furtive whisper, 'who is also his ward – Vanessa. Well, he calls her his niece, but actually I think she's the daughter of his cousin, who died in childbirth. Anyway, the thing is, way before the brothers moved to this country, Victor had already sent Vanessa here, to boarding school. She's your typical society girl now – all pearls and teeth. Actually, I'm being catty, she's pretty enough. But spoilt rotten by Victor, by all accounts.'

'Is that her photo he has on his desk?'

'Yes, that's right. You know, I do believe that girl is the only thing he truly cares for in this world.'

'The chink in his armour?' said Harley, passing the lad a cigarette and sparking one up for himself.

'You could say that.'

'So, let me guess.' Harley made a quick check himself for any eavesdroppers. 'You found out that Spiru Manduca has been schtupping this Vanessa, right?'

'Exactly!' Stimps was unable to contain his excitement. 'Ooh, I can see why you're a sherlock. Yes, I happened to be going through some things in Spiru's office, and I came across—'

'Hold on. *Going through some things?*' Harley raised an eyebrow.

'Come on now. A boy's got to make a living. Anyhow, the long and short of it is that they meet regularly, in a little flat in Conduit Street. Just imagine what Victor would do to him if he found out. His precious little Vanessa, the virgin princess, with his own brother. It's simply too delicious to contemplate.'

'What exactly *did* you tell Spiru? That you knew the when and the where?'

'Oh God, no! I just let it slip that I'd guessed he had a thing for her. No details. Didn't have a chance. The brute was on me before I could draw breath.'

'That's good.' Harley sat back and took a long drag on his Gold Flake. 'Yeah, that's real good. But we need some hard evidence. A little insurance policy. And I know exactly the man to provide it.'

'Fantabulosa! But, whatever you do, please make sure my name's kept out of it. I don't think I'd survive another set-to with that brute.' Stimps made another tentative exploration of his neck then swallowed the last of his gin. 'I look forward to seeing that bastard get his comeuppance.'

Just then, Juney popped her head into the Snug.

'Telephone call for you, George.'

'Who is it?'

'Your mate, John,' she said, with a theatrical wink.

'Tell him I'll be right there.'

Harley shook hands with the dilly boy.

'Thanks a million, Stimps. You might have just saved my life with that tip-off.'

'Any time. But remember, you didn't hear it from me, right?'

Up at the bar, Harley dragged the candlestick telephone set away from the little cluster of drinkers.

'Hello?'

'George? Franklin, here. Listen, something important has come up. Can you be at the Lyons Corner House on Coventry Street tomorrow at six?'

Harley checked his pocket diary. 'Yeah, looks like I'm free. Why?'

'As part of my background checks on Brendan Collins I contacted that professor chap, Osbert Morkens – the one from that radio programme that Cassina was on? It turns out that Morkens taught both Collins and Cassina at university. I played down the Collins angle, telling him it was Cassina I was interested in, but before I'd had chance to ask any questions, he was asking to come and see me in person, saying he had some important information for me.'

'Really? What? And he wants to do it at the Corner House? Why can't he just come into the nick?'

'Professor Morkens has become a bit of a public figure recently. Had an article on him in the *Radio Times* last month, apparently. He's worried what it'll look like if he's seen coming into the station. I was all set up to do it myself, but the super has called me in for a meeting tomorrow afternoon. It appears the top brass are getting a bit jittery about the lack of progress in the case. I can't wiggle out of it, I'm afraid, and it might run on. Do you think you could see the professor for me? If it is something of any substance, I don't want Quigg to get wind of it before we've had a chance to check it out. I've already briefed Morkens that you're working alongside me as a private consultant on the case. Actually, he liked the idea of the additional level of discretion.'

'Well, alright. Let's hope he's got something useful, eh?'

24

CYNTHIA EASED BACK on the seat with a small sigh of relief. Even though the cup of tea she'd been presented with looked rather anaemic (annoyingly, she'd begun to develop a taste for Harley's more robust version of the beverage), she was thankful for the chance to rest her aching feet. This was the third children's home they'd visited that day – though you wouldn't have guessed it from the level of evangelical zeal which Emily Fairfax still seemed able to muster.

'I must say, Mr Lloyd,' said the young woman, sitting primly next to Cynthia on the settee in the Master's office, 'as well as maintaining the physical welfare of the children, I am most impressed with the way you minister to their spiritual needs. I believe we witnessed genuine enthusiasm on the part of the students in that Bible class.'

'Thank you, Miss Fairfax,' said Lloyd, unable to avoid a little self-congratulatory preening of his walrus moustaches. 'Of course, our duty is not only to house, clothe and feed our young inmates, but also to school them towards being useful members of society. As you know, I personally believe the Gospel holds the answers to most of the difficult question life might throw our way.'

'Mr Lloyd is a treasured member of our congregation at St Luke's,' explained Emily, giving a beatific smile while squeezing tight her eyes – a habit which Cynthia had always found mildly irritating in her friend's sister, but now, having spent the whole day with her, was really beginning to grate on the nerves.

'That picture on the wall there,' said Cynthia, indicating a photograph of a group of children all clutching identical suitcases and waving to the camera. 'Some kind of holiday trip for the children?'

'Ah! No. Not exactly.' The Master removed the photograph from the wall and brought it closer for inspection. 'This is the latest group to benefit from our child migrant programme. These children here are waving goodbye to their old life, Miss Masters, and with it all the old hardships and lack of opportunity. You see, they're just about to board the train ready to take them down to Southampton, from where *HMS Jervis Bay* would transport them halfway around the world to embark on an exciting new life in Australia.'

'Goodness! Australia?' said Cynthia, taking hold of the picture. 'But some of these children look awfully young.'

'I believe the programme is open to children from three to fourteen.'

'It's a government-backed scheme,' explained Emily, reassuringly. 'Fully endorsed by all the leading churches and charities. I think, to date, it has sent as many as ten thousand children from deprived backgrounds off to happier lives in Canada and Australia.'

'Really? And where do they go when they arrive there?'

'Oh, some are sent to farm schools, where they are taught the necessary skills for a career in agriculture. Others are housed with loving families on homesteads in the countryside, all of whom have been vetted beforehand.'

'Are they then adopted by these new families?'

'I believe some might be,' said Lloyd.

'Orphans, then?'

'Not all of them, no,' said Lloyd, who had now developed a slightly defensive tone.

'And the ones that aren't orphans – are the parents in agreement with this arrangement?'

Lloyd gave a little condescending chuckle. 'I'm afraid, Miss Masters, the kind of domestic family model you might be imagining simply does not exist for most of these children. This scheme offers a huge chance for them to secure their future away from a life of deprivation and neglect.'

Cynthia studied the picture again, running her fingertips across the row of young smiling faces. 'How long does it take?'

'The voyage? Oh, quite some time,' said Lloyd. 'Six weeks, I believe.'

'Six weeks... and does anyone from the home go with them?'

'My goodness, no! We couldn't spare anyone from the staff for such a long time. We run on an incredibly tight budget here.'

'Then who looks after them on board?'

'Oh, they're in quite safe hands, I assure you,' said Emily. 'Each party is escorted by two Sisters of Galilee.'

'Sorry?'

'Nuns, dear. Why don't you give Cynthia one of the pamphlets we had printed, Mr Lloyd? I believe that would answer most questions about the scheme.'

After rummaging around in a cupboard for a while, Lloyd produced a small pamphlet, on the front of which was a replica of the photograph of the waving children.

'For the migrant groups sent from our own stable of homes, we get local businesses to act as sponsors,' continued Emily.

'The sponsors provide the train tickets for the transfers to Southampton, and the suitcases, suitable clothing, et cetera. The pamphlets themselves were donated by one of our sponsors. We're rather proud of the success of this scheme, actually.'

'I see,' said Cynthia. 'Might I keep this?'

'Of course,' said Lloyd. 'But, I didn't quite catch your interest in these matters. Are you considering joining Miss Fairfax in her charitable endeavours?'

'Come, come,' said Emily, squeezing her eyes tight once more. 'I know we're in need of all the helping hands we can get, but we mustn't pressurise poor Cynthia. It's a lot to take in. She's only just begun to test the water, so to speak. Haven't you dear?'

'Indeed,' said Cynthia, trying to adopt an earnest expression. 'But I must say, it's extremely important work you're all doing here. These children are the nation's most precious commodity and it's hugely reassuring to see that they're in such safe and caring hands.'

'Well, well,' said Lloyd, puffing his chest out and making his moustache dance with a little purse of his lips. 'Merely following one's duty, don't you know.'

'Yes, I can see that,' said Cynthia, studying in closer detail the row of innocent faces gazing back at her from the photograph.

* * *

Harley slipped a coin into the gloved hand of the attendant who stood in the entrance of the Regent Palace Hotel.

'Much obliged, George. What you after?'

'Burlington. Is he in?'

'He's in the Rotunda Lounge,' said the doorman, touching the peak of his cap as Harley walked past into the foyer. 'Through the swing doors at the back.'

The room was busy, with most of the tables occupied by parties in evening dress – smoking, drinking and talking so loudly that it was a struggle to hear the prosaic efforts of the tea-dance band stationed on the small dais in the corner. The Corinthian columns and classical mosaics on the floor afforded the place an air of grandeur but, for a seasoned professional such as Harley, it was easy to spot the seedier elements among the upmarket punters: the elegant woman in the slightly risqué evening dress, for example, who would be escorting at least one of the tipsy middle-aged men at her table to her room, just as soon a she'd negotiated a decent rate; or the 'whizzer' – part of a team of pickpockets, who was distracting the elderly gent with her coquettish moves, so her colleague might relieve him of his fat wallet; and over by the island of potted tropical plants, toying with his monocle as he observed the room with professional interest, was Walter Prescott, aka Burlington Bertie, confidence man and blackmailer extraordinaire.

Burlington was one of the many friends and associates of Harley's whose dubious morals he chose to ignore – there was simply no other way to function as a sherlock in the underbelly of the city. Besides, he was no judge, no jury; it was hard enough to adhere to his own strict code of conduct, without worrying about anyone else's.

'How's it going, Bertie?'

'Not bad, Harley. Not bad at all.' Burlington, immaculate in his tuxedo, flashed a charming smile. 'To what do I owe the pleasure?'

'I need a favour.' Harley offered a cigarette. 'And I need it done quickly.'

'Matter of life and death? That kind of thing, eh?'

'Could be.'

'Whose?' asked Burlington, lighting both their cigarettes.

'Yours truly. Hence the urgency.'

'Ah! Sorry to hear that, old bean. What's the job?'

'Gathering intelligence on an adulterer. I want the comings and goings of the guilty couple, and – most importantly – I want photographic evidence.'

'Life and death, you say?' Burlington took a thoughtful puff of his cigarette. 'Curiouser and curiouser... the when and the where?'

'A couple of nights a week, at a little flat in Conduit Street,' said Harley.

'Child's play, old thing. Got the exact address?'

''Fraid not.'

'How about a likeness of the little lovebirds? I'll get my best man on it.'

Harley shook his head. 'Uh-uh. Nobody else. I need you to do this in person.'

'Really? So, who exactly am I to spy on?'

Harley leant in to whisper in Burlington's ear, at which point the monocle dropped from the conman's eye.

He took a quick swig of his Martini.

'Are you completely sure this is a wise move, old man?' he said in a whisper. 'You're surely not thinking of putting the black on the Spider's little brother, are you?'

'No, Bertie. Even I'm not that stupid. Just think of it as a little insurance. You up for it? I need it done pronterino, mind – those mugshots could save my life.'

Burlington swirled his finger around in his cocktail for a moment as he considered the proposal, then he re-engaged his charming smile.

'No sooner "S" than "D", old chum. After all, you've been good to me in the past. A friend in need, and all that. But if it does go wonky, make sure they bury me in evening dress. Chin chin!'

Burlington polished off his Martini and waggled his empty glass at a nearby waiter.

'Care to join me?'

'Sorry. I've got a lot on. Maybe another time, eh?'

Harley stood up and tipped his hat. 'Well, thanks, Bertie. Let me know when you have something for me.'

25

As Harley pushed his way through the gilded doors of the Lyons Corner House on Coventry Street, he was immediately assailed by a heady mix of floral scent and confectionery. He always felt the same coming into these grand tea houses. It was like being spirited away to the ballroom of some sham ocean liner – one populated exclusively by dull-eyed members of the lower middle classes, convinced they were enjoying the epitome of luxury and culture beneath the grandiose chandeliers.

He tapped out a Gold Flake and headed down the staircase to the basement level. He'd not met Osbert Morkens before, but it didn't take him long to spot the professor – with his domed bald head and full set of tweeds, the academic stood out a mile among all the provincial couples and bored shop girls.

'Professor Morkens?'

'Mr Harley?' Morkens shook his hand and pointed at the chair opposite. 'Please take a seat. Can I get you anything?'

'No, I'm fine, thank you.'

'I must say, these places are rather Modernistic, aren't they? I usually have my supper at my club when I'm in town, but a student brought me here a few months ago and I thought it might be rather fun to come back.'

More likely you didn't want the Old Boys at the club knowing you were associating with the likes of police officers and private detectives, thought Harley.

'Now, are you sure you won't have anything? The scones are rather good.'

'Well, I might just have a splash of tea.'

'Of course. There you are. You be mother.'

'So, Professor,' said Harley, once he'd helped himself to some tea. 'DCI Franklin tells me you might have some information for us.'

'Yes. Rather worrying business.' Morkens sat back in his chair and plucked at his white goatee beard. 'I'm not totally convinced I'm doing the right thing here. Wouldn't want to get the lad into any trouble, you know.'

'Alasdair Cassina?'

Morkens nodded. 'You see, I read about DCI Franklin in the newspaper, Mr Harley. I know which case you're investigating. Damn serious affair… with a noose waiting for someone at the end of it, I'd imagine.'

'Possibly. If we get it right.'

Harley took a sip of tea, keeping his eye on the academic.

'Well then – you can understand my reticence.'

'I can assure you, this is off the record. Just think of it as having a little informal chat.'

'Confidential?'

'Of course. And anything you tell me will be thoroughly investigated before we approach any of the individuals concerned.'

'Yes, yes. I see. I suppose one has a moral duty in these circumstances.'

'There is that as well.' Harley took his notepad out and

smiled reassuringly. 'Where do you want to start?'

Morkens pushed aside his plate and leant his leather-patched elbows on the table, clasping his fingers together.

'Well, a few days ago, I was telephoned by Brendan Collins.'

'Cassina's literary agent? He was your student at Oxford, wasn't he? Where you are Professor of…' Harley consulted his notes. 'Ancient History.'

'I see you've done your homework. Yes. I also taught Alasdair Cassina.'

'Cassina was a student of Ancient History?' asked Harley, jotting something in his notebook.

'Yes. *Classics* we tend to call it. The study of the languages, culture, religions and history of societies of the ancient world. But I only taught Cassina for a year, you understand, before he switched to English Language and Literature. Anyway, I'd had a brief reunion with Collins at the Savoy Hill studios recently – Cassina and I were guests on *The Social Looking Glass*. Don't know if you heard it at all?' The professor looked expectantly at Harley.

'I did. I thought you were a calming influence.'

'Well, thank you. It did get a bit fraught. But, you see, before the broadcast Collins approached me with his concerns about Cassina.'

'Concerns?'

'He'd been displaying increasingly erratic behaviour; a mild form of mania from what I could make out. Then, three days ago, Collins telephoned me at my college. Said he was in Oxford on business, and could he come and see me? Said it was urgent. Now, when Collins was an undergraduate, I got to know him quite well. Both he and Cassina were part of my little storytelling club, the Blind Bard Society.'

'How would you describe Collins? What's his character like?'

'His character? Oh, he was always a favourite of mine. Someone you could rely on. A wise head on young shoulders. But when he walked into my rooms on Friday evening, he was a complete nervous wreck. It took a couple of stiff drinks before I could get him to talk.'

Harley leant forward. 'Nervous? About what exactly?'

'Well, you see, he showed me this…'

Morkens unclipped his battered leather briefcase and placed a sheet of paper on the table. On it was a complex geometric design – a lozenge with rudimentary crenellations, and a number of small circles and cross shapes suspended from two curved branches. Below this was a short line of text in some foreign alphabet.

'Now, where are those damned glasses?' said the professor, searching through the pockets of his jacket and waistcoat.

'They're, erm…' Harley pointed to the half-moon spectacles perched on top of Morkens' domed head.

Morkens laughed. 'Losing my marbles, I swear I am. Now then…' He took a pen from his top pocket and pointed to the diagram. 'Any idea what this is?'

'It looks like a sigil, to me – a magical symbol.'

The professor sat back in his seat, a look of astonishment on his face.

'How on earth do you know that?'

'My Uncle Blake,' said Harley, with a little embarrassed chuckle. 'He was into all that stuff. I've got some of his books on the subject. Some of them are quite old.'

'How old, exactly?' said Morkens, the white outcrops of his eyebrows twitching in curiosity.

'I'm not sure. Why?'

'Well, you might have something of great interest there; something extremely valuable. Perhaps you might let me see them one day? Hold on.' He tugged at his beard again. 'Blake, did you say? Blake Harley?'

'Yes.'

'He wasn't a fellow of the Royal Geographical Society, by any chance?'

'Yup! Until they kicked him out,' said Harley with a wry smile.

'Most extraordinary. Do you know, I believe I once met your uncle. A fascinating character from what I remember.'

'He was that. Started off life as a costermonger's son. Became a soldier, explorer, a big game hunter, an inventor...' Harley proudly counted off on his fingers. 'And, if you believe all the stories, even a spy.'

'Is he still with us?'

'I'm afraid not. He went missing in Peru in 1911, just after discovering Machu Picchu with Hiram Bingham's expedition. They never found a body. He was legally declared dead in 1918. You know, by the time he went missing, he'd mastered around twenty languages and had published over thirty books. Not too bad for a street urchin from the Old Nichol Street Rookery, eh?'

'I should say not.'

'Anyway, that's why I recognised that as a sigil,' said Harley, realising he'd got a little carried away. 'Amongst his many hobbies, he had an interest in the occult. I inherited most of his library, you see. There's one particular book I remember with pages of those symbols in it. Something about King Solomon.'

'Probably *Lemegeton Clavicula Salomonis, The Lesser Key of Solomon*,' said Morkens, nodding. 'Rather apt you should mention it. You see, that book is a grimoire, concerned with demonology. This symbol here would be in it; it's the sigil for the demon Belial. But Collins copied this from the cover of a different book altogether, a nasty little thing called *The Grimoire of Valentinus*.'

'Valentinus,' repeated Harley, making notes.

'Yes. One of the early Christian Gnostics, from the second century. But the grimoire was only named after him, you understand. It's most likely to have had its origins in the thirteenth century. It is written in Samaritan Aramaic. This would no doubt have added a level of authenticity to its provenance – Simon Magus and some of the other early Gnostics were from Samaria, you see. But the author of *The Grimoire of Valentinus* was almost certainly a Cathar.'

'Cathar?'

'Part of a heretical sect which flourished in Southern France from the middle of the twelfth century until the fourteenth century – when they were massacred, by papal decree, during the Albigensian Crusade.'

Warming to his subject, Morkens now adopted the didactic tone he reserved for his lectures.

'Like many of the Gnostics, the Cathars believed in a dualist universe. Two gods – one good, one bad. Observing that life on earth usually contained a fair amount of evil, the Cathars refuted the idea that such a world could have been created by a good god. Instead, they attributed its creation to *Rex Mundi*, the King of the World. A chaotic god of material things. Some went on to identify this *Rex Mundi* with the Old Testament Jehovah – who often appears in the scriptures as savage and vindictive. Whereas the sublime God of the New Testament ruled serenely, from the spiritual realm.'

'I can see why the Pope would have got a little hot under the dog collar over that,' said Harley.

'Ah, but you see the *Valentinist* Cathar sect, of which the author of the grimoire was almost certainly a member, took the whole premise one stage further. They denounced Jesus as the evil offspring of the wicked god, and rejected Judeo-Christian moral values, reasoning that the commandments had been handed down by Jehovah with the sole intention of helping Moses and the other Old Testament prophets to subjugate mankind and keep him enslaved. In their view, the only way to escape this mortal imprisonment and attain salvation was to rebel against all conventional moral codes. They also disapproved of childbirth, claiming that procreation helped to swell the number of souls enslaved by Jehovah in the material world. In fact, they encouraged any form of sexual intercourse which would not result in conception – sodomy, fellatio, that kind of thing.'

Harley looked over at an adjoining table, where an elderly dowager and her female companion were looking on with ashen faces. He held his hand up in apology, then leant forward on the table.

'Maybe we should skip some of the more graphic details, Professor?'

'Good grief! I do apologise, I completely forgot where I was for a moment.'

'That's alright. So, what? These Cathars just did what they wanted? Wreaking havoc wherever they went?'

'The Valentinists were just a small, extremist, sect. The majority of Cathars lived an ascetic, abstemious life. Many of them were vegetarians, to whom killing any living thing was abhorrent. But these Valentinists refuted the idea that a soul could attain redemption by simply leading a sin-free life. They believed that this kind of spiritual redemption could only be achieved by gnosis – divine knowledge received through an inspiration from God. Once someone had received gnosis he became part-god himself, and so was impervious to corruption from any act that he might commit. And one of their main methods of attaining gnosis was through ritualistic magic.'

'Hence the grimoire.'

'Exactly.'

Morkens now leant across the table, lowering his voice.

'This abhorrent little book combines two of the Valentinists' main tenets – the revulsion of procreation and the attainment of gnosis through magic. It is an instruction manual, Harley, accompanied by the most horrific diagrams. An instruction manual for arcane rituals, which almost exclusively involve the torture and sacrifice of young children.'

Harley gave a sigh and tipped his hat back an inch or so.

'And I take it Brendan Collins told you that Cassina is in possession of this *Grimoire of Valentinus*?'

'Not just in possession of it – he's using it as inspiration for his new novel. Collins is worried that, with Cassina's growing notoriety, this new work of his will become some kind of handbook for lunatics, encouraging violence against children.'

'Surely the publishers wouldn't allow such a thing?'

'I wouldn't underestimate Alasdair Cassina. That young man has an exceptional mind. I wouldn't put it past him to be able to present such a subversive message in a form that was somehow palatable to the censors. He also has complete faith in the loyalty of his readers – regards them as fervent followers in a rather messianic way. Collins believes that, if pushed, Cassina would have the book privately published and distributed among his network of devotees.'

'Is that the only thing Collins is worried about?'

'I don't follow.'

Harley leant forward, lowering his voice.

'You know which case we're investigating here. Do you think there's a chance that Alasdair Cassina could be the Nursery Butcher?'

Professor Morkens removed his glasses and sat thinking for a moment, tapping a long index finger on the table.

'Cassina may be showing worrying signs of some kind of messiah complex. But these theories on morality that he postulates in his work, although disturbing to many, are purely theoretical. I'm not sure he has the disposition to enact actual violence in the real world, but I couldn't be certain that Collins doesn't believe him to be involved somehow.'

'Has he said as much?'

'Not in so many words,' said Morkens. 'But he did remind

me of a connection between Cassina and Rupert Dawson, whose house in Clapham the first victim was found in.'

'What?' said Harley, sitting up. 'Jessica Dawson's husband? What connection?'

'Dawson was an undergraduate at Brasenose, at the same time as Collins and Cassina.'

'They knew each other?'

'Yes. Not well. Dawson belonged to a far more sporty set. But Collins reminded me that Cassina had developed a certain enmity towards Dawson when they were students. Apparently there had been some kind of drunken spat once, during which Dawson had belittled Cassina in front of his friends. He was a rangy, athletic type, I seem to remember.'

'Hardly a reasonable motive for planting the corpse of a child in his house.'

'I agree. But Collins seems to think it significant. That's why I felt an obligation to contact Mr Franklin.'

Harley drew on his cigarette.

'Let's just say, for argument's sake, that Cassina *is* involved with the murders. That it's some kind of deranged philosophical experiment. Do you think, in such circumstances, he could pressurise Brendan Collins into helping him?'

'If that were the case, why would Collins discuss his concerns about Cassina with me?'

'I don't know,' said Harley. 'A cry for help, maybe?'

'You know, I'm beginning to think that this whole thing was a mistake. Just the very idea that two Oxonians, successful young men from good families, could be at all connected to such heinous crimes—'

'With respect, Professor,' interrupted Harley, 'I don't think where they went to school is going to exclude them from our investigations.' *But the fact that Collins' old man is a government minister might*, thought Harley. 'But, anyway, this is all just supposition. As I said, we're just having an informal chat here.

We don't have any evidence to prove either of them might be involved. And I promise you, everything you've shared with me today will be treated with the utmost confidence.'

'Well, that's reassuring. Thank you.'

'One more thing. You spoke about these Valentinists rejecting the accepted moral codes of society. I can see how this would fit in with the themes of Cassina's books – the questioning of morality in *A Reflection in the Ice*, and all that. But you don't really think he believes in these magical rituals, do you? After all, as you said, he's an educated man.'

Morkens regarded Harley with a smile. He looked amused, patriarchal, as if Harley had just suggested something naive.

'Ritual has been fundamental to religious practice since the dawn of time,' he said. 'There are millions of *educated* people who believe that, during Mass, the consecrated bread and wine are changed into the body and blood of Jesus Christ. Such faith is at the very essence of human society.'

'Faith in sacrificing children to attain some kind of mystic wisdom?'

'Such practices held sway for millennia. In civilisation terms, they have only very recently been rejected.'

'But that's just it – now they have been rejected. We're no longer in the thirteenth century. How can a man like Cassina, who lives in the modern world of automobiles and wireless telegraph, believe in such things?'

The academic sat up and held out a hand.

'*There are more things in heaven and earth, Horatio, than are dreamt of in your philosophy!*' He chuckled. 'You know, I believe they still talk about my Hamlet in the Brasenose Dramatic Society. Anyway, we don't know for sure that Cassina *does* believe in such things. Collins merely said that he was using the grimoire as inspiration for his new book. Although it is my opinion that such arcane texts shouldn't be regarded flippantly. Many have suffered serious psychic damage from messing with occult practices.'

The professor looked at his watch and then signalled for the waitress.

'Anyway, I'm afraid I must be off to catch my train. I'm not sure if any of this has been of any use?'

'Yes, very useful, thank you,' said Harley, closing his notebook and standing up. 'Will you be available if I need to follow up on anything?'

'Of course,' said Morkens. 'Here's my card.'

If the private detective had looked behind him as he weaved his way through the linen-clad tables on his way out, he might have caught a glimpse of someone scrutinising his movements, someone who now slipped away from his own table to shadow Harley as he made his way up the sweeping staircase. Someone he'd seen once before – outside Madame Leanda's Duck Lane clinic – in a black Homburg hat, with a doughy complexion and thick, pebble-lensed spectacles.

* * *

When he got back to Bell Street, it struck Harley that the house felt colder than usual. On entering the kitchen, the reason for this became obvious. Someone had smashed one of the small panes of glass in the back door, probably in order to slip the lock.

He stood quietly, trying to attune to any strange sound that might be coming from the house. He then lit an oil lamp and, grabbing the stout shillelagh he kept propped up by the kitchen fireplace, began to make a stealthy search of the downstairs rooms. He was relieved to find that none of Uncle Blake's curios appeared to be missing; in fact, apart from the broken window, nothing seemed to have been disturbed at all. On the first floor it was the same story – no open drawers, no emptied closets; definitely not the usual screwsman's job. He lit the gas lamps on all floors and began to make a second, more thorough check of the house. By the time he'd reached the attic room, he was beginning to wonder whether the window hadn't been smashed in some innocent accident. Maybe some of the local kids had lobbed a cricket ball over the garden fence by mistake?

Then, just as he was about to leave the room, something in the corner of his eye caught his attention: the four photographs of Brendan Collins, given to him by Madame Leanda, were missing from the blackboard. He could see where the chalked *No.1 Suspect* next to Collins' name had been smudged by the thief's hurried hand.

Harley made a quick analysis of the situation: compromising photographs of the son of the Parliamentary Under-Secretary of State for the Home Department mysteriously disappearing after a break-in. There was one obvious solution – MI5. After all, this was exactly the kind of job that Harley might have been sent on as a field agent.

Well, alright. No serious damage done. He already knew what Collins looked like, and Franklin had made it clear that they were never going to be able to use the photographs in a court case. Just another hurdle in a bloody long steeplechase.

Just then Moloch padded into the room, demanding his supper with a baritone mewl.

'And where were you when you were needed, you old cove? You're supposed to be guarding the gaff when I'm not here.'

And with that Harley followed Moloch's slow swagger downstairs to prepare supper for them both, and to pour himself a strong whisky and soda.

26

'**GEORGE! PUT A** coaster under that teacup, would you, please? I've only had that piece a few weeks.'

With a sigh, Harley removed his cup from the elegant octagonal table.

'Walnut?' he asked, running his fingers over the rippled grain of the polished veneer.

'Amboyna.'

'Never heard of it.'

'Indonesian, I believe.'

'Expensive?'

'Don't be gauche, darling. Now, will you come over here? I thought you said you only had a short while before you had to leave.'

'Yeah, sorry. My mind's elsewhere. I didn't kip too well last night.'

'I'm not surprised, with that break-in at your place. Have you reported it to the police yet?'

'I'm seeing Franklin later. I'll tell him then.'

'Be sure you do. Listen, don't you think you ought to spend a few nights here?'

'No,' Harley smiled reassuringly, as he joined Cynthia on the chestnut leather sofa. 'I'm quite capable of looking after myself. And I don't want you worrying yourself silly, either.'

'I'm just supposed to regard this as the norm, I expect. Living around all this jeopardy?'

'Jeopardy? You're not in any danger, Miss Masters. I won't let anything happen to you.'

'Actually, it was your safety I was thinking about.'

Harley smiled and closed his eyes for a moment, resting his head back on the seat.

'Well, I'm a big boy now,' he murmured.

He took a deep breath, savouring the perfume of the richly patinated leather, mixing luxuriously with the sweet notes from the lilies in the Lalique vase on the sideboard. It was almost possible – ensconced, like this, within the tasteful elegance of Cynthia's apartment – to believe that all was right with the world; that there were no homicidal lunatics, roaming the midnight streets, snatching innocent children—

'George! Are you listening to me?'

'Hmm?'

'I thought you wanted to talk about my visit to the children's homes?'

'Yes. I do. Sorry.' Harley sat up and tapped out a Gold Flake, lighting it with Cynthia's large green onyx table lighter. 'So, come on. Let's see, now. You were saying on the phone that you thought it unlikely the children were disappearing directly from the homes?'

'Yes. Not impossible, but unlikely, in my opinion.'

'Because?'

'Because everything's so regimented at these places. There are registers, systems in place. I don't think it would be that easy for a stranger to just walk in and kidnap a child. Certainly not on multiple occasions.'

'What if they weren't strangers? What if the management were in on it?'

'For what reason?'

'I don't know – financial?'

'What, selling the children? To murderers? Pederasts? That all sounds rather far-fetched to me. Besides, I don't think there's any need for inventing such conspiracies. Not when the reality is so extraordinary. Here, look at this.' She handed Harley the pamphlet she'd been given about the children migrants' scheme.

Harley read through the text, his frown deepening the further in he got.

'This is insane! It's what they used to do to convicts. Some of these kids are as young as five!'

'I know. It does seem awfully cruel, doesn't it? Those poor children. Whatever must go through their minds on that long voyage? But I must say, Emily did seem convinced they'd ultimately lead happier lives out there.'

'Here we go,' said Harley, stabbing at the page. 'Homesteads, farm schools. They're basically being sent out to the colonies as slave labour.' He took a long draw on his cigarette and scanned through the rest of the pages.

'No!'

'What is it?'

'This list of sponsors. Look – *Rivista Publishing Ltd*. They printed this pamphlet. That's Victor Manduca's firm.'

'Manduca?' said Cynthia, giving a little involuntary shudder. 'But surely they wouldn't allow that awful pornographer anywhere near those children?'

'You know, I think you might have stumbled across gold here, Cyn.'

Harley whipped out his notebook and began scribbling furiously. But when he got to the back page of the booklet a curious look came over him. 'There's something else here.'

'What do you mean?'

'Take a good look. What does this remind you of? The layout of the text. The typeface. The quality of the paper.'

'Sorry. I don't follow,' said Cynthia.

'I'd need to compare them properly when I get back to my place, but to me this looks incredibly similar to the booklet you picked up at that Black Sabbath in Belgravia.'

'The AOU manual? Well, we already know Manduca's involved with that little cabal. I saw him there, remember?'

'Yeah, but this might be the proof we need. He's so slippery, that one. We'll need hard evidence to bring him in. Hold on a second.' Harley flipped to the front page, which featured the photograph of the group of children, holding suitcases and waving at the camera. 'Do you have a magnifying glass anywhere?'

'Actually, I do. I've one mounted on a stand. For my tapestry work.'

'Tapestry?'

'Oh, don't look at me like that. It's a perfectly normal hobby.'

'If you say so.'

Cynthia got up and fished around for a bit in the sideboard. 'Here you are. What are you looking for, exactly?'

'This kid here, the one at the back.' Harley swung the large magnifying glass into position. 'His face is partially obscured, but… Oh, fuck!'

'Please, George! There's really no need for that type of language.'

'Oh, I assure you there is! You see this little boy here? I've seen his face before.'

'Where?'

'In the autopsy photographs, from the Butcher's first victim in Clapham.'

'Dear Lord!' exclaimed Cynthia, clutching a hand to her throat.

* * *

Harley swung the motorcycle and sidecar combination into Meard Street and parked up outside the Shabaroon. Before the war, motoring had been the privilege of the wealthy enthusiast and the upper classes. However, the wartime demand for armoured cars and other military vehicles had transformed the industry and, by peacetime, this new technology had finally come into the reach of the common man. For Harley, his Norton motorcycle symbolised the exciting potential of the post-war years, as much a mark of the new social freedom as the growing popularity of the jazz music he was so fond of.

As he climbed off the bike, he heard the sound of footsteps on the cobblestones behind him.

'Mr Aitch! Hang on a mo!'

Alfie Budge came to a sliding halt in front of Harley, bent over double with his hands on his knees. With all the exposure to city pollution and his nascent tobacco addiction, the little cockney sparrow's lungs weren't best equipped for prolonged bouts of exercise, and it took a good while for him to regain his breath, coughing, spluttering and swearing his way through the recovery.

'Better out than in,' he said, delivering a particularly nasty gobbet of phlegm on the ground at his feet.

Having fully recuperated, Budge now gave a whistle as he regarded the motorbike. 'Cor! What a beaut. That yorn?'

'Yup! Norton CS1,' said Harley. 'There's been a couple of winners at the Isle of Man TT riding these, you know. Climb aboard. See how it feels.'

Budge clambered up astride the leather saddle, his diminutive figure dwarfed by the powerful machine.

'So, you got something for me, Squib?'

'Yeah, it's about Whelks.' Budge grabbed the handlebars and crouched forward, mimicking the illustrations he'd seen in the boys' annuals. 'I reckon we might be onto something.'

'Really? What've you got?'

'Last couple of days he's broken his routine. During the day, he's usually with Mori the Hat, right? Everywhere Mori goes, he goes too. That's our Benny – like a bleedin' shadow. But for the last two days he's nowhere to be seen. Not around Adler, anyways.'

Budge sighed and patted the gleaming petrol tank with a dreamy look in his eye.

'Come on, son! Let's have the rest of it. Where's Benny going, then?'

'Oh yeah… erm, somewhere in Seven Dials, we reckon.'

'Where exactly? Come on! This is important.'

'Alright!' said Budge, with a defensive twitch of the elbows. 'We'll get you an address, don't you worry. We almost had 'im last night. Boots Naylor was right on 'is tail but, as he was making his way up Shaftesbury Avenue, he spotted some bogey who had collared him last month, so he had to drop back. You know Boots Naylor?'

'No, I don't know Boots Naylor. And I don't want to know him either. What I want is for you to find out where Benny Whelks has been going.'

'Yeah. And we're gonna do that for you, only…'

Here it comes, thought Harley.

Budge bit his lip. 'Well, we're gonna need a little more dough.'

'What for?'

'Well, I wanna double up on the crew, so as we don't lose him this time.'

'Go on. How much?'

The little wide boy screwed up one eye as he performed some mental arithmetic.

'Another five bob should do it, for the next couple of days.'

Harley gave the lad an old-fashioned look, then produced the money from his pocket.

'There you go. But listen. I'm expecting an exact address, got it?'

'Got it,' said Budge, clinking the coins in his grubby hand. 'It's a beaut, alright,' he added, giving the bike another pat.

'Well, get me a result on Whelks and I'll take you for a spin.'

'You sprucing me?'

'Course not.'

'Alright, Mr Aitch. You're on.'

'Right, scarper! I've got to see a man about a dog.'

* * *

'There you go,' said Juney, plonking down two foaming pints on the bar top.

'Thanks.' Harley wiped a splatter of froth from his newspaper.

'I see you've been reading about that missing kid in Limehouse. Poor little mite. They're saying it's definitely the Nursery Butcher again.'

'Well, there's nothing to indicate that at the moment, Juney. You should take everything you read in this rag with a pinch of salt.' Harley rolled up the *Daily Oracle* and stuffed it into his pocket.

He took the drinks over to DCI Franklin and indicated the back of the pub with a nod of his head. 'Let's go through to the snug. It's a bit more private in there.'

'So, listen,' said Harley, once they were safely ensconced behind the relative privacy of the snug bar's frosted glass, 'I've got something that needs urgently looking into.'

He took a sup of his beer and then handed Franklin a sheet of paper from his notebook.

'HMS *Jervis Bay*?'

'That's right. She set sail for Australia out of Southampton on the second of March. There was a group of twenty-five kids from children's homes on board that day. Part of a child migrants' programme. You've got a full list of their names there. Do you think you could get someone to check whether they all arrived safely?'

'In Australia? Well, I'd imagine that might take some time. But, in theory, it should be possible. Why?'

'Because one of the kids in that group bears an uncanny resemblance to the poor bastard who had his head sewn on to our first victim. Look.'

Harley handed the policeman the pamphlet Cynthia had given him.

'I don't know,' said Franklin, squinting closely at the photograph on the front page. 'It's difficult to say for sure.'

'Really? Personally, I think it's a pretty strong resemblance. But let's find out if they all got there safely first. If they did, then there's no further action. If they didn't, then I reckon I might have a good idea where that monster's been getting his victims from.'

'What makes you think they were taken from the ship?'

'Because of a certain person's association with the migrants' programme.'

'You know I'm going to need more than that.'

'Let's just say I'm not quite prepared to commit to the theory just yet. Once I give you the name, there's no going back.'

'I see, one of your more nefarious associates, eh?'

'Not an associate. Definitely not an associate.'

'Well, one of the reasons I wanted you on the case in the first place was for your wider reach behind enemy lines. Alright,' said Franklin, placing the paper in his inside pocket, 'I'll get someone on it straight away.'

'Good. Now, what about that hat box? Any progress there?'

'Bespoke, possibly last century. The maker's label is missing. Our killer probably bought it second-hand. From the quality, I'd say the original owners would have been people of some social standing.'

'What?' Harley scoffed. 'And they couldn't possibly be killers, right?'

'Justice is blind, as far as I'm concerned. If you had enough evidence to prove it was the Archbishop of Canterbury, I'd have him in for questioning.'

'So why aren't we going after Collins then?'

'Because we haven't got enough evidence yet. We need everything tied up neatly with a bow before we bring Collins in for questioning, otherwise yours truly will be directing traffic at Piccadilly Circus for the last few months before my retirement. With Collins' family connections we'll have just one bite at the cherry. Now then, to the matter in hand.'

Franklin popped the clasp on his briefcase and handed Harley a buff-coloured folder.

'What's this?'

'Sir Bernard Spilsbury's report on his re-examination of our victims.'

Harley grabbed the folder and began to eagerly pore over the typed sheets inside. It didn't take him long to stumble across something that caught his eye.

'Hold on! He's saying here the head found in that hat box on the tram had been preserved in alcohol beforehand. The other two weren't like that, were they?'

'No,' said Franklin. 'And if you continue to read on, you'll see that Spilsbury believes it to have been preserved for some considerable time – possibly even years. The decomposition had taken place relatively recently, following its removal from the preservation fluid, but there's no telling when the original death occurred.'

'What? But that doesn't fit with the pattern. What's this monster up to?'

'It gets stranger. In the first two heads the brains were intact, but with this third specimen the cranium has been stuffed with a wad of cloth.'

'Yeah, a fine piece of embroidery, apparently,' said Harley, continuing to read from the report. 'Possibly depicting a scene from the Book of Revelation.'

'Well, Sir Bernard may be the leading pathologist in the country, but he's no textiles expert. We've sent the cloth off for analysis by specialists at the British Museum.'

'Good. Keep me updated on that. What else has our boy Spilsbury discovered?'

'Oh, there's plenty more in there, you'll see.'

It took a full one and a half Gold Flakes for Harley to absorb all the relevant facts of the post-mortem report, and when he finally closed the folder, he had a spirited glint in his eye.

'So, here we have our victims, presented at three different locations.' He kept his voice low so as not to be overheard in the saloon bar. 'In each case, decapitated heads have been left with a different body. In two cases they've actually been sewn on.'

'Damn abomination,' said Franklin.

'Agreed. Still, that doesn't stop our boy Sir Bernard from gleaning some clues from them. Chronic lower respiratory infection in two of the victims, which could indicate a history of malnutrition. But none of the torsos were by any means wasting away. In fact, they all showed a decent amount of fat. Then there's this bit of Spilsbury magic. On the first two heads, there's a band of latter growth of hair indicating a period – a month or so before death, he says – in which the victims enjoyed a far more nutritious diet. What do you think? Is this bastard fattening them up before he kills them?'

Franklin gave a weary sigh and a slowly shook his head. 'It's like something from the Brothers Grimm.'

'And maybe that's no coincidence.' Harley paused to take a long, thoughtful drink of his beer. 'So, presumably he has the resources to house and feed these kids. That tells us he has a certain prosperity. Whereas our victims, on the other hand

– chronic malnutrition, callouses on their hands and feet, the fact that no parent has claimed them…'

'All indications of poverty.'

'Exactly. I reckon the reason we can't identify the bodies is because these kids were invisible to begin with.'

'Possibly living on the streets.'

'Or perhaps snatched from a children's home?' said Harley.

'Hence your line of enquiry with the child migrants' programme. I see.'

Franklin pondered this for a while, gently tapping the stem of his Bulldog briar against his teeth.

'And these children's homes, they'd be local to London, do you think?'

'Why not? There are plenty to choose from in the Smoke. Why go further afield?'

'Surely those in charge would notice they'd gone? After all, the authorities running such institutions have a responsibility for the welfare of their wards.'

'That's why I want you to check out those kids from the *Jervis Bay* voyage. It would be the perfect opportunity to grab them.'

'I see.' Franklin took out his tobacco pouch. 'What about little Eddie Muller?' he said, beginning to fill his pipe. 'How does he fit into your theory? All indications are that he's from a loving working-class family. Granted, they're not Rockefellers, but even so.'

'Well, it's only Enoch Craster who's making a connection between the Muller kid and our man.'

'Him and the millions who read his column. I'm waging a public relations war with this one. I can't afford to dismiss the disappearance of an innocent – and damned photogenic – six-year-old out of hand just like that.'

'Well, I sincerely hope little Eddie turns up on his mother's doorstep with only a couple of grazed knees to show for his troubles. But, if you want to use me to best effect, I can't be getting distracted with every missing persons case that drops on your desk… or keep being ambushed by soddin' DI Quigg.' Harley tipped his hat back a couple of inches. 'I told you we needed to tread carefully with the Manducas. That little stunt of Quigg's has put me in some seriously hot water – a distraction I could do without at the moment.'

'And as I've told you, George, I hauled him over the coals for it.' Franklin put a match to the bowl of his pipe. 'Quigg's dangerously ambitious. I'm afraid there's a limit to the control I'm going to have over him. You'll just have to watch your back.'

'He's as bent as a dog's hind leg is what he is. I swear Manduca's cut a deal with him – I saw them give each other the old Freemasons' handshake. And as for watching my back, I thought *you* were supposed to be doing that?' Harley took an irritated puff of his smoke. 'I take it Manduca's not been charged with anything?'

Franklin shook his head. 'Let off, scot-free.'

'What a surprise. So I really do have to watch my back.'

'I'm not saying you're on your own with this,' said Franklin, with a reassuring smile. 'Of course, I'll do my utmost to protect you. I just need you to understand I haven't got a magic wand to make it all go away.'

'Alright. Just don't be surprised if you get a call to say some dead sherlock has been hauled out of the Thames. Anyway, talking of magic wands, after what Morkens told me about Cassina's interest in the occult, how do you want to play it with our literary double act?'

'We followed up the Dawson connection with some of the other Brasenose students of the time. It pans out. I think I definitely have enough to bring Cassina in for questioning now.'

'And Collins?'

The policeman thought for a moment.

'Honestly, George? If your theory about the break-in at your place is correct, and given who his father is... well, I can't see how we can make any kind of move against Collins without risking getting into very hot water with the top brass. Not until we have some kind of usable evidence.'

'But surely, once you've questioned Cassina, wouldn't it be perfectly reasonable to go and have a follow-up chat with his literary agent, to discuss your concerns about his client? I could do it if you want.'

'You'll do nothing of the sort!' said Franklin. 'I don't want you going anywhere near Mr Brendan Collins, not unless I've given you a direct order to do so. Is that clear? I'll think about whether it's reasonable to follow up with him myself, after I've spoken to Cassina.'

'You're the boss,' said Harley, with a little dismissive shrug. 'Presumably I'm allowed to do a little sniffing around in the background? We've already established that whoever is responsible is keeping these kids somewhere before doing away with them. I'd like to see if our literary boys have links to any suitable premises.'

The policeman nodded. 'I suppose so. But, for God's sake, tread carefully. Oh, I almost forgot.'

Franklin rummaged around in his jacket pocket.

'Here's that copy of the keys found on the victims you wanted.'

Harley fingered the cast iron. It was a pleasing Georgian design, with a quatrefoil bow and intricate, maze-like wards. Like the key from a fairy-tale illustration.

'Thanks. And this is an exact copy, right?'

'Just as you asked for.'

Just then Juney appeared behind the bar.

'John? Telephone call for you – urgent, apparently. You'll have to come around the other side to take it.'

'Right you are,' said Franklin, downing the remains of his pint before making his way out to the saloon bar.

He returned a few minutes later, with a concerned look on his face.

'Problem?' asked Harley.

'They've found another body. Washed up in the docks at Limehouse.'

'Is it the Muller kid?'

'I don't know. That's all I have at the moment. I'd better get off there now.'

'I'll come with you. I've got the bike outside.'

'No, better not. Apparently Quigg's already there. Best you keep a low profile.'

'Alright, I'll wait here. But telephone me as soon as you find out, won't you?'

27

For most of the morning, the sky had remained a sodden grey, like a dirty rag hung out to dry over the city. But as Harley gazed out over the river from the Victoria Embankment, the sun suddenly made a fleeting appearance, casting a fan of brilliance upon the water. He looked down at the swirling eddies picked out in the patch of light and thought about the body he was about to view in the Scotland Yard morgue. He'd seen bodies hauled out of the river before, bleached and ruined by the same turbid waters that now rushed past a few yards below him.

At least this new grisly offering from Old Father Thames wasn't little Eddie Muller. Despite their initial fears, the corpse washed up in the Limehouse docks had turned out to be the remains of an adult female. Franklin had asked him to attend the morgue, as – the policeman had added intriguingly – he thought Harley might be able to shed a little light on the identity of the deceased.

He flicked his cigarette butt into the river and crossed over the street, tipped his hat to the bobby at the gates, and entered the imposing brick edifice that was Scotland Yard.

'Sorry to have to drag you along to this, George,' said Franklin, greeting him in the waiting room of the morgue. 'Not the most pleasant of activities, I know.'

'Well, I've got lunch planned with Solly later. So I can drown my sorrows if it all gets too harrowing.'

'It won't have been your first, I'll warrant.'

'Sadly not. But I'm curious to know why you think I'll be able to identify the body.'

'Ah! Well, you see, our unfortunate victim didn't have many possessions upon her person – we no doubt lost some things to the current. But, luckily, we managed to retrieve her purse from one of her skirt pockets. Among its contents were a number of business cards and a sodden, folded page from a memo pad. The business cards were pretty intact, but the ink on the memo was all but washed away. However, we have managed to decipher some of the message. And it mentions you by name.'

'Really? What does it say?'

Franklin flipped open his notepad.

'From what we can make out, it says: *Dora*, then something unintelligible, then *George Harley 2.30pm*.'

Fearing he might already have guessed the answer to this next question, Harley asked, 'And the name on the business cards?'

'Madame Leanda,' said the policeman. Then, with a little embarrassed cough, added, 'Member of the Berlin Institute of Sexology.'

'Jesus, no!' said Harley, tipping his hat back.

He slumped down into one of the chairs lining the room, trying hard to repel the image of the beautiful Leanda stretched out on a slab. That exquisite creamy skin now mottled and puckered by immersion in the cold water; the strawberry blonde hair matted with green river weed; the deep blue eyes milky with the cast of death.

'I'm sorry, George. I didn't for one moment think it would be a personal friend. I just assumed, from the nature of the business card, that… well, it was someone you'd come across professionally.'

Harley gave a sigh. 'She was. I only met her twice. But she'd made quite an impression.'

His mind began to race, joining the dots of the recent developments in the case.

'You know,' he said, putting a hand instinctively to his gut. 'I've got a horrible feeling I might somehow be indirectly responsible for this woman's death.'

Franklin's brow furrowed.

'How so?'

'Madame Leanda was my source for those photographs of Brendan Collins, and for the information about his violent sexual fantasies. I told you I thought that MI5 were behind the break-in at my place; well, I'm now beginning to think they could also be responsible for making sure that Leanda was permanently silenced.'

'Are you seriously suggesting that a government department would assassinate an innocent member of the public, purely to avert some kind of political scandal?'

'I—' Harley began to respond, but realised that this wasn't the time or place to venture down that particular rabbit hole. 'Forget I said anything. To tell you the truth, this has really knocked me sideways.'

'Would you like a moment? Before we…'

'No,' said Harley, resignedly. 'Come on. Let's get it over with.'

'Here you are, then,' said Franklin, proffering a bag of boiled sweets. 'Cough drop. Suck on one of these and light up a cigarette – little trick I've picked up over the years. Makes the whole affair a little more palatable.'

It was customarily cool inside the morgue, with the usual vinegary tang of formaldehyde and faint, gamey base note of decay. Harley took a long pull of smoke – cooled by the menthol of the sweet – then followed DCI Franklin towards the sheeted form on the slab in the middle of the room.

Their echoing footsteps on the flagstone floor seemed too conspicuous somehow, violating the solemn silence of the place.

Puffing regularly on his Bulldog briar, Franklin made a quick check on Harley and then gave the nod to the lab attendant.

Harley held his breath as the sheet was slowly pulled away from the body.

And then let it out with an immediate sense of relief.

Even with the marbled taint of decomposition, and the bleached and sloughed skin on the extremities, it was obvious the deceased was at least ten years older than Leanda. She was thin and wiry, with a harsh, Germanic jawline.

'That's not her,' he murmured, with a sigh. Then he rubbed his mouth, stifling a smile. 'It's not her.'

'Are you sure?'

'Positive. Believe me, if you'd have met her, you'd know.'

'Well, now we have to discover—'

Franklin was interrupted by a knock on the door. He indicated for a young CID officer to enter.

'What is it, Watkins?'

'I've managed to get that file, sir. On the Leanda woman.'

'Well done, lad! DC Watkins here remembered the name, you see, from an arrest last year. Is there a photograph, Watkins?'

'Yes, it's here somewhere. There we are.'

DCI Franklin held up the mugshot for comparison with the victim on the slab.

'Well, George. I'd say, allowing for conditions, this is definitely the same woman, wouldn't you?'

Harley checked the photograph then took his trilby off and scratched his head.

'Bugger! If *this* is Madame Leanda, then who the hell have I been talking to?'

'Wait a minute,' said Franklin with a black look, pulling Harley aside so they wouldn't be overheard. 'Are you telling me that Collins' alleged perverted fantasies about murdering children have all been some kind of hoax?'

'Well, there are still those photographs of him togged up in the sailor suit.'

'Purely circumstantial,' said Franklin. 'A little odd, but hardly criminal. And absolutely no evidence of him harbouring homicidal thoughts.'

'Well, I'll admit it weakens the case for Collins being our killer, but—'

'Weakens the case?' exclaimed Franklin. 'It's clearly a hoax. An out-and-out fit-up!'

'Maybe you're right,' said Harley, his brain still whirling from the revelation. 'We need to get this body positively identified by Dora to make sure, though.'

'Oh, I intend to do that. But, mark my words, you've been duped. There's someone out there posing as this Madame Leanda, and whoever it is has some vested interest in fingering Brendan Collins as the Nursery Butcher. Which probably means she's somehow connected to the killings herself. Good grief! Just think if we'd have hauled Collins in as a suspect on the strength of that false lead. The son of the Under-Secretary for the Home Department!'

Harley shook his head. 'Is that what's worrying you most about this? Ruffling the feathers of the Old Boys' Club?'

Franklin bit on the stem of his pipe. 'Yes, it is! And for bloody good reason! Now, I suggest you forget that chip on your shoulder for once and get back out there and clear up this mess!'

As he headed for the door with his tail between his legs, Harley conjured the deep azure of those mesmerising eyes. *Alright, you devious bitch*, he thought, crunching up the remnants of his cough drop. *Just who the hell are you?*

Back outside, he crossed the road and headed north along the Embankment. Discovering the true identity of the bogus Madame Leanda was definitely a priority now, but he had one more pressing problem to deal with first.

Slipping into a public telephone box, he tapped out a cigarette and dialled the operator. 'Townley 252, please,' he said, sparking up as he waited to be connected. 'Bertie? It's George. I was told you had something for me. Please tell me it's those smudges of Spiru and his niece. It is? Well, that's the best news I've had for a long time, mate. Can you meet me up West? I'm meeting Solly at Renzo's. I'll stand you lunch.'

* * *

Later that afternoon, as Harley turned into Wardour Street – having just enjoyed a protracted lunch with Solly Rosen and Burlington Bertie – another burst of sunlight managed to battle its way through the city clouds to bathe the pavement in an inviting glow. Like many of its salacious denizens, Soho in the early afternoon was a lazier, shabbier version of its night-time self; quietly resting for a few precious hours before once again painting on a lurid face with which to entice the punters. Feeling a little sleepy from the wine he'd had with his meal, Harley now raised his face to the sunshine and closed his eyes to soak up this rare moment of tranquillity.

He found his thoughts wandering back to the conversation he'd had with Cynthia, about his decision to become a private detective. Perhaps she was right? Maybe he could turn his hand to something else, something that didn't involve dealing with the violent and unhinged, and all the other shades of lunatic he came across while plying his trade in the murk of the city. It had once been his dream to open a club. Well, why not? He had a few connections with the scene – he was good friends with Jumpin' Johnson Munro, one of the hottest horn players in the country. Perhaps they could start something together? Have a few acts come over from the States? Cynthia could move into Bell Street – after all, there was plenty of room. Or, if she didn't want to leave her own apartment, maybe he could move in there, rent out his place?

Harley was still in the midst of these domestic musings when he was yanked back into stark reality by the stab of a pistol thrust painfully into the small of his back.

'Number's up, sherlock,' growled Spiru Manduca into his ear. 'Keep your mouth shut and walk slowly to the car.'

28

STILL DROWSY FROM the soporific, Eddie Muller sat silently in his chair, mesmerised by the reflections of candlelight gleaming softly in the impressive array of silverware.

'Elbows off the table, there's a good boy.'

There was a time when he'd been frightened by the funny leather goat mask the man wore. But now he found its never-changing expression strangely comforting. And if he squinted, he could make the pattern of its horns, drooping ears and snout into a five-pointed star – just like the wooden ornament that hung in the window at Christmastime.

The goat man placed a bowl of trifle before him.

'And how are your new clothes?'

Confused by the question, Eddie looked down at himself. Hadn't he always worn this sailor suit, with its trim collar and fresh smell of the laundry room? Not wanting to say the wrong thing, he smiled and nodded earnestly.

'Of course, you were suitably grubby when you first came in – deliciously so. All part of the glorious transformation.

Eat your dessert now, there's a good boy. I'm sure your sister would be delighted with such a treat.'

Eddie stuffed a spoon loaded with custard and cream into his mouth, and tried to picture Milly, but all he could muster were a few vague elements. A shrill laugh, the smell of pear drops, the crusted scab on a knee.

'You really are quite beautiful, my child,' continued the goat man, pouring himself a glass of wine from a glistening decanter. 'As pretty as an angel. It's curious that such beauty can blossom amongst the wretched and destitute, like a lotus in the mire. It's because of this quirk of nature that you have been chosen, Edward – as the beautiful often are. Chosen for a fate as honoured as that of… oh, Lisa del Giocondo, say, or maybe those two little street urchins, gazing into the baker's window, used by Raphael as models for his cherubs in *The Sistine Madonna*.'

Pleased with this analogy, the man raised his glass and took a delicate sip.

'You see, if one has lived well, the astral body evaporates like pure incense, ascending towards the superior regions. Sounds rather enticing, don't you think?' He noticed Eddie was coming to the end of his dessert. 'Would you like some more?'

After spooning more trifle into the bowl, his hand caressed the child's sticky cheek for a moment, then gently pinched the flesh. 'And do drink up your Hippocras, dear boy. We wouldn't want you having nightmares again, would we?'

29

FORMED BY MOOR Street, Old Compton Street, and Charing Cross Road, the Moor Street triangle was one of Soho's murkier little enclaves; a nest of drinking dives and slovenly apartments, stacked above a handful of jaded shop fronts. The triangular courtyard behind the buildings served as both a meeting place for dubious transactions and a quick escape route. A neat disappearing act could be performed by entering a premises in one side of the triangle, slipping out the back door, across the yard, and then out into one of the other streets. Just such a trick had been performed by Spiru Manduca, when he'd frogmarched Harley out of his car with his Beretta pushed firmly into the private detective's back. Harley guessed this was to confuse any passers-by who might be foolish enough to later come forward as eyewitnesses to his kidnapping.

It irked him that he'd been so easily jumped in the street – like some greenhorn mug, standing there mooning over his judy. It was also obvious that Spiru and his sidekick intended to deal out some serious punishment. If it had been a simple case of putting on the frighteners, it would have already happened in the back of the car.

Now he needed to concentrate on staying alive.

He stood in the gloom of the Moor Street yard with Manduca behind him. The Maltese had one hand on his shoulder and the other holding the pistol. Andre the heavy hadn't caught up yet – he'd be parking the car somewhere out of sight, Harley guessed.

'Listen, Spiru. Before your oppo comes back, I've got something you need to see, something important you'll—'

'Shut it, Harley! That ain't going to work with me.'

Manduca's breathing sounded laboured, his voice jittery: adrenaline, probably – a bad sign for someone with his finger on the trigger.

Harley looked around him in the gloom.

Had he really survived all that murderous trench warfare to die with a bullet in his back in this dingy courtyard, surrounded by cigarette butts and the rotting garbage of dismal lives?

Maybe. But not without a fight.

He slowed his own breathing and emptied his mind, the blood singing in his ears.

Manduca's hand on his shoulder – that was good, a point of reference, of contact.

If he were fast enough, he could—

'Sorry,' said Andre, suddenly appearing out of an adjacent fire exit. 'There was a copper in Greek Street, I had to take it up to Soho Square.'

'Let's get on with this. Get the door. It should be unlocked.'

* * *

The first-floor apartment had been converted into a photographic studio for the Manducas' pornography business.

Lights on tripods had been arranged around a painted backdrop of a Turkish harem. There was a mobile clothes rail, strung with a selection of elaborate lingerie – confections of spangles, lace and feathers, and, on the back wall, an alarming array of fetish paraphernalia: rubber mackintoshes and helmets, riding crops and bull whips.

'Interesting place you've got here,' said Harley. 'You decorate it yourself?'

'That's right, you keep joking, you smug bagħal.' Manduca parted the heavy curtains to check the street for passing bobbies. 'All the way to the grave.'

Harley shot a glance at Andre. He noticed the sidekick was looking a little jumpy. Well, that was something to work with.

'Come on, Spiru, don't be melodramatic. We both know you're not going to kill me.'

'No? Depends on whether you tell us where those negatives are.'

'Is that what all this is about? I told you, I haven't got a clue about any negatives. The bogeys must have them.'

Manduca shook his head. 'No, they don't.'

'Is that what your mate Quigg told you? I wouldn't trust that shicer.'

The gangster's face retained its stony glare.

'What are these negatives of, anyway? Someone important? Something compromising?'

Harley caught the briefest glimmer of a reaction.

'You working the black on someone? More of the old two-way mirror snaps from Madame Leanda, eh?'

Spiru's breathing began to quicken again, his hand gripping the pistol with increasing pressure.

'Last chance, sherlock. Leica film canister, in a brown envelope. We know it was at Turpin's place. Where is it now?'

Harley held his hands out. 'Don't know what you're talking about, pal.'

'You know, my brother is a proud man. Bringing the coppers into our business, like that? And now refusing to hand over those negatives? Well, Victor thinks you're trying to make a fool of him. He's asked me to take care of you.'

'And he knows you've interpreted that as creasing me, does he? Andre, you alright with this, are you? Accessory to murder?'

Andre shrugged. 'Spiru's in charge.'

But the heavy was just a little too slow to adopt his nonchalant expression; Harley could see he hadn't been privy to Spiru's plans.

'And what do you reckon Mori's going to think about your little idea?'

'Adler?' Manduca chuckled. 'What would a villain of his calibre care about some tin-pot sherlock?'

'We go back a long way. It was Mori who set me up with the sit-down with your brother.'

'He's right,' said Andre. 'Victor told me that—'

Manduca waved his gun to shut him up.

'So, you're big pals with Mori the Hat, are you?'

'That's right. In fact, when you picked me up, I'd just left him and one of his boys. We were having some grub together.' Harley turned to Andre with a smile. 'How do you feel about helping to off one of Mori the Hat's pals? You got the stomach for that, Andre? Don't you think that's the kind of thing to bring down a little heat on a fella's head?'

'What say we just check in with the boss about this?' said Andre. 'I mean, Adler's crew? We don't want to get on the wrong side of those boys.'

'Have you swallowed this idiot's story?' said Manduca, with a sneer. 'He's just clutching at straws. Shivering in his boots.'

'Ring him,' said Harley, nodding at the telephone set sitting on a small desk by the door. 'They'll still be there. Renzo's in Berwick Street. Get the number from the operator. Call Mori, ask him for his blessing to snuff out one of his pals.'

Harley tried to keep his voice calm, secretly praying that Solly Rosen hadn't changed his plans for a second dessert.

Manduca laughed. 'Even if your little story is true, why would we do that? See, I don't believe you *are* pals with the Jew, but even if you are? Well, I'm going to make you just disappear.' He snapped his fingers. 'Who's to know who did it?'

'Well, I hate to criticise your work, Spiru, but jumping a bloke on Wardour Street in broad daylight? Not exactly professional, is it? There's going to be all sorts of people who saw that go down. It's bound to get back to Mori sooner or later, probably already has. We call him the All-Seeing Eye.'

Andre had begun to look decidedly queasy. 'Maybe we should call the restaurant? Just to make sure. Victor would blow a fuse if he thought we'd—'

'Alright!' said Spiru, starting to lose a little of his own confidence. 'If you're mug enough to be taken in by this, then maybe you need the lesson. Call the fucking place. The sooner you find out this joker's pulling your żobb, the sooner I can get back to making him go away. Maybe then next time you'll listen to me.'

'I just think Victor would want us to check this out, that's all,' said Andre, walking to the telephone.

'Oh, Victor will get to hear all about this, don't you worry.'

While his sidekick rang the switchboard for the number, Manduca pulled up a stool and sat covering Harley with the Beretta. 'And you, sherlock, maybe you should take the opportunity to make peace with your god.'

Harley stayed silent. He'd taken a gamble but, if his luck was in, he might have just bought himself a way out of this. Composure was the thing now. He fixed the Maltese with an old-fashioned Shoreditch stare.

'Hello? Is that Renzo's?' Andre pushed the receiver of the candlestick telephone to his ear. 'I'd like to speak to one of your customers – Moriel Adler… Yes, that's right, Adler… He isn't…? Oh, but… Yes, yes, put him on, please.' He covered the mouthpiece and whispered across the room, 'Adler isn't there, but his boy Solly Rosen is.'

'Not looking good for you, is it, Harley?' said Manduca.

'Mori's a busy man,' said Harley. 'He's not got time to be hanging around all day over lunch. But Solly will fill you in. Just ask him about me.'

'Solomon? Solomon Rosen? It's Andre here… Andre Calleja… I work for the Manducas… That's right, the Spider.' Andre's smile dropped from his face as he turned to find Spiru scowling at him. 'But, you know, Victor doesn't really like to be called that… What? Oh, yeah, well, listen, do you know a sherlock by the name of Harley…? You do? And was Harley there with you for lunch…? With Mr Adler? Yeah? Alright… Well, we're here with Harley, you see, and he was saying that… No, you don't need to know where we are… Because I don't want to tell you, that's why… Now, calm down, it was an innocent enough question… You—'

'Moor Street, Solly!' shouted Harley. 'First-floor photographer's studio!'

'Shut it!' yelled Manduca, leaping off his stool. 'Jesus, Andre! Pull your finger out your arse and put that phone down!'

Andre hammered at the receiver cradle to cut the line, then threw the telephone set on the table as though it were a venomous snake.

'He's telling the truth,' he said, obviously flustered by the news. 'Rosen said they'd all had lunch together.'

Good boy, Solly, thought Harley.

'I think we should forget this. I mean, messing with one of Mori Adler's pals?'

'That's right, Andre,' said Harley, nodding benignly. 'You're speaking sense there. This is all just one big mistake. I had nothing to do with that raid. It was that poisonous cowson, Quigg. And I certainly don't know anything about that roll of film. But no hard feelings, eh? I'm happy to let bygones be bygones, so—'

'Shut it!' said Manduca, walking over to Harley, the pistol clenched tightly in his hand. 'Let a man think.'

Andre rushed over to the window. 'We should go,' he said, nervously inspecting the street below. 'Renzo's is just around the corner. They'll be here any minute.'

'Wait a moment...'

'Alright if I smoke?' asked Harley.

'Just keep your hands where I can see them. Andre, pat him down.'

But Andre was otherwise occupied, alternating between checking his watch and peering through the curtains. 'We got to go. You heard him. It's all just a big mistake.'

'I swear, Andre, if you don't pipe down, I'll put a slug through *you*. Hands up, sherlock!'

'*Hands up?*' said Harley, smiling now. 'Hands up? I reckon you've been watching too many films, Spiru.'

'Be quiet. Let's see what you've got in there.'

Keeping the gun trained on Harley's gut, Manduca began to frisk him for weapons. It was when he was delving into the private detective's inside pocket that he found the brown envelope with SM written on it.

He narrowed his eyes, weighing the packet in his hands.

'What the fuck is this? Those are my initials.'

'Oh, just a few family snapshots,' said Harley.

Manduca tore across the top of the envelope and pulled out a wad of photographs – all depicting his latest clandestine liaison in Conduit Street with his brother's ward, Vanessa.

The gangster's face blanched. He glanced furtively back at his sidekick, who was still preoccupied with checking the street for Adler's men.

'Andre, change of plan,' he said, struggling to swallow, his mouth suddenly dry. 'Maybe you're right. After all, we don't want to go stirring up the hornets' nest. Go bring the car around. I'll be down in a little while.'

'Really? You mean it?' said Andre, visibly relieved.

He dashed over to the door, but stopped, his hand on the knob. 'You're not going to do anything silly now, are you? I mean, you won't have time to move the body, they'll know it was us.'

'No. I just want a few words with our friend here. Just to smooth things over, see?'

'Alright, that's good. Yes. Smooth things over. Don't be too long, though. I'll wait for you in Old Compton Street.'

'Can I smoke now?' asked Harley, when they were alone. 'Jacket pocket, left-hand side. Take one for yourself, if you like.'

'Not until you start talking. What is this? A shakedown? I ought to kill you for having these.'

'But you're not going to, are you? See, after Quigg's raid I knew you'd come after me sooner or later. So I thought it wise to take out a little insurance policy.'

'Who squealed to you? Was it that fucking nancy boy?'

Harley feigned ignorance. 'Who? Hold on – what, that little lavender I caught you trying to throttle? You mean he knows as well? Blimey, you really ought to be a bit more careful.'

'How did you find out?'

'I'm a sherlock – it's what I do. I find things out. I'm good at it. But I never divulge my sources.'

Manduca pressed the Beretta up under Harley's chin. 'What's to stop me shooting you and taking these with me?'

Harley sighed. 'Do us both a favour. Put the gun away. Come on, we haven't got much time and I need to explain something to you.'

The Maltese pushed his face close into Harley's. He was on the cusp of saying something, but then stepped back, pocketing the pistol.

'That's better.' Harley tentatively pulled out his packet of

Gold Flake with a finger and thumb, keeping his eye all the time on the Maltese.

'I reckon you should just put this one down to experience, mate,' he said, after a long drag on his cigarette. 'I'm telling you, I had nothing to do with the police raid, and I really don't know anything about any negatives. But listen, I bear no grudges.'

He paused to pick a few tobacco strands from his tongue, watching Manduca closely, trying to gauge his reaction.

'What's going to happen now, Spiru, is that you're going to let me go and then you're going to convince your big brother he's got it all wrong about George Harley.'

'And why would I do that?'

'Because I've put copies of those photographs in the hands of a brief, with instructions that, should I disappear, they get sent to your brother. That's why.'

Spiru closed his eyes and sighed. He took a moment to process this information.

'If you go squealing to Victor about this, I *will* kill you. You do know that?'

'I don't doubt it. But only if Victor doesn't get to you first.'

Just then there was a loud banging from the floor below.

'That'll be Mori's crew,' said Harley. 'You'd best be off. Is there a back way out?'

Manduca nodded. 'I'll lose them in the triangle.'

'Off you go then. I'll square it all with Mori. You'll be alright.'

The Maltese hesitated for a moment, fighting against his instincts to flee.

There was another round of loud banging from the ground floor.

'Fuck it!' Manduca hastily pocketed the photographs. 'Alright, I'll see what I can do with Victor. But I swear, if you double-cross me, Harley…' And with that he was away, disappearing out of a door hidden behind the backdrop.

There was a loud crash from the hallway, followed by thunderous footsteps up the stairs. Soon, Harley found himself staring into the comforting countenance of an out-of-breath Solly Rosen.

'Late as usual,' said Harley. 'The party's over, Sol,'

'I thought you was in schtuk, Georgie.' Rosen bent over to catch his breath. 'Sorry – big lunch. Where are they?'

Not for the first time, Harley silently thanked the fates for delivering him such a useful pal as Solly Rosen.

'They've all run away. Thanks to you. Just like when we were kids.' He gave a playful punch to one of Rosen's huge biceps.

'Well, you'd do the same for me,' said Rosen, a little sheepishly.

He rolled the well-developed muscles in his shoulders and took a look around the room.

'I take it that your little Maltese problem has gone up a notch?'

'No, no. On the contrary.' Harley allowed himself a little self-satisfied grin. 'In fact, I think we might have just made it go away for good.'

'Garn! Really? What happened? They let you off 'cause you promised to pose for one of their smutty books?' Rosen winked and nodded towards the bondage gear on the wall.

'You're a funny man, Solomon Rosen. A very funny man.'

30

Following his eventful day, Harley was enjoying the restorative embrace of an unusually deep sleep when he was roused by a loud and persistent knocking on his front door. He rushed downstairs, bleary-eyed, and opened the door to discover that, while he'd been sleeping, a heavy mantle of saffron-coloured fog had once again descended upon the city.

Alfie Budge was at the doorway, his elbows and shoulders all a-jangle as he rubbed and stomped in the damp night air, trying to impart a little warmth.

'Thank gawd, Mr Aitch! I thought you weren't never coming.'

'What are you doing here at this time of night, Squib?'

'What d'you think I'm doing? I've been waiting for you to answer the bleedin' door, ain't I? It's taters out here!'

'Must be important.'

Budge nodded solemnly. 'Deadly important.'

'You'd better come in then.'

'No time. It's Benny Whelks. Come on!'

'Where are we going?'

'Seven Dials. We've found out what he's been up to. And it ain't good. It ain't good at all.'

'Alright, slow down. What do you mean?'

'What I mean is, I reckon there's a good chance that Benny Whelks is the bleedin' Nursery Butcher!'

* * *

Having promptly changed out of his pyjamas, Harley was now on his way with the young ragamuffin to Seven Dials. It would normally have been a twenty-minute stroll from Bell Street, but the journey had now to be conducted through streets murky with thick, yellow-brown fog. The polluted air seemed to close in around them, blurring the streetlamps to a shimmering string of will-o'-the-wisps, and transforming the familiar to something unearthly, like streets in a dream, full of unknown threat.

'I gotta be honest with you, Mr Aitch,' said Budge, straining to see ahead of him in the gloom, 'these pea soupers always give me the collywobbles.'

'You'll be alright,' said Harley. 'It's only weather.'

'Yeah, but what's lurking in that weather? That's what worries me. Hold on! What was that?'

'What?'

Budge clutched at Harley's sleeve.

'Listen. There!'

'That's a whinny.'

'A what?'

'A horse, whinnying,' said Harley, batting away the lad's hand. 'Probably just some carter, doing night deliveries.'

'Sounds like a bleedin' banshee to me.'

'It's the fog, it does weird things to the sound. There it is again. See? Just a nag. Come on, stop being so milky.'

After twenty minutes or so navigating through the gloom – with Budge growing increasingly anxious – they finally found themselves entering a narrow alleyway off Great Earl Street.

'Alright,' said Budge, slowing down. ''Ere we go. The lock-up's just around this corner.'

'What's the matter with you, son? You look like you've seen a ghost.'

'I'm bleedin' petrified, that's what. I mean, the job was dangerous enough to start with: having to shadow that nutcase Benny Whelks. But now we've found out he's the Nursery Butcher, well…'

'Let's not jump to conclusions. We don't know anything for sure yet.'

Budge stopped defiantly in his tracks and wiped his ruddy nose on the back of his hand.

'Listen, you don't have to be no sherlock to figure this one out. Me and Boots have been watching Whelks go in and out that lock-up. We've seen him take in food *and* a coil of rope; and Boots swears blind he saw him come out with bloodstains on his shirt. *Bloodstains.*' He gave a little involuntary shudder. 'Then, tonight, just before the fog set in, I managed to pluck up enough courage to sneak up and stick my lughole to the door. And I swear to you – I swear on my old mum's grave – I could hear someone *sobbing*. All muffled like. As though their mouth was gagged. I'm telling you, he's got little Eddie Muller in there.' Budge began to wring his hands in agitation. 'And if we don't get the poor little bastard out, that maniac is gonna come back and chop his head off. And then he'll rip his heart out. And then he'll—'

'Alright, Alfie! Take it easy, son. Breathe, now. That's it. Nice long breaths.'

Having managed to control his attack of nerves, Budge began wrestling with his voluminous cap.

'Need a smoke,' he said, searching through the lining. 'Had a roll-up in here somewhere.'

'Here you go.' Harley passed him a Gold Flake.

'Much obliged,' said the lad, just about holding it together. He put the shaking cigarette to his lips and let Harley light it for him.

'Tell me, how do you know Whelks isn't in there right now?'

'I don't.' Budge drew greedily on the cigarette. 'But we followed him when he came out, right? He hopped on a trolleybus to Shadwell, where his digs are. That was eleven o'clock, so I figured he was off home for the night.'

'Sounds reasonable enough. Alright then, you'd best get off home.'

'No sprucing?' The relief on the little cock sparrow's face was a sight for sore eyes. 'You don't need me to hang around, then?'

'No, I'll take it from here. You'll be fine getting home, will you?'

'Yeah, yeah, course.' Budge looked about him nervously. 'Only...'

'What is it?'

'Well, you, er...'

'Spit it out, son, I've got work to do here.'

'Well, there *was* mention of a bonus.'

Harley gave him an old-fashioned look. 'Not too petrified, then?'

'Come on, Mr Aitch. Business is business!'

Harley placed the money in Budge's outstretched hand, then smiled and took off his scarf.

'There you go,' he said, folding it gently around the street urchin's scrawny neck. 'You've done well tonight, son. Get yourself off home to bed.'

But Budge stood his ground, rubbing nervously at his raw nose.

'Thing is, I hate to think of him all trussed up like a chicken in there, ready for the oven. D'you promise, if it is little Eddie, that you'll get 'im out safe?'

Harley looked at the lad's ashen face and gave a sigh.

'I'll do all I can, Squib. But I can't promise he'll be alright. Life ain't like that, son. You should know that by now.'

'S'pose you're right. But we can always hope, can't we? Ah, well.'

Budge kicked at the ground, took one last watery-eyed look at the forbidding alleyway, and then was off, to be quickly swallowed up by the dirty-yellow night.

Harley took a cautious peek around the corner. There it was – the entry to the lock-up: a double set of wooden doors with a small yard in front of it.

If Budge were right, and Benny Whelks did have the Muller boy tied up in there, then it shouldn't be too hard a job – under cover of the thick fog – to extract him and spirit him away to safety.

So long as Whelks wasn't in there as well.

If he were, then Harley would certainly have his work cut out for him. Even with all his experience, he knew Whelks would make for a formidable opponent. Although relatively slight in build, the chiv-man was driven by a shark-like killer instinct, and, once engaged, was almost impossible to put down. And he always kept that gleaming cut-throat honed to perfection.

Before leaving the house, Harley had equipped himself with a leather pouch which contained a pared-down version of his field kit. From this he now removed a small tube of Benzedrine tablets – standard issue when he'd been in Military Intelligence. He chewed down a couple of the pink tablets to chase away the last remnants of sleep and transferred his brass knuckles to his jacket pocket.

As he crept towards the lock-up, Harley noticed his footsteps returned a curious echo, as though someone were close by, mirroring his movements. He turned and took a few steps back, trying to discern any sign of a figure in the gloom. But there was no one there. He put it down to an effect of the weather and resumed his cautious approach.

At the lock-up doors he saw, with some relief, they'd been secured by a large padlock – this obviously meant that Whelks had yet to return. Although substantial-looking, Harley recognised the device as an old 'cast heart' lock – a bit of a museum piece which shouldn't present too many problems.

As far as picking locks was concerned, George Harley had been trained by the best – Chimp Mason, the renowned cockney 'screwsman', or housebreaker, something of a folk hero in the less-salubrious drinking establishments of the East End. When he'd first decided to become a private investigator, Harley had engaged Mason – a childhood friend of his and Solly's – to train him to pick a selection of household locking devices, reasoning that such a skill was bound to come in handy in his chosen profession. This wouldn't be the first time he'd put this training to good use.

He was just removing his set of lockpicks from the pouch when a thought occurred: *the Nursery Butcher's key*.

He dug out the copy of the key which Franklin had given him and held it up, comparing the quatrefoil design to the small curlicues engraved on the padlock. He was encouraged to find there was some similarity in the motif. After all, if the key did match, not only would it unlock the door, but also the puzzle as to the identity of the child killer.

Swinging the brass cover away from the keyhole, Harley inserted the key and turned.

Nothing.

He tried it the other way.

No give, whatsoever.

Disappointed, he went back to his pick set. As expected, he had the old lock snapped open within a minute or so.

It was just as Harley was standing to remove the open padlock that the harrowing blow to the back of his skull was delivered.

Stumbling to one knee, he instinctively pistoned an elbow back, but his attacker was on him like a wild animal, clamping a sodden rag over his mouth with a vice-like grip.

The pungent odour was immediately recognisable – butyl chloride, the 'death drop'. In the few brief seconds before he lost consciousness, Harley struggled with all his might against the weight pinioning him to the wet ground. But it was futile – he was too compromised.

As he succumbed to the noxious chemical, he found himself feeling strangely comforted by the thick yellow fog, which seemed to have somehow found a way into his skull, to caress his brain into sweet, velvet oblivion.

31

HARLEY AWOKE TO a prevailing sense of nausea and the mother of all headaches. When his stomach had settled enough, he opened his eyes to find his vision blurred.

He was lying on his side. On attempting to move, he discovered his ankles and wrists were tightly bound.

'You awake, G-G-G-George?'

The unmistakable stuttering of Benny Whelks.

Harley took a few deep breaths, trying to clear his head, preparing for the worst.

'St-stay st-still. I'll g-get you up.'

In no position to resist, Harley allowed the gangster to hoist him up into a sitting position and haul him back against the wall. Once the giddiness induced by the movement had subsided, he blinked away the mist from his eyes and took stock of his surroundings.

The lock-up was much bigger than it had appeared from outside. The illumination was provided by a series of foul-smelling paraffin lamps. There was also the pervading aroma of engine oil, large patches of which stained the concrete floor. The combination of smells soon begun to turn Harley's stomach. Whelks stood before him, that graveyard face attempting a smile.

'Thought I'd done for you there. Didn't recognise you in the sm-sm-sm-smog.'

'Jesus! What did you clout me with?' asked Harley, his voice sounding strangely hoarse.

Whelks produced a small rubber-coated cosh from his pocket.

'Corporal Dunlop, eh? And then the old death drop. I s'pose it could have been worse – could have been that cut-throat of yours. I mean, people don't tend to wake up from that, do they, Benny?'

Whelks placed a defensive hand to his jacket pocket, a small tic beginning to worry his left eye.

Harley silently cursed himself. What was he doing, trying to spiel an automaton like Whelks?

'Listen. What are the chances of you cutting me loose, eh?'

'N-n-n-not just y-y-y-yet.'

The stuttering had increased – never a good sign with Whelks.

'W-w-w-what are you d-doing here?'

'I'm being a sherlock, Benny. It's my job.'

Harley snapped his head around as a haunting moan emanated from the shadows to his right.

'What the fuck was that?'

Whelks placed a finger to his lips and fixed Harley with a shark-eyed stare, as he grabbed one of the oil lamps from the floor.

As he made his way across the room with the lamp, the corner became slowly more illuminated, until Harley could see clearly where the moan had come from.

There he was. Gagged and bound to a metal chair. Blindfolded. Stark naked. Covered in bruises and dried blood.

Brendan Collins.

Once Whelks had placed the light on the floor beside his prisoner, Harley could also see that taped to the wall behind him were the photographs of Collins that had been stolen from Bell Street.

With his foggy brain beginning to clear, the private detective quickly pieced together the parts of this particularly nasty Whelks-shaped puzzle.

'No, Benny!' he shouted, trying to struggle to his feet. 'You've got it all wrong, mate! Let me explain.'

'Ch-ch-ch-cheese it!'

Harley was immediately silenced by the sight of the gleaming blade in the gangster's taut fist.

'There's your B-B-B-B-Butcher. I c-c-c-caught him for you.'

Whelks untied the blindfold.

Collins had the terror-filled eyes of a cornered animal.

The chiv-man began to tease the agent's nipple with the blunt edge of the cut-throat.

'I saw it all on that board in your attic. Everything he's done to those k-kids.'

Whelks pockmarked face was alive with tics now.

'F-f-f-f-fattening them up.'

He gave a small nick to the Collins' stomach, immediately producing a thin trickle of dark blood which began to well in the crease of his thigh.

'T-t-t-t-taking their little hearts.'

With a deft hand Whelks marked a heart shape on the pale chest, just deep enough to draw more blood.

'And all that d-d-d-dirty stuff he d-d-d-d-does.'

Up until now, Collins had sat petrified in his seat, his eyes glued to the vicious steel blade glinting before him in the lamplight. But now that Whelks had begun to playfully tap the flat of that blade against his flaccid penis, he struggled furiously against his restraints, a strange mewling sound coming from his gagged mouth.

'Enough!' shouted Harley, who had finally managed to push himself up against the wall and was now shuffling awkwardly over to the corner. 'You've got it all wrong!'

It was probably the after-effects of the butyl chloride, but it seemed to Harley that Whelks' next move defied the laws of physics – like some kind of apparition. One moment the chiv-man was crouched over the whimpering Collins, the next he was suddenly behind the detective, the cruel blade of the cut-throat pressed lightly against his Adam's apple.

'I'll c-c-croak you too,' he hissed vehemently. 'I'm gonna t-t-take his head, see? But first he's going to tell me where the Muller k-k-k-k-kid is. When I slice off that cock he'll scream like a stuck p-p-pig. Too noisy for the daytime, see? That's why I came back. The weather's p-p-p-p-perfect for such w-work.'

Whelks stood for a moment with his eyes closed, recovering from such an uncharacteristically long speech, the razor still pressed against Harley's throat.

Then, with a ghostly balletic leap, he was back at his victim's side.

Holding the steel blade to the agent's eyes as a mimed warning – as though the wretched man needed any reminding of the jeopardy he was in – he reached behind and untied the gag.

Collins watched with startled eyes as Whelks slowly and deliberately pulled on a leather glove, then pinched the limp penis between his thumb and forefinger.

'Where's the k-k-kid?'

'What kid?' Collins' voice was childlike, barely a whisper. He stared in abject terror at the razor poised above his stretched-out cock.

Watching this play out from a few yards away, Harley's mind scrabbled for a plan. He flipped from one scenario to the next, but there was nothing. Over the last few days he'd become resigned to the fact the literary agent was just a patsy.

Why would anyone go to such elaborate ends as to kill the real Madame Leanda and replace her with a stooge if it wasn't to direct attention away from the real killer? And if Collins wasn't the Nursery Butcher, then how could he possibly tell Whelks where Eddie Muller was? And what could Harley do to intervene? Even with all his faculties intact, any attempt to overpower a razor-wielding Benny Whelks was going to be a tall order – with his hands and feet bound it would be sheer suicide. All he could do was stand there impotently in that dismal gloomy space and watch the horror unfold – with the sickening knowledge that, in some way, he was partly responsible for it.

Over in the corner Whelks had lowered his head to shake off a flurry of tics and, as he raised it again, his face – lurid in the sickly glow of the oil lamp – was the stuff of nightmares.

He tilted the razor, reflecting a strip of light across Collins' eyes.

'One more ch-chance. Where… is… Eddie… M-M-M-Muller?'

Collins opened his mouth wide, saliva stringing at the corners, his head turning in a slow shake, trying to negate the inevitable.

A tear trickled down his cheek.

But no sound came out.

Whelks nodded once. Stretched another quarter inch from the agent's penis. Angled the blade, and—

'Benny! Put that thing down, son! You don't know where it's been.'

The shock of Mori Adler bursting into the lock-up produced a high-pitched yelp from Collins and had Harley stumbling over onto his knees.

Whelks, however, retained his hold on Collins' Hampton, his left eye now twitching in a frenzied Morse code as he stared in confusion at his boss.

Adler removed the cigar from his mouth. 'Benjamin,' he said, his voice now moderated to a calming, paternal purr. 'That'll do, son. Put the razor away. We'll have a little chat and then decide the best course of action. You asked me to come over here, remember? Alone? Well, here I am.'

Whelks closed his eyes, gave a weary sigh and then folded the razor's blade back into its mother-of-pearl body.

'There's a good lad.'

Adler closed the door and gave the lock-up a quick once-over. He walked over to Harley, who had managed to manoeuvre himself to a sitting position again.

'You look a bit tied up at the moment, George. You had a falling out with our Benny?'

'I was following a lead, on the missing Muller kid. Made the mistake of breaking into this place. Next thing I know I'm seeing stars and sucking on a handkerchief-full of death drop.'

'Shame on you. Getting caught out like that. You want to up your game, son.'

'Yeah, well. He's like a soddin' phantom, that one, ain't he?'

Harley had begun to relax a little, but now his heart skipped a beat as Adler produced a large flick knife from his jacket pocket. The mobster loomed in close, bringing with him a cloud of Havana smoke and expensive cologne.

'Mori, listen. I—'

'Schtum!'

Adler sliced through the ropes securing Harley's hands and feet.

'Get up out of the dirt. You'll ruin your suit. That's a nice bit of schmutter, that.'

Harley struggled to his feet and began to explore the tender, egg-shaped lump on the back of his head.

'So, what do we have here?' Adler was now standing over the pitiful-looking prisoner, who was still wide-eyed and shaking from his recent ordeal.

'He's the one, b-b-b-boss,' hissed Whelks, zealous hatred in his eyes. 'The N-Nursery B-B-B-B-Butcher.'

'Never! This schmendrik?' said Adler, incredulously, blowing smoke into Collins' face as he leant in to get a closer look at the photographs taped to the wall.

'Please help me,' whispered Collins, openly weeping now. 'I can get you money, anything. Please.'

Adler retrieved the discarded gag from the floor. 'Stick that back in his mooey, Benny. Just while we have our little chat.'

'Can I speak?' asked Harley as Whelks muzzled Collins.

Adler held his large hands out, showing a flash of gold in his grin. 'We're all friends here, ain't we?'

'Listen. We've got a right royal mess on our hands, here, and that's stone ginger. See, Benny took it upon himself to break into my gaff, so as he could—'

'Wait a minute!' Adler pointed at Whelks with his Romeo y Julieta. 'He did what?'

'He broke into my place, in Bell Street. Least, I'm assuming it was him.'

'Benjamin? Is this true?'

Whelks nodded, placing a hand to his twitching cheek. 'It's that M-M-Muller kid. It's been eating me up. I w-w-wanted to know whether they had any leads.'

'What, are you meshuggener? Why would you do such a thing? George is like one of our own. Would you do the same to Solomon, or Big? You want I should break into *your* gaff, go through your things, eh? Well?'

'C-c-c-course not, Mori.'

'No. Of course not. I'm disappointed, Benjamin. Very disappointed. This, I don't expect from my right-hand man.'

Adler took off his trilby to rake his fingers through the thick waves of oiled hair.

'Alright, George,' he said, positioning the hat back on, just so. 'Please continue.'

'Well, it's a long story, but the crux of it is that I'd been given a false lead about our friend here being a possible for the Nursery Butcher.'

'S-s-s-s-suspect n-n-number one, it s-said!' protested Whelks.

'Schtum!' barked Adler. 'I won't tell you again. Go on, George.'

'Well, this lead turned out to be a load of old madam. A malicious fit-up.' Harley looked at Whelks as he said this. 'No substance in it at all. But the false information was still there, mixed in with all the other case notes in my attic at Bell Street.'

Adler nodded. 'I see, so Benny does his little screwsman turn, sees this false lead, and puts two and two together to make five. Am I right?'

'That's about the size of it.'

'The ph-ph-ph-ph-photographs,' murmured Whelks.

'Yeah, what about these mugshots?' said Adler peering at the print of Collins bent over the rocking horse, and then at the one of him dressed in the sailor suit. 'I mean, if he's innocent, what's all this malarkey?'

'My guess is it's just an unhappy coincidence; one that was taken advantage of by the shicers who fed me the moody lead. See, I think our friend here likes to indulge in a bit of sexual masochism.'

'Excuse me?' said Adler, punctuating his question with a smoke ring. 'Sexual what?'

'Masochism. He likes getting spanked, pretending he's back in the nursery.'

'I see. One of the rubber mackintosh brigade, eh? Public schoolboy?'

'As a matter of fact, I think he is.'

Adler took a long draw on his cigar.

'Got a name, has he?'

'Brendan Collins,' said Harley.

From the reaction in Collins' eyes, the revelation of his identity seemed to have caused him as much anguish as Whelks' razor.

'What does he do, this Brendan Collins?'

'He's a literary agent.'

The mobster sniffed and then tapped a large plug of ash from the end of his Havana.

'So, let me summarise. We have Mr Brendan Collins here, a civilian – innocent of any crime that we know of – who Benny has kidnapped, held under unlawful arrest, and exposed to a prolonged bout of mental and physical torture, all because he got the wrong end of the stick after a little spot of housebreaking – is that about the size of it?'

'You should have been a brief, Mori.'

'Don't be flippant. This is a serious matter.'

The mobster slid a large beringed hand into the inside of his jacket. When it reappeared, Harley was horrified to see it held a Mauser semi-automatic pistol.

'What are you doing?' asked Harley, carefully.

'I'm afraid we're going to have to off him.'

'What?'

'Mr Brendan Collins,' said Adler, waving the gun at the tied-up literary agent, who had begun to hyperventilate. 'After all, he's clocked our faces. If he goes to the bogeys with this, they'll collar Benny and throw away the key. And likely do the same to me and you. It's unfortunate, but he's going to have to disappear.'

'Unfortunate?' said Harley, feeling his nausea returning. 'And what about me? You going to off me as well?'

'Don't be ridiculous. You're staunch, everyone knows that. You're quite safe.'

'Oh yeah, apart from being an accessory to the murder of an innocent man,' said Harley. The throbbing in his head had increased to a sickening level. 'Listen, Mori. Put the gun away. You can't kill him.'

'Oh, yeah? Why's that then?'

'Because, if you do, it'll be the beginning of the end.'

Adler chuckled ominously, then pointed the pistol at Harley. He cocked his head like an inquisitive Great Dane.

'Says who?'

Harley sighed. 'Brendan Collins, as well as being the literary agent for Alasdair Cassina, is also the son and heir of the Right Honourable Sir Hugh Collins, Parliamentary Under-Secretary of State for the Home Department. He's one of theirs. The son of a government minister. If he disappears, they'd never let it go. They'll hunt us all down like dogs. After all, Benny's good, but who's to say nobody saw him take Collins off the street?'

Adler lowered the Mauser. He glowered at Whelks, arranging and rearranging his grip on the gun as it hung by his side.

'What have you fucking done, Benny? And don't you dare say sorry, you asterbar!'

The mobster paced the room for a while, chewing on his cigar.

'I might have a solution,' said Harley, walking over to Collins, showing his empty hands to Adler and Whelks. 'A way out.'

'What way out, Einstein?' said Adler. 'There ain't no way out. Whatever happens, old rubber mackintosh there has seen our faces. And even if he does relish a bit of punishment, he's hardly going to turn the other cheek after what Benny's dealt out to him, is he?'

Harley plucked the photographs from the wall and handed them to Adler.

'But you've got *these*. Can I take off his gag for a moment?'

Adler narrowed his eyes, then nodded.

'Brendan,' said Harley, placing his jacket over Collins' lap and then crouching down so their eyes were at the same level. 'I know this must have been traumatic for you, and it can't help to discover that it's all because of a misunderstanding, but you're a bright lad. You've heard our predicament here. Tell me honestly: what would happen if those photographs were made public?'

Collins stared at the floor. 'I'm engaged to be married. I'd be ruined.'

Harley looked up at Adler.

'And your old man's political career would no doubt suffer from such a scandal, right?'

Collins gave a little juddering intake of breath, then nodded quickly.

Harley stood up. 'There's your way out, Mori.'

Adler stood smoking his cigar for a while, quietly contemplating the series of photographs. Then, to Harley's relief, he pushed the Mauser back into his inside pocket.

'We'll take a gamble on your plan.' He tapped Harley out of the way and crouched down in front of Collins, his knees cracking like rifle shots. 'But listen up, Mr Brendan Collins. If I get even a sniff of this being reported to Scotland Yard – and, believe me, my friend, I've got eyes and ears everywhere – then I'll personally make sure Benjamin finishes the job he started here. Got it?'

'Yes, of course,' whispered Collins.

'Alright, Benny. Untie the man and get him his clothes. I've got the Bentley outside; we'll take him over to Doc Shandy's and get him checked over.'

'No!' said Collins. 'No doctors! There'll be questions.'

'Bright lad,' said Adler, beaming again now. 'It reassures me to hear you talking about confidentiality. But don't you worry about Doc Shandy – he's our tame medic, see. Whether he's sewing 'em up or signing their death certificate, he never asks questions.' Adler tapped the side of his Roman general's nose.

Harley sparked up a Gold Flake, grimacing a little at its effect on his delicate stomach.

'Listen, Mori. Before you go, can I have a quick word with Brendan, in private?'

Adler pointed his chin at Harley and contemplated this request with a furrowed brow. Then he grunted. 'Why not? I suppose we owe you something for all this palaver. No funny tricks, though. Benny and me will be just outside, in the car.'

Once he'd helped Collins into his clothes, Harley gave him a cigarette and sat him back down in the chair.

'All I can say, fella, is you'd better not turn out to be the bleedin' Nursery Butcher.'

Harley was expecting an emotional reaction from Collins. But he just looked beaten. Dead-eyed.

'Of course I'm not,' he said mechanically.

Somehow this sounded even more genuine than an impassioned plea of innocence.

'No. But you think your good mate Alasdair Cassina might be, right?'

This did stimulate Collins a little, bringing the fear back to his eyes.

'Listen, Brendan. This is going to sound unbelievable after what's just happened here, but I'm actually a private detective, working alongside the police on the Nursery Butcher investigation. Now, I'd fully understand if you refuse to cooperate, but I want to ask you about Alasdair. Did you know he was being questioned about the Nursery Butcher case?'

Collins had become unresponsive again, staring at the ground, the cigarette smoke spiralling up from his shaking fingers.

'I know you've been through the mill here,' said Harley. 'I wouldn't be asking if it wasn't important. You see, I'm becoming convinced there's some kind of conspiracy to mislead this investigation. To point the finger at you and Cassina. But I need proof. We are talking about child murder here.'

'Yes,' said Collins eventually, after a long pause. But he continued to avoid Harley's gaze. 'I did know the police wanted to speak to Alasdair. I'd only just heard about it when… when that thug out there, jumped me.'

'We've spoken to Professor Morkens,' said Harley. 'We know about that book you found at Cassina's flat – *The Grimoire of Valentinus*.'

Collins now looked up, concern back in his eyes.

'He told you about that?'

'Oh, I don't think you should be too hard on the professor. He felt he had a moral obligation to say something.'

'What a mess,' whispered the agent. He covered his face with his hands. 'What a damned fool I've been. When those photographs get out, I'll… it'll be the end of…' His shoulders began to judder with sobbing. 'Barbara…'

Harley put a hand on his arm.

'They're not going to get out – as long as you don't go to the police about your abduction. It's a Mexican standoff.'

'Oh, yes?' Collins sat up, wiping the tears from his eyes. 'And where did *you* get the photographs from? Who's to say there aren't other copies out there?'

Harley took a drag on his Gold Flake. 'I'm not going to lie, I can't promise you that.'

'No. You can't. But it hardly matters anyway, seeing as I'm likely to have my throat cut as soon as I get into that motor car.'

Harley shook his head. 'No. Mori's a lot of things, but he ain't stupid. He heard what I said about your father.'

'You'll forgive me, Harley, if I don't share your unwavering confidence in your friends.'

'What if I come with you?' asked Harley. 'To Doc Shandy's?'

Collins nodded fervently, the tears threatening his eyes again.

'Alright then. But just one more question before you go. That book, the grimoire – have you any idea where Cassina got it from?'

'I know exactly where he got it from,' said Collins in a hushed tone. 'Somebody called Perrine.'

'Perrine?'

'A damned bad influence, in my opinion. Alasdair's been pretty cagey about this chap, but I'm convinced he's been getting some of his more outlandish ideas from him. God knows where they met. He really does seem to have some kind of hold over Alasdair.'

'Got a description?'

'Looks somewhat like a tramp. Mutton chop whiskers. Most extraordinary-looking.'

'Wait a minute.' Harley took out his notebook and flicked back to the entries he'd made when quizzing Cynthia about her visit to the AOU meeting. 'Here we go – this Perrine fella, does he wear a big trench coat and a battered old beaver hat?'

'That's him.'

'And you think that Perrine gave Cassina that grimoire?'

'I know he did.'

'Tell me – have you ever heard of something called the Ancient Order of the Unicursal?'

Harley watched Collins' eyes, but they didn't seem to register any significance to the name.

The agent shook his head then stood up, a little stiffly, wincing at a pain in his back. 'One question, you said. I'm afraid we shall have to continue this some other time.' He looked anxiously towards the open door. 'If there'll be another time, that is.'

32

EDDIE AWOKE TO the caress of a fingertip drawn lightly across his cheek. The bedroom was warm, a vigorous fire crackling in the grate. Outside, the wind buffeted the house, hurling rain against the old leaded lights like handfuls of wet rice.

'Wake up, Edward,' said the man, sitting on the edge of the bed, his dark eyes reflecting the flickering fire through the holes in his burgundy leather goat mask. 'I need to go away again. Your lunch is over there, on the tray. Make sure you finish it all up, won't you?'

The goat man stood up and walked over to the window, placing his long pale fingers against the glass.

'You know, you've become rather a favourite of mine. I've enjoyed our time together.'

He turned his gaze back to the bed. 'On the tray, you will also find a key.'

A particularly loud squall thrashed against the house as if in reaction to this statement. Eddie sat up in bed, rubbing the sleep from his eyes as he peered over at the dressing table.

'Now, dear child, this is *not* the key to your freedom; why would you seek such a thing, after all? Where could you possibly go after this? Rather, it is the key to the adjacent chamber, in which reside some of your predecessors.' He glared at Eddie, his sonorous voice suddenly filling the room, joining the swell of the storm outside. 'I forbid you to enter that room, Edward. Do you understand? *Forbid you.*'

The pale fingers now caressed the child's warm cheek.

'Its inhabitants would not make for entertaining playmates. I forbid, and yet… the choice is still yours, the key at your disposal. Do you understand?'

Eddie coughed. He tried to find his voice. 'Please, I… I don't wanna go back in the cage.'

The goat man chuckled.

After the door had closed on the bedroom, after the bolts had been drawn, Eddie wriggled back down under the protection of the covers. Before long he was asleep once more, his mind gently lapped by the waves of soporific drugs as he slipped back into strange dreams, of talking goats and fiery angels with shining armour.

33

'SAY THAT NAME again.' DCI Franklin's voice was faint and crackly on the other end of the telephone.

'Hold on, the money's running out.'

Harley fed another penny into the slot.

'Perrine. Elderly bloke. Large trench coat, battered old beaver hat and bushy whiskers. Cynthia clocked him at the AOU meeting. Mean anything to you?'

'No. But I'll have it looked into. Perrine, you say? Got it. By the way, your chum Dora has now positively identified Madame Leanda's body. Rum sort, that Dora, even for a street-walker.'

'Don't let her hear you call her that. Courtesan to the rich and famous is our Dora.'

'I see.' Franklin gave a little disapproving cough. 'Well, we now have it confirmed that whoever gave you those photographs of Collins was certainly *not* the late Madame Leanda. We need to track her down, George.'

Damn the woman! He still couldn't hear the name without conjuring those deep blue eyes and the Theda Bara curves.

'Believe me, I intend to.'

'Now, listen. About that group of kids from the children's homes, on board the HMS *Jervis Bay*.'

'Yes?'

'We've now heard back from the Sisters of Galilee.'

'Who?'

'The nuns who escorted the children on the voyage.'

'And?' asked Harley, with anticipation.

'They confirmed that all the children who boarded the ship on the second of March in Southampton arrived safely in Melbourne forty-two days later, and are now either boarded with foster families or enrolled in the farm schools.'

'Bugger!'

'Hold on. The thing is – the *Jervis Bay* passenger list for that voyage doesn't tally with the list of children's names which you gave me. It's short by two. Two young orphans who were never on that ship. Edwin Todd and Ronald Cleary.'

'Jesus! So, finally, we have names for two of our victims.'

'Well, let's not jump to conclusions. All we know is they didn't turn up for the voyage. They might have just decided to play truant in order to avoid being shipped out to the colonies. And no one could blame them for that.'

'But that photograph. One of them is a dead ringer for our first decapitated head.'

'I'm afraid you're the only one entirely convinced of that. It's not that clear an image.'

'What?'

'Listen, I have officers researching the boys' records, seeing if we can't get our hands on any other likenesses of them to confirm your theory. But, in the meantime let's concentrate on our current leads, shall we?'

'It feels right to me.'

'Noted. But we need to have the evidence. Time will tell. Now, Brendan Collins.'

'What about him?' asked Harley, with a little trepidation.

'I tried to contact him, but it would appear he's gone AWOL. Missed a few important meetings, apparently. Makes me a little nervous, I must say; given what's been going on.'

'I wouldn't worry too much.' Harley tried to sound as nonchalant as possible. 'I'm sure he'll turn up.'

'Well, let's hope so. Cassina's been kicking up a stink since I had him in for questioning. Threatening all sorts of legal action. I'd like to speak to Collins, see if we can't calm him down a little.'

'My guess is it's all bluster. I've met Cassina's type before. They give it the big "I am", but, when push comes to shove, they're terrified of the thought of actually spending any time inside a police cell.'

'You still think he has no involvement in the murders?'

'I know Collins was a false lead. But Cassina? I really don't know now. There's something linking all these players together – Victor Manduca, von Görlitz, our moody Madame Leanda, this character Perrine. I don't think he actually carried out the murders, but I'm beginning to accept the possibility that Cassina might be involved somehow.'

'I think I might agree with you there,' said Franklin. 'By the way, I'm sure you've seen all the sentimental claptrap the *Daily Oracle* has been printing about Eddie Muller's disappearance. Well, against my advice, the super has publicly acknowledged the possibility that he might be a victim of the Butcher.'

'On what evidence?'

'I know, I know – but there it is. Now, in her statement, the mother mentions a fellow called Treamer. Take this down.'

'Hold on.' Harley took out his notepad and pencil. 'Go on; Treamer, right?'

'Yes, Horace Treamer. Works as a rent-collector and estate agent in Limehouse. Treamer & Son, they have an office just off Commercial Road. According to Rose Muller's statement, this Treamer made a visit to the house on the day of the boy's disappearance, about the rent arrears. But when I quizzed her about it, she became quite anxious. Inexplicably so. In my opinion Rose Muller knows something about Horace Treamer that she's holding back. I had one of my officers go to question him but, by all accounts, he's a slippery character. Denied knowing anything of any relevance. This Treamer has no official record, but there are rumours – receiving stolen property, extortion, that kind of thing. Nothing substantiated, but all reasons to make him a person of interest.'

'You want me to take a closer look at him?'

'Exactly. After all, I understand you might have some useful connections in the Limehouse area?'

'Let me see what I can dig up.'

'Thanks. But go easy now. The Muller case is hot property in the press at the moment, thanks to that blasted Enoch Craster. We can ill afford to give him any further ammunition to attack us with in one of those damned articles of his.'

'I hear you. Alright, I'd better get on.'

'Hold on, George, there's one more thing. The specialists at the British Museum have now analysed that fragment of embroidery packed into the preserved head found on the tram.'

'And?'

'Well, it looks like Sir Bernard was on the money. The embroidered image does indeed depict a scene from the Book of Revelation, chapter thirteen. I'm looking at a photograph of it here. It's some sort of mythical creature, like a lion, but with seven heads, holding a staff with a fleur-de-lis on it. Damned odd! I looked the chapter up. I have it jotted down here somewhere. Ah! Here it is: "And I saw a beast coming out of the sea. It had ten horns and seven heads, with ten crowns on its horns, and on each head a blasphemous name." I thought this bit might be relevant, listen: "One of the heads of the beast seemed to have had a fatal wound, but the fatal wound had been healed. The whole world was filled with wonder and followed the beast." What do you think? Does it tie in with any of your theories? I know you were looking into references to decapitations in the Bible.'

'I don't know. I'll need to research it further. Let me write that down. Chapter thirteen, you said?'

'That's correct.'

'And did they give any indication as to its age, where it might have come from?'

Harley heard the characteristic tapping of Franklin's pipe stem against his teeth. 'They did. And that's where it gets even odder. You see, the embroidery is exactly the same image as that shown in one of the panels in what's called the *Apocalypse Tapestry*, a rare French medieval piece commissioned by the Duke of Anjou in the fourteenth century.'

'Where is this tapestry today?'

'Well, it's not really widely known about, but it's in Angers Cathedral.'

'So, presumably, in order to make his copy, our killer has either visited Angers, or has some interest in medieval history.'

'But that's just it. The embroidery found in the child's skull isn't a modern copy. In fact, the specialists at the British Museum can't even be sure if it doesn't predate the original. It's possibly some kind of test design for the larger piece. According to them, it's an exquisite example of French embroidery from the 1300s. Priceless, apparently.'

Harley tipped his hat back an inch or so. 'This bugger is too clever for his own good. With a bit of luck, he'll end up tying himself up in knots. Alright. Let me deal with this Treamer character first and then I'll take a look at the history of this Apocalypse Tapestry. Keep me updated from your end.'

Harley terminated the call, then dialled the operator.

'Hello? Could you put me through to the Lotus Blossom restaurant in Limehouse… Thanks…'

'Lil? It's George... Oh, can't complain... Yeah, she's good, thanks... Listen, Lil – what do you know about a character named Horace Treamer...? Really? Go on...'

* * *

''Fraid this one's almost over,' said the usherette.

'That's alright, my dear,' said Enoch Craster, directing his comments to the young woman's prominent cleavage. 'I'm here to meet someone.'

'Suit yourself,' she said coolly, her expression balanced somewhere between supercilious and bored. She ripped his ticket in half and gave a perfunctory tug at the heavy curtain.

The reporter made his way cautiously up the aisle of the darkened cinema. On the screen behind him, the Flying Scotsman hurtled past as a young woman struggled desperately with a set of railway points – another lacklustre part-silent British production, as intimated by the sparse audience attendance. Still, those who had forked out for a sixpenny seat seemed suitably engaged. Their expressionless faces were bathed in the screen's silvery aura, anaesthetised for a while from their mundane lives.

Craster felt his way along to the back row and squeezed into one of the seats. Within a minute or so – just as the anonymous note had indicated would happen – he was tapped on the shoulder with a rolled-up copy of *The Times*.

'Thank you for coming, Mr Craster,' the stranger murmured as he sat down. His accent suggested a certain level of refinement – the tang of stale spirits and unwashed clothing suggested otherwise.

'I just hope you're not wasting my time here, friend. I'm a busy man.'

'Oh, I warrant by the end of our conversation you'll think your sixpence well-spent.'

Craster gave a dismissive sniff and pulled out his notepad. 'So, come on then – what's this "red-hot tip" that's going to make my career? I believe that was the phrase you used in your note.'

'It's as simple as this. I am going to give you the Nursery Butcher.'

'Oh, yes?' The journalist's sneer was wasted in the dark. He sighed as he put away his notebook again. 'Do you know how many crank letters we get sent every day, from lunatics purporting to know the killer's identity?'

'I wouldn't have a clue. Nor do I care. I'm no lunatic, Mr Craster. Far from it. And I'm not merely going to reveal his identity. I'm going to lead you right to him. Expose him in his lair, surrounded by the carcasses of his victims.'

'Are you, indeed? And why on earth should I believe you, Mr...?'

'Ah, no. No names just yet, I'm afraid. I shall require some assurances about my protection first. As for proof, well now, let me see...'

Craster's eyes were getting accustomed to the gloom, and he could just make out the man rummaging in the inside pocket of his shabby overcoat. The fellow had the dishevelled appearance of one of the many unfortunates that could be seen tramping the streets of late. Craster guessed he was somewhere in his late sixties – though it was difficult to be certain in the dim light. Obviously he was some kind of alcoholic fantasist.

'Here we are. This ought to do it.'

Craster squinted at the small, striped tin which had been placed in his lap. 'Humbugs?' He gave it a shake and began to prise the lid off.

'It's evidence that will prove to you I'm telling the truth.'

'Really?' The journalist fished out something wrapped up in a muslin cloth. 'What is it exactly?'

'A toe. Removed from the victim left in the butcher's shop.'

The small squeal of disgust that Craster emitted had a good number of heads turning around in the surrounding seats.

'A pathologist should be able to verify it as a match. I also have photographs of the scenes and other evidence to verify my information. But we must move quickly. Strike while the iron is hot.'

'Really? And erm...' Craster quickly dropped the withered digit back into the tin. 'What is it you'd want in return, exactly?'

'For turning King's evidence against the killer, I'll need full assurances from the authorities of my immunity from prosecution. For leading you to the biggest scoop your paper has ever had? For that I shall require money. Filthy lucre. And lots of it. Enough to move far away from this wretched Gehenna and start my life anew. Could you arrange that, do you think?'

'Well, my boss, Lord Rainsworth, is a very rich and powerful man,' said Craster, quickly regaining his composure at the realisation of the significance of such an exclusive. 'If what you say is true, my friend, then I don't see why we can't fulfil everybody's dreams.'

'That's good. Yes, that's very good indeed.' The old man nodded enthusiastically and began to drink greedily from his hip flask.

34

DEVOID OF ANY empathy with the young victims – or, indeed, of any burning compulsion to see justice done – Detective Inspector Aloysius Quigg saw the Nursery Butcher investigation as nothing more than a wonderful opportunity to both further his career and achieve the fame and recognition he felt he so rightly deserved. The only obstacle he faced was the stodgy professionalism of DCI Franklin. That and the fact that his network of cronies and informants had, as yet, failed to offer up any plausible suspect on whom a charge might be made to stick. He had therefore been delighted when his fellow Lodge member, Enoch Craster, had informed him of the exciting meeting with Martin Perrine at the Astoria Picture Theatre.

'Good Lord, Quigg!' exclaimed Superintendent Banks, as Quigg now relayed this compelling news to his superior. 'If what you say is correct, then we have him.' He indicated the seat before him. 'Sit, sit. Now, you say, as well as the missing digit, this character is conversant with facts about the case that hadn't been made available to the press?'

'Indeed, sir. He has photographs of the scenes – *before* the victims were discovered.'

'Before? And how are we to be certain that this scoundrel doesn't have blood on his own hands, eh? After all, he's asking for immunity from prosecution, is he not?'

'Well, sir, that might well be the case…' Quigg paused to arrange his fleshy jowls around an ingratiating smile. 'But one would imagine it's more by *association*, wouldn't you think? He can't be our main protagonist. Otherwise, what on earth would induce him to come forward in the first place?'

'True enough, I suppose.'

'No, it's much more likely he's associated by circumstance. And I think, in situations such as these, we must think of the greater good, sir. Heaven knows, I'm the last person to allow a felon off the hook, but if granting him immunity leads to a swift apprehension of the main architect of these murderous atrocities, then, well, I think we owe it to the great British public to see it through, don't you?'

'Quite right, quite right,' said the superintendent, nodding earnestly. 'What's the fellow's name again?'

'Perrine. Martin Perrine. Probably a pseudonym, I would think. Can't find anything on him in our records.'

'Hmm, I see.' The superintendent tapped his pen thoughtfully against his blotter. 'Of course, the whole thing will need to be handled carefully, Quigg, vis-à-vis the press, et cetera. We can't be seen to be doing deals with criminals, whatever the outcome.'

'Of course, superintendent.' Quigg leant his elbows on the desk and tented his hands, as though thinking deeply about the problem for the first time. 'With that in mind, I propose we give exclusive rights to the *Daily Oracle*. After all, it was Enoch Craster who brought us the lead in the first place. I've worked with the fellow in the past. I can vouch he'll be completely receptive to our direction. Perrine obviously has a certain amount of trust in Craster, to go to him as his first point of contact.'

'Well,' said the superintendent, 'you'll have to square it with DCI Franklin first.'

'Ah.' Quigg leant back in his chair and tapped his fingers against his lips.

'You have a problem with that?'

'Well, sir, it's just that I know there's some bad blood between Mr Craster and Detective Inspector Franklin. Some minor misunderstanding in the past.'

'Detective *Chief* Inspector Franklin.'

'Yes, of course. Only, we wouldn't want a clash of personalities to scupper our chances with such an important case, would we, sir?'

'Well, I—'

'No. I wonder if it might be more prudent for *me* to deal with this directly. Perrine has intimated that he requires a certain level of… well, *hospitality*, I suppose you would call it, before he reveals all the details of the murders. I know the *Oracle* are willing to foot the bill for these expenses – better that than the good old British taxpayer, hmm? He has also suggested that he would feel most comfortable making his revelations directly to Craster. I could work in tandem with him to procure the statement, and when we have the necessary evidence, well, then we can apprehend the murderer. At that stage, obviously, DCI Franklin could take charge again. If you felt it necessary.'

'It sounds a little unorthodox. However, as you say, if it leads to the arrest of the Nursery Butcher, maybe it warrants a little bending of the rules. After all, one should always be open to initiative.'

'Quite so, sir. And if it all turns out this Perrine has been leading us up the garden path? Why, then DCI Franklin will be left untainted by the whole fiasco, and he'll be free to continue the investigation along other lines.'

'I must say, that's an extremely selfless attitude, Detective Inspector.'

Quigg attempted a look of humility but found he couldn't quite carry it off.

'One tries one's best, sir.'

'Very well, Quigg. Proceed as planned, but with caution. And I want regular updates. If you manage to pull this off, man, it'll be quite a coup. But God help us if it all goes wrong.'

* * *

Harley dropped down into the small back yard off Commercial Road. He stayed crouched for a while, watching the back elevation of the building, checking for any sign of habitation. He silently cursed the cloudless night sky above him, which was flaunting a large theatrical full moon, bathing the yard in a silvery glare. Where was the London fog when you needed it? No screwsman worth his salt would go out on a night like this. But he hadn't the luxury of waiting for more accommodating weather. It had been clear from Limehouse Lil's appraisal of Horace Treamer that the rent-collector was exactly the kind of mercenary lowlife to associate with kidnappers and pederasts – if the price was right. Moreover, Lil was certain that one of the properties the Treamers looked after was the St Stephen's Home for Homeless Boys, in the East India Dock Road. This shicer definitely warranted closer inspection.

Satisfied that his entrance into the yard had gone unobserved, Harley now cautiously made his way towards the building. Reasoning that the rent-collection business would, from time to time, necessitate the storing of large amounts of cash on the premises, Harley knew there was a good chance the back door – and possibly the windows on the ground floor – would be secured with some kind of bars. The first-floor windows, however, were another story; it looked like they hadn't seen a new coat of paint in years – which meant, with a little luck, the frames would be rotten enough to yield to a little coaxing with a screwdriver.

A few minutes later – with the aid of a strategically placed dustbin – Harley had clambered up onto the flat roof and forced the catch on the stairwell window. He now stood on the first-floor landing, waiting for his breathing to calm, and listening for the creak of a floorboard or the opening of a door – anything that might indicate a nightwatchman having been alerted to the break-in.

A quick scan of the ground floor confirmed his suspicions as to the security precautions of Treamer & Son. All the rear doors and windows were locked and barred, and there was a large, impressive-looking safe in the rear office – obviously where the firm kept their cash box and any confidential client information. Equally well secured was a wall-mounted key cabinet, which no doubt housed the keys to the various properties the company was responsible for.

Harley checked his watch, giving himself a ten-minute window to perform a search of the premises. He then lit a small stub of candle he'd taken from his field pack and began to systematically sift through any paperwork that had been left out on desks or in unlocked drawers. After five of his allocated minutes, it had become obvious that, regardless of what might be said about his moral character, Horace Treamer was extremely disciplined in keeping his confidential business papers under lock and key. A little frustrated, Harley now made his way into the front area and began a search of what looked to be the receptionist's desk.

Here his luck began to change. On top of the in-tray was the office diary.

He quickly turned to the date of Eddie Muller's disappearance. There were a few names and times, but nothing that held any obvious significance to the case. He began to flick back page by page, until – on an entry just over a week before the Muller boy was taken – he discovered something that he knew might well turn out to be the missing domino piece to set all the other clues tumbling together in a beautiful chain of connectivity:

2.00pm. Cruickshank's Yard. Mr Perrine.

Harley checked his watch again, then made directly for the key cabinet. The locking device wasn't something he recognised – no doubt Chimp Mason would have it sprung before you could say 'Jack Robinson', but he didn't fancy taking a chance on working on an unknown mechanism for half an hour or so in such a risky environment. Obviously, he could wrench the thing off the wall and jemmy it open. But then he'd run the risk of arousing sleeping neighbours or a passing bobby; and, besides, the idea was to extract the keys to the property without it being noticed – not until it was too late, anyway.

He decided to take a punt on human nature. He went back to the receptionist's desk, opened the top right-hand drawer and pushed his hand right to the back.

There it was – a small key. You could always rely on the laziness of human routine.

Back in the rear office Harley had the key safe unlocked and the bunch labelled 'Cruickshank' in his pocket in under a minute. He was just relocking the cabinet when he heard voices outside.

Two people: a woman and a man.

Perhaps they were just using the doorway for a convenient spot to smooch in on their way back from the pub?

No. A key in the lock!

The voices louder now, in the lobby.

Harley ducked down behind the desk and retrieved his brass knuckles from his pocket.

'What's all this, Horace?' The woman's voice was coarse, slurred a little by drink. 'You promised me a hotel this time.'

'Gladys, please. You'll wake the neighbours.'

'Don't you Gladys me! I told you, I want a bit of duck down under my arse, not a bleedin' writing desk!'

'Shush! There's something wrong here. That light...'

With a sinking feeling Harley realised he'd left the candle stub burning in the ashtray on the reception desk.

'Who's there!'

Although this was shouted with gusto, there was a tremolo of fear in Treamer's voice.

'I-I warn you, I'm armed, you know!'

Harley slid on the knuckleduster and quietly rose to his feet.

He held his breath, trying to hear the footfalls above the hollow ticking of the office clock.

A floorboard creaked. They were close now.

He slipped quietly to the wall behind the door and watched as the handle was teased down, the metallic ping of its spring sounding improbably loud in the tense silence.

He weighed the heavy brass in his hand.

The clock ticked on.

Somewhere further along the road a dog barked.

The handle eased up again.

''Ere! Where you off to now?'

The woman's loud voice made Harley start.

'To get the police!'

Treamer sounded further off now – back out by the lobby.

Then, as quickly as it had appeared, the danger passed. Harley gave a deep sigh of relief as he heard the stumbling clickety-clack of the drunken woman's heels pursuing the faint-hearted rent-collector down the street.

35

THE ZINC-COLOURED moon continued to shine down on Limehouse, galvanising the rooftops and the skeletal jibs of the cranes and derricks. All was silent, save for the musical creak of timbers from the merchantmen anchored cheek by jowl along the waterfront.

Harley struck a match and cupped the flame in his hand. He checked his watch again. He'd had Cruickshank's Yard under observation for twenty minutes now, and there'd been no sign of movement whatsoever. In fact, the whole dead-end backstreet looked like it hadn't been visited in years – the perfect location, no doubt, for Perrine's nefarious dealings.

Harley knew he should probably have called it in to Franklin, but he also knew the wheels of justice turned slowly, and by the time the policeman had obtained the necessary warrant, Treamer would no doubt have discovered the missing key and tipped off Perrine and his associates. He now had a limited window of opportunity to search the warehouse and secure any evidence linking Perrine to the murders. And, of course, there was also a slim chance that he might discover little Eddie Muller in there.

He crushed his cigarette beneath his heel and slipped across the street, keeping tight to the shadows.

It didn't take long for Harley to identify a partially detached panel in the rickety fencing – this offered little resistance, once he'd applied enough pressure. He waited for a moment to see if the noise would arouse any response. Then, after a minute or so without any sign of movement, he squeezed into the ramshackle yard, navigating his way through the piles of old packing crates and sodden hessian sacking to make a slow and silent circuit of the building. After finding nothing of immediate interest, Harley made his way back to the front of the building and crouched by the entry doors, where, using the keys from Treamer's office, he quickly unlocked the two sets of padlocks and lowered the heavy chains quietly to the ground. He checked the surrounding area once more, then slipped inside and pulled the door to behind him.

Harley cupped his hands over his closed eyes for a few seconds, to help them adjust to the dark. From his trench-raiding days he knew it took several hours for the human eye to reach its optimal night-vision sensitivity, but he found this trick usually helped with the immediate transition.

Silence.

The meagrest of light leaked in through a handful of grime-encrusted windows.

On first impressions it appeared that, apart from the odd broken crate, the warehouse was deserted. Of course, someone might just want it to appear that way; someone lying in wait, ready to attack.

With the reassuring heft of his knuckleduster on his fist, Harley now took a few tentative steps forward, each one carefully paced, pausing to listen before taking the next. After his eyes had adjusted a little more to the gloom, he began to cautiously make his way over to an object he could see standing against the wall to his left.

A large crate, perhaps? Whatever it was, it was covered in a greasy tarpaulin. He caught a whiff of a distinctive smell – the acrid ammonia of stale urine.

Harley decided to risk striking a match. Preparing himself for the worst, he gathered the corner of the tarpaulin in his free hand and yanked it up.

He saw the bars of a cage, like at the circus, the floor strewn with soiled straw.

And, just visible in the far corner, a dark shape.

The match burnt out.

Before lighting another, he dragged the heavy cover all the way off and onto the floor.

There was a scuttling behind him, accompanied by a few murine squeaks.

He moved to the far corner of the cage, crouched on his haunches, bundled three matches together and struck them alight.

A child's green jersey. Ragged, soiled.

When the Muller kid had gone missing, he'd been wearing tweed knickerbockers and a green jersey.

But where was little Eddie now?

The matches fizzled out.

Harley was just rummaging in his pocket for more when he heard the warehouse door creak open behind him. He spun around, his muscles tense – to be blinded by an electric torchlight, aimed directly in his face.

'Police! Step away from that now! And keep your hands where we can see them!'

* * *

'This is ridiculous,' said Harley, as he was frogmarched towards the black Wolseley, his wrists handcuffed behind his back. 'I've told you what this is all about. Why aren't you in there, searching the place?'

'Because we're busy pinching you, Harley.'

'For what, exactly?'

'Breaking and entering, for starters.'

'I told you – I found it unlocked.'

'Oh, yes? Like you found Treamer's office unlocked? Save it for the beak.'

'You've got to be kidding me! I'm working on the Nursery Butcher investigation. Get hold of DCI Franklin, at Vine Street. He'll straighten all this out. But first, you need to get back there and retrieve that evidence, and you need to search for—'

Harley was promptly silenced by a vicious blow to the ribs with a truncheon.

There was a brief struggle but, with his hands shackled, he was quickly overpowered and bundled into the back of the Q car, where he found himself sandwiched between two more bogeys, wearing standard-issue beige gabardines. Soon the deep purr of the Wolseley's engine was speeding them through the dockside backstreets and out onto the East India Dock Road.

'Why ain't we going to Limehouse nick?'

Harley's query was met with stony silence. He decided to try a mollifying tone.

'Come on, lads. I've just discovered evidence that links that location to the missing Muller kid. He might still be in there. Or at least there might be evidence which could lead us to him.'

'Us?' said the bogey in the front passenger seat.

Harley now recognised him as DC Webbe – a copper he'd had trouble with in the past.

'Whatever you think you've found, it's of no odds. Personally, I don't know why Franklin brought you in on this case in the first place. But that's irrelevant now. You see, not only has our DI discovered the true identity of the Nursery

Butcher but, as of an hour ago, said suspect's premises were being raided. I wouldn't be at all surprised if, as we speak, the perverted bastard is already safely under lock and key in Vine Street. We can find out where the Muller kid is from the horse's mouth.'

'Your DI? Quigg, by any chance?'

'That's Mr Quigg to you,' said Webbe.

So that explained the special treatment.

'Who's this new suspect that Quigg's identified?'

'That's police business,' said Webbe, turning to face the front. 'Now, shut it! Unless you want another taste of the billy club.'

36

HE WAS SOMEWHERE cold, wet. His fingers dragged through the slimy clay of the shell crater. He opened his eyes and hauled himself to a sitting position, checking arms, legs... all still in working order.

A thunderous roar ripped the sky as the howitzers began a second barrage of covering fire to support the advance. He cursed and scrambled around in the filthy pool of stagnant water for his Lee-Enfield. Just as his hand struck against the metal of the rifle's bolt, a magnesium flare exploded above his head, flooding the gloom of the crater with its stark light, revealing a small figure huddled in the mire – little Eddie Muller in his green jersey, clutching his knees to his chest, terror in his eyes.

* * *

'George! Wake up!'

Harley awoke to the holding cell at Vine Street Police Station, where he'd spent a troubled night, trying to snatch the odd forty winks amid the usual raucous cabaret of pugnacious drunks and foul-mouthed tarts, enjoying their overnight accommodation courtesy of the Metropolitan Police.

He struggled to sit up. There was a nagging crick in his neck and his ribs were heavily bruised from the blow from Webbe's truncheon.

Standing over him was DCI Franklin, holding a mug of tea.

'John,' he croaked, massaging his face.

'Bad dream?'

'Something like that,' said Harley, taking hold of the cup. 'Nice of you to finally turn up.'

'I'm sorry. But I've only just found out you were in here. We've had rather a busy night.'

The policeman was looking older, somehow, the usual confident gleam missing from his eye.

Harley took a sip of the tea and rummaged in his jacket pocket for his smokes. 'What's the story?'

'Let's get you out of here and then I'll explain the whole thing. I've managed to swing it with the super to get the charges dropped. Luckily, last night's events have left him in a good mood, but it still took a damn sight more grovelling than I should be doing at my age. I'm not going to lecture you, George, but you placed me in a very compromising position by breaking into that warehouse like that.'

'I found Eddie Muller's jumper there,' whispered Harley. 'In a soddin' *cage*!'

'Really? Where is it now?'

'God knows. Quigg's clowns frogmarched me out of there without even a second glance at the place. It's probably been scrubbed clean by now.'

Franklin rubbed his brow.

'Well, we'll have to look into that, of course. But I'm sure you could do with a wash and brush-up yourself. Let's get you booked out and then we can—'

'Oh no! I'm not going anywhere until you tell me what the hell's going on here. That shicer Webbe said that Quigg has identified the murderer. Well? Who is it?'

Franklin sighed, then sat down on the wooden bunk next to Harley and pulled out his pipe.

'Alasdair Cassina. I suppose it shouldn't come as a surprise. But I don't think either of us really believed he could be the killer; a man like that. I must say, though, there's plenty of compelling evidence. You know, as well as the Dawson connection with the Clapham victim, we now have links to the other two sites of victim discovery.'

'You have?'

'Yes. In Cassina's novel, *A Reflection in the Ice*, the anti-hero, Father Cassidy, has his immoral epiphany whilst waiting to be served in a butcher's shop. And the route of the Number 81 tram – on which our third victim was found – takes it one street away from Cassina's Mayfair apartment.'

'Tenuous bollocks!' exclaimed Harley. 'Who came up with that old madam? Quigg, I bet. Is that all you've got?'

'No,' said Franklin, wearily. 'That's just the icing on the cake. The rest of it is irrefutable, I'm afraid.'

'Has he confessed?'

'In a way, yes.'

'What does that mean?'

'When we raided his apartment last night, we found Cassina dead in bed. Beside him was the corpse of a blond child, a boy of about six—'

'Eddie Muller?'

'No, no. Not the head, anyway. The same MO, you see – head stitched on to a different body, heart ripped out, toes missing...'

'Jesus Christ!'

'The body we've yet to identify. But we're pretty sure the head belongs to Ronald Cleary.'

'Cleary? Wasn't he one of the missing kids from the *Jervis Bay* passenger list?'

'Yes. It appears you were right about the children being taken from the migrants' programme. We've now obtained clearer images of both the missing boys from the children's home's records. As well as identifying Cleary as Cassina's last victim, it's also been confirmed that the head found at the Dawson residence belonged to the other missing lad, Edwin Todd. Just as you said.'

'I bloody knew it!'

'There's to be a full review of all the children signed up for the migrants' programme, to see if the other victims can be identified.'

'How did Cassina die?'

'A single bullet wound to the chest. We've yet to get the autopsy results, but it certainly looks like suicide. Probably knew that the game was up. The revolver was still in his hand. In his typewriter was a full confession to the murders, documenting his obsession with occult practices and sexual perversions. It makes grim reading, I can tell you. There was also a black magic circle painted on his floorboards and detailed descriptions of the preparation of the bodies in the draft of his new novel.'

'That's convenient.'

'What do you mean?'

'A typewritten suicide note? Could have been written by anyone.'

'You think the suicide was staged?' Franklin shook his head. 'I don't think so. We have a key witness who has identified Cassina as the Nursery Butcher.'

'Brendan Collins?'

Franklin frowned. 'What makes you say that?'

'Well, he had concerns about Cassina,' said Harley. 'He went to see Morkens about that occult book.'

'I see. No, it wasn't Collins. Unfortunately, Brendan Collins is currently lying in Guy's Hospital, in a coma.'

'What?'

'He attempted to take his own life last night. Swallowed a sleeping draught and stuck his head in an unlit gas oven.'

'Well, that's a bit of a coincidence, ain't it?' said Harley. 'Two suicides in the same night?'

'Oh no. There's absolutely no doubt about Collins. His suicide note was handwritten. Mainly an apology to his fiancée, Barbara. It appears he feared he was about to be blackmailed over some rather unsavoury indiscretions. Didn't want the shame reflecting on the family name.' Franklin tapped the stem of his pipe against his cheek. 'More than likely something to do with those damned photographs, wouldn't you say? Not heard any more about them, have you?'

'No. Nothing,' said Harley, trying to sound nonchalant. He prodded self-consciously at the still-tender lump on the back of his head. 'But listen, if it wasn't Collins, then who fingered Cassina?'

'That fellow you were looking into, Martin Perrine.'

'Perrine?' exclaimed Harley, spilling his tea. 'You're kidding me! It's him I now fancy for the murders. That shicer's connected all the way through. It was Perrine who rented the warehouse from Treamer – which, I'll remind you, is where I found Eddie Muller's jersey!'

'I've no doubt he's involved. In fact, my money's on him being some sort of pederast. But that's irrelevant now, since he's been granted full immunity from prosecution.'

'On whose say?'

'Quigg's, with full backing from the super.'

'What? How comes that bastard's calling the shots now?'

Franklin shrugged dejectedly.

'And what do *you* make of this Perrine? Is he credible?'

'I couldn't say. I haven't been allowed to interview him yet.'

'You haven't been *allowed*?' Harley looked at him sceptically.

'Mr Perrine is being looked after by the *Daily Oracle*,' said Franklin. 'They've put him up in a swanky hotel – Brown's in Mayfair. For his own protection, apparently. He voluntarily approached Enoch Craster in the first place, you see. Quigg has granted the paper exclusive rights. So the *Oracle* is paying for his board and lodging. The whole thing's most irregular.'

'Most irregular? It stinks to high heaven.' Harley stood up and began to pace the cell, processing this new sudden turn in events. 'What the fuck's going on here, John? I thought you were the leading officer on this case.'

Franklin winced. 'Well, that appears to be in some dispute.'

Harley was about to push the point harder, but seeing the look of defeat in the policeman's eyes he thought better of it.

'Listen, have you still got enough clout to get me into the crime scene, do you think? So, I can have a look around?'

'Cassina's apartment? Yes, I think we can manage that, as long as we're discreet. But we'd better get a move on. As far as DI Quigg is concerned, bar writing the final report, the whole case is done and dusted.'

Harley grabbed his hat and jacket from the wooden bench. 'Well, let's just see about that, shall we?'

* * *

Blanched sunlight filtered through the net curtains, illuminating the chaotic mess of the master bedroom. On the bed – royal-sized and opulent – the sheet was pulled back to reveal the shocking rosehead of a bloodstain, its distinct blackened heart radiating out to more nebulous petals of purple-crimson. Around the bed, the thick-pile carpet was strewn with tangled clothes, discarded newspapers and dirty plates. The top drawer of the dresser had been yanked open, a snake's nest of ties spilling over its edge. On the writing desk by the window, the black-lacquered Underwood typewriter hunkered down, insect-like, amid a cluster of empty bottles and overflowing ashtrays.

Harley took stock of the scene before walking into the room, carefully stepping over the items on the floor. The air had a stale, sickly sweet tang to it.

'That magic circle, or whatever it is, is on the floorboards in the sitting room,' said Franklin. 'Hidden by the rug.'

'Alright. Let's do this first.' Harley nodded towards the writing desk. 'Why is that in the bedroom? He's got a study next door. Do you think it's been moved?'

Franklin held his hands up. 'Your guess is as good as mine.'

Harley walked over to the bed and looked down at the bloodstain.

'One shot, you say?'

'Of course – a suicide.'

'Did they retrieve the slug?'

'Apparently so. Lodged in the carpet behind the bed there.'

Harley walked around to inspect the hole in the floor. 'That's quite an angle. Was he bare-chested, or shot through clothing?'

'He had a nightshirt on,' said Franklin, looking puzzled. 'But that's not going to affect the trajectory, is it?'

'No, of course not. But most suicides place the gun against their naked flesh. And the most popular choice of target is the head, at the temple – right for the right-handed, left for left. Next most popular is in the mouth. Under the chin is unreliable – most people will flinch when they pull the trigger, often resulting in just a glancing blow. But a single gunshot to the chest? There's a big chance of getting that wrong. With a shotgun, maybe; but a revolver?' Harley shook his head. 'No. That don't sound right to me. You need to get them to check for powder burns.'

'Are you really thinking this was a murder? What motive? Revenge for the killings?'

'You're talking as though you're convinced that Cassina was the Nursery Butcher.'

'Aren't you?'

'No, I'm not,' said Harley. 'And I won't be until I've seen a bit more evidence than just a typewritten confession.'

'Much as it grieves me to think Quigg might have had the solution handed to him on a plate, I don't think there's any denying that Cassina is our man. Perrine has presented us with a missing toe from the victim found at the butcher's shop. And photographs taken at the scene in Clapham and at St Giles Circus.'

'Which surely incriminates *him* as the murderer?'

'No, George.' Franklin was beginning to sound thoroughly demoralised now. 'He took them from Cassina. Along with the most compelling piece of evidence: a draft of his new novel. You see, Cassina was in the habit of dating each chapter of a manuscript as he finished it.'

'Sounds odd.'

'Apparently, these authors all have their own little quirks.'

'Typed?' asked Harley, nodding at the black Corona on the desk.

'The manuscript was. But the dates are written in by hand.'

'Alright. Go on.'

'Well, there's a large section of the story – dated before the first corpse was revealed in Clapham – that describes Cassina's protagonist carrying out ritualistic murders on children that match, to the letter, the techniques used by our Nursery Butcher. There's no doubt about it, Cassina's our man.'

Harley walked over to the window and pulled aside the net curtain. Outside, slate-grey clouds were gathering above the city, muting the already feeble sunlight. He closed his eyes for a moment, smoking, thinking.

'I need to see it.'

'What?'

'That manuscript. Can you do that?'

Franklin gave a sigh. 'I suppose so. But I'm not sure what you're expecting to find.'

'Well, nor am I, but let's give it a go, shall we? For Eddie Muller's sake.'

The policeman removed his hat and undid the stud on his collar. 'I don't know,' he said, slumping down on the chair at the dressing table. 'If I'm honest with you, I'm looking forward to washing my hands of the whole sordid affair. When you think about the suffering those poor kiddies must have gone through.'

'Yeah, and might *still* be going through, if you've got the wrong man. I wouldn't up sticks and retire to Whitstable just yet. My gut tells me the real Nursery Butcher is still out there, contemplating his next move. Probably over room service at Brown's, courtesy of the soddin' *Daily Oracle*. I mean, we've not found little Eddie Muller yet, have we? That shicer Perrine has got to be made to talk.'

Franklin held his hands up, seemingly defeated.

Harley turned his attention to the bed.

'D'you have any crime scene photographs yet?'

'Yes, as it happens. The boys in the lab rushed them through. Hold on.'

Franklin retrieved his Gladstone bag and handed Harley a folder. The private detective took a seat at the writing desk, where he sparked up a Gold Flake and spent the next few minutes studying the photographs.

Having scanned through the whole morbid collection, he returned to one particularly uncanny image: a photograph of the dead Cassina, slumped on a bank of pillows, with the child corpse beside him. The young, cherubic face – painted in stage make-up, and depicted in stark contrast in the black-and-white print – was turned to the author as though gazing lovingly at him, a seam of coarse stitches ringing the slender neck like an ugly choker. The effect was like that of a publicity shot for some macabre ventriloquist act.

'What's this in Cassina's hand?'

'The gun?'

'No, this... here.' Harley stabbed at the print with his finger.

'Haven't got my reading specs with me.' Franklin took the photograph and held it at arms-length, squinting. 'Ah, yes. That's a picture book.'

'A picture book?'

Franklin nodded. 'It's as though he'd been reading to that poor dead child before he shot himself. Homicidal lunacy, I'd say.'

'Or part of the careful staging of the scene. Where is it now?'

'The book?'

'Yes, the book!' Harley was beginning to get a little frustrated with the older man's despondent mood.

Franklin sniffed and walked over to the bedside table. 'Why it's here,' he said. 'This is it.'

'Don't touch the cover!'

He joined Franklin at the bedside.

'*Mother Goose Nursery Tales*, Charles Perrault.'

Harley took a pencil from his jacket and flipped open the book.

'Do we know which story it was turned to?'

Franklin shook his head. 'Sorry, no. Do you think that's significant?'

'Yes, I do.' Harley went back to the crime scene photographs. 'Look there. It's about halfway through, I'd say.'

Restricting his touch to the edge of the pages, he began to flick through the fairy tales, until he came to a page with a small splatter of blood on its corner.

'Bingo! There we go – *Bluebeard*. Hold on! *Bluebeard*. Isn't there a key in that story? You know, that the wife is forbidden to use?'

'I don't recall, George, sorry.'

'Was there a key found in the child's mouth this time?'

'No, this time it was in Cassina's mouth.'

Harley laughed sarcastically.

'So, let me get this straight. When you discovered Cassina's body, in his mouth was a key, in his right hand he had the gun and, in his left, he had this book?'

'Yes, that's right. As it is in the photograph.'

'And we're meant to believe he continued holding this book while also positioning the muzzle of the gun against his chest, taking his final look at the world and pulling the trigger?'

'Well, that bloodstain would suggest it was close to the body when the bullet entered the chest. And the book was definitely in his hand when we broke in last night so, if it was suicide, then—'

'I'm not buying it. This was no suicide. No soddin' way! That key, the book and the gun were all placed on Cassina after he was shot. This whole scene was posed. And that means the Nursery Butcher is still out there somewhere, gloating.'

'You can't possibly know that for certain. What about—'

'That bastard's toying with us,' interrupted Harley. 'The whole way this has been staged – the corpse of the kid, the bedtime story – he's sending us a message here. One that he thinks we're too dumb to work out.'

Franklin gave a long sigh and shook his head. 'Well, I'm afraid I'm not going to be able to help you pursue your theory. I've been asked to step back from the case while Quigg finishes up.'

'What about finding little Eddie Muller? Surely that's still a priority?'

'Of course. But without any solid leads they'll be concentrating on any clues they can find in Cassina's things.'

'Any solid leads? I found the kid's jersey in a cage, in a building rented by your chief informant! How much more solid do you want? You need to be interrogating that shicer Perrine to find out who's really behind these murders.'

Franklin shook his head. 'The superintendent won't go for that. In Cassina's confession he states that nobody else was involved in the killings. As far as the Met is concerned, the Nursery Butcher is no longer a threat to society. I'll obviously do what I can to supply you with information, where possible. But if you really want to investigate the possibility that the killer is still out there – and, by the way, I don't think I agree with you there – then I'm afraid you're on your own.'

'Well, at least I know where I stand. Anyway, it won't be the first time.'

'And you need to stay this side of the law,' said Franklin, wearily. 'I shan't be able to spring you so easily next time.'

'I'm a big boy now,' said Harley, setting his hat on his head. 'I can look after myself. Right, let's have a look at this magic circle and then I need to see that manuscript. I take it you can still do that at least?'

37

IT WAS ANOTHER busy morning in Whitechapel High Street. A line of trams flanked each side of the central reservation, while cars, trucks and horse-drawn vehicles vied for position in the main road. Street traders added to the clamour, hawking their wares on the pavement with jovial banter. And here and there, small huddles of young men, confiding in Russian and Yiddish, gathered outside cafés which bustled with hungry workers.

Cynthia stopped to adjust her shoe strap outside a display of hats and dresses – 'The latest West End fashions, at East End prices.'

'George, do slow down a little! I'm going to twist an ankle at this rate.'

'Sorry. But you know how important this is.'

'And you really think he's going to be able to help, do you? Solly's uncle?'

'I dunno,' said Harley. 'But my guess is that the book placed in Cassina's hand wasn't chosen at random. There's a message in it somewhere. And there's no one who knows more about books than Nate Rosen.'

'I still can't get over it. Alasdair. I mean, I knew he was a little odd, but… well, to think we were once friends.'

Harley pulled Cynthia close and kissed the top of her head. 'Try not to think about it. You'll drive yourself barmy. Anyway, as I said, he was no saint, but I'm convinced he wasn't our killer.'

'But what about his manuscript? You must see how the police would find that compelling evidence. You said it yourself, it was all in there – the age of the children, the beheadings, the stealing of the hearts. And, to be honest, I can see why Franklin wasn't overly convinced by your theory about the typewriter ribbon.'

Harley gave a frustrated sigh.

'That's because the soddin' Met needs to be dragged kicking and screaming into the twentieth century. And anyway, it wasn't the ribbon I was talking about. It was the type blocks – those little slugs of metal with the raised letters on them. Even on the same model, they're always slightly different on each individual typewriter. Those differences show in the typed text – it's what's called a print indent. I'm no expert, but the section in that manuscript describing the ritualistic killings looks to me like it was typed on a different machine. And as for the dating of each chapter – why would anyone do that? Apart from our killer, in a desperate attempt to convince the police the bogus section in that manuscript was genuine. It stinks.'

'Well, Scotland Yard seem satisfied with it.'

'Yeah, I know. That's why we need to get to the bottom of this *Bluebeard* connection. Come on, the shop's just up here. You'll like the old fella, he's interesting.'

On entering the shop, they were greeted with the sweet, musty-almond aroma of second-hand books – hundreds of which were crammed into the shelves and piled in teetering towers across the floor.

'Gosh!'

'Looks like chaos, right?' said Harley. 'But I bet Nate knows where everything is.'

'Well, perhaps not everything,' commented a voice from behind a nearby stack. Its owner appeared a few seconds later – a diminutive old man with a white beard, wearing a black velvet yarmulke and a pair of half-moon glasses. 'One day a machine they will invent, to perform such work. But for now, ah! I must rely on my ancient brain, so help me! George, my dear boy, how are you?' The smile was warm, the handshake surprisingly firm for his age. 'And this must be Cynthia. It's a pleasure, my dear.'

Uncle Nate took the stub of a pencil from behind his ear and made a quick note on the flyleaf of the book he was holding. 'So,' he said, glancing at a fob watch nestled in the slack pocket of his cardigan. 'Time for tea, yes?'

Soon they were ensconced in the back office, each with a small glass of black Russian tea.

'Nu. Solomon told me there was something you wished to ask me?'

Harley nodded. 'It's for a case I'm working on, Nate. What can you tell me about the fairy tale *Bluebeard*?'

'*Bluebeard*? Wait one moment...' The old man returned a few minutes later, holding a large, leather-bound tome. 'Here he is,' he said, opening the book to show a striking illustration. 'This is how Gustave Doré saw the villain, presenting the keys to his young wife, you see?' He turned the book towards Cynthia. 'Look at the eyes, my dear.'

'It's truly frightening,' she said. 'Evil.'

'Indeed. Doré was a genius, no? But the tale itself? Let me see...' The bookseller twisted a finger into his beard. 'Well, it is a French folk tale, first collected by Charles Perrault in his

Histoires ou Contes du Temps Passé, of course. Of the original source I am not certain, but there are numerous similar tales in other cultures. Shakespeare alludes to an English version called 'Mr Fox' in his *Much Ado About Nothing*, you know.' He paused to take a sip of his tea. 'Anyway, it is a cautionary tale, like *Little Red Riding Hood*, and so forth. This one, well, it warns of...' Uncle Nate gave Cynthia a little melodramatic mime of shock, 'the dangerous curiosity of Woman. The tale has similarities to the temptation of Eve.'

'Only this one turns out to have a slightly happier ending,' said Harley.

'Perhaps,' said the old man. 'Although, some may argue that being expelled from Paradise...' He shrugged. 'Maybe, for the gift of moral reasoning, this is a fair price to pay, no? Ah, but that's a whole other conversation.'

He sat back in his chair and pushed his spectacles up onto his forehead. 'So, you know the story, yes? Our heroine arrives at the sumptuous castle of her new husband, Bluebeard, whom she has agreed to marry – despite the worrying stories of the mysterious disappearance of his previous wives. I think, perhaps, her mind was distracted. All those great riches, eh? A heavy purse makes a light heart. Anyhow, her new role she embraces: the Lady of the Manor. And why not? Soon, Mr Bluebeard, he announces he must go away on business – after all, where does she think all the riches come from in the first place? So, he hands her the keys to the castle.' Uncle Nate pointed to the Doré illustration. 'He knows what he's doing, this Mr Bluebeard. Look at him. And those keys, they are a symbol, yes? I will spare your blushes, my dear, but even in Doré's illustration it is obvious. This is a cautionary tale for girls, remember? So, the husband lays down the law, as husbands like to do.'

Uncle Nate sat up and stuck his thumbs in his cardigan pockets, setting his face in a dramatic frown. '"Fatima," he says

– for Perrault has modelled his villain on the Mohammedan, but more of that later – "Fatima, here are the keys to all the rooms in the castle. Also, to the closets that house my jewels, my silver plate and all my coin. With these keys, my wife, I grant you the freedom to *act as you wish*. Open doors, enjoy the finery, indulge yourself and your family – for is this not your home as well as mine? But *this* key, my dear," and he holds up the last one on the ring, "this key belongs to the closet at the end of the long gallery. This, my wife, you must *not* enter for all the world. You should disobey me in this? Then expect a suitable punishment. So says your husband, Bluebeard, to whom you are duty bound."'

The bookseller paused to take another sip of tea.

'Of course, every little boy and girl hearing this story would know what must happen next. With the flame of curiosity burning inside her, Fatima invites her friends to the castle for a party. And what a time they have. They open each of the rooms, with wonder and delight. Oy! Such riches. In awe, they are, of the good fortune that has befallen their young friend. And no doubt a little jealous too, hmm? But where is Fatima herself? Where? Why, of course, she is scurrying along to the forbidden room, to do exactly what she has been told not to.'

'What else could she do?' said Cynthia.

'What else, indeed,' said Uncle Nate, with a nod. 'Ah! But such horror she finds inside. The floor a swamp of clotted blood, in which wallow the corpses of young women – the previous wives of our industrious Mr Bluebeard. In her panic to get away, she drops the key, and so seals her fate. For, try as she might, she cannot remove the bloodstain from it.'

'The mark of her sin,' said Cynthia, with a raised eyebrow. 'I see what you mean by your reference to Eve.'

Uncle Nate smiled and nodded slowly. 'So, the husband returns, discovers the blood on the key – the evidence of his wife's betrayal – and says, "Very well, madam, since you are so fond of this chamber, you shall take your place among the ladies there." He takes out his scimitar to cleave her beautiful head from her body. But the clever girl buys some time by asking leave to pray before she dies. Surely, he won't deny her this? However, instead of praying, she secretly meets with her sister – and asks her to summon their brothers. Following the convention of such tales, the brothers arrive just in time and lop off our villain's head. Fatima inherits his vast fortune, and we're once again at the happily-ever-after.'

'What's the significance of the blue beard, do you think?' asked Harley.

'Well,' said Uncle Nate. 'Beards are associated with the lustful goat: the Devil. And, after the crusades, also with the Saracen. In Islam, beards have a great symbolic value, you understand. And remember, in Perrault's time, the courtiers were all clean-shaven. So, the beard would have been a symbol of the foreigner, or of the peasant. A brute even. Indeed, the word for beard in French is?'

'*Barbe*,' said Cynthia.

'Yes. See how close that is to *le barbare*, the barbarian.'

'But why a *blue* beard?' asked Harley.

'Hmm...' the old man once more twisted his finger in his own beard. 'Blue... It is the colour of the ocean and of the heavens. It can stand for knowledge and the mysterious, perhaps? And of course, to a Frenchman, like Perrault, it is synonymous with raw meat.'

'*Un steak bleu*,' said Cynthia.

'Exactly. It would be unlikely that Perrault would have missed this connection – even subconsciously.'

'So,' said Harley, pulling out a notepad. 'We have a cautionary tale.'

The old man nodded. 'One that warns of the fate of broken promises.'

'But she doesn't actually get punished in the end, does she?' said Cynthia.

'Ah, but the lesson is there, nonetheless, my dear, in the fate of her unfortunate predecessors.'

'And we have a possible reference to the garden of Eden,' continued Harley, making notes. 'With Bluebeard representing the serpent, the Devil.'

'Also, possibly God,' added Uncle Nate. 'Since what he prohibits is the discovery of knowledge.'

Harley raised his eyebrows, a little surprised. 'Alright,' he said, adding it to his notes.

'And, of course, after everything else, *Bluebeard* is a deliciously dark tale of horror and gore,' said Uncle Nate. 'A predecessor of the Penny Bloods, or Penny Dreadfuls of the last century, pandering to the keen appetite for sensation and murder that seems always to be gnawing away at the belly of the common man.'

'Much like the tales of Jack the Ripper,' said Cynthia.

'There you go,' said Harley still scribbling in his notebook. 'Now we're getting somewhere.'

'But George,' said Uncle Nate, retrieving his glasses from the top of his head. 'Might I ask something? Solomon hinted that you might be helping the police with this dreadful case.' The old man hesitated, wringing his hands. 'The child murderer – this Nursery Butcher. Is that correct? Of course, I'll understand if you can't say.'

'No, it's alright. Yeah, that's the case. The Nursery Butcher.'

'And for this you ask about *Bluebeard*?'

Harley nodded.

'Then, my friend, I think there is a much more relevant connection: Gilles de Rais.'

'Why does that name ring a bell?' asked Harley. 'Go on.'

'Baron Gilles de Rais was a French nobleman, from the fifteenth century. A chevalier, a Marshall of France, and a brave companion-in-arms to Joan of Arc, no less. This individual, you understand, was one of the wealthiest, most cultured men of his time. Unfortunately, he was also a supremely evil sadist, who developed an insatiable appetite for the defilement, torture and murder of young boys. Throw in with this his experimentation with the conjuring of demons, the masquerading as a devoutly pious character… well, you can see we have quite the villain, no? When he was eventually brought to trial, the full scale of his atrocities was revealed. With the help of his loyal entourage, de Rais had slaughtered hundreds of young children over the years, their bodies consumed in the vast fireplaces of his castles or discarded in the cesspits on his estates. Through the centuries the details of his crimes became blurred, and so he became a bogeyman with which to scare naughty children: the Bluebeard of legend, and, some say, the inspiration for Perrault's homicidal villain.'

Harley put down his notepad and lit a cigarette. He stood up and began to smoke voraciously, lost for a moment in thought.

'Do you have any books on this fella?'

'Hmm, I don't think so. But you want I should check?'

'Please.'

When the old man had left, Harley turned excitedly to Cynthia.

'I knew it! This *Bluebeard* thing can't be a coincidence. Can you remember Cassina ever mentioning this Gilles de Rais character?'

She shook her head. 'No. But if everything Nate is saying about him is true, I'm surprised he's not more widely known.'

'Yeah. He should be rubbing shoulders with Dr Crippen and the rest of them in the Chamber of Horrors, right? But you know, the name does ring a bell, somehow.'

'We all know what you're like, with that encyclopaedic brain of yours. You probably read a line or two about him in a book once.'

'Well, let's hope Nate has something more on him.'

But when the old man returned, he was empty-handed.

'I'm sorry. But, you know, I think I might be able to solve the puzzle of why you thought you knew the name. You see, this is just the sort of thing your Uncle Blake was interested in: dark and menacing tales of ghouls and dybbuks.' He chuckled and gave his head a little waggle. 'I was always trying to persuade him to part with certain treasures from that vast collection of his. You know I'm almost certain he had a book on de Rais. You still have his library, yes?'

'Some of it's still packed away in tea chests, but most of it's out in the study. I use it as a reference library sometimes.'

'Then go home, my friend. Maybe there, God willing, you'll find the key to this mystery. And help bring this modern-day Bluebeard to justice.'

38

'HAVE YOU SEEN this?' asked Cynthia, following Harley up the stairs back at Bell Street. He turned to find her holding up a copy of the *Daily Oracle*, the front page of which was emblazoned with the headline BLACK MAGIC IN MAYFAIR!

'Why on earth did you buy that?'

'This exclusive story they're running on the murders.'

'You mean that old gammon fed to them by this fraud Martin Perrine?'

'Oh, I know I shouldn't, but I can't help myself. I need to try to make sense of it all – how Alasdair could have possibly been involved in something so... so *horrific*.'

He sat her down on the stair next to him. 'Listen, Cyn, I know this is all a bit of a shock, but you're not going to get any sense out of that rag.'

'Look.' She opened the newspaper to reveal a dramatic half-page illustration, depicting a group of revellers in evening dress, surrounding a candlelit altar. 'They've turned the murders of those poor children into some kind of vulgar pot-boiler. Black masses, orgies.'

'Well, that's that hack Craster for you,' said Harley.

'But there must be *some* truth in it. After all, we know Alasdair was experimenting with occult rituals – there's the pentagram on his floor and the grimoire.' Cynthia fingered the beads of her necklace anxiously. 'And then there's von Görlitz and his awful Unicursal society. Remember, I saw Perrine there.'

'Well, it's good copy, ain't it? It's all the rage at the moment – séances, clairvoyants, esoteric societies.'

'You know, I think it's to do with people turning away from the Church,' said Cynthia.

Harley tutted and carried on up the stairs. She hurried after him, up to the third-floor study where he kept his reference library.

'What are you tutting about? Listen, I'm not the greatest fan of the Church, but I do think, for a lot of people, religion serves an important purpose. It gives them comfort. Without it there's a hole – a hole that needs to be filled by something.'

'Something *spiritual*?'

'Yes, something spiritual. I don't know why you find that so funny. It's fundamental to civilisation.'

He shrugged. 'Well, I reckon a lot of this renewed interest in spiritualism is to do with the war – all that death and destruction; sons and husbands taken overnight; families devastated. People need to make sense of it somehow. As if that were possible. So, they pay good money to a bunch of shysters who claim they're in touch with their loved ones on the other side.'

'I agree, there's been an upsurge in that kind of thing since the war,' she said. 'But visiting a medium, attending a séance – it's hardly the same as joining a coven or celebrating a black mass, is it?'

'Maybe not,' said Harley. 'But I think it's still connected. Anyway, this ain't going to get us any closer to finding the true identity of the Nursery Butcher, is it? Come on.' He cocked his thumb towards the racks of book shelving. 'Let's get on with it.'

'So, we're looking for anything to do with this Gilles de Rais, yes?' asked Cynthia, sitting down on the faded Persian rug and running her hand along the row of book spines on one of the lower shelves.

'Or Joan of Arc, I suppose,' said Harley, mounting a set of rickety old library steps. 'Seeing as de Rais served with her. You start with the Occult section, and I'll do History.'

'Why am I covering the Occult? I hope you're not trying to insinuate anything, Corporal Harley.'

'As bewitching as you are, it's actually because a lot of the books in that section aren't in English, and your French and Latin are far better than mine,' said Harley. 'Which wouldn't be difficult, seeing as mine are virtually non-existent.'

'What about that embroidery piece found in that poor child's head? The medieval Book of Revelation tapestry? Are we also looking for references to that? It seems to me to be in a similar category as Gilles de Rais.'

'If it comes up, all well and good,' said Harley. 'But don't look especially for it. I'm not convinced it's not just some kind of red herring.'

After searching through the book titles for a while, Cynthia sat back on her haunches. 'Good grief! It would appear Fedor von Görlitz and his Belgravia coven have nothing on the Harley clan. Was your Uncle Blake some sort of warlock?'

'Hardly – he was the son of a costermonger from Bethnal Green. Why?'

'All these books on black magic. *Clavicula Salomonis, Le Petit Albert, Le Dragon Rouge*...'

'Grimoires.'

'Exactly,' said Cynthia, holding up an ancient-looking tome, bound in embossed leather. 'Instructions on summoning demons and casting spells. Did he believe in all this mumbo jumbo?'

'I don't think he believed in magic, not in a literal sense. But he was fascinated by folklore, rituals, superstitions – and he passed a bit of that on to me, to be honest. He reckoned that, on his travels, he'd experienced some bloody strange things – things that couldn't have a scientific explanation.' Harley sat down for a moment on the top of the library steps. 'Mind you, Uncle Blake was never one to let the truth get in the way of a good story.'

'Do you think there might be a chance of him turning up again one day?'

Harley shrugged. 'I doubt it. It's been eighteen years now since he went missing. You know, he's probably the most fascinating person I've ever met. I think I told you that Dad died when I was sixteen?'

'Yes. And your mother – when you were away in France, wasn't it?'

Harley nodded. 'Yeah, the Spanish flu took Mum. But before that, when Dad went, Uncle Blake became a real role model, you know? I mean, we didn't see him much because of his travels. But when he did come home, the stories he used to tell…' He smiled and shook his head. 'He'd have me mesmerised for hours.'

'He certainly sounds like a remarkable character. Maybe you should—' Cynthia stopped, mid-sentence. 'George, look!'

'What?' asked Harley, scrambling down from his perch.

'Here – two books on Gilles de Rais.'

'Never!'

'Yes – look.'

Harley grabbed the books from her. '*The Condemnation of Gilles de Rais*… and, what's this one, in French?'

'Let's see… *The Trial of Gilles de Retz*… I'd imagine that's just a different spelling. *The Trial of Gilles de Retz of the House of Laval*.' She flicked through the book to get an idea of its contents. 'It looks like it's a record of his trial. The original was in Latin, apparently… and there's some commentary on the crimes.'

'Can you translate it alright, d'you think?' asked Harley, already fervently scanning the pages of the other book, which was in English.

'I think so, yes.'

There followed a period of industrious silence, broken only by the turning of thick, aged paper.

A few minutes later, Harley slammed his fist against the top of the steps.

'Got you, you fucker!'

'George, please!' exclaimed Cynthia, with a disapproving look. 'Must you swear like that?'

'I'm sorry. But you've got to hear to this. Listen. "Amongst those who aided de Rais in his detestable work was the notorious old woman, the procurer of young children, *Perrine Martin*, nicknamed *La Meffraye*."'

'Perrine? Gosh! That can't be a coincidence. But listen, I think I've just found something more important here—'

'Martin Perrine,' continued Harley, interrupting. 'I knew it!'

He suddenly noticed Cynthia was scrutinising some newspaper cuttings that had fallen out of the book she was reading.

'What was the name of the professor chap on that wireless programme?' she said excitedly. 'You know, the one debating with Alasdair and the vicar?'

'Morkens. Osbert Morkens. Why?'

'Listen to this: "Tenth of February, 1910. Sotheby's Auction House was the scene of a furious bidding war yesterday, as book dealers, antiquarians and amateur historians sought to become the proud owner of a rare cache of ancient books and manuscripts that once belonged to the infamous Satanist, the Breton Baron Gilles de Rais. The items – believed for centuries to have been lost to the annals of time – were discovered by chance by a shepherd, after following one of his heavily pregnant ewes into a cave near the Château de Tiffauges, once de Rais' home and the site of many of his atrocities. There he discovered a large chest, partially buried, and sealed against the elements with beeswax.

"When the hammer finally fell on the prized lot, the bidding had reached a staggering £750 – far exceeding the average price of a large family home in the London suburbs. The new owner of this dubious treasure is a Doctor Osbert Agamemnon Morkens, a lecturer in Ancient History at Oxford University." And look,' continued Cynthia, holding up the newspaper cutting. 'His name has been ringed.'

'Give it here.' Harley took the article from her.

'There's another cutting here. This one's from the *Oxford Times*, a year later: "Following on from his successful series of public lectures on the life of the notorious French nobleman, Gilles de Rais, Professor Osbert Morkens of Brasenose College today sets out for Tiffauges in Brittany, where he will lead a privately funded archaeological dig in the grounds of the ruined local fortress, the Château de Tiffauges. In the fifteenth century, the château was the scene of black magic, torture and murder at the hands of the villainous de Rais, who killed dozens of young boys, and is believed to be the inspiration for the French fairy tale *Bluebeard*. The professor and his team will attempt to locate the whereabouts of a secret underground chamber, used by de Rais for his alchemical experiments, with the hopes that any findings might go some way in explaining why a member of the French nobility and former companion-in-arms of Joan of Arc, would take such a dramatic descent into depravity and madness." And look, someone's written a note here in the margin: "*Has he found them?*" Found what, do you think?'

'I don't know. But that's Uncle Blake's writing,' said Harley. 'Morkens told me that he'd met him once.'

'Who? Your uncle? But that's—'

'Yeah, I know – weird, right? And these cuttings – it's like Uncle Blake was keeping tabs on him and his associations with Gilles de Rais.'

He came down off the library steps and began to pace the floor.

'Jesus Christ, it *is* him! It's Professor Morkens! Morkens is the Nursey Butcher, and that shicer Perrine is the one who's been going out and pinching kids off the streets for him, just like Perrine Martin did for the Baron.'

He lit a cigarette and began to smoke feverishly.

'But you know what? Those milky bastards at the Yard will never buy this. They're not going to pinch a sodding Oxford professor. I mean, people of that calibre couldn't possibly be criminal lunatics, could they? No doubt he's a friend of the Commissioner; probably a bleedin' Mason as well. No. I'm going to have to go after him on my own, catch the shicer with blood on his hands. That's the only way to convince these clowns!'

'Calm down, you're beginning to worry me.'

'I'm sorry, but I told them that Cassina's suicide was staged – this bastard Morkens thinks he's so clever, so clever he can play with those little kids' bodies as though they're just clues in some public school treasure hunt. Well, I've got your number now, Professor. Let's see how clever you are with a set of brass knuckles in your face.'

'Please promise me you'll be careful. If Morkens really is the Nursery Butcher, then… well, you said it yourself, he's obviously some kind of criminal lunatic. There's no telling what he could be capable of.'

'I think I can handle some dusty old academic, don't you?'

'What was it your old CO used to tell you? "Never underestimate the enemy"? That sounds like jolly good advice to me, Corporal Harley.'

'Fair point,' he said, walking purposefully to the door. 'Come on, then!'

'Where are we going?' asked Cynthia, scrambling to get up off the floor.

'Your place. I need to use your telephone to try and track down where Morkens is right now.'

39

EDDIE MULLER PULLED the tartan blanket up to his chin and wiped a chubby hand across the condensation on the car window. The outside world streamed past: fog-smeared streets with serried rows of stucco houses, wide pavements, tall plane trees, iron railings and lamp posts as black and glossy as liquorice. Had they told him where they were going? He couldn't quite recall. Things had become very confusing lately.

Still woozy from his morning sedative, Eddie rested his head back against the cool leather. He closed his eyes and scratched his cheek, still sticky from the box of Turkish Delight he'd gorged on in the parlour before they'd left. Within a few minutes he'd drifted off to sleep.

He awoke to a hand on his knee. It was the other man, the one with the funny voice and the wolf mask. A foreigner, German. A 'Fritz', as his Uncle Bert called them. "Never trust a Fritz, Eddie." Though this one seemed nice enough and had fascinating eyes, eyes that made you feel a little dizzy, if you looked at them long enough.

'Edward? We're here, little one.'

Then he was being led through a grand entrance, his new patent leather shoes clip-clopping on the polished tiles. He clung tightly to the man's large hand, the back of which was covered in coarse black hair.

Inside the dining room a large spread awaited him: tea and orange juice, egg sandwiches, sardines on toast and cake. Lots of pink cake. He hoisted himself up onto one of the Queen Anne chairs and a heavily laden plate was put in front of him. He lost himself for a while in the serious work of eating.

When he'd finished, he pushed the empty plate away.

The man with the fascinating eyes laughed heartily. 'My, my. What a big appetite you have.'

Eddie smiled dreamily, both cheeks now as sticky as each other.

'So, we will let your stomach settle a little, then a bath for you, young man. You have a big day ahead of you tomorrow.'

Eddie was about to argue that it wasn't bath night, but then realised that this might not be true. He nodded slowly and sat back in his chair to stare at the pretty ceiling.

His guardian had to go to check on something and asked Eddie to sit quietly 'like a good little boy' until he returned. But when he left, something made the child follow to the door and quietly turn the porcelain handle. As he peered out into the hallway, he caught sight of the man entering another room. A glimpse of the strange occupants of this room made Eddie chuckle, but also gave him a funny feeling in his tummy.

They were the strangest-looking adults he'd ever seen. All naked, displaying their flawed, grown-up bodies, all hair and paunches and nether regions, as Nanny Muller called them. And some of them wore masks as well – cats and owls and foxes, and other animals that he couldn't put a name to. They must be about to play some kind of party game.

What a strange house this is, thought Eddie, trotting back to the table for another helping of cake.

40

HARLEY SAT AT the piano in the living room of Cynthia's elegant apartment, a lighted cigarette in one hand and the telephone receiver in the other. Cynthia sat watching him from one of the roll-backed Chesterfield armchairs, sipping anxiously at a large sherry.

Hearing a click on the line, Harley pushed the receiver tight to his ear. He'd been waiting five minutes to be connected and had been about to give up.

'Fellowes speaking.'

The voice on the other end was as dry and laconic as he remembered it: Constantine Fellowes, the senior ranking official who, on many occasions during a short but eventful career in MI5, had been Harley's point of contact for logical – and sometimes life-saving – advice.

'It's Harley, Fellowes, George Harley.'

There was a sigh, followed by a short but meaningful pause.

'And just how did you manage to get put through to me, Harley?'

'Good old Fellowes. Not "How are you, George? Good to hear from you!" If I told you how I got hold of you, you'd feel obliged to sack someone. So, I'm afraid that's going to remain a secret. I seem to remember you like secrets.'

'And what, exactly, do you need me to do for you?'

'What makes you think I need you to do anything?'

'Of course you need me to do something for you,' said Fellowes, without emotion. 'As you know, I'm an incredibly busy man, and I wouldn't normally entertain such a request…'

'But?'

There was another pause on the line.

'But if it concerns your current investigation into the series of child murders, attributed to the so-called Nursery Butcher, then I might consider complying. So, what is it?'

'I bet you know what I had for breakfast as well, don't you, Fellowes?'

'You have thirty seconds. I'm timing.'

Harley quickly referred to his notepad.

'Professor Osbert Agamemnon Morkens, born January tenth, 1874. Currently holds the Camden Professorship of Ancient History at Brasenose College, Oxford. You taking this down? What am I saying? Of course you're taking this down.'

'Congratulations, Harley, you have piqued my curiosity. An interesting suspect – I take it he *is* a suspect?'

'Could be.'

'But I thought the Met had caught their nasty little child murderer?' said Fellowes, shedding a little of the indifference in his tone. 'A case of Scotland Yard applying their usual due diligence to an important investigation, is it?'

'Yup.'

'I see. My commiserations. But you only have yourself to blame. After all, you did resign from the Firm. Now, what is it you wish to know about Morkens?'

'I'm trying to track down his whereabouts, as a matter of

some urgency. I've just managed to sweet talk the head porter at his college – a surprisingly leaky old cove, given his position.'

'Indiscreet?'

'Well, the bloke didn't know me from Adam, but I only had to claim to be an acquaintance of the professor's for him to share the comings and goings of half the faculty at the college. It turns out that Morkens has been on a leave of absence over the past few weeks, engaged in research for his new book – that's the story he's given, anyway. So, he's not been staying at his rooms on campus much. Chummy said the professor told him he intended to spend some of the time at a country residence he'd inherited; somewhere down in Kent, he seemed to think it was.'

'And you need me to get you an address, is that it?'

'Exactly. The place sounds like a prefect hideaway for a mass murderer to me. Shouldn't be too much of a stretch for His Majesty's Secret Service, should it?'

'Couldn't you ask your new pals at Scotland Yard?'

'Probably. But there's no way they'll be able to do it as fast as you. Besides, there's too many rotten apples in that particular barrel. There's no guarantee that our friend Morkens wouldn't get wind of it.'

'I see. And how soon do you need this by?'

'Preferably in the next hour.'

If Harley hadn't known better, he'd have sworn he'd heard a faint laugh on the other end of the phone. But, of course, it was well known that Constantine Fellowes never laughed.

'Listen – we still haven't located the Muller kid,' said Harley. 'Who knows? He could be down there right now, at the mercy of this monster. I need to put a stop to this bastard as soon as possible.'

'Very well. I'll see what I can do. Stay at this number.'

* * *

'So, Aloysius,' said Enoch Craster, lounging in his chair in the smoking room of Brown's Hotel as though such plush elegance were something he experienced on a daily basis, 'things seem to be going swimmingly well, wouldn't you say? I hear the powers that be are considering rewarding a certain detective inspector for his part in bringing the Nursery Butcher's reign of terror to a close. Promotion, is it? Or a gong?'

'Well, one really shouldn't speculate,' said Quigg, his face a little flushed from the port and lemon he was sipping at in the manner of an old maiden aunt. 'Besides, having the opportunity to protect the innocent from such heinous crimes is reward enough.'

'Pull the other one,' said Craster, a sly half-smile appearing on his rodent-like countenance. 'You're lapping it up, you old dog. Of course, you've got yours truly to thank for this. Did you like the way I pointed out to our readers that the reason Cassina did away with himself was because he "*felt the vice-like grip of the Metropolitan Police closing in around his neck*"?'

'Well, it *is* a plausible theory,' said the policeman, a little flustered. 'Anyway, you can't say the story hasn't been good for your own career.'

'Indeed, it has. My serialised exclusive on Perrine's account of Cassina and his black magic antics has seen the paper hit record-breaking circulation figures. Our competitors haven't had a look in.'

'The story certainly seems to have captured the public imagination. How long will you run it for, do you think?'

Craster leant forward in his seat, lowering his voice.

'Well, here's the thing. I've just done a rather exciting deal with a publishing house. I'll run some more articles in the *Oracle*, some side stories and background on the characters. But I intend to save the juiciest bits, like the horrifying denouement in Cassina's Mayfair penthouse, for a feature-length book. That's why we're here today – just need to make sure old man Perrine is on board, explain to him that, if he plays ball, we're both going to end up incredibly rich men.'

The journalist gave a smug wiggle of the eyebrows, then sat back and folded his hands on his chest.

'And where do I come into this, exactly?' asked Quigg. 'When you called, you mentioned something about needing my assistance?'

'Ah, yes. Well, what could be a better ending to this whole affair than the sensational discovery of little Eddie?'

'I'm sorry?'

'Eddie *Muller*! The kid that's still missing? You know – one of those innocents whose protection is supposed to be your sole motivation?'

Quigg's dewlap quivered as he cleared his throat. 'Of course, yes, Edward Muller.' He covered his embarrassment with a slurp of port and lemon. 'But, up until now, Perrine has only hinted at knowing anything about the Muller child. Do you really think he knows more?'

'Oh, I'm certain that old rogue knows much more than he's letting on about a lot of things. And I'm convinced he knows that little Eddie is already dead; hence his reticence in discussing the matter. But I'm not interested in helping him incriminate himself, Aloysius. That'll be like killing the goose that lays the golden eggs. That's where you come in. We'll work on him together, tease the information out of him. And all the way you'll be reassuring him that, whatever he discloses, there's no fear he'll be prosecuted for any crime. If we manage to pull it off, you'll be handsomely rewarded. And I'm talking about ready cash, not just some bit of tin on a ribbon to hang around your neck. So, what say you, my friend? Are you in?'

Quigg glanced around at the affluent guests, feeling a little uncomfortable with the nature of the conversation. But nevertheless, he nodded enthusiastically, his dewlap swinging turkey-like below his hangdog jowls.

'Jolly good,' said Craster. He consulted his watch. 'Where is the old duffer?'

'Perrine?'

'Yes, he's already twenty minutes late.'

Craster signalled to a young porter who was crossing the room.

'Sir?' said the lad. He was a jaunty, affable type with a face full of freckles.

'We're here to meet one of your guests. I wonder if you wouldn't get a message to him, tell him we're waiting?'

'Of course, sir. Which name was it?'

'Perrine, Martin Perrine.'

'That'll be room 326, the newspaper account?'

'That's right,' said Craster.

'Gone out, I'm afraid, sir.'

'Are you sure, son?'

'Oh yes,' said the porter. 'Quite distinctive, ain't he, Mr Perrine?'

Craster fished a coin out of his pocket and gave it to the lad. 'Could you just check with reception, see whether he left a message for us?'

'Of course, sir. Right away.' The porter touched his cap and then sauntered off to the reception, whistling a breezy rendition of 'Chinatown, My Chinatown'.

He was back in a couple of minutes with a puzzled look on his face.

'Well?' asked the newspaperman.

'Seems that Mr Perrine checked out this morning, sir.'

'He what?'

'Checked out, sir. With his luggage and everything. Didn't settle up, on account as the paper was paying.'

'Did he leave a message?' asked an uncharacteristically worried-looking Craster. 'A forwarding address?'

The young porter shook his head. 'Sorry, sir. Not a thing.'

41

'So, it looks like this is it,' said Harley. 'Pluckborough Mote. It's in East Charping, Kent.'

They were back in the kitchen in Bell Street. On the table, alongside the teapot, teacups, crusts of sandwiches and a curled-up Moloch, was a small pile of books from Harley's reference library. These included *Burke's Peerage*, *Who's Who*, *Historical Buildings and Ancient Monuments*, *A Walking Tour of Kent*, *The Buildings of England* and other similar works which Harley felt might prove useful.

'He inherited it from his mother, the Honourable Jocasta Mary Shalcomb,' continued Harley, reading from his notes of the conversation with Fellowes. 'Daughter of the third Viscount Shalcomb. Does that mean Morkens has a title?'

'Probably not,' said Cynthia. 'As the daughter of a viscount, the mother's would have been a courtesy title. As such, it wouldn't have been passed down to her children.'

'I might have guessed he'd have something to do with all that bollocks.'

'I'm well aware of your views on the peerage,' said Cynthia, interrupting him before he could get into full flow. 'But let's get back to the case in hand, shall we? What was the property called, Pluckborough…?'

'Pluckborough Mote.'

Cynthia leafed through a couple of the reference books before stopping at an entry in *Historical Buildings and Ancient Monuments*.

'Here we are: "*Pluckborough Mote. The ruins of a medieval moated manor house… the origins of the house date from circa 1350… earliest recorded owner was William Langley, High Sheriff of Kent… by the mid-fifteenth century, the building had fallen into ruin, with its stones subsequently carried away to build other houses in the neighbouring district…*"'

'Doesn't sound like it,' said Harley, pouring out some more tea. 'A farmhouse, Fellowes said.'

'Here we are. "The grounds also sport a handsome seventeenth-century *farmhouse*, once home to Henry Chillick, a minor poet and litterateur, part of a notable Kentish family, whose members included MPs and a governor of Bombay."'

'That's it.' Harley unfolded a large map and spread it out on the table, disturbing a disgruntled Moloch, who flashed a withering stare at the detective before slumping down onto the kitchen floor. 'Sorry, mate, but some of us have work to do. Right, here it is. East Charping. It's about ten miles out from Tunbridge Wells. On the bike I'd say that's about an hour and a half away.'

'You're not going down there on your own, are you?' Cynthia looked worried. 'If Morkens is the murderer, why, you don't know what he's capable of. Wouldn't it be better to pass the information on to John Franklin?'

'I told you – it'd be a waste of time. The fire's gone out in his belly. All he wants now is to collect his gold watch and settle down by the seaside with the missus.'

'Well, you can't really blame him, can you? But why does it have to be you?'

'Who else?'

She sighed. 'And what if something happens to you? What then?'

'You can't think like that, can you? You just get on with it.'

She snatched up his packet of Gold Flake and lit herself a cigarette. 'Well. Let me tell you, *I'm* thinking like that. I'm sure it all sounds very heroic, but you know, actually, I think it's quite idiotic for you to go down there on your own. It's probably not even crossed your mind what it might mean to *me* if you didn't come back… well, has it?'

'Now you're being melodramatic.' Harley began to fold the map up.

'Melodramatic?' Cynthia closed her eyes and drew a deep breath. 'You know, I'm not even sure it is about rescuing little Eddie Muller.'

'And what's that supposed to mean, exactly?'

'Oh, forget it!'

'No, come on, I want to hear this.'

'Well – the fearless war hero, George Harley, putting the world to rights for us all; courageously tackling—'

'You know what? I've changed my mind.' He grabbed his hat and began to walk out of the kitchen. 'Save it till later. I've got things to do.'

'George!' she called out after him. 'George, wait! Can't you at least get Solly to go with you?'

But the only reply was the slamming of the front door.

* * *

By the time Harley was thundering out of the London suburbs on his Norton the night was drawing in and the weather threatening to turn. Before long he found himself motoring through driving rain, thankful for his thick trench coat, leather helmet and goggles. The waterlogged road forced him to reduce speed, the black tarmac glistening in the meagre spread of the headlight. He passed the dim silhouettes of trucks and coaches, looming out of the murk like mythical beasts. Finally, after what seemed like an age, he was turning off the A21 and plunging into a network of winding, unlit back roads. On more than one occasion he had to stop to consult the map, using the small torch from his field kit, which he'd stashed under a rain cover in the sidecar. Twice he had to double back to take an alternate route. But at least by this stage the rain had begun to subside and before long the clouds were scattering to reveal a nickel-coloured moon.

The motorbike's headlight threw stark, claw-fingered shadows ahead of him on the tree-lined lanes of Kent, its gleam reflected from the undergrowth here and there by mysterious, feral eyes. The drive was treacherous in places. He fought against the pull of deep, claggy ruts and had to swerve the heavy motorbike combination to avoid sprawling puddles and startled pheasants careening across his path. Eventually he came across a road sign which indicated the way to East Charping: before long, he'd arrived at an ancient gatehouse, with *PLUCKBOROUGH MOTE* engraved upon a stone panel.

Harley killed the engine and took a moment to hide the Norton in a thicket of blackthorn bushes. He ditched his helmet, gloves and goggles, and slung the field kit across his shoulder. Then, using a thatch of tangled ivy as a ladder, he climbed over the boundary wall and followed the driveway, keeping to the deep cover that ran alongside it. After a few minutes' trek he came across the sprawling farmhouse, which was flanked by a cluster of outbuildings.

He made a quick recce of the premises. The outbuildings seemed unoccupied; there were two lights burning on the ground floor of the farmhouse, but no sign of any vehicle parked in the vicinity – though there were relatively fresh tyre tracks in the mud of the drive. He was just about to test the lock on the back door of what appeared to be the kitchen when he heard the sound of a car approaching along the drive. Pocketing his torch, he darted across the yard, taking up position in the gap between the house and an old potting shed.

The car was an Alvis 12/50 Sports model. Top of the range – an expensive piece of machinery. With just the pale moonlight for illumination, and with its convertible roof up, it was difficult to see inside; but once it had been parked close to the house, Harley had a clear view of both occupants.

The passenger was the first to get out. Judging by the crumpled old beaver hat, the bushy whiskers and shabby overcoat, this had to be the dubious informant Martin Perrine. Perrine was closely followed into the house by the driver, someone who Harley recognised immediately – the strange character in the Homburg and thick pebble-lensed glasses he'd bumped into outside Madame Leanda's clinic.

He felt an exciting rush of adrenaline. If this was the kind of company the professor kept, then it was almost certain his hunch about Morkens and the farmhouse had been on the money. Surely, he was now close to unravelling the puzzle? And, who knew? With a bit of luck, maybe even rescuing little Eddie Muller.

But, of course, there was one problem: he was outnumbered – three to one, if Morkens was home. And although two of the company might be elderly individuals who were probably strangers to physical violence, the third of their number, Homburg, was an unknown quantity. He'd have to tread carefully, that was for sure.

Having waited until the new arrivals had disappeared inside the farmhouse, Harley now crept out of his hiding place, hugging the wall of the building as he made his way towards the kitchen window.

He heard laughter, conversation.

Risking moving a little closer to the window, Harley bobbed his head up briefly to get a closer look.

Inside, Perrine and Homburg had been joined by a third person; not Morkens, but a female, her back turned to the window, the gaslight in the kitchen casting her in silhouette.

The woman was laughing, her shoulders shaking in mirth.

He watched Perrine touch a hand to the woman's cheek and, as she placed her own hand on top of it, Harley caught a glimpse of a jawline that looked familiar.

Is that you? he thought. *Come on. Turn around.*

As though she could hear his thoughts, the woman turned to the sink, her face in full sight of the window, and she gazed into the courtyard as she filled a glass with water from the tap.

Harley quickly dropped out of sight. But, before he did, he'd had a clear view of that beautiful face, with its deep blue eyes and exquisite complexion.

Madame Leanda! Or, at least, the woman posing as her.

He slunk back to the relative safety of a large rhododendron, behind which he could keep a safe watch on the occupants of the kitchen without the risk of being seen. He felt strangely deflated by the revelation – although it had been obvious that the mysterious strawberry blonde was somehow involved with the subterfuge surrounding Brendan Collins and Cassina, there had been a part of him that had hoped she'd turn out to be an innocent victim, coerced into the conspiracy by Manduca or the German von Görlitz. But watching her now, laughing and joking with Perrine – a man responsible for the framing of Alasdair Cassina as the Nursery Butcher, and possibly even for his murder – well, it seemed beyond doubt that she was an integral part of the murderous cabal.

But Harley's despondent musings were cut short.

He watched as the femme fatale's place at the window was taken by Perrine, who now stood at the sink and began to remove not only the shabby overcoat and crumpled hat, but also the greasy hair and overgrown sideburns – obviously just theatrical adornments, applied with spirit gum. Tossing the blue spectacles on the draining board, he ran the tap, and began to lather a small cake of soap. Having vigorously washed his face and neck of the fake grime he'd used to give his alter ego a dishevelled look, he placed a fresh towel over his face, patted it dry and then removed it – to reveal the domed head and white, caprine beard of Professor Osbert Agamemnon Morkens.

42

HARLEY CROUCHED IN the darkness, contemplating his next move. His head was whirling from the revelations of the last few minutes. Why on earth had Morkens been posing as Martin Perrine? And the fake Madame Leanda and Homburg – how did they fit into the picture exactly?

One thing was for certain – he was doing no good skulking outside in the dark. The decision now was to either fall back and regroup with reinforcements, or grasp the nettle and carry on single-handedly. It was at moments like this he found himself questioning his self-enforced mandate to refrain from carrying a firearm. Though it didn't take long for his conscience to offer up images of ruined faces in battle fatigues or the double-leafed trapdoor of an execution chamber as a stark reminder of the rationale behind this decision. So, what was it to be? Drive off to try to locate a public phone box in the slim hope of convincing DCI Franklin to muster some troops for a raid? A tall order, considering it was the middle of the night and the policeman had already warned him he'd be on his own if he persisted with the investigation. Or steal into the farmhouse – alone, and armed only with a knuckleduster – with the hope there were no more of the professor's accomplices inside?

The sound of a door opening drew Harley's attention back to the farmhouse, where he now saw Homburg and Madame Leanda leaving by the kitchen door. He pulled further back into the undergrowth as, with a wave to Morkens – who stood watching from the kitchen window – they climbed into the Alvis and set off back down the drive.

Now it was an easier decision.

Harley waited until the car had disappeared and Morkens had left the kitchen, then crept over to the back door and deftly slipped the latch with his strip of celluloid. He put on his brass knuckles, gave a cautious glance behind him and stepped inside.

The kitchen led on to a low-ceilinged passageway, which opened out into the main entrance hall. The stairwell was a dark affair – all oak panelling and barley-twisted balusters – which led up to the first floor and down to the gloom of a basement level below. He could see a light on the floor above, and reasoned there was a good chance that Morkens would have retired to a bedroom for a change of clothes. He decided to scout out the basement level.

To his dismay, Harley found the ancient stair treads groaned with the slightest weight, so each step he took had to be slow and cautious. Once he'd reached the basement lobby, he was presented with a choice of three doors, but it was the central one which stood out immediately as warranting investigation, secured as it was by a hefty padlock. The room beyond obviously had something to hide.

But it was also the age and design of the padlock that caught Harley's attention. It looked like a museum piece. Georgian, at a guess – surely a perfect match for the ornate quatrefoil keys the Nursery Butcher had left within the mouths of his victims?

He fished out his copy. Slipped back the brass keyhole cover. Inserted the key. And twisted.

The padlock snapped open with a satisfying click.

Now the game was on.

Inside it was pitch-black and he quietly closed the door behind him before resorting once more to his torch. A flash across the walls revealed a row of three gas brackets and, before long, he had these lit – though the light they cast was barely adequate to illuminate the long, vaulted cellar.

The first thing he noted was the smell: mould and damp, but something else beneath this – cloying and sickly-sweet. Across the left-hand wall was a long bench, busy with laboratory paraphernalia: Bunsen burners, rubber tubing, alembics and other assorted scientific equipment. On the wall opposite there was a large inglenook fireplace and in the middle of the room, dominating the space, was a roughly hewn table – more like an oversized butcher's block than a piece of domestic furniture. Against the wall, facing the door, sat the most alarming of the room's contents: three metal cages, their floors strewn with dirty straw. Harley dashed over to inspect these, flashing his torch into the dark corners, hoping to see Eddie Muller cowering inside. But he was frustrated to discover all three were empty.

He turned back to the table. The surface was rough, scored in many places, stained and unpleasantly greasy to the touch. Was this where Morkens had butchered his young victims? Had this dank chamber been the last thing they'd seen, shut off from the world, in a gloomy old farmhouse buried within ancient woods?

Harley put this thought to the back of his mind and continued with the search. Beneath the table he found a shelf stacked with large, leather-bound volumes. To improve the lighting, he put a match to a pair of giant, burgundy-coloured pillar candles, which stood nearby on iron stands, and then pulled out a selection of the books.

They were obviously old; a collection of colour plates, accompanied by a few pages of Latin text. Esoteric scenes, timeless and strangely alluring: a green lion consuming the sun; a noblewoman nursing a toad to her breast; archers shooting crossbows in a graveyard. There were many other images, somehow familiar to him, triggering some distant memory like the snatched fragment of a long-forgotten nursery rhyme.

He became strangely immersed in the pictures and, as he pored over the ancient tomes, the light in the room seemed to dim a little, and the colours of the illustrations glowed in contrast, shimmering before him on the page. He also noticed the sickly-sweet aroma growing stronger and more complex – musk and spice, and something else, gamey, organic.

Harley closed his eyes for a moment and was immediately assailed by a series of strange visions: the flickering of candlelight on damask silks; bejewelled fingers wielding ancient swords; a grimacing mouth glistening with the grease of roasted meats. Then he found the images were fading... fading to an ebony, infinite darkness.

His eyes remained closed. All was silent, the velvet silence of cathedrals.

After a while, he began to make out the strains of distant music: a haunting melody played on some kind of flute, naive and melancholic. And under this music there was something else, a faint menacing whisper.

Another vision now swirled into focus, stark, lifelike: the demonic baron, Gilles de Rais, in this very basement. Stripped to the waist before a roaring fire. Sweat streaming down his pale chest. Flames dancing in ecstatic, jet-black eyes. Beneath him, on the blood-drenched table, the naked corpse of a fair-headed child, his torso opened to reveal glistening, purple viscera; his innocent, cornflower-blue eyes locked on Harley's, the little mouth pleading, pleading...

Harley snapped open his eyes in a nauseating panic. His gaze was immediately drawn to a shelf, high up above the fireplace, half in shadow. He fumbled for his torch, aware that his actions were clumsy, as though he were drunk. He pointed the shaking beam of light at the shelf, and took an involuntary step back, resting a hand against the table to steady himself, his mouth filling with saliva.

There, staring back at him from the misty contents of large specimen jars, were the preserved heads of children. Thirteen of them. All with the cornflower-blue eyes of the victim from his hallucination.

Now Harley suddenly remembered why he was there: Morkens, the Nursery Butcher, and little Eddie Muller. He remembered Cynthia's warning. And he now knew, beyond any doubt, he was in the lair of a homicidal maniac.

And he was about to lose consciousness.

43

HARLEY AWOKE TO find himself slumped against the wall on the cold flagstones. The gas lamps were at half-jet, leaving large areas of the cellar in deep shadow. His mouth was dry and there was a painful throbbing in his temples. More worryingly, he found his hands were bound behind his back, secured to a pipe which ran at low level along the wall.

'Fuck! Not again,' he murmured, kicking out in anger and pulling against his restraint.

From somewhere off in the shadows there came an ominous chuckle.

'Welcome, Mr Harley. Welcome to my Bloody Chamber.'

'You're laughing now, you bastard. But this is where your little game starts to come crashing down around your miserable head.'

'Well, I certainly admire your spirit,' said Morkens, walking into view, a sinister smile on his lips. 'Although, I'd say that's a little optimistic, wouldn't you? Given the way things have turned out.'

The professor appeared taller somehow, more physically commanding than when they'd met before. He'd changed into a long-flowing robe of Eastern design, an embroidered smoking cap covering his bald head. And there was something in his jet-black eyes that put Harley in mind of a Caravaggio exhibition that Cynthia had once taken him to. Something wicked, ancient. It occurred to him that this was the real Osbert Morkens, and the affable academic he'd met in the Lyons Corner House was as much a false identity as Martin Perrine.

'Terribly bad luck, intoxicating yourself like that with my candles.' The professor traced a slender finger down the solidified rivulets of wax. 'Rather potent, aren't they? I developed them to help induce the Sleep of Siloam – a trance-like state, to help new initiates comprehend spiritual enlightenment.'

Harley used his feet to push himself to a sitting position against the wall; an act that caused Morkens to produce a small handgun from the folds of his robe.

'I'd advise you quash any ideas you might have of heroic attempts to escape, dear boy.'

The revolver was an antique-looking, brass-framed affair. A short .22 calibre, Harley guessed. Not the most accurate of firearms, but still fatal at such close range.

'You know the police are on their way,' said Harley, resting his head back against the wall. 'Racing here, as we speak, to drag your sorry arse to jail. We know all about your sick little games, you see.'

'Oh, yes? And which little games might those be?'

'This fixation you have with that lunatic Gilles de Rais. Leaving all those clues, like some giddy little flapper on a treasure hunt.'

The professor's features darkened. He gave a pensive tug at his white goatee.

'Those oafs at Scotland Yard wouldn't have figured that out. What assistance have you had?'

'Assistance? Don't flatter yourself, Prof. The keys in the kiddies' mouths? Cassina's suicide? That *Bluebeard* book – I mean, it's all a bit heavy-handed, ain't it? I s'pose it's understandable, really. You're obviously bright, but I guess you just lost a bit of perspective. All you maniacs get caught up with your little perverted obsessions, don't you?'

'Perverted obsessions?' Morkens thumped his fist on the long bench, on which the macabre collection of specimen jars had now been lined up. 'Look on my works,' he hissed, twisting a number of jars so that the pitiful heads faced Harley. 'Look at them! *Look!* Perverted obsessions? Hold their stare, you deluded creature. Do you think…'

Morkens checked himself. He took a few deep breaths, inhaling through his nose, then pulled out a small pill box and placed a black lozenge on his tongue. When he spoke again, he was calm once more, measured.

'They're exquisite, don't you think?' He caressed one of the jars with his long, elegant fingers. Inside the glass, fronds of golden hair settled lazily in the preserving fluid, the cherubic face looking strangely tranquil, as pale as alabaster. 'If you ignore the blanched flesh at the neck, you could almost be looking at busts from the old masters – Donatello, perhaps. Or Cellini. The boys were chosen carefully, you understand, in order to match the originals.'

'What do you mean, the originals? You've done this before?'

'No, no. I mean the Baron's fine work.' He walked along the bench, running his hand along the line of jars. 'Of course, I had to decant them from the old vessels, replace the embalming fluid; a laborious process. Trial and error. Regrettably I lost one dear boy before I'd perfected the technique. But I put him to good use, of course – gifting him to you in that hatbox on the tram. The body I used belonged to this little chap here, I believe.' Morkens tapped the glass jar at the end of the line. 'Quite a conundrum for you, no doubt, that preserved head? And what did you think of the Baron's choice of stuffing? Such exquisite taste. *La tapisserie de l'Apocalypse*. You know, I believe it to be one of the original samples of Hennequin de Bruges' design. Of course, the originals might all have similar cerebral embroideries; all chosen with symbolic intent, of course. Just look at them, Harley. Look at them closely – I defy you to tell the difference between the victims of a few weeks ago and those little ones who have had their beauty preserved for *centuries*!'

'The Baron? Are you trying to say that's what you found, in the grounds of that castle in France? The heads of Gilles de Rais' original victims? From when was it, the 1400s? I don't believe you.'

'Oh, it's quite true. But...' Morkens stepped closer. 'How do you know about the dig at Tiffauges? Who's been talking?'

'You'd be surprised,' said Harley, keeping a close watch on the killer's face – if he was going to get out of this alive, it was imperative to judge Morkens' reactions, so he could gauge how to play him. 'When it comes down to the nitty gritty, you'll find you can't trust anyone nowadays.'

Morkens stood for a moment, fixing Harley with a penetrating gaze, the gas jets reflected in miniature in his dark eyes.

Then he suddenly clapped his hands, bellowing a laugh.

'Of course! Your uncle! It was Blake Harley who told you about the archaeological dig, wasn't it? And did he also tell you about the auction of the Baron's library?'

'Oh yeah. At Sotheby's. I s'pose that's where you first got turned on by it all, was it? Rummaging through all those dirty pictures in those old books? Gilles de Rais' blow-by-blow account of how he fiddled about with little boys?'

The professor took a step towards him, levelling the pistol at his face.

'You know, your uncle was also bidding for that collection in the sale room that day. Maybe the great man wasn't quite who you thought he was, hmm?'

Then he laughed and lowered the gun. 'You know, in your own coarse little way, you're not far from the truth. You see, the secrets in de Rais' journal, the ancient knowledge gathered in those books and manuscripts he had collected over his lifetime, *were* a revelation to me. They galvanised my mind, like a bolt of lightning. My immediate reaction, as an academic and antiquarian, was to publish a paper based on my discoveries, in order to refute the vulgar image of the bloodthirsty pederast and bungling occult dilettante that has been foisted on the Baron through the centuries. But, you see, the more I read of his elevated studies in alchemy and Gnosticism, the more I realised I could never reveal such powerful secrets to the public.'

Morkens paused for a moment to pop another of the black lozenges into his mouth.

'Oh, I'll admit it was humbling. Here was I, suddenly privy to a wealth of arcane wisdom, the pursuit of which had been lost to man since the dawn of the so-called Age of Enlightenment. How could I possibly share it with the masses? It would be like casting pearls before swine. And then I came to the passage in his journal, describing that chamber at Tiffauges, constructed underground to contain all his most sacred possessions, to keep them safe from his oppressors as the Duke of Brittany's net closed in.'

'Come on then, what *was* in there?' asked Harley, keen to keep Morkens talking so animatedly. 'Apart from those poor kids' heads, I mean.'

'Ah no!' The professor wagged a long finger at him. 'Such things aren't for the likes of you, I'm afraid. You lack the metaphysical training, you see. As do most.'

Morkens sighed as he sat down on a stool, placing the gun on the bench behind him. 'Alas, we now live in such a boorish, literal world.'

He turned the nearest jar, so that the preserved head was facing him, and tapped on the glass with a fingernail.

'You know, the press described my killings as bestial. They are quite wrong, of course: a beast could never be as cruel as man. You see, the pleasure comes from design, not from instinct. Take the wolf – does he know the ecstasy of torture? Of torturing *children*?' Morkens' eyes fluttered, his sensual lips pursed at the memory. 'Of course not. He knows nothing of their delicious defencelessness, has never experienced that delectable moment when they realise they have no refuge, no saviour.' He lifted the lid of the jar and teased the floating flaxen hair. 'You talk of perversion? Obsession? No, my friend, this is ritual. Ritual and *artistry*. First the concept, the design. Then the selection of the victim. Only the most beautiful, you understand – one would get no pleasure from murdering an ugly child. Then the preening, the fattening up…' Morkens suppressed a chuckle. 'The playful fights. Everything choreographed. A kind of theatre, almost. That exquisite excitement as you watch them move from childlike joy to surprise… to *outright terror*.' His face darkened once more, his breath quickening. 'Then teasing them back, explaining – oh so earnestly – that you were only joking, that you didn't mean to scare them so. And how they do so *want* to believe it, with all their heart. How they convince themselves that you're really their friend. Even though they see the angry welts already rising on their lily-white skin.'

Morkens grasped his temples and closed his eyes momentarily, trying to still his panting.

'You're insane,' whispered Harley.

The professor held out his hands and smiled.

'Insane? Perhaps… when judged against your banal

pedestrian values. But that's neither here nor there. After all, I am the undisputed emperor of *my* world.'

Harley was doing his best to suppress his disgust at the killer's maniacal gloating. 'That's all very interesting,' he said. 'But tell me: the locations you chose to leave the bodies at. The house in Clapham, I get – after all, you made sure to point out the connection between Cassina and Dawson to me yourself, at the Lyons Corner House that time. But the other two?'

'I didn't want to make it too obvious. But our friend Perrine is very persuasive. He pointed out to Quigg and Craster the significance of the butcher's shop in Alasdair's little novel. As for the tram route connection? It was pure chance. They concocted the link themselves. We just needed somewhere easily accessible.'

'We?'

Morkens chuckled. 'You shan't draw me on that.'

'But why did you choose Cassina as your patsy in the first place?'

'You're the detective – you tell me.'

'Something to do with the kind of books he wrote? Maybe you thought his reputation as an *enfant terrible* would make him a credible suspect.'

'*Enfant terrible* – how fitting. Yes, our late novelist was the perfect example of entitled ennui, wasn't he? And so handsome, of course. As you managed, somehow, to stumble across my Bloody Chamber, I'll let you into our little secret. After all, you shan't have the opportunity to share it with anyone.'

Morkens flashed another of his sinister smiles.

'Our plan is that, in death, Cassina will become a kind of antihero for the cult of youth. A Valentino of apathy and chaos, if you will. A beacon to all those poor lost souls, attending their cocktail parties and gallery openings, gyrating in the latest inane fashion to their nigger minstrel bands.' He gave a little wistful sigh. 'I'm afraid the young are all doomed, aren't they? Doomed, sooner or later, to catch that virus, spreading like wildfire amongst them.'

'Virus?'

'Metaphorically speaking, you understand. Oh, come now, Harley, you must see that Western civilisation has reached a dead end? It is sick! Moribund.'

Morkens had started to become agitated again.

'Over the years it has become corrupted – predominantly by the tainted kiss of Christianity, but also by the Enlightenment, by democracy, by the so-called freedom of the masses. This rot has been allowed to spread through society, unchecked. And when you have a diseased plant, why, you must chop it out, root and branch. Burn the infected material. Start again by planting anew!'

'And you reckon you're the man for the job, do you?'

The professor closed his eyes, crunching the lozenge between his teeth and swallowing before he continued.

'I am merely the architect. Others must enact the process.'

'Like that charlatan, von Görlitz?'

'Oh, Fedor is no charlatan. Granted, he might have started out in the carnivals, but he is one of the most naturally gifted mesmerists I've ever met. And now, with the aid of my careful mentoring over the years, he has become a most powerful mage; one not to be reckoned with lightly. Herr von Görlitz may well go down in history as one of the greatest prophets of the New Era.'

'New Era?' scoffed Harley.

'Yes. One which will require a certain amount of heralding in; for which *I* have provided the design – in the artistry of my exquisite murders and in the instructions hidden within Cassina's unpublished novel.'

'A novel which will always remain unpublished.'

'Oh no. On the contrary, dear boy.' Morkens eyes were wide now, showing his excitement. 'Rumours of its existence will spread; we'll make sure of it. The manuscript will be leaked. Unauthorised editions printed. It will become the stuff of legend: the Author of Chaos, leaving a murderous legacy for the generations to come. Oh, it was easy enough to tip Cassina in the right direction with his work – introducing him to the tenets of Valentinists, et cetera. But he's far more useful to us dead. You see, the section we have now inserted in his manuscript frames the Nursery Butcher murders as just a part of Cassina's magnum opus: the quest to re-educate the lost generation in the futility of modern Western society. Once his cult begins to flourish, the young will clamber to re-enact the murderous rituals depicted in his book, just as they clamber to learn the latest dance craze from America. Of course, this isn't our only stratagem. We have other irons in the fire – in Europe, in Russia. Sowing our seeds of destruction here and there. You see, only when man has sunk to the very depths of the moral abyss will the world be cleansed. Then we shall have our *tabula rasa*, a clean slate on which to draw the design of a new world, perhaps reflecting elements of those great civilisations of antiquity, unfettered by democracy and the confused morality of modern man. To this end I have been dripping my exquisite poison, distilled from the teachings of our exalted Baron – both here and abroad – in preparation for such a recalibration. And I'm please to say it is already having some effect. Having turned their backs on God, people are so open to beguilement, you see.'

'And what about your bogus Madame Leanda? That strawberry blonde with the Hollywood curves. I wouldn't have guessed she was your type, Morkens. How does she fit into your little cabal, eh?'

The fierce glare returned to the professor's eyes.

'We won't talk of her.'

'Really? Why's that, then? You were happy to—'

'Enough!' shrieked Morkens, grabbing for his gun.

'Alright,' said Harley. 'Easy now. I get it.'

Sensing the professor's mood change again, he quickly scanned the room for anything that might aid in his escape, his mind racing through different strategies to placate his clearly unhinged adversary.

'Maybe you could educate me on something?' he said, trying a lighter tone. 'See, what I don't understand is, if you've got this grand scheme, why take the risk?'

'Risk?'

'Your little trail of breadcrumbs. For example, leaving those keys that could lead anyone straight back to your little playroom here.'

'Not anyone,' said Morkens, looking distracted for a second, as though something had just occurred to him. 'Anyway, they won't do, not after today. We are about to create Cassina's own little Bloody Chamber, you see. Far away from here. Dressed with a cage, a chopping block…' He nodded at the jars. 'We'll relocate some of the children there. The padlock is intended for *that* entry door. And when Perrine hints of the existence of such a place, those gullible fools, Craster and Quigg, will be persuaded to try the keys on the door, et voilà! Well, you see how the legend will grow.'

'I think I get you now, Morkens. You think you're smart, invincible even – but you're not *sure*, are you? Were you testing fate, securing your own door with that lock? Like a kid seeing how high he can climb a tree before he gets stuck or falls out. Is that why you go out in that fancy dress outfit?'

'Hmm?'

'Disguising yourself as that tramp, Martin Perrine – another of your little Gilles de Rais clues, of course.'

'Why am I also Perrine?' Morkens shrugged. 'Because it amuses me to be so. And, of course, it was a way of directing things without being personally associated with the crimes. You must admit, it's worked admirably. After all, your colleagues at Scotland Yard are now convinced that Alasdair Cassina was the Nursery Butcher, are they not?'

'Not for long.'

'I disagree.'

'What about the real Madame Leanda? Why did she have to die?'

'Ah! An unfortunate necessity. By chance she happened to recognise one of my associates from Berlin and started to spread scurrilous rumours about him.'

'So, von Görlitz and his little outfit *are* wrapped up in all of this.'

The professor smiled archly. 'When we searched the woman's clinic, we were amused to find her little archive of compromising photographs. Then you turned up, out of the blue, wanting suggestions for possible suspects. It was all too irresistible.'

'You know Brendan Collins tried to kill himself over those photographs.'

Morkens shrugged again. 'Nature has a way of correcting her own mistakes, sifting the wheat from the chaff.'

'And what about their little hearts and toes? What are you doing with those, you mad bastard?'

'Tut-tut. You shan't rile me that easily, you know.'

'No, come on, humour me. I'm curious – what do you do with them?'

'They're ingredients. With rare and powerful effects. For my *lamiarum unguenta*.'

'Come again?'

'You are familiar with the works of the Numidian, Apuleius…? No, of course you're not. What was I thinking. Really, I don't have time for this. Now, why don't we—'

'Where's Eddie Muller, Professor?' interrupted Harley, sensing he was losing the initiative. 'I don't see him in your disgusting little collection there.'

'Oh, the delectable Edward is quite safe. For the time being. As a matter of fact, a great honour awaits the child.'

'You shicer. What are you going to do to him?'

'I don't see why it should matter to you. Why don't you let it go, dear boy? After all, you must realise you're going to die here tonight.'

Harley gave a dismissive sniff. 'Maybe. Maybe not. The thing is, though, Prof, for all your arrogance, thinking you can run rings around us all, you gave yourself away in the end, didn't you? Playing your little treasure hunt, thinking you were so much smarter than the rest of us. Well, looks like you've fucked up this time, old son.'

'I think that's enough idle chit-chat. Now, you need to explain in detail how you identified me as the murderer, and who else might know.'

'I told you – everyone on the case knows. You'll be getting a knock on the door any minute now. Getting your collar felt by CID, like any other grubby little kiddie-fiddler. Why don't you do yourself a favour? Untie me now and give up little Eddie Muller. I promise I'll put in a good word. I'm sure any judge would look favourably upon it if you handed him over unharmed.'

'Oh dear, how tiresome,' said Morkens, with a sigh. 'You can't truly expect me to believe you would have come here alone if the authorities were aware of my involvement in the murders?'

He moved to stand over Harley, directing the gun at the private detective's face as he pulled a small golden pot from his robe.

'*This* is my *lamiarum unguenta*. My associates are due to return soon. Either you tell me voluntarily what I wish to know, or,' he waggled the pot, 'I'll have them hold you down as I apply this precious ointment to your skin. You see, it has powerful hallucinogenic properties. Just the merest of traces would produce strange and harrowing visions. But I shall smear enough on your *grubby* little temple to induce the wildest of psychoactive reactions. You'll be plunged into a personal hell, tormented by a host of demons summoned to do my bidding. And when its powerful effects begin to fade, you'll awake to find yourself stretched out upon my dear old chopping block.' Morkens paused to run a fingernail along his moist lip. 'You know, in a way, I rather hope you do refuse to tell me. One develops a taste for such things, you know.'

While they had been talking, Harley had been scanning the room, searching for anything that might offer a means of escape or act as an improvised weapon. As it was, his chances appeared slim, but he knew that if he were going to act, he needed to do it now, while Morkens was still alone.

'Alright,' said Harley, with a sigh, trying his best to look downcast, frightened. 'Get my pack, it's over on the table there. I'll show you how I worked it out.'

The professor thought for a moment, took a step to the side so he could check that Harley's hands were still tied behind him and then went over to the table.

With his back turned, Harley seized the moment. He quickly pulled in his feet, rocked onto his haunches, and gave an almighty yank on his bonds.

As he'd hoped, the lead pipe came away from the wall and snapped, releasing him.

Morkens turned as he heard the commotion behind him; but not quick enough. Though his hands were still bound behind his back, Harley was now free to launch himself, head-first, into the child-killer. The two men careered into the laboratory bench, test tubes and alembics crashing around them. Morkens hollered as the wind was knocked out of him, his gun clattering to the flagstones.

With the gas hissing loudly from the ruptured pipe, the lights – now starved of their fuel – quickly dimmed. Within seconds the cellar was in complete darkness.

Harley heard a low groan – evidently Morkens had been hurt in the fall, but there was no telling how long he'd be out of action. Using his elbow, he felt clumsily around on the floor, soon locating what he'd been looking for – a shard of glass from the broken lab equipment. He manoeuvred it towards his hands and begun to cut away at the bonds around his wrists.

'Help!'

The professor's first shout was weak, unlikely to be heard outside the room. But after a bout of panting, he yelled again, this time with more vigour: '*Help me! Down here, in the cellar!*'

Harley stopped cutting at his bonds for a moment and listened intently in the dark. He could hear some movement from across the room, but it was difficult to gauge exactly where Morkens was.

The gunshot was explosive, thunderous in the enclosed space. The flare from the barrel illuminated the room for an instant, showing the crazed, bloodied face of Morkens, steadying himself against the wall. Thankfully he was aiming towards the fireplace and hadn't seen where Harley lay. But the shot had obviously grabbed the attention of someone upstairs – urgent footsteps could now be heard on the floor above.

Harley continued to cut frantically at the rope, aware that Morkens' associates would be with them within seconds, his fingers sticky with blood from where the broken glass had dug into the flesh.

Another deafening shot in the dark, closer this time, ricocheting dangerously off the stone floor, just a foot or so from his head.

He scrambled for cover behind the table.

Morkens fired again.

There was a loud *wumph* as the jet of gas from the broken pipe ignited, flaring the cellar with a ferocious light.

When Harley's eyes had adjusted to the glare, he saw the maniacal professor was standing astride him, thrusting the barrel of the .22 at his chest with a shaking hand.

There was the sound of hurried steps from outside the door.

'Now we'll have *your* pretty head in a jar, Harley!'

44

MORKENS' FACE WAS delirious in the infernal light of the flaring gas pipe. The bloodied forehead, those black eyes burning maniacally, the mouth set in a grimace of rage – Harley reasoned that finally, after so many perilous adventures, he might truly be staring into the face of death. The professor's cadaverous hands were shaking wildly, one pointing the gun at his chest, the other fumbling with the lid of the golden pot.

He glanced at the door, waiting for the handle to turn.

Time slowed.

He felt his mind slip into the space he'd cultivated in the trenches. A place devoid of emotion, indifferent to any future beyond the next few seconds. He knew the security of his sanity relied wholly on his remaining resolute in this mindset. There was a slim chance that opportunities for escape might present themselves, but the likelihood was that he would die in the next few hours, following a bout of torture at the hands of Morkens and his cronies. The only control he had now was how he chose to react to this fate.

He closed his eyes and began to control his breathing, steeling himself for the ordeal ahead.

The door opened and Morkens turned to greet the new arrival with a smile – a smile which quickly vanished from his deranged face.

'Drop the gun, Professor,' said John Franklin. He gripped a torch in one hand, and in the other his service revolver, which he was pointing squarely at the child-killer's chest.

'And if I don't?' snarled Morkens, flecks of spittle spraying from his mouth.

'If you don't, he'll put a bullet in your gut and then I'll tear your fucking head off!' yelled Solly Rosen, storming into the room behind Franklin, wielding an iron bar in his huge fist.

'An ending undoubtedly messier than a quick drop on the hangman's noose,' added Franklin.

'Oh, mark my words, gentlemen, I shan't be going anywhere near a hangman's noose,' said Morkens, dropping the gun and holding his hands up in the air. He was once more the picture of composure, his face set with the calm confidence of the patriarchal academic.

* * *

'I've never been more pleased to see your big ugly mug,' said Harley, pulling greedily on a Gold Flake as he and Rosen stood in the kitchen, watching a handcuffed Morkens being led into the back of a Black Maria by the local Kent constabulary. 'Did Cynthia call you?'

'Yeah, only she couldn't get hold of me at first, hence the delay.'

'Well, seems I was out cold for a good part of that, so I was none the wiser.'

'How come?'

'It's a long story, Sol. I'll give you the full rundown later, over a pint.'

Rosen grinned. 'Yeah, I reckon I won't be putting my hand in my pocket for years after this little rescue, eh?'

'Alright,' said Harley. 'Don't get carried away. I had it all covered. It was just taking a little longer than expected.'

Rosen laughed heartily. 'Had it all covered? What, trussed up like a Christmas turkey with a barker stuck up your conk? Don't give me that old madam.'

They were both still laughing at this when Franklin came back in.

'Glad to see you've managed to retain your sense of humour. After what we found in that damned chamber of horrors, I'm not sure I'll laugh again for months.'

'Gallows humour. You know how it goes. So, any sign of the Muller kid?'

The policeman shook his head. 'I'm afraid not. What makes you think he's still alive? Something Morkens said?'

'Yes. He could have been lying, I know, but… well, just hoping, really.' Harley took another drag on his cigarette. 'Or maybe I'm just trying to justify almost getting topped by that maniac.'

'I'd say the justification is in getting a dangerous killer off the streets and ensuring no other poor victims are tortured and dismembered,' said Franklin. 'We're all indebted to you for that, George. And I can't begin to apologise for not backing you on this in the first place. I should have listened to you when—'

'Don't,' interrupted Harley. 'I've had enough long speeches for one day. You got here in the end, that's the important thing. And right in the nick of time, an' all. By the way, you sure these woodentops have searched thoroughly enough for Homburg and our mysterious strawberry blonde?'

'They're giving the grounds another going over as we speak. But if they had returned, my guess is they'd have made themselves scarce as soon as we arrived. So much for honour among thieves. We'll circulate their descriptions. Hopefully they'll turn up sooner or later.'

'Well, Morkens certainly thought it was some of his oppos coming down the stairs. I'm only guessing it was those two. And you need to raid that AOU headquarters in Belgravia. That shicer von Görlitz is in it up to his ears. That might even be where they're holding the Muller kid.'

'Don't worry, I've telephoned it all in to the Yard. I'd imagine they're knocking up some sleeping magistrate as we speak, to get the warrant signed.'

'Let's just hope Madame Leanda and her chum don't tip them off before you get there,' said Harley.

'We'll get to the bottom of it all in the long run.' Franklin took off his gabardine and hat and hung them on the coat rack. 'Right, the boys from the Yard should be here in a short while. I think I'll make a start on collecting some of this evidence. God alone knows what more we'll find in this damn charnel house. They've already discovered what looks like a pile of old bones in a well out there. And under the sink there was a large pestle and mortar, containing a shrivelled-up heart and what looks like a child's toenails.'

'Stop it, would yer?' said Rosen, pulling a face.

'Let's hope it isn't little Eddie,' said Harley. 'I could stomach all this a bit better if we found him alive, you know?'

Franklin noticed how drained the private detective was looking. 'We've got this covered, George. Why don't you and Solly head back to town? You can take my car. I'll go back in one of the Q cars.'

'But I've got the bike, outside, I—' began Harley.

'You're in no fit state to ride that thing. I'll have someone bring it back for you in the morning.'

'You know, I might take you up on that,' said Harley, suddenly realising how exhausted he was. 'But listen, John – don't go lighting any bloody candles in this place, especially purple ones. And, obviously, if you do find any traces of the kid—'

'Then I'll be in touch straight away,' said Franklin. 'Now, you get yourself off home. I'll see you some time tomorrow to take a statement. And, George?'

'Yes?'

'Thank you.'

* * *

Solly climbed into the driver's seat and reached across to tousle Harley's hair.

'Well, I reckon you did it again, Georgie boy. Another murderous cowson locked up where he belongs.'

Knowing the reputation of some of Rosen's associates, Harley found his enthusiasm a little puzzling, but he smiled, nonetheless. 'Didn't find the kid, though, did we? God knows what's happened to the poor little sod.'

'He might turn up yet, you never know. But listen – what did that shicer mean when he said he wouldn't be going anywhere near a hangman's noose? He going to top himself, d'you think?'

'No, I don't think so, not for a minute. Our professor has a far too high opinion of himself for that.'

'What did he mean then?'

'Well, he's a bright lad, ain't he?' said Harley. 'Either he's already working on an escape plan, or…'

'Or what?'

'Or he's going to pull in a few favours from the Old Boys' Club.'

'Come off it,' said Rosen, shaking his head. 'They'd never let him off. After what he did to those kiddies? There'd be a riot.'

'Maybe you're right. But his lot make up the rules to the game, don't they? I wouldn't be surprised if he doesn't find some way to save his ruddy neck.'

45

IT WAS FRIDAY night and festivities were in full flow. A generous fire burnt in the saloon bar grate, charging the room with a gloriously vinous and yeasty atmosphere, and the trio of tipsy musicians clustered around the upright piano was laying down a convivial soundtrack for the earnest work of communal intoxication; all of which made the prospect of leaving the Shab's cosy embrace at the end of the night a dismal prospect, but, thankfully, one that seemed to advance further into the future with each successive round of drinks.

Jovial as this might all appear, the Soho pub was still no environment for the demure or faint-hearted. Hal Dixon had already evicted two Piccadilly daisies, who, experiencing a run of bad luck, had snuck in from the cold to try their luck amongst the pub's punters. Archway Asta – once a great beauty, now a broken melodrama of a woman who seemed to survive on cadged drinks and crumpled bags of peppermint creams, had given her monthly performance of scrambling onto the bar, half-naked, to announce her suicidal intentions. As usual,

Juney had wrestled the six-penny bottle of iodine from her lips and covered her in an overcoat, before arranging a taxi to take her home (which was Asta's motivation for these regular performances in the first place). Half an hour previously, the local beat constable – the formidable PC Trent – had attended a particularly blood-soaked fistfight in the public bar between two inebriated cabbies. And there was also the all-too-familiar rumour doing the rounds that the Elephant and Castle Boys would be in the vicinity later that night to continue their ongoing turf war with Mori the Hat's gang. But all this was to be expected. If you wanted decorous elegance, you'd do better at some other, more genteel, establishment – the Café Royal, say, or the Ritz. This was the Shabaroon in Soho, on a Friday night.

'Gosh, I swear I should feel more sozzled than I do,' said Cynthia. She rested her head back on the banquette, exposing the exquisite line of her neck.

'The night's still young,' said Harley.

Cynthia narrowed her eyes at him, then smiled. 'You know, they're all so proud of you. I haven't been allowed to buy a drink all night. That nice old man over there bought this last round. He thought I was your wife.' She giggled at the sound of this.

Harley looked across to the table where the individual in question sat, surrounded by a group of serious-looking young men in wide-lapelled jackets. He held his drink up in a toast of thanks.

'That *nice old man* is Wally Lynch.'

'Who?'

'Before Mori Adler, there was Eric Coleridge, and before Eric Coleridge there was Wally Lynch. He's retired now, but that *nice old man*, as you call him, used to be one of the most dangerous villains in London.'

'Well, I don't think we've got anything to worry about. He thinks you're simply marvellous for capturing Morkens. They all do.' She rested her head against his shoulder. 'You're a local hero, Corporal Harley.'

Harley swallowed the rest of his whisky. 'You try telling that to Rose Muller.'

'Oh dear, has she been in touch again?'

'Another letter this morning. Urging me to go over all the evidence again, to try to work out where little Eddie might be. Says her old man has turned to drink over it.'

'And you say the police didn't find anything at the farmhouse that might indicate he was ever there?'

'Nothing,' said Harley. 'And by the time the coppers had got to the AOU place in Belgravia it had been cleared out. Added to that, it seems that Fritz von Görlitz has got some kind of diplomatic immunity through the embassy. And there's no trace of Homburg or the bogus Madame Leanda. It's not looking good. All we have is that jumper from the warehouse. The chances of finding the poor little bugger alive are pretty slim. If only I could—'

But his words were stifled by Cynthia's forefinger, pressed against his lips. 'Shush.'

She moved in closer, bringing with her the subtle blend of her Gizemli scent and sweet vermouth. In the rosy light from the lampshades, her face had a striking, luminous beauty. It was possibly an effect of the whisky, but for a moment she appeared slightly unrealistic amongst the Shab's bawdy patrons; elegant and stylised, a Lempicka portrait sprung to life. She replaced the finger with her lips, which were surprisingly hot and moist. Suddenly her tongue was in his mouth, probing and insistent.

His heart kicked in his chest.

Then she had pulled away and was clasping his face in her hands.

'Why don't we?'

'Sorry?'

'When he thought I was your wife, it made me feel…' She rubbed her nose with the heel of her hand, then looked at him earnestly. 'Corporal Harley, will you marry me?'

He shook his head. 'You're drunk.'

She scowled and grabbed his face again. 'I've never been more sober in my whole life. I shall ask you just one more time – well, will you?'

Harley thought back to the moment in the cellar: Osbert Morkens grinning maniacally, holding the gun to his chest; then further back, to harrowing night-time raids across no man's land; coming to in the cold slime of a shell crater, the sky thundering above his head. The stink of death and the squalor of trench life. The numbing futility of those lost years, lost comrades.

He placed a firm hand on Cynthia's, feeling its faint tremble. He gazed into the hazel-green beauty of her eyes, and knew, for just this once, he would defy his gut instinct.

He swallowed, his throat suddenly dry, and then said, 'Yes. Of course I will, Miss Masters.'

It's fair to say that Juney, Dixon and PC Trent had their work cut out for them at closing time that night. The revellers were eventually persuaded to move the party on elsewhere, and the night descended into some kind of broiling, Hogarthian dream. It was, by all accounts, a night to remember (although, of course, many of those involved didn't); a night which spawned a plague of hideous hangovers and earned itself a rightful place in Soho folklore

46

A month later

IT WAS SUFFICIENTLY early in Alberto's café bar to find a few of its overnight clientele still huddled over cups of overly sweetened tea and milky coffee. Harley looked around at the mixture of faces. Here were the citizens of the nocturnal city, whose lives went unnoticed by the majority of the populace. Here you could see the furtive glance of the recently unemployed, and the sickly pallor of the hungry and the conquered, but also the defiant, gimlet eye of the petty criminal and the resigned, stoicism of the veteran jane.

The café's corpulent Italian chef, Pietro, emerged from the kitchen through the beaded curtain, his left eye screwed up against the smoke from the ubiquitous cigarette stuck to his thick bottom lip. He unceremoniously plonked down the plate of food and the two steaming mugs of tea on Harley's table, then wiped his hands on the grubby tea-towel tucked into his apron string.

'Thanks,' said Harley.

'Prego,' said Pietro. But then, that's all Pietro ever said.

Harley pushed the egg and chips across to the pale young man sitting opposite him. 'There you go, Tommy. Get that down you.'

Tommy Harkin was a dilly boy. Smarter than most of his associates, he tended to keep his mouth shut and his eyes and ears open – a useful trait that had led Harley to include the lad in his retinue of reliable informants.

'Thanks, George,' said Harkin, mopping eagerly at the egg yolk with a slice of bread. 'I've been trolling all night without a sniff of trade. So, what's this little chicken's name again?'

'Julian Bartlett. He's sixteen.' Harley placed a small photograph on the sticky Formica. 'Been missing for about six months now.'

The dilly boy stuffed a forkful of chips into his cheek and nodded, chewing ravenously. 'Oh, *her*. Oh yes, I know that one.'

'Where?'

'*Where?* Oh no. The first question is *how much?*'

'Let's say half a crown.'

'And smokes?'

Harley smiled and nodded. 'Alright, I'll throw in some smokes.'

Harkin looked on expectantly until Harley produced a pack of Gold Flake, then snaffled one of the cigarettes and lit it immediately.

Harley put the money on the table. 'Come on then. Where did you see the kid?'

'Well, the first time was when he was trying his hand with the Soho Square boys,' said Harkin, pocketing the coin and picking up a limp chip. 'You know what they're like at rounding up all the little waifs and strays.'

Harley gave a sigh. 'How long's he been working the streets, then?'

'Oh no, she didn't last. Not cut out for the trade, poor thing. You have to be bold to survive out there, as I'm sure you know.' Harkin gave a little dismissive shake of his head, then dragged a tress of red hair behind his ear. He leant forward, conspiratorially. 'No, the last time I saw our little friend was at one of those cod tea parties, given by that vile Reverend Morley.'

'Who?'

'The priest at St Rufus's, behind King's Cross.'

'Yeah, think I've heard of him. Takes in charity cases, right?'

'Yes, well, he's always in Soho, trawling the streets on the premise of saving our lost souls. But he also throws these tea parties in the church hall; "gathering his flock", he calls it.'

Harkin blew out a plume of smoke, disdainfully.

'Lays on a load of free jarry. Those without a doss for the night get to bunk down at his. Where, of course, they get touched by more than just the Holy Spirit, if you know what I mean—'

The lad broke off abruptly, distracted by something he'd seen through the café's shop window. Looking alarmed, he grabbed at the packet of cigarettes, took a last gulp of tea and started for the exit.

'Oi! Where are you going?'

By way of explanation, Harkin nodded towards a figure standing in the street outside, then slipped furtively out the door.

Harley turned to see DCI Franklin entering the café – an arrival which prompted the instant departure of another three of the café's patrons.

'Something I said?' asked the policeman, as he took Harkin's vacated seat.

'You just cost me half a crown. It must be a chore being so popular.'

'Oh, it's something you soon get used to as a copper. How've you been keeping?'

'Yeah, good. Busy, actually.' Harley caught a look in Franklin's eye. 'You alright?'

'Oh, yes, thanks. Plodding along, as usual. Counting down the days until my retirement. By the way, I had an update on our little German warlock yesterday.'

'Von Görlitz?'

'Yes. It's been confirmed he's still in Berlin. But I'm afraid we've little chance of getting him over again for questioning. It seems Herr von Görlitz has some important friends in extremely high places.'

'The slippery bugger. What about Homburg and Leanda?'

Franklin shook his head. 'Vanished into thin air. Possibly in Berlin with von Görlitz. I can't help feeling I've let the public down somehow.'

'I know what you mean. And still no sign of Eddie Muller. Maybe that's good news, in a way. No body I mean.' Harley took a drag on his Gold Flake. 'At least we collared that maniac, Morkens. Talking of which, the trial starts next week. Let's hope the bastard gets the drop, eh? As a witness, I'm guessing I won't be able to watch until after I've testified?'

'Well, that's actually what I've come to see you about.' Avoiding Harley's inquisitive look, the policeman pulled out his pipe and began to fill it from his tobacco pouch.

'Don't be telling me he's taken the coward's way out and topped himself.'

'No, no. Nothing like that. Morkens has changed his plea to guilty. There isn't going to be a trial.'

'Aright,' said Harley, nodding. 'Alright. But that can't mean he'll avoid the death sentence. Not after what he did. Unless—'

'Unless it's deemed he was insane at the time of the offence.'

'I thought that shicer might try to pull something like this. But I've looked into this.'

Harley pulled out his notebook and flicked through to the relevant page. 'Here it is. "*In such a case the defendant must be suffering from a defect of reason. The defect of reason must be caused by a disease of the mind and be such that the defendant didn't know what he was doing; or, if he did know what he was doing, didn't know the act was wrong."* None of which applies for Morkens. As far as I'm concerned that shicer is as—'

Franklin puts his hand up to calm Harley.

'Listen, I'm just telling you how it is. Last week Morkens instructed his defence team to offer a plea of guilty, citing the mitigating circumstance that he had been ordered to murder the children by…' Now Franklin pulled out his own notebook. '…by a demon serving the ancient Ammonite god, Moloch.'

'Moloch?'

'He's mentioned in the Bible, apparently. Something to do with child sacrifice.' Franklin noticed Harley's look of concern. 'Is that significant?'

'I'm well aware of the Biblical reference. It's just that Moloch is also the name of my pet cat, remember? I named him after an engraving my Uncle Blake had hanging in his study. He was into all that kind of stuff. But what I want to know is, how Morkens…' Harley made a fist, his face colouring with anger. 'Jesus! If that bastard has had someone snooping on me, I swear I'll—'

'We don't know that, George. Let's just put it down to coincidence for the moment, shall we?' Franklin put a match to his pipe and took a couple of puffs. 'The painful truth is that the medical johnnies have examined our professor and are convinced he's not faking his symptoms.'

'What?'

'They've offered a diagnosis of criminal insanity. The Home Secretary has intervened and placed him under an immediate reception order. He's off to Broadmoor in the morning.'

'You've got to be joking!'

'Morkens is fifty-six. He's very likely to spend the rest of his life incarcerated in there. And Broadmoor Lunatic Asylum is no Savoy Hotel, I can tell you.'

Harley shook his head. 'No. That bastard's playing us. Pulling in favours to save his neck.'

'What do you mean, pulling in favours?'

'It's that bleedin' Old Boys' Club, ain't it? It was stone ginger this would happen. I knew it! Just think about it: Osbert Morkens is an Oxford professor, the grandson of a viscount. The Home Secretary? The judge? They probably all belong to the same sodding private members' club. I bet if you looked into it, you'd find some connection.'

'Well, I for one am not going down that particular route.'

'More than your job's worth?'

'Damn right! And if you know what's good for you, you'll leave well alone. That's the kind of hot water that even your chum Moriel Adler couldn't get you out of.' Franklin stood up. 'Now, you're obviously upset about this, so I'll—'

'Listen,' Harley lifted his hands, 'I'm sorry. I didn't mean to fly off the handle like that. Please, John, sit.'

The policeman relented and Harley ordered a mug of tea for him.

'Maybe there's an upside to this,' he said, sparking up a Gold Flake.

'Go on.'

'Well, if Morkens isn't going to hang, we can have another pop at him; try to find out what happened to little Eddie Muller. And any other victims that we don't know about yet.'

Franklin closed his eyes and gave a little shake of the head. 'George. Don't you think you've done enough? Morkens is going to stay locked up in that asylum for the rest of his life. Can't you now just forget him? Concentrate on forging a new life with that beautiful fiancée of yours? A case like this, all the horror, the perversion… well, it can start to get inside your head. Taint everything around you.'

'And what do I tell Rose Muller when she comes knocking, eh? Explain that I've given up looking for her little boy because it was upsetting me? Sorry, it don't work like that.'

'All I'm saying is appreciate what you have right now. Cynthia, your house, your friends, the strength in your arm, that robust mind of yours. One day they'll all be gone.'

Harley was about to respond, but Franklin held up his hand while he sucked on his pipe and thought for a moment. Then, having recovered what he'd been searching for, said:

'Make the most of what we yet may spend,
Before we too into the dust descend,
Dust into dust, and under dust, to lie,
Sans wine, sans song, sans singer, and – sans End!'

'That's good. I'll give you that one,' said Harley, smiling. 'What is it?'

'*The Rubaiyat of Omar Khayyam.*'

'Fitzgerald?'

'Well done.'

'Yeah, Uncle Blake was big into that.' Harley crushed his cigarette into the ashtray. 'So, can you get me a visit to Broadmoor?'

The policeman sighed. 'If you insist. After all, I'm back in favour with the super again – thanks to you.'

'You don't have to come, if you don't want to. Just get someone else from CID to escort me.'

'As if I'm going to let that happen.'

'Appreciated.' Harley looked at his watch. 'Listen, I need to get off. I'll check in with you in a couple of days' time.'

'By the way? How's Cynthia? Well, I hope.'

'Yeah, she's good. Everything's just dandy, thanks,' said Harley, getting up to pay Pietro.

But as he made his way out into the grey drizzle of the morning, Harley began to mull over Morkens' reference to Moloch; soon coming to the conclusion that he wouldn't be fully convinced everything was *just dandy* until he'd spoken to his fiancée, checked on his old tomcat, and closely inspected all the external locks and window catches at his place in Bell Street.

47

HARLEY AND CYNTHIA flung themselves down on the park bench, laughing after their romp up the hill. They sat in silence for a moment, catching their breath, making small clouds in the crisp autumn air. In front of them was a sweeping vista: the wide swell of Greenwich Reach, with the river flexing its muscles as if already sensing a briny tang in the air; the grimy, dockland sprawl of the Isle of Dogs; and beyond, glimpsed above the span of Tower Bridge, the majestic crown of St Paul's, nestled amongst its drab environs. Behind them, Sir Christopher Wren's proud little onion-domed observatory stood sentinel over Time – resembling a Baroque doll's house when compared to his mighty cathedral and the elegant Naval College below.

'What about that for a view then, Cyn?'

'Stunning! As is *this*.'

Cynthia held her hand up, displaying the Georgian engagement ring Harley had given her: a rose cluster of diamonds – an heirloom he'd inherited from Uncle Blake.

'I'm glad you like it. I bet it's got some exciting backstory. It was itemised as "the countess's ring", and knowing Uncle Blake, well, there's bound to be some intrigue behind it.'

'How romantic,' she said, with a sigh as she made the gemstones glint in the autumn sun.

'It's a little loose, though,' said Harley. 'We need to get that seen to. Don't want you losing it.'

'That'll be easy enough to remedy.'

Cynthia pulled up her coat collar and rested her head on Harley's shoulder, looking out again at the view. 'It's mad to think of all those people, living out their lives, crammed around the river like that. And yet, most of the time you have no sense the river's there at all.'

'Liquid history, someone once called it.' Harley lit two cigarettes and passed one to Cynthia. 'Old Father Thames. I always imagine him Poseidon-like, with this long beard and a trident, keeping watch from the shadows beneath one of the bridges.'

'Just think of all the things he must have seen,' said Cynthia. 'Over all those centuries. Romans, Celts, Druids... way back when it was a savage place.'

'Some would tell you it still is.'

Cynthia laughed and stood up to take in the view of the park.

'Wasn't Henry VIII's palace in Greenwich?'

'Yeah. He was born here, as was his daughter, Queen Bess. Over there, there's an ancient oak named after her; it was already four hundred years old when she was born.'

'And it's still there?'

'Yeah. She used to have picnics in its hollowed-out trunk. Apparently, Henry once danced around it with her mother.'

'Poor old Anne Boleyn,' said Cynthia.

'She'd have been taken to the Tower by barge, from just down *there*,' said Harley, pointing.

'Just think of that journey. How awful for her.' Cynthia put a hand to the back of her neck and gave an involuntary shiver. 'I think someone's just walked over my grave.'

Harley laughed and pulled her back to the bench.

'You know, when I was a kid, I came up here and picked a leaf from a bush.'

'For most people that wouldn't be extraordinary.' She gave him a playful poke in the ribs. 'But, coming from Shoreditch, it was probably the equivalent of an expedition to Outer Mongolia.'

'Very funny. Do you want the story or not?'

'I do. Please continue.'

'Right. So, this leaf had a real perfume, you know? Sweet and herby. Magical, somehow. Smelt a bit like Pears' soap, if I remember right.'

'Probably sweet bay.'

'Yeah? Well, anyway, I held this leaf to my nose, closed my eyes and…'

'And what?'

'Nah, you'll only laugh.' He drew on his Gold Flake and let out a plume of smoke into the cold air.

'I promise I won't. Do go on.'

'Well, I could suddenly see them all: Queen Elizabeth and her ladies-in-waiting, riding out side-saddle through the trees. Could hear them laughing, all beautiful and decked out in all that fantastic clobber, you know? Queer, ain't it? I've never told anyone that before. Maybe I've remembered it wrong.'

She turned and gave him a kiss on his cheek, his stubble prickling her lips.

'I think it sounds magical. We have such amazing imaginations as children. It's a shame in a way that we have to grow up.'

She sat up and looked at him.

'What do you believe in, Corporal Harley?'

'Blimey! That came out of the blue. Do you mean in a religious way?'

'Well, yes, I suppose I do.'

Harley shook his head, took the last drag from his cigarette and threw it into the bushes. 'Virgin births? Miracles? Resurrections? I don't believe in any of that old bollocks. It's all just made up.'

Cynthia sighed. 'I know. I know, but…'

'But what?'

'Well, I'm not quite sure what I'm trying to say, really. But the idea that we're sitting here, on the same piece of earth that all those generations of humans have walked on.' She put her hand to her cheek and looked around her. 'Just thinking that Queen Elizabeth might have sat on this very spot is crazy enough, but to go back through all those centuries, medieval, Romans, Celts and beyond…'

'What, you think there's some kind of design to the whole thing? That we're playing a role in someone's story, is that it?'

She shook her head. 'No, that's not what I mean. I think what I'm talking about is some kind of *connection*.' Cynthia stood, grabbing Harley's hands and pulling him up.

'What's happening now?'

'Just listen, will you? Now and again, when I'm playing the cello – sometimes on my own, but more often when I'm with the orchestra – well, I get *lost* somehow, in the music. And at that moment it's as if I've slipped out of the gown of *me*, of Cynthia Masters. Sloughed off my skin, if you will – like a snake. Oh, it's difficult to explain, but at that moment I understand I'm just part of a whole. Do you see? A tiny mote in some infinite and everlasting light of the universe.' She placed a finger on his lips. 'Don't laugh.'

'I'm not laughing.'

'Swear?'

'Cross my heart and hope to die.'

'What *is* that then? Is that religion? Spirituality?'

'Some kind of brain disease, I'd say.'

She punched him hard on the arm.

'Pax!' he said, holding his hands up, laughing. 'Seriously, though. That's just art, ain't it? That's humans for you. It's like when you get lost in a good book. Or you're haunted by a painting. No one said that wasn't magical. It's just not *magic*.'

'What about when you gaze at a night sky full of stars? Or a sunset? That's not art.'

He narrowed his eyes, considering this. 'No. But it probably comes from the same mechanism in our brains. There's bound to be some evolutionary advantage to appreciating beauty.'

'Your boy Darwin again? You know, I'm not sure science can answer all these questions… and I'm not sure I'd want it to if it could.'

He grinned at her.

'What?'

'Nothing. Just you.'

Cynthia smiled one of her generous smiles and Harley became lost for a moment in those hazel-green eyes. And in that instant, he realised that she'd managed to penetrate the last layers of the thick carapace he'd fashioned over the years. A shield he'd started work on as a youth on the streets of the East End, then had added to throughout the war years, his subsequent time spent with MI5 and as a private detective. There was now the two of them: George and Cynthia. A simple enough concept to grasp – the notion behind so much art and literature through the ages, the mainstay of popular culture; but one that made his head reel a little, now he was experiencing it in the raw. He felt compelled to pull her in tight.

He cupped her jaw and kissed her, tasting the scent of her lipstick, the slight saltiness on her tongue. They pressed into each other, oblivious now to the city vista and the autumnal chill. He slipped his hand within her blouse, an urgency rising between the two of them.

Cynthia stopped suddenly, pulling away from him.

'Sorry.'

'No, it's not that. Over there! I saw someone. Someone spying on us.'

'What?'

Harley pushed his way through the dense tangle of shrubs. He searched carefully in the hedgerow and behind the trunks of the mature chestnut trees. After a while, he returned, thick clumps of mud on his shoes.

'Nobody there. Are you sure you saw someone?'

She nodded, still looking a little anxious.

'Don't worry. It'll just be kids, I expect. Or some sad pervert out for a thrill in the woods.'

'The thing is, I think I saw the same man yesterday.'

'Where?'

'Outside my apartment. He wears a grey Homburg and thick-lensed glasses.' She put her hand to her throat, defensively. 'Do you think it might be that fellow? Morkens' man?'

'No, I'm sure it's just a coincidence,' said Harley, trying to hide his concern.

He surreptitiously patted his pocket to check his brass knuckles were there, then glanced once more at the shadows amongst the trees. 'Come on. It's getting a bit chilly now. Let's get you home and have a spot of tea, eh?'

'Is there something I should know?'

'No. It's nothing. As I said, it's probably just some pervert, getting a cheap thrill.'

But as they made their way back down the hill, Harley kept a keen eye out for anyone following them.

* * *

'Do you really have to go to see that hideous creature tomorrow?' asked Cynthia, after supper at Bell Street that evening. 'I can't help thinking it's somehow unhealthy – to be in close proximity to such, such… depravity.'

'You sound just like Franklin. Listen, it's just one day. One more chance to find the Muller kid. I can't bottle out on that now, can I?'

'I suppose not.'

'And when this is all over, I promise, we'll go away somewhere for the weekend.'

'Paris?'

'Well, I was thinking more Brighton, but, yeah, why not? Paris.'

'Fabulous!' she said with a smile.

'Hold on,' he said a little sheepishly. 'I've got something for you.'

'What on earth is it?' asked Cynthia, looking in the old biscuit tin which Harley had placed on the dining table.

He took out an object wrapped in cloth and began to unfold it. Cynthia soon realised the wrapping was a German imperial flag.

'A souvenir, from the war. It's a Luger P08 semi-automatic.' He turned the pistol around so she could get a good look at it, but kept the barrel pointed towards the floor. 'I took it off a Fritz during my first trench raid. An Unteroffizer – a corporal – not much older than me. All his pals were caught off guard, but this bloke… well, he took three of us out with this. Nerves of steel. I kept it as a reminder.'

'I thought you didn't approve of guns in civilian life?'

'I don't… usually,' he said, rubbing the back of his neck. 'Listen, don't read too much into this, but I want you to keep it with you, while I'm away tomorrow.'

'Don't be ridiculous! I'm not having that thing in my apartment. Hold on, is this to do with that fellow in the bushes? I thought you said it was just a coincidence?'

'And I still think that. Only…'

'George, is there something you're not telling me? Because I'd really rather know all the facts. Do you think I'm in some kind of danger?'

'I don't know. But there's a possibility that Morkens has had someone spying on me.'

'And *me*?'

'I know, I know. Listen, there's always a slight chance you'll get some fallout from a case. Usually, I'm alright with that, because… well, normally I've only got myself to worry about. But it would be stupid to take any chances. So…' He smiled, a kind of guilty schoolboy smile. '*Please!* Just keep it with you in the apartment.'

Cynthia scowled at him for a moment, smoking silently. Then she gave a deep sigh and held out her hand.

'Come on then. I suppose you had better show me how the wretched thing works.'

48

'Just a moment, George,' said John Franklin, placing a hand on Harley's arm as he was about to get out of the Yard's black Wolseley, 'Silent Six'. 'There's something I need to tell you before we go in there.'

It had been a long, uneventful drive out from the capital, and they were now parked up outside the castellated gatehouse of the Broadmoor Criminal Lunatic Asylum – Franklin having finally secured the interview with Osbert Morkens which Harley had been so insistent on.

'I was going to wait until after we'd seen him. But... well, I've been mulling it over during the journey, and I think it's best you're forewarned before we go in there; in case, as is my hunch, it has something to do with the professor.'

'What are you talking about? Is there something I should be worried about?'

'Possibly,' answered Franklin, after considering the question for a while. 'Here. Take a gander at that.'

The policeman handed Harley a mugshot of an

unsavoury-looking character with protruding ears, defiantly sneering at the camera. 'Recognise him at all?'

'No. Should I?'

'He's not your mysterious stalker in the Homburg hat?'

'Definitely not. Homburg's an odd-looking cove – graveyard complexion, thick, pebble-lensed glasses. This fella's far too pretty. Who is he?'

'A nasty little Maltese villain named Silvio Baldacchino. Our boy Silvio has a bit of a reputation back home in Valletta. He's got a charge sheet as long as your arm: extortion, kidnapping, wounding with intent.'

'Charming. So, why are you carrying his smudge around with you?'

'Baldacchino had his collar felt two days ago,' said Franklin, beginning to fill his Bulldog briar with tobacco. 'Getting off the channel ferry at Dover. It was a routine customs check, apparently, but he panicked; made a dash for it. He was attempting to enter the country on a forged passport – poorly forged at that. When they searched his suitcase, they found a loaded revolver and an envelope. An envelope containing a photograph of you, along with your name and address.'

'What? You're sprucing me!'

Maltese? thought Harley. *It couldn't be the Spider, surely?*

'I'm afraid not. I've seen the evidence myself. Customs and Excise duly turned him over to Special Branch, who, I'm reliably informed, took him into one of their ghost cells in the basement of their HQ at Hyde Park Corner and… well, applied a little pressure, let's say, to get the lad to cough.'

'Good boys. And?' he asked, tentatively.

'And cough he did.'

Franklin struck the match he'd been holding and was lost for a moment in a small cloud of aromatic smoke.

'According to Baldacchino,' he continued, after winding down his window, 'your old friend Victor Manduca was behind it.'

'That can't be right.'

Harley's mind whirled through the possibilities. He knew the photographs of Spiru and Vanessa were still safely locked away in his solicitor's office in Moorgate. Spiru would never risk having his clandestine affair exposed to his murderous brother. Did that mean he wasn't privy to the hit? It must do… well, alright… that meant he still had some control over the situation. A simple phone call to Spiru and the younger Manduca would do anything, come hell or high water, to stop another sanctioned hit on him. Wouldn't he?

'It was the Spider alright,' said Franklin. 'But, according to Baldacchino, he was only meant to wound you. To frighten you off.' The policeman tapped the stem of his pipe against his teeth. 'But then, I suppose, he would say that, wouldn't he? So, I guess that's no real consolation.'

'Yeah, thanks for pointing that out,' said Harley, pulling out a Gold Flake and snatching up the box of matches Franklin had left on the dashboard.

'The *good* news is, we rounded up Victor Manduca and his gang immediately. Early morning raid. They're still locked up in the cells as we speak. Not to be released until I give the nod.'

'I'm not sure the order would have come directly from Victor,' said Harley, still calculating it all as he puffed on his cigarette. 'As far as he was concerned, everything was back to normal. Sure, he'd been implicated in the case; but we hadn't been able to make any charges stick, had we? Fundamentally he's a businessman. A despicable, immoral, ruthless businessman, no doubt. But a businessman nonetheless. His ultimate goal is the gelt. I'm not sure he'd rock the boat like that after the waters had calmed down so much for him. Maybe the order for the hit came from that shicer von Görlitz?'

'Maybe. Or perhaps from our friend the professor in there?'

'Go on.'

'Well, as it happens, I'm as doubtful as you are about Victor Manduca being the instigator of the plot. But he obviously organised it. And the reason I don't want him and his gang released until I give the word is because I don't want anyone in the know to get a message to Morkens that Baldacchino has been apprehended. If it *was* the professor who commissioned the attack, then he might be a little more forthcoming in our interview if he still believes it's going ahead.'

Harley blew a long trail of smoke through his nose.

'You know what, John?' he said, shaking his head. 'You're not as green as you are cabbage-looking. That's some smart thinking there.'

'Oh, I've been known to have my moments.'

'Whatever will they do without you when you retire down to that B&B in Whitstable, eh? Alright, then. Let's get this over with.'

Harley got out of the car and grabbed his hat from the back seat. He ran his fingers through his hair, shot his cuffs and killed his Gold Flake beneath his heel.

'The last time I had a parlay with this character,' he said, standing on the gravel drive and looking up at the imposing redbrick edifice, 'I was chained to a pipe with a .22 in my face.'

'Come on, George,' said Franklin, placing a reassuring hand on the younger man's shoulder. 'I've a feeling you need to do this. Not just for little Eddie and those other poor kids, but also for your own peace of mind.'

* * *

'Well, so far, I'd say he's been the model patient, Inspector Franklin,' said Principal Attendant Johnson.

Behind him, the winter sun broke through the clouds above the sweep of Berkshire countryside framed by the large arched window. If it weren't for the high perimeter wall which cut through the terraced gardens, the vista might have been mistaken for that of a sleepy country estate rather than the grounds of a high-security institution.

'Each inmate is different, of course,' continued Johnson, with the air of a man describing his favourite hobby – stamp collecting, say, or birdwatching. 'Depending on their respective condition – whether a patient is subject to moral deficiency, melancholia, mania, violent seizures – these will all have an effect on their behaviour, of course. But there's usually an initial period of readjustment, a settling-in as it were, when they can be prone to display violent expressions of their frustration at losing their liberty.'

'But Morkens has displayed no such behaviour?' asked Franklin.

'None at all. I suppose it might be a question of breeding.'

This provoked a little snort of derision from Harley. 'Or it might just be because he's faking it all. That he is, in fact, as sane as you and me.'

'I'm afraid that's a question for the medical staff, Mr Harley. My concern is to keep the inmates here secure, and, of course, to look after their welfare.' Johnson gave a slightly patronising smile before taking a pinch of snuff from the pewter box opened on the blotter in front of him.

'And has he made any mention of his victims whilst he's been here?' asked Franklin. 'In particular, the whereabouts of a child called Edward Muller?'

'No, not to my knowledge.' The principal gave a trumpeting blow on his handkerchief and then made a show of consulting the large clock above his head. 'Well now, I'm afraid I have a meeting of the trustees I must prepare for, gentlemen, so, if you have no further questions, perhaps we might…?'

'Of course,' said Franklin. 'How long can we have him for?'

'Professor Morkens has all the time in the world nowadays, Inspector. You may take as long as you like. But I must warn you, he has stipulated that he will only grant an interview to Mr Harley here, on his own.'

'What?'

'I'm afraid those were his express wishes. Of course, should you wish, you will both be granted access to his cell. But I doubt it would be very productive. He was quite adamant about the matter.'

* * *

'I've got to admit this shicer is getting my goat,' said Harley, as they followed the warder down a set of meandering corridors. 'First the stuff with Moloch, then that bastard Homburg lurking about. Now he's asking for me personally.'

'Don't let him get to you. Remember, we're here to try to determine what happened to little Eddie Muller.'

'I know, I know.' Harley took a long pull on his Gold Flake. 'It's just this bastard's got a knack of getting under my skin.'

Before long they had stopped outside a cell at the far end of a dreary corridor. Franklin turned and placed a hand on Harley's shoulder.

'Listen, I trust you to do a professional job. The chances are slim that we'll get anything more from Morkens, but it's certainly worth a try. Just don't let him get inside your head.'

Harley killed his cigarette beneath his heel, then removed his hat and combed his fingers through his hair. Even though the asylum corridor was chilly and damp, there was a sheen of perspiration on his forehead. He'd been plagued all morning by a strange apprehension, like a cold slug of lead lodged beneath his breastbone. A feeling that had been exacerbated by the news he'd be conducting the interview with Morkens alone. He understood this was just his subconscious playing tricks with him, that he'd allowed the idea – encouraged by the sensationalist popular press – of the professor as some kind of supernatural force of evil to get inside his head. Morkens was just a homicidal egomaniac, a deluded sexual pervert. The fact that the man possessed an above-average intellect and a smattering of charisma was by the by. He had no occult powers, no mind-control skills. Such things simply didn't exist. Here was just another murderous shicer, out to scratch his own filthy little itch. The world was full of them, right?

Then why was it that, for the past few nights, he'd dreamt of the child-killer's pale face, leering out from inky darkness, the eyes menacingly transformed by the horizontal pupils of a goat?

'Is this us, mate?' he asked the warder, nodding at the studded oak door.

'Yes, sir. This is Professor Morkens' cell. But, before you go in, I need you to hand over any weapons you might have on you. Just as a precaution, you understand, sir.'

The warder was a few years older than Harley and the sight of the man's nervous pallor beneath the peak of his cap didn't do anything to alleviate the sinking drag he felt in his chest. He produced his set of brass knuckles.

'There you go. I'll want 'em back, mind. What's your name, mate?'

'Smythe, sir,' said the warder, pocketing the knuckleduster.

'Tell me, Smythe, do you attend to this particular inmate?'

'Yes, sir. All this wing, sir.'

'And what's he like, would you say?'

Harley noticed the man's furtive glance towards the door. '*Like*, sir?'

'Morkens. Is he well-behaved? Does he ever talk to you?'

'You'll be quite safe, sir. Owing to the violent nature of his crimes we have him manacled for your visit.'

'That's not what I meant. I was just wondering whether he'd ever discussed anything with you, his crimes, or—'

The warder shook his head quickly, a look of panic in his eyes. 'I wouldn't know anything about that, sir. You'll have to take it up with the principal.'

Without further ado, Smythe flipped the inspection plate, peered into the cell and then selected a key from the large bunch which hung from a ring on his belt.

The door opened with a low groan of its hinges.

'I'm afraid I'm going to have to lock you in, sir. But don't you worry – me and your colleague will be right here throughout. Just call if you need any assistance.'

Harley took a moment to reshape his hat, then placed it back on his head, shot his cuffs and stepped into the child-killer's cell.

* * *

The cell was small and dim. Twelve foot long by eight foot wide; the only light provided by a gas bracket fitted with a soiled, vellum lampshade. Against one wall was a metal-sprung bedframe, covered in a thin horsehair mattress. Harley could just make out a figure sitting at a small table, akin to a school desk, in front of the bed. It took a while for his eyes to adjust to the light but, when they had, he saw that Morkens had his elbows on the desk and his manacled hands pressed to his cheeks, the fingers fisted – apart from the two thumbs, which were stuck up like horns on either side of his face.

The two men regarded each other for a while, the only sound to be heard the hiss of the gas lamp and the distant, pitiful lament of a troubled inmate. Finally, Morkens lowered his hands and gestured to the other chair at the table.

'Why don't you sit, Harley? You look ill at ease.'

'I'll be alright standing.'

'As you wish. So, I take it you're here to continue our little chat. We were somewhat interrupted last time, were we not?'

Morkens' feminine lips drew a smile, his eyes pitch-dark in the gloom.

Harley felt a cold knot tighten in his chest.

'Yeah, you were lecturing me on the artistry of murder. I remember Cassina was banging on about that in the radio show you did together. Was it you who first put the idea into his head?'

'Perhaps. Not directly, though, of course. Rather via my associates.'

'Your associates?' Harley pulled out his notepad.

'Come now. You don't expect it to be that easy, do you?'

'The principal said you'd agreed to an interview.'

'And so I have. But you must understand, it's to be on my terms.'

Harley took a scornful look around the cell. 'On your terms, eh, Prof?'

Morkens gave a little murmur of amusement, though his smile had now disappeared.

'Why don't you sit?' He rattled his manacles. 'They have me well secured. You'll be quite safe. Sit and we'll have a civilised conversation. You can tell me what you expect to learn from your visit and, assuming it's a reasonable enough request, I'll give it due consideration.'

The professor placed his hands flat in front of him and waited.

Harley bent down to check under the table, then called out towards the door, 'You still out there, John?'

Franklin spoke through the inspection plate. 'Still here, George. Everything alright?'

'Yeah, just checking,' said Harley, as he pulled back the chair and sat down.

'There now, isn't that better?' said Morkens.

Harley took out a pack of Gold Flake and offered it across the table.

The professor began to pull at a cigarette with his pale, thin fingers, but then pushed it back. 'Perhaps you'd choose first, dear boy?'

'Come on. It's only a smoke,' said Harley with a laugh. 'We don't all go around poisoning each other, you know.'

He sparked up a cigarette for himself then tossed the pack back to Morkens. He held the match out, on his guard as the child-killer leant across the table to light his cigarette.

'Thank you.' Morkens exhaled two thin plumes of smoke through his nostrils. 'Not my brand, but a civilised act, nonetheless. So, there we are. I'd say we're off to a good start, wouldn't you? Tell me, what is it exactly you'd like to learn today? You're a little rough around the edges, but I can see you've got a decent-enough brain. There's much I could teach you. It just takes a willingness of—'

'Eddie Muller,' said Harley, interrupting. 'Is he still alive?'

Morkens closed his eyes and let out a sigh. 'Oh, you disappoint me, dear boy. Here I am, offering you a unique opportunity, to be the one to share with the public the story of my great work. The story of the century. And the only thing that concerns you is the whereabouts of some guttersnipe child.'

Harley dearly wanted to tell Morkens that no one cared. That he was just another lunatic, locked away in a warehouse of lunatics; just another statistic in the principal attendant's books. He wanted to say that those headlines in the press would soon be no more than soggy chip paper. But, of course, he knew if there was to be any chance of discovering the whereabouts of the Muller child, he'd have to play audience to this megalomaniac's rantings. And besides, if he were honest, wasn't there just a small part of him that wanted to hear more of Morkens' story? Wanted to know what possible justification this well-educated product of the upper classes might have for the horrific violation of innocent children?

Harley regarded the professor's dark eyes, burning now with feverish arrogance. He surreptitiously put his fingertips to his chest, to touch the tightness there.

'Do you really think people see your crimes as art? The mutilation of those little kiddies? I've got to tell you, even though the evidence on the streets might be to the contrary, the great British public have a soft spot when it comes to children. Sorry to burst your bubble, pal, but you're no hero out there.'

'Of course I'm not. I'm the *Nursery Butcher*; and apparently now the *Beast of Brasenose* – I'd loved to have seen the look on the dean's face when he read that headline.' Morkens laughed as he nodded towards a collection of newspaper articles, pasted on the cell wall. He rested back in his seat and brought the cigarette to his lips. 'As you say, I have spoken to you of the art of murder, but, you know, the real motivation for my craft is science.'

Harley raised his eyebrows. 'Science?'

'Oh, I'm not talking about the science of the physicist and the mathematician – mere puzzle-solving exercises for the classroom. Such science just asks: How? What I speak of is the Great Work. The path to enlightenment. The answer to the eternal question: Why?'

'Science can explain "Why?"' said Harley. 'Why does the sun appear to set every night and rise again every morning? Science can explain that. That's a "Why?"'

Morkens smiled. 'We're not in the public house now, Harley. You're just playing with semantics. You may call that an explanation, but it's merely a description. All your science has achieved are descriptions of greater and greater complexity; such phenomena as the sun rising and setting remain as magical to modern man as they did to the ancients – more so, in some cases.'

Harley snorted.

'You don't agree? Let me put it another way. Your science says to you: "Understand, and you will believe." But the Great Work teaches us: "Believe, then you will understand." Your science, for example, could never disprove the existence of God.'

'There we go. I was wondering when you were going to bring him into it.'

'Oh, don't get me wrong. When I talk of God, I'm not referring to that pale Nazarene or indeed any other manifestation rumoured to have walked amongst us. The living have no use of true religion; it is for beyond this realm. If there *were* a Lamb of God, believe me, he wouldn't make visits, wouldn't sully himself in the mire. Regardless of what the scriptures might tell you.'

Harley took a hard pull on his Gold Flake. He knew he shouldn't get drawn into this argument, but somehow he couldn't help himself.

'What do you mean by God, then?'

Morkens leant forward. 'If you knew it, you could teach it to me; and when I knew it… I should no longer believe it.'

Harley chewed this over for a bit.

'So, you just believe, without knowing what you believe in?'

Morkens shook his head. 'No, no. It is *you* who do not know what I believe, and I believe it *precisely* because you do not know it.'

'I thought we weren't playing with semantics,' said Harley. 'You still haven't told me who this God is.'

Morkens closed his eyes for a moment, beginning to appear agitated. 'To quote the great Eliphas Levi: "*God is He whom we shall eternally learn to know better and, consequently, He whom we shall never know entirely.*"'

He rested back in his chair again, tenting his hands under his chin. 'Would you agree that, after each successive step forward, your science is always checked by yet another problem, another prize veiled in mystery?'

'Well, it's only a mystery until we've discovered the answer, right? Then we move on to the next question. That's progress.'

'Is it?' Morkens began to raise his voice, bringing his bound hands up. 'Mark my words: one day – perhaps in this century

– your scientists will stumble across a puzzle so tangled that they'll be reduced to simply responding, "We will never know." And where will that leave you? Your science is a mere Tower of Babel. You may continue to build it up, to the wonder of those who shield their eyes as they gaze up at its lofty heights. But it will never touch the heavens. Never! Whereas we followers of the *true* science, we have learnt to *believe*... and our faith illuminates the mystery with burning aspirations!'

This last sentence was yelled with passion, prompting the warder to look through the inspection plate.

'Everything alright in there, Mr Harley?'

'Yeah. All good, thanks.'

'Ah, dear Smythe,' said Morkens, flashing a predatory look at the door. 'So considerate.'

Harley shook his head. 'Believe in *what*, exactly? Black magic? Devil worship? Satanism?'

Morkens laughed. 'Such terms should be left in the nursery, or in the pulpit. Man makes his devils from the cast-off gods of lost civilisations. What is this devil worship you talk of? Nothing but a patchwork quilt, strung together from scraps of ancient beliefs. A system corrupted, misunderstood. We must first cleanse the gods of antiquity of all the dust and grime they've acquired through the centuries before we can see them shine again in all their terrifying brilliance.'

Harley thought back to Franklin's account of the professor's confession, about his mention of the ancient god Moloch. Perhaps it *was* just a coincidence after all? Nothing to do with his old tomcat. He felt the weight lift a little in his chest.

'Alright, I think we're going a bit off track here. I'll ask you that question, now, Professor, if you like. Not the *how* but the *why*. Why murder little children, defile their dead bodies, and remove their heads and hearts? What's that got to do with this "great work" of yours?'

'You really want to know? I warn you, man, these things are not to be made light of.'

'What, the mutilation of little children? Oh, don't you worry, I get that.'

The professor closed his eyes for a moment, tugging on his white goatee as he took some deep breaths.

'Very well.'

When Morkens opened his eyes again, Harley realised he'd never seen such dark irises before; in the dim light of the cell, they merged as one with the pupils. The effect was disquieting, but also mesmeric.

'You see, Man is made of three parts. After death, that inside him which is of the divine returns immediately to the divine.'

'Do you mean, to heaven?'

'Some may call it such. There are other names for it,' said Morkens, dismissively. 'Once this divine element ascends, it leaves behind two corpses: one terrestrial and the other aerial. One – the corporal body – already devoid of life, succumbing quickly to corruption and decay, the other – the astral body – still animated to a certain extent, but destined to fade slowly, to be absorbed back into the forces that produced it. Do you follow? Now, if one has lived a carnal life – and few men can say otherwise – then this astral body holds him prisoner, still seeking the objects of its lusts, wishing to return to life, return to the carnal. *It torments the dreams of young girls and bathes in the steam of spilt blood.*'

Morkens had leant forward to deliver this phrase. Harley noticed that his breath smelt of liquorice, and something else, something herbal.

'Ah, but a *child's* astral body... well, that is innocent and untainted; a pure incense which ascends slowly, joyously, towards the superior regions.' Morkens closed his eyes briefly and drew in another deep breath. 'Such is the elixir of true knowledge, the Universal Medicine.' He sat back in his chair with a look of pride. 'And it is the process of capturing such a volatile and treasured essence that I have perfected in the terrible alembic of murder. But not murder at the hands of drunken passion or of bloodthirsty rage. No, only in the beauty of a murder enacted as art.'

Harley crushed his dog-end under his foot, trying to mask his feeling of disgust. 'So, why hasn't anyone else heard of this *essence* of yours?'

'What? Why, of course they have. Von Reichenbach, Newton, Mesmer – many have tried to study the astral body. It has been given divers labels through the years: magnetic fluid, Odic force, aether, ectoplasm. But now, of course, your precious scientists dismiss it out of hand; they think that which cannot be measured must not exist. As if they could quantify such an essence with their slide rules.'

'But *you* have, you say.'

'Indeed.' The arrogance returned to the child-killer's eyes.

'How?'

Morkens shook his head. 'Such things cannot be easily explained. It would take days just to lay down the groundwork in order for you to even begin to understand.'

'That's convenient, ain't it? And you did this all on your own, did you?'

Morkens nodded. 'Of course, I had immense help from the Baron's teachings. And, as I have said, I have associates for other branches of my studies. But the Great Work takes patience, devotion, solitude. Of course, it is not devoid of risk. It can result in nervous disturbance; insanity, even.'

You don't say, thought Harley.

'Such experiments are only for the strong-willed, you understand. They should be avoided by women and the young, those of a nervous disposition. One must possess perfect self-control, have a command of fear... I venture you might make a likely initiate. If you so wished.'

'You're alright. I'll give it a miss, I think.'

'But why?'

'Why? Why not go around murdering little kids, you mean?'

Morkens gave a patronising smile, as though listening to a child. 'One of the first lessons for the initiate is to seek out their true path, to learn that no self has value but your own.'

'Christ! We'd be in a fine old mess if we all went around thinking that.'

'Come now. All human action is ultimately motivated by self-interest. We just encourage the initiate to be honest about this, to cast off the shackles of their inhibition.'

'What a load of old madam,' said Harley, shaking his head.

'Madam? I don't follow.'

'Rubbish. Flannel. Nonsense. People are always doing things to help each other. It's how society works.'

'No. It's simply that society has programmed us to believe that doing good for others is a virtue. Therefore, our motivation for such charitable acts is merely to satiate our need to feel and appear righteous. And so, alas, we waste so much of our precious time in this life conforming to these unnecessary, restrictive social norms.'

'Listen,' said Harley, 'there are sound, logical reasons for people not to harm each other. Evolutionary reasons. If we were all just murderous savages, the human race would have become extinct centuries ago.'

'I was speaking of doing good to others. Man is prevented from doing *harm* by his fear of divine retribution.'

Harley shook his head. 'Maybe once. But the Church has lost its grip on the world.'

'You'll find they have simply swapped their gods for dictators, for governments, for the State. The fear of retribution remains.'

'So, hold on, you reckon that nobody ever cares about others for charitable reasons, that we only do each other good turns to make ourselves feel better? And the only thing that stops us from doing harm is the fear of punishment?'

'You put it most succinctly, dear boy.'

'I mean, I thought I was cynical, but… listen, that might be true for some. But not for everyone, not for most people.'

'Your credence does not affect its veracity. What would you say fuels your desire to know the whereabouts of little Edward Muller, for example?'

'Do you really need to ask?'

'I'd like to hear your explanation. Humour me.'

'Well, to spare him and his parents any further suffering – if he's still alive.'

'And if he's not?' The professor's eyes were alight once more.

'Then… well, to return his remains to his poor, grieving mother, so she can mourn him properly, give him a decent burial.'

'Yes. And then the great George Harley becomes the folk hero of London.' Morkens held up his manacled hands, his voice rising to a crescendo. 'The saviour of the dispossessed!'

'That's bollocks. And you know it.'

'Do I? What if such a prize was to cost you something personally?'

Harley thought about the Maltese gun for hire, Baldacchino, now languishing somewhere in a cell. He just managed to stop himself from smiling. *Here it comes*, he thought. *Not such a genius now, are you, Professor?*

'The job always involves a certain risk.' He shrugged. 'It comes with the territory.'

'Ah, yes – the *job*. A Sherlock Holmes for the Jazz Age, is that how you see yourself?'

'Don't knock it. I was good enough to collar you, weren't I?'

The condescending tone wasn't lost on Harley. He'd been lashing out against such arrogant entitlement all his life – and he knew that to rise to the bait was a mistake. But he just couldn't help it; never could. Not when his dander was up. And boy, was it up now.

Try and have me settled by some snotty-nosed Maltese hayseed, would you? he thought. *Well, you've ventured into my world now, Prof.*

'I s'pose that might be a bit galling for you, eh? That it was little old George Harley who unravelled your master riddle and got you pinched? You being an Oxford man and all. The grandson of a viscount. You went to all the right schools, know all the right people, belong to all the right clubs...' Harley sniffed and looked around the cramped cell. 'Look where it all got you.'

The predatory look returned to the professor's face. 'This personal cost we're talking about – you'd be prepared to expose yourself to such risk, would you, in securing the return of young Edward? I suppose it would be small beer to such a selfless champion of the people.'

'You can unleash your attack dogs if you like. It wouldn't be the first bit of roughhouse I've had to deal with. Besides, I know a few canine types myself.'

Harley sat up in his chair and rubbed his hands, feeling he needed to take back control of the interview.

'So, enough of the old gammon. You going to give me Eddie Muller, or what?'

Morkens grunted, reflecting on this. 'Well, I said I'd consider your request, and that's exactly what I intend to do.'

'When will I know?'

'Oh, soon enough. But before you go, perhaps I might ask *you* a question? Of a philosophical nature?'

Harley looked at his watch and then nodded. 'You can ask. I might not answer, though. Try me.'

'I've been told you see yourself as an atheist.'

'Told by who?'

Morkens dismissed the question with a wave of the hand. 'What *is* it you believe in, George? About the nature of Man, say? Are we mere animals, without design, as your scientists would have it? Or could you allow yourself to believe we possess souls, trapped in these ugly, bloody carcasses of ours? Are we single, autonomous entities? Or...'

The professor leant forward, his eyes flashing with piercing brilliance. He grinned, showing his teeth, which were far from perfect: they were strangely curved and of an odd, grey tinge, the colour of mushroom flesh. Harley held the feverish glare of those black eyes and waited for him to finish.

'... just a tiny mote in some infinite and everlasting light of the universe?'

On hearing Cynthia's words – first spoken to him in an intimate moment, repeated now by this depraved maniac in his squalid cell – Harley finally lost the little restraint he had left.

'You fucking shicer!' he hollered, wrenching Morkens up by the lapels of his asylum jacket. 'I swear, if you touch a hair on that girl's head, I'll—'

'Help!' screeched Morkens. 'Murder! Warder! Save me! Save me!'

Harley found himself being hauled backwards out of the cell while the professor writhed on the floor, rattling the chain of his manacles, his face now the very epitome of raving lunacy – black eyes blazing, his cheek slick with spittle.

'Alright, George. Easy now,' said Franklin, holding him up against the wall of the corridor while Smythe wrestled with the lock. 'I warned you he'd try to get inside your head, didn't I?'

'It's Cynthia. The bastard was on about Cynthia!'

'Has he threatened her? What did he say, exactly?'

'He... well, he...' Harley shrugged off the policeman's hands and straightened his jacket. 'He repeated something she'd said to me. Something no one else could have known... except that bastard Homburg, lurking in the bushes. He must have been closer than I thought. That shicer's up to something.'

'We'll look into it. Did you get anything on Eddie Muller?'

'Possibly,' said Harley. 'Possibly. Come on, I'll tell you all about it in the pub. I need to get out of this bleedin' place.'

As Smythe led them back down the corridor there came a loud banging on Morkens' cell door.

'A word of advice, Harley!' yelled the professor in a clear, confident tone. 'Be careful what you wish for, my friend!'

The maniacal hyena-laugh resounded off the brick walls, taunting them all the way out to the block stairwell.

49

'*THERE WERE EXTRAORDINARY scenes in New York today, as Wall Street was overwhelmed by a deluge of investors rushing to offload their stocks on a chaotic market, spiralling out of control. The wild crashes occurred at the very opening of the Exchange, as, amid scenes of confusion and disorder, a huge volume of stocks was offered in an opening rush to sell. Experts are predicting billions of dollars will have been wiped off share prices by the close of trading later today...*'

'Blimey, Moloch, d'you hear that?' said Harley, ruffling the shabby coat of his old tomcat, curled up on the sofa next to him. As he got up to turn off the wireless, Moloch regarded him irritably with his one chartreuse-coloured eye, as if to say *What significance have such human trifles to me?*

'I mean, not that I feel any great sympathy for them Rockefeller types,' continued Harley, who'd developed a habit of talking to his cat during his years of living on his own at Bell Street. 'But if it's as bad as they're saying... well, it's stone ginger it'll trickle down to the man on the street.'

Just then there was an urgent knock on the door. Harley put down his cup of tea and went to answer it.

'Squib.' He looked down at an out-of-breath Alfie Budge, leaning against the door frame, his little pigeon chest heaving like a blacksmith's bellows. 'To what do I owe the pleasure?'

The young Budge waved an envelope. 'Got this… for yer… Mr Aitch,' he said, breathlessly. 'Bloke said it was important.'

'What bloke was this, then?' said Harley, plucking the letter from Budge's hand.

'Dunno. Never seen 'im before. Bit of a queer cove.'

'How so?'

'Sneaky-looking. Mumbled a lot.'

'What did this fella look like?'

'Let's see, now.' Budge screwed up one eye and scratched at his unruly mop of red hair as he thought. 'Mackintosh, Homburg titfer and a pair of specs that would make a librarian blush.'

'*Homburg?*' The smile disappeared from Harley's face. 'Where was this?'

'You alright, Mr Aitch? Nuffin' wrong is there? Only, I—'

'*Where?!?*' barked Harley.

'He was hanging around in the foyer of the Astoria, Charing Cross Road,' Budge blurted out, accompanied by a little nervous jerk of the elbow. 'Don't think he'd been in to see a picture, though. Just lurking there, I reckon. Nabbed me as I went past. Knew me by name. Though, for the life of me, I don't know the geezer from Adam.'

'That everything?'

The young lad nodded earnestly, standing sheepishly now, with his hands thrust into his pockets.

Harley ripped open the envelope.

The message was succinct. One line. Typewritten on a heavy-bond paper.

> *You will find Edward Muller at Flat 9, Laurel Mansions, Hampstead.*

Harley pocketed the letter, grabbed his jacket from the newel post and searched out his notebook. He copied some things onto a fresh page then tore it out and thrust it into Squib's grubby hand, along with a handful of loose change.

'Listen carefully and do exactly as I say. Run to the nearest phone box and ring the Bentornato. It's the Italian restaurant in Frith Street.'

'I know it.'

'Just *listen*! Ask for Solly Rosen. Say it's important. If he ain't there, try the Twelve Ten club. You've got both the telephone numbers there. Tell Solly to meet me at the Hampstead address I've written down for you. Tell him I said he was to drop everything and get there as soon as he can. *As soon as he can* – got it?'

'Got it,' said Budge, with a serious look on his little freckled face.

'Good. Then ring Vine Street nick and ask for DCI Franklin.'

'Hold on. But—'

'Schtum! I ain't got much time here. Ring Vine Street and ask for John Franklin. Tell him—'

'But Franklin's dead,' interrupted Budge.

'What?'

'I heard it from Larry the Screever, who heard it from PC Trent. Died in his sleep, Monday night. His ticker just gave up the ghost, apparently. S'pose he was getting on a bit.'

'Dead? You sure?'

Budge nodded. 'Like I said, Mr Aitch, heart attack.'

'John!' Harley raked his fingers through his hair as he thought for a moment. '*Bugger!* Alright. Make your priority getting hold of Solly. When you've delivered the message, do your best to track down PC Trent – he knows you, don't he?'

'That he does.'

'Good. Tell him we'll need some boys in blue at that address. Tell him it's to do with the Eddie Muller case.'

Budge's eyes widened as he let out a low whistle. 'Eddie Muller? Morkens' victim? Is the poor little bugger still alive then? You found 'im, have yer?'

'What are you still doing here, Squib? Scarper!'

Galvanised by the weight of both his assignment and its remuneration in his pocket, the young messenger sped off wheezily down the road, in search of the nearest Post Office telephone kiosk.

* * *

The journey from Bell Street to Hampstead was a blur. Usually a careful driver, Harley now pushed the Norton to its limits, hurtling dangerously through sidestreets, only just wide enough for the sidecar combination, in order to avoid traffic on the busier roads. After an almost disastrous encounter with a brewer's dray while negotiating the back alleys of Somers Town, he decided it would probably be safer to rejoin the main road.

As he gunned the Norton along Chalk Farm Road, his mind reeled with the possible significance of the recent turn of events. First there was the death of John Franklin – ostensibly from natural causes, but something in Harley's gut said otherwise. Then there was the reappearance of Homburg. But by far the most worrying development – and the one that had caused the return of that tightness beneath his breastbone – was that Morkens had arranged to have Eddie Muller delivered to Cynthia's flat.

50

THE LIGHT WAS beginning to fail as Harley pulled into the drive of the red-brick mansion block, the wind whipping up flurries of dead leaves as clouds tore across the darkening sky with the threat of a storm. He threw his leather helmet and goggles into the sidecar and rushed up the rain-slick steps, adrenaline quickening his heart as his brain raced through possible scenarios of what he might find inside. He knew Cynthia had planned to leave the previous night for a concert in Hamburg, and so hoped that meant she was safely out of harm's reach, but what about Eddie Muller? Was he about to discover the child's dismembered corpse? His head in a hat box? Or was the whole thing a trap? Would Homburg be waiting inside with a mob of armed thugs?

Letting himself through the common entry door with the key Cynthia had given to him on the day after their engagement, he avoided the caged lift, instead taking the stairs two at a time, vigilant to danger, checking behind him to make sure no one was following; up to the second floor, pausing outside the apartment door, catching his breath, checking the frame for any indication of a forced entry, placing his ear to the wooden panel to listen for signs of a struggle.

Nothing.

He fitted his brass knuckles, eased the key into the lock, listened once more at the door – and then threw it open.

For all his speculation the scene that greeted him was a jarring shock.

There, looking incongruous in Cynthia's chic, modern hallway, stood little Eddie Muller, dressed in a black sailor suit. Harley guessed it was Eddie Muller, anyway – it was difficult to match the pudgy youngster he saw before him with the skinny Limehouse ragamuffin in the police photographs. The boy stood pigeon-toed, the striped hook of a candy cane protruding from the pocket of his reefer jacket. There was the look of abject terror on his face – haunted eyes clamped wide open, cheeks running with tears, and his glistening bottom lip quivering uncontrollably. But the immediate concern was Harley's Luger semi-automatic which the child clutched tightly in his chubby little hands, summoning all his strength to keep it pointing at the private detective's chest.

'Alright now, mate,' said Harley, quickly pocketing his knuckleduster and holding his hands up. 'I'm one of the good guys.'

He took a tentative step into the hallway – and watched the little fingers hook over the Luger's trigger.

'No need to be afraid now. It's all over. It's Eddie, ain't it?'

The terrified boy gave an almost imperceptible nod.

Harley broke eye contact for a second to check those fingers again – he knew what a light touch the Po8's trigger had. He took another careful step forward.

'I bet all you want to do is go home, Eddie, see your old mum, eh?'

Harley let his hands drop, smiling now, nodding sympathetically.

'That'd be good, wouldn't it? Why don't we telephone her now, Eddie?'

Another step.

'Get her round here?'

At the first sign of the gun's barrel dropping Harley pounced. He pulled the sobbing child in close, grabbed the pistol and pushed the safety catch on.

'Alright, fella. We're alright, now,' he said, bending down to put himself at the same height as Eddie. 'Tell me, son, is there anyone else here? Anyone we need to be worried about?'

It was then that Harley noticed the blood on the bare flesh above the top of the boy's stocking.

'You hurt, mate? What have they done to you?'

He gently pushed Eddie back a little, pulling up the leg of his shorts to get a better look. But there was no wound.

'Where's this blood from, son?'

The child gave a little whimper, like a scolded dog.

Harley now saw the mess on the carpet. A trail of bloody footprints, leading from Cynthia's bedroom.

He stood up and used the gun to point with.

'What's in there?' His voice was barely above a whisper now. 'Come on, Eddie, you can tell me.'

He grabbed the boy's shoulder, shaking him now.

'Eddie!'

But Eddie just stood there, forming a little O with his mouth, shaking his head, showing the whites of his eyes.

Harley slipped the safety catch back off the Luger. He took a deep breath and began to walk towards the bedroom – a walk he was destined to repeat again and again through the years, the theme of a thousand nightmares to come.

Unlike the many other perilous situations he'd found himself in before, Harley now struggled to keep a clear head, to distance himself from the fear. This was Cynthia, his Cyn... and his shield was down.

But surely there was still a chance he was mistaken? That the blood on the carpet and the horror in little Eddie's eyes were due to… to what? The slaughter of another child? Another kiddie's head in a hat box? Would that really be better?

Yes. Better than *that*.

Walking down the corridor, Harley's mind replayed Morkens' words to him: *Be careful what you wish for, my friend!*

He stood outside her bedroom, trying in vain to calm his rapid breathing.

He somehow summoned the courage to tease open the door, the gun held out before him.

A large dark stain on the teal-coloured rug.

A form lying in the bed, covered with the bedspread.

No.

His hand shook. Lifting the cover…

No, no, no, no, no.

A naked body. *Her* body. The skin ashen from *pallor mortis*, waxwork-like, fragrant with her Gizemli perfume; beautiful, in a way – until it met the shocking butchery of the wound.

'Cynthia.' The whisper left his lips. Unheard.

Now he was on his knees, covering his eyes, hollering. A long, painful cry – feral, enraged. His mind reeled with the visceral horror of it; this macabre desecration; a desecration *he'd* visited upon her – a reward for his pride and arrogance.

Be careful what you wish for, my friend!

Harley stood up, stripped the covers, yanked boxes from beneath the bed, hurled open the wardrobe doors, ransacked the bedroom, the bathroom, searching for it, searching for *her*.

Not there. Where? Where!

Now he was in the hallway again, clutching at the collar of Eddie's sailor suit, shaking him violently.

'Where have they put it? Where is it? Where is it! *Say something, you little bastard!*'

Here it was, the prize he'd paid for with Cynthia's life – and more. This little fatted calf. A part of him wanted to clout the chubby little face, smack away that stupid look of bewilderment.

Harley felt the weight of the Luger in his hand; saw again his hand pulling back that bed cover…

He raised the pistol.

The shout from behind him took him by surprise. Then he was up against the wall, the powerful forearm pushing into his windpipe.

'What's the fuck's the matter with you?' said Rosen, prising the Luger from Harley's hand. '*George!* Snap out of it? D'you hear me?'

It took a second or two, but Harley's eyes came back to the room.

Rosen relinquished his stranglehold and went over to comfort Eddie.

'Alright, son. Old George there was just mucking you about. He didn't mean anything by it. Uncle Solly's here now.'

He swooped Eddie up in his bear-like arms and turned his attention back to Harley.

'What happened here, mate?'

Harley pointed vaguely in the direction of the bedroom.

'Cynthia. In there. They've…'

He paused, unable to form the words, feeling nauseous, his head pounding as though it were about to crack. He took some deep breaths.

'She in there, is she?' Rosen began to walk towards the bedroom.

'*No!* Don't go in there, Sol, please. Not yet. Not with the kid. She's… Cynthia's…'

Harley slid slowly down the wall, his hands over his face.

'They've taken her head. They've taken her fucking head!'

Little Eddie Muller gave a whimper. He hooked his arms around Rosen's neck and whispered in his ear: 'Please, Uncle Solly. Please don't let 'em take *my* head.'

51

SOLLY ROSEN BOUNDED up the front steps of Harley's house. He took a moment to prepare himself – swept a comb through his thick black hair, shot his cuffs, adopted an affable grin – and then rapped enthusiastically on the knocker. All this good cheer was purely for effect; inside he was desperately worried about his good friend. When he'd called round the previous week, Harley had answered the door with deep shadows beneath his bloodshot eyes and a perceptible shake to his hands. He had also refused Solly entry.

Cynthia's murder had obviously hit Harley hard – you didn't have to be a sherlock to work that one out; not to mention the death of John Franklin, for which Harley also blamed Morkens – although, quite how someone could induce a heart attack in a fella while cooped up in the loony bin some thirty miles away was beyond him. Grief hit people in different ways, he knew that, he was no schmo – despite what his Marni said. But Georgie Boy, reduced to such a state? The bloke had a DCM, for God's sake! He'd come through the big shemozzle in France without so much as a bloody nose. Not to mention the countless scrapes he'd been in since. George Harley was as tough as old boots, everyone knew that. But what was it his old bubbe used to say? *Some of the sweetest fruit lies beneath the toughest skin, Solomon.* Or maybe that meant something else?

Having confused himself, Rosen left the thinking alone for a while and had another go on the door knocker. Still no reply. He was just trying to peek in through the parlour window when the front door of the adjacent house opened.

'What you playing at, Solomon Rosen, lurking around out there?'

It was Harley's formidable neighbour – Vi Coleridge, the widow of the late Eric Coleridge, former boss of Mori Adler's Soho gang.

'What, me, Mrs C? Er… nothing, honest.' The one-time British middleweight champion was suddenly reduced to a naughty schoolboy caught with his hand in the biscuit barrel – an effect Violet Coleridge often had on the male of the species.

'Come to see George, dear?'

Rosen nodded and moved across to lean on the dividing wall. 'To tell you the truth, I'm a bit worried about him. Is he in there?'

'I don't know,' said Vi, crossing her arms beneath her ample bosom. 'I did him a little steak and kidney pudding last night. Left it on the doorstep, as he wasn't answering. The empty plate was there this morning, so he must have eaten it. Unless one of the local tykes has had it away, of course.'

'They wouldn't dare. Imagine what you'd do to 'em, eh?'

They both had a little laugh at this, then Vi laid a hand on Rosen's arm.

'I wouldn't bother him if I were you, son. Let sleeping dogs lie for a while, eh?'

'Well, you'd know best, I s'pose. But, I've been thinking, see – they couldn't find her engagement ring, right? How can we be certain it was her? With her, you know, with her... her head missing?'

'Please, Solomon! I'd rather you didn't.'

Rosen shuffled his feet. 'Yeah, course. Sorry.'

He rubbed at his square jaw and looked up at the window again.

'He will pull through this, won't he?'

'It'll take time. And there are no guarantees, mind. But George is made of strong stuff. And he has good people around him; good people who'll need to support him, when the time is right.' She cast him a gimlet eye by way of warning. 'But with a bit of luck, in the end, George will be alright. He's just got to find his own way through it, that's all.'

* * *

The reason that Harley hadn't answered the door at Bell Street, was because at that precise moment he was in the depths of Soho, sitting in the office of Victor Manduca, where the Spider had discovered him on returning from lunch.

Manduca now regarded the private detective, who sat slumped behind the ornate desk, looking dishevelled, with a three-day stubble and no shirt collar.

'Mr Harley. An unexpected pleasure. Do we have some business to attend to? Or perhaps you were just passing and thought you'd drop in?'

'Business,' murmured Harley, pulling himself up in the seat.

'I see.' The large bovine eyes flickered over the Luger pistol which lay on the desk, within easy reach of Harley's hand. 'Might I have my chair?'

'You can sit there.'

The Spider's fleshy jowl wobbled as he cleared his throat.

'Very well. But I hope this won't take long. I have a busy schedule this afternoon.'

'That all depends on you, Victor.'

Harley snapped to attention as the door opened, snatching the gun from the desk.

'Come in,' he said, aiming the Luger at Spiru, who stood frozen in the doorway. 'The more the merrier. That's it. Close that door, now.'

Spiru took in the situation with some alarm.

'Why is this bagħal here?' he murmured. 'What's he been saying?'

'Oh, I just want some information,' said Harley, smiling. 'And I've got something to trade for it, an' all.'

Victor Manduca sniffed disdainfully. 'Very well, let's hear what you have.'

Harley took a few moments to savour the exquisite look of trepidation on the younger Manduca's face, knowing the gangster would think he was about to reveal the clandestine affair with his brother's ward.

'Those negatives you were asking about? I might have a possible lead.'

'The negatives?' said Spiru, with obvious relief.

The Spider's eyebrows arched in surprise. 'Indeed? And in return?'

'Two things. The first is I don't want to have walk around this city – *my* city – worrying every minute that some hayseed lowlife from Malta is going to creep out of an alley and stick a barker in the back of my head. You need to understand that, even six foot under, I can cause you a whole bucketful of woe. Got it?'

'Well, seeing as that last enterprise – the commission for which came from elsewhere, you understand – ended in a rather excessive amount of attention from the authorities, I think I can agree with such terms,' said Manduca, magnanimously.

'Spiru?' asked Harley, miming taking a photograph.

'Alright! Agreed,' said Spiru, nodding desperately behind his brother's back.

'And your second condition?' asked the Spider, languidly inspecting his fingernails.

'The whereabouts of a certain individual.'

Manduca held out his enormous hands in supplication.

'If this is about Fedor von Görlitz, then I'm afraid you're far too late. I happen to know he returned to Berlin over a month ago. Besides, Fedor is extremely well-connected. You wouldn't—'

'This ain't about von Görlitz,' interrupted Harley. 'I'll get to that shicer later.'

'Who, then?'

'Poisonous-looking geezer. About five ten. Pasty complexion; thick, pebble-lensed glasses. Always wears a Homburg.'

The brothers exchanged a glance.

'Very well,' said Victor, after a moment's consideration. 'Let's hear your lead on the negatives.'

'And you'll give Homburg up?'

'If your information is worthy of it.'

Harley nodded and sparked up a Gold Flake.

'I have it on good authority that Sonny Gables' son, Teddy, has been flogging smutty prints, made from some of those photographic plates of yours that were confiscated by the bogeys from Turpin's flat. The plates were sold to Teddy by a bent DC in C Division called Fred Drake. If Drake held back some of the plates, he might also have the thirty-five millimetre canister. Or he could have passed it on to Teddy.'

'And why are you so happy to turn grass all of a sudden?' asked Spiru.

'I'm past caring, d'you see? You'd do well to take that on board, Spiru.' Harley pinched the bridge of his nose. 'Past caring.'

'You do realise you may have just sealed the fate of these two individuals?' purred the Spider in his syrupy voice.

Harley took a long drag on his smoke and shook his head. 'Not my concern. Drake's a bent copper and Teddy Gables is an idiot without an excuse. So, come on, give me the lowdown on Homburg.'

Victor Manduca gave a little reassuring nod to his brother and then said, 'The individual you are referring to is a soldier of fortune, a gun for hire, from Berlin. I don't know his real name, but he is known to his associates as Mr Whispers – a satirical little sobriquet awarded to him on account of the injury to his vocal cords that he suffered during the war.'

'Fighting on which side?'

'I believe he is Bulgarian.'

'Figures,' said Harley. 'And where can I find this joker?'

'Whispers did travel back to Berlin, I believe. But I heard that he's back in town, lodging above the social club in Manette Street. But take care if you intend to visit him there. The place is a nest of vipers – a magnet for anarchists and troublemakers in exile. He's bound to have a loyal dog or two keeping lookout for him.'

'Much obliged,' said Harley, standing up with the Luger in his hand. 'Now, both of you stand over there so I can keep an eye on you as I leave. And Spiru? Remember our little conversation, eh? Don't get any funny ideas.'

'Your little conversation?' asked Victor, when Harley had left.

'Search me,' said Spiru, adopting an innocent look. 'You saw the state he was in. Looked like he hadn't slept for days. But why did you give Whispers up so easily? Won't that come back to bite us?'

The Spider gave a hearty laugh, the thick folds under his chin rippling in waves.

'My dear brother, Mr Whispers is a trained assassin, whereas Harley? Well, he's just some wide-boy private detective, with a war souvenir for a weapon.' He unwrapped a caramel and popped it into his fleshy mouth. 'The poor fool doesn't stand a chance.'

52

THE FIGURE IN the cream-coloured mackintosh emerged cautiously from the dark green Austin Tourer, which was parked in Manette Street with its engine idling, the plume from the exhaust adding to the turbid mist which hung heavy in the night air. He peered about him in the fog for a moment. Then, satisfied his arrival had gone unobserved, he pushed the thick-lensed spectacles back up to the bridge of his nose, adjusted his Homburg hat and made his way cautiously towards the social club, the lights of which glowed invitingly ahead of him in the gloom.

The smoky, clamorous room was packed with the usual cabal of raucous young men, fogging the windows with their drunken polemics. The newcomer pulled his hat down a little lower and pushed his way through the crowded tables. At one point, a well-built individual in a leather-peaked worker's cap grabbed at his arm and muttered something in German. But he ignored this, carrying on determinedly towards the door that led to the rear staircase.

Having successfully reached the first floor without being intercepted, Harley removed the pebble-lensed glasses and rubbed at his eyes. Working quietly in the darkened stairwell, he peeled off the mackintosh which covered his own overcoat and popped out another two Benzedrine tablets from the tube in his pocket. He then disengaged the safety catch on the Luger, knocked gently on the door to the apartment and took a step back.

'Guten Abend, mein Freund,' he said confidently, waiting for the slightest movement of the door handle.

* * *

Having parked the stolen Austin in a quiet alleyway, Harley reached over to the back seat and put two fingers to the unconscious Mr Whispers' carotid artery, worried the dose of butyl chloride he'd administered might have been a little too generous. Satisfied that his captive was still alive, he checked the handcuffs were still secure, before bringing him round with a bottle of sal volatile.

After a prolonged bout of coughing, Whispers brought up a little watery vomit then struggled to a sitting position.

'Where are we?' he asked in a hoarse mumble, squinting against the glare of a nearby gas lamp.

Harley fished the Bulgarian's spectacles from the footwell and hooked them in place for him, then fitted the Homburg to his head.

'There, you're all set. Out you get. We're going for a little walk.'

Still groggy from the drugging, Whispers made slow progress from the alleyway to the dockside but, after a while, he was revived a little by the cold wind coming in off the river.

'What is that smell?' he said, a pained look on his ashen face.

'You should be used to that, pal, with the company you keep. That's good, honest shit. The excrement of millions of Londoners. We're at Beckton Sewage Works.'

Whispers gave him a puzzled look, his pale grey eyes glistening like molluscs in the magnifying lenses of his spectacles.

'Listen, Harley,' he rasped. 'I won't insult your intelligence by denying any involvement in what happened. But you must understand, I was only engaged to surveil you and the girl, to track your movements. I can't be held responsible for what they did to—'

'Schtum!'

Harley pointed to a large ship, anchored at the dockside. 'Over there.'

'This is a waste of time, my friend. I really can't imagine how I could be of any use to you.'

Harley pulled the Luger from his waistband.

Whispers sighed and trudged reluctantly towards the ship.

'Climb down,' said Harley.

The Bulgarian peered over the side, tracking a fixed metal ladder which led down into the empty cargo hold. He shrugged, holding up his cuffed hands.

Harley forced Whispers to his knees, then released one of his hands from the manacles – an old pair of Victorian Darbys which the private detective kept for special occasions; solid restraints, reliable, untraceable. Dragging Whispers to his feet again, he shoved him roughly towards the ladder.

Whispers did his best to make slow work of climbing into the hold, cursing to himself quietly all the way down, the loose manacles clanging loudly against the metal rungs.

'Back! Further!' shouted Harley, once the Bulgarian had made it to the bottom, directing him away from the base of the ladder.

Then, with the pistol trained on Whispers, he made his own, swifter, descent into the hold.

Harley took a moment to catch his breath, sparking up a Gold Flake while he regarded his adversary.

Before he'd been shanghaied, the assassin had been relaxing at home. Now the bite of the damp night air was beginning to take effect. Standing there shivering in his shirtsleeves and house slippers, with his trademark Homburg, strangely enlarged eyes and deathly pallor, it was hard to believe this man could ever pose any kind of serious threat.

But then he smiled – an arch imitation of a smile, one that revealed a cunning cruelty.

'Is it justice?' The whispering was inveigling, serpent-like. 'Is that what you seek? I understand you are a believer in such things. The professor explained this to me. I assure you, my friend, this little charade won't bring you justice.'

'Come over here, you shicer.'

Whispers held his hands up in supplication and made a little mewling sound. 'Alright! Alright! I capitulate. Hand me over to your police friends. I go willingly. After all, shame on me, you caught me off my guard.'

'I said, get over here.'

'Believe me, Harley, the girl's death wasn't—'

The shot from the Luger was explosive in the echoing confines of the hold. The bullet ricocheted off the steel wall above the head of the Bulgarian, who now fell to his knees with trembling hands held high, the frantic flickering of his eyes magnified in the lenses of his glasses.

'Last chance,' growled Harley. He smiled as he watched Whispers scuttle awkwardly towards him on all fours.

'There's a good boy.'

Hauling the villain against the wall by his collar, he quickly reached down to clamp the open manacle to the bottom rung of the ladder.

'Now. Two questions. The first is, who was the woman posing as Madame Leanda?'

'No, no, my friend,' croaked Whispers, cuffing his dripping nose. 'Believe me, you don't want to mess with that one.'

Harley dug the barrel of the Luger in below the Bulgarian's ribs.

'Spill your guts, you maggot, or I'll do it for you!'

'Alright, alright! Her name is Oona.'

'Oona? Oona what?'

'That's all I know. Just Oona.'

'Where will I find her?'

'I don't know. Truly, I don't. I've seen her three times, four maybe. You must understand, I was brought over to deal with specific things only. To silence the real Madame Leanda and…'

'And?' said Harley, delivering another vicious dig with the pistol barrel. 'What else? The kids?'

'No! Not killing them…' Whispers licked nervously at his lips. 'Only helping to plant one of the bodies. The one on the tram.'

'And was she involved with that? This Oona? Planting the bodies?'

'I don't know. I know nothing more about her… only… only that she's different from the rest of them.'

'The rest of who?'

'The professor's associates. The AOU brethren.'

'Different how?'

The Bulgarian gazed up at him, a manic zeal appearing in his huge watery eyes.

'Because she's not afraid of him, Harley. Think of that! She's not afraid!' Whispers attempted a chuckle, which immediately degenerated into a fit of coughing.

Harley took a step back in disgust.

'Alright. Enough of that bitch. Now, you shicer, *now* you tell me where it is.'

'Where what is?'

Harley spat and then reached inside his overcoat to pull out a wooden club, on the end of which was a lead ball studded with cruel spikes.

'I hear you served, Whispers. Albeit on the wrong side. So, you might recognise this.' He wielded the weapon, feeling the heft of it. 'It's a trench club. Saved my life on more than one occasion, this. Now, I'll ask you again, where is it?'

Whispers shook his head, managing a weak smile. 'We both know you're not going to use that. Nor will you shoot me.'

'No?'

'No. After all, how would you dispose of me? You could never carry me up that ladder on your own. Now, why don't you release me and we can go to your police friends, hmm? I told you, I'm perfectly willing to—'

The vicious blow to his thigh silenced him immediately. The spikes of the trench club pierced the flesh, soon producing a sodden scarlet bloom on the flannel trousers.

Whispers gawked at Harley with wide, astonished eyes, whimpering as he clamped a hand to his injured thigh.

'You haven't thought this through, man! I'll be discovered, when they come to load the ship.'

Harley pushed the Luger back into his waistband then took a pull on his cigarette, flicking the ash onto the Bulgarian's hat.

'No, you won't. See, this is what they call a Bovril boat – a sludge vessel. Every day they fill up with tons of shit from this sewage plant and take it out to sea, to dump it in the Barrow Deep, in the outer Thames Estuary.' He twirled the trench club in his hand. 'That's the cargo destined for this hold you're in, sunshine. And such a cargo isn't loaded. It's pumped in… from up there.'

Whispers' blinking gaze moved skyward to where a huge outlet pipe was suspended over the ship's hold.

'Every day, in and out. It's routine. Some bloke back there pulls a lever and she starts pumping. They could probably do it with their eyes closed. So, you see, no one's going to discover you down there. When that pump starts you're going to slowly drown; drown in a flood of liquid shit. And I can't think of a more fitting end for a bastard of your calibre.'

With a low moan, the Bulgarian gave a futile yank to the handcuffs which bound him to the ladder.

'But I'll give you one chance to save that rotten skin of yours,' said Harley.

'Yes?' said Whispers, eagerly.

'You need to tell me the truth, now. And you'll need to be quick.' Harley looked at his watch. 'You've only a few minutes left.'

'What is it?' hissed the assassin, wincing as he tried to sit up a little. 'I have no loyalty towards them. I'll tell you anything. Anything!'

'Alright then. Where is it?'

'What? Where is what?'

'You know what, you bastard! The thing you took from her.'

'The head? That? The girl's head? It really wasn't me. You must believe that. But, yes! I can tell you where it is, if that's what you want. Just let me up first. Let me out of here and we can discuss this.'

Harley took the key to the handcuffs from his pocket. He dangled the key chain in front of the blinking, watery eyes.

'You've got a matter of minutes. Now, where the fuck is it?'

Whispers glanced nervously at the outlet pipe above him. He licked his dry lips as he clasped at his injured leg.

'Von Görlitz! Von Görlitz took it, back to Berlin. But I know where. You see? You need me after all. I can lead you to him. Just let me up, now. Please, man! I've told you where it is. Let me up. After all, this isn't what you want. This isn't justice!'

Harley looked down at the grovelling assassin, thinking how childlike he appeared in the emptiness of the hold.

He closed his eyes for a moment, summoning the memory of little Eddie Muller stood in that hallway; the trail of bloody footsteps which led to Cynthia's bedroom.

'Maybe not justice,' he murmured. 'But it'll do. For now, anyway.'

He then tossed the key to the far corner of the hold.

'No!' hissed Whispers. 'You won't do it! You're just trying to scare me! You can't leave me here to die, man. Please!'

But Harley was already scrambling up the ladder.

'Please, Harley! I'll tell you something about *her*, about Oona! Something important! Come back!'

'Sorry, Whispers,' said Harley, looking down from the edge of the hold. 'You'll have to speak up, I can't hear you.'

He then quickly retreated to the rear of the dock, where he turned his collar to the damp chill and stood watching the ship from the shadows.

The lights strung in a ghostly festoon along the waterfront cast the vessel in an eerie light in the fog-laden air. He felt strangely detached from his surroundings, as though watching a film at the cinema. He'd killed before; brutal, hand-to-hand affairs in dank trenches, the stink of his adversary's breath in his face, terror staring back at him from youthful eyes. But this was different.

There was a noise behind him. The crunch of gravel underfoot?

He whirled around, struck once more by the sense of looming danger hiding in the shadows, back there, between the stark, industrial buildings.

Just then the banshee's wail of a steam whistle jerked his attention back to the waterfront. He turned to see the mighty pipe judder once in the air on its steel cables, before disgorging an explosive torrent of liquid sewage into the hold of the ship.

The stink swept over him in a sulphurous wave – the breath-taking stench of hell. The clamour of tons of excrement battering the steel walls of the hold was like the bellowing of some primordial river beast, magically resurrected from the ancient Thames mud. He stood for a moment, overwhelmed by the sheer violence of the scene, imagining Whispers tugging frantically at his manacled wrist, futilely trying to escape the suffocating tide of ordure, a muted scream distorting his anaemic face.

Then, as quickly as it had begun, it was over. The large pipe settled on its steel cables, the last few clumps of waste falling from its edge into the hold.

All was silent on the dockside, save for the muffled lapping of the muddy water, and the intermittent creak and groan of the ship's hull.

Harley pulled his cap down low on his face and crept back out to the dockside.

The hold was almost full, the faecal sludge reaching to the second rung of the ladder. He watched with his handkerchief clamped to his nose as a cluster of bubbles broke the surface, closely followed by something larger, something which rolled to upright itself in the filthy ooze.

It took Harley a few seconds to recognise it as Whispers' Homburg.

'Auf Wiedersehen, you shicer,' he mumbled, before darting off into the shadows.

Having abandoned the stolen Austin at the docks, he now had to make it on foot back to the high road, where he'd parked his motorcycle combination earlier in the day. As he trudged through the murky backstreets, the fog began to gather again, wreathes of it, swirling around the lamplights like spectral ivy, reducing their illumination to inverted Vs in the haze. And along with the fog there crept back to him that gnawing sense that something was out there, observing, waiting for him in the shadows.

Then, as he passed a narrow side alley, he froze in his tracks...

There! A pale face, watching him from a bay window. He stood, locked in its unnerving stare, his hand moving to the Luger stuffed into his waistband.

There was something uncanny about the features, vague and distorted somehow. He felt the hairs rise on the back of his neck, his frayed nerves stretching to breaking point, the blood singing in his ears. It was as if he knew instinctively that here, finally, he would confront the mysterious threat he'd felt for so long, that monstrous presence in the dark.

Harley raised the pistol and took a cautious step into the side alley, fully expecting the figure to disappear from sight. But, instead, it seemed to move closer to the window, to push its ghostly face against the misted glass.

Steeling himself, he rearranged his grip on the gun and rushed forward.

Then he stopped, gurgling a hollow chuckle.

He could see now that the bay window was the shopfront of an antique shop; and that this personal demon staring back at him, its features distorted grotesquely by the warped surface of an old flyblown mirror, was none other than George Harley himself, with his dishevelled hair, bloodshot eyes and unkempt stubble.

Harley pocketed the Luger and gave a sarcastic salute to his contorted reflection.

'Abyssinia, Corporal Harley. You mug!' he said.

Then, like an urban fox, he slunk off into the hazy gloom of the night.

GLOSSARY OF SLANG

I have endeavoured to use authentic slang in *Midnight Streets*. As well as referring to contemporary fiction of the period, the following dictionaries of slang proved invaluable:

Captain Francis Grose, *A Classical Dictionary of the Vulgar Tongue* (London, 1931)
Eric Partridge, *A Dictionary of the Underworld* (London, 1949)
Jonathon Green, *The Cassell Dictionary of Slang* (London, 1998)

Abbreviations

backsl. Backslang: a type of slang where the written word is pronounced backwards (e.g. 'yob' for 'boy').
Pol. Polari: theatrical cant first used by actors, circus folk and fairground showmen. Later taken up by the gay subculture.
rhy.sl Rhyming slang: a variety of slang where a word is replaced by a phrase (usually clipped) which rhymes with it (e.g. barnet = barnet fair = hair).

Rom. Romany: the language of the Romany people (Gypsies). An Indo-European language related to Hindustani.
Yid. Yiddish: the historical language of Ashkenazi Jews, based on German dialect with added words from Hebrew, Polish, French and English.

Abyssinia Goodbye ['I'll be seeing you!']
asterbar A bastard [semi-backsl.]
baghal A bastard [Maltese]
bogey CID detective ['Old Bogey' = the Devil]
bubbe Grandmother [Yid.]
cackle Empty chatter, gossip [the sound made by a hen]
cheese it! Shut up! Stop it! [a corruption of 'cease it!']
chiv A knife, a razor [Rom. chiv, chive, knife]
chiv-man A criminal apt to use a knife or razor as a weapon [see chiv]
cod Vile [Pol.]
Corporal Dunlop A short rubber truncheon [Dunlop is a rubber-tyre manufacturer]
cowson A general insult, similar to 'son of a bitch'
dilly boy A teenage male prostitute [abbreviation of Piccadilly, which was well-known for its prostitution]
dimp A cigarette end saved for future smoking [from the dimple pinched into it to snuff it out]
dinarly Money [Pol. Spanish *dinero*, money, Italian *denaro*, money]
dorcas Someone who is caring, generous [Pol. The Dorcas Society was a ladies' charitable church association]
factory A police station
fantabulosa Excellent [Pol. 'fantastic' + 'fabulous']
gammon Chatter, nonsense, cheating patter [perhaps from tying up a ham]
gelt Money [Yid. *gelt*, money]
hampton The penis [rhy.sl Hampton Wick = prick]

ikey, ikey-mo A Jew [derogatory; from 'Isaac' + 'Moses']
jane A prostitute [rhy.sl jane shore = whore; Jane Shore – mistress of Edward IV]
jarry Food [Pol. Italian *mangiare*, to eat]
judy A woman, a girl [from Punch and Judy]
kite The stomach [from British dialect *kyte*, womb, stomach]
lavender, lavender boy A male homosexual [possibly from the lavender water they used]
London Particular Thick, acrid, London fog, caused by air pollution (see 'pea souper')
lumbered Arrested
madam, a load of old Nonsense, rubbish; flattery [possibly from shopkeepers' patter: 'Of course it will, madam']
manor A police district; a policeman's beat; a wide-boy's patch [from 'Lord of the manor']
meshuggener Crazy, a crazy person [Yid.]
milky Cowardly, scared [allusion to its white colour]
mooey The mouth [Rom. *mooi*, mouth]
mott A woman, girlfriend, prostitute [from Old Dutch *mot*, whore]
nark A police informer [Rom. *nak*, nose]
nix Nothing [from German *nichts*, nothing]
nymph of the pave A prostitute
oily A cigarette [rhy.sl oily rag = fag]
omi-polone A male homosexual [Pol. Italian *uomo*, man; *pollo*, chicken]
on velvet To be well off, living in clover
pea souper Thick, acrid, London fog, caused by air pollution. Often a yellowish-green colour (note: pea soup was often made from yellow split peas)
penny dreadful A sensationally written pamphlet or book, usually documenting lurid 'true crime' tales, sold for one penny.
Piccadilly daisy A prostitute [Piccadilly was well-known for its prostitution]

pinch To steal/to arrest
ponce A pimp, a man 'living off immoral earnings' [from French Alphonse, or possibly *pont* or *pontonnière*, a prostitute who works from the arches of a bridge]
pronterino Quickly
put the squeak in To inform on
rosie Tea [rhy.sl rosie lee = tea; Gypsy Rose Lee - American stripper]
schmendrik A clueless mama's boy [Yid.]
schmo A fool [faux Yid. Alternative to the more vulgar **schmuck**, penis]
schmutter Clothes [Yid. *shmatte*, rags]
schtuk Trouble, bother [despite its appearance not a Yiddish word; possibly 'stuck' adapted to a Yiddish model]
schtum Quiet, silent [Yid. *shtum*, dumb, voiceless]
schtup To have sexual intercourse [Yid. to stuff, to fill]
screever A pavement artist who draws in coloured chalk [Italian *scrivere*, to write]
screwsman A skilled house-breaker [screw is criminal slang for a skeleton key]
sherlock A private detective [Sherlock Holmes]
shicer A lowlife, good-for-nothing [Yid. *scheisse*, shit]
smudge A photograph [the blurred effect seen in many cheap photographs of the time]
snow-bird Cocaine-user
spieler An illegal gambling club [German *spielen*, to play]
spruce To tell lies, to cheat, to flatter [i.e. 'sprucing up' the facts]
staunch Trustworthy, loyal, safe; able to keep secrets
stone-ginger An absolute certainty [Stone Ginger was a celebrated champion racehorse in New Zealand; the meaning is emphasised by the use of stone to mean 'absolutely'—e.g. stone blind, stone-cold sober etc.]
taters Cold. [rhy.sl taters in the mould = cold]
trade A prostitute's clients

troll Of a prostitute, to work the streets looking for punters [Pol.]

wide Sharp-witted, shrewd; also (of clothing) flash, ostentatious [wide awake]

wide-boy Petty criminal, wheeler-dealer, minor villain

work the black To blackmail

yok A gentile, a non-Jew [backsl. Yid. *goy*, from the Hebrew *goy*, a nation]

żobb The penis [Maltese, vulgar]

ACKNOWLEDGEMENTS

I owe huge thanks to my agent, James Wills, for all his mentoring and expert advice, to my editor, Rufus Purdy, for all his enthusiastic contributions (and for really 'getting' Harley's world) and to the fantastic team at Titan Books, especially Olivia Cooke and Isabelle Sinnott (UK), and Katharine Carroll (US), who have worked so tirelessly behind the scenes on this book's promotion. Special thanks must go to Hermione Ireland at Byte the Book, without whose early championing of George Harley this novel probably wouldn't ever have seen the light of day. Finally, I'd like to thank Susie, my wife, for her everlasting support, and all those family members, friends and work colleagues who have encouraged me over the years in my endeavours to become a novelist (you know who you are). Abyssinia!

ABOUT THE AUTHOR

Phil Lecomber was born in Slade Green, on the outskirts of South East London. Most of his working life has been spent in and around the capital in a variety of occupations. He has worked as a musician in the city's clubs, pubs and dives; as a steel-fixer helping to build the towering edifices of the square mile (and also working on some of the city's iconic landmarks, such as Tower Bridge); as a designer of stained-glass windows; and – for the last quarter of a century – as the director of a small company in Mayfair which specialises in the electronic security of some of the world's finest works of art.

For more fantastic fiction, author events,
exclusive excerpts, competitions, limited editions and more

VISIT OUR WEBSITE
titanbooks.com

LIKE US ON FACEBOOK
facebook.com/titanbooks

FOLLOW US ON TWITTER AND INSTAGRAM
@TitanBooks

EMAIL US
readerfeedback@titanemail.com